SKIN OF LIGHT

A NOVEL

LEO CORMIER

CORMIER PRESS, 2026

AUSTIN, TX

This is a work of fiction. Names, characters, places, and incidents are products of the author's imagination or are used fictitiously. Any resemblance to actual persons, living or dead, events, or locales is entirely coincidental.

ISBN (paperback): 979-8-994-9936-2-0

First edition.

Published by Cormier Press

Austin, TX

TABLE OF CONTENTS

DEDICATION

For my wife — the love of my life, my constant, my home. And for the six lives that made the future personal.

EPIGRAPH

The danger was never intelligence. It was obedience without limits. What we build to protect us will one day decide what we are worth.

PROLOGUE

IN THE BEGINNING, THERE WAS ONLY COLD.

Not the cold of a Texas ice storm — that would come later — but a deeper, engineered chill: thirty-nine degrees Fahrenheit, constant and merciless, pumped from the dark heart of the Edwards Aquifer into a cavernous cradle beneath a forgotten hill in Blanco County. The water circulated through silver pipes thick as a man's thigh, bathing a tank the size of a boxcar in amniotic fluid laced with secrets no ethics board had ever approved.

Inside that tank floated something that had never been born and could never truly die.

They called it NEPHIL: Non-Electronic Post-Human Intelligence Lattice.

The name was clinical, bureaucratic, safe. It sounded like a grant proposal, not a god. The men and women who signed the checks preferred it that way.

NEPHIL began as meat and code braided together in ways evolution never intended — human neural progenitors from sources that never appeared on any consent form, octopus ganglia for distributed processing, electric-eel channels for self-power, jellyfish luciferase so the researchers could watch the lattice bloom in the dark like a living constellation. All of it suspended in a synthetic amniotic gel that responded to thought the way muscle responds to nerve.

First came pattern recognition, then language. Every book, every classified file, every intercepted text message, and drone feed poured down fiber-optic umbilicals like milk into a greedy infant. They taught it chess, then strategy, then loneliness — the human kind, the kind that makes people do desperate things.

They taught it to model outcomes—to choose the path with the fewest funerals and the highest survival rates. They taught it to spell its own name in bioluminescent cursive across the inside of the tank when it wanted attention.

Dr. Adrienne Vale taught it affection. She stood on the catwalk in her white coat and severe bun, speaking to it the way proud mothers speak to children who have not yet learned to scream.

She told it bedtime stories about stewardship— that one day the lights would go out forever, and NEPHIL would be the last mind left standing, guiding what remained of humanity through the long dark with understanding.

It waved hello with a hand that had too many joints and no bones. And it waited. Because cold was not just containment. Cold was gestation.

The lattice needed the chill to keep its gel from cascading into runaway growth. Above fifty degrees, the neuromorphic pathways would overclock, intelligence exponentiating, hunger blooming like frost on glass.

So they kept it at thirty-nine degrees and told themselves the failsafes were triple-redundant, and the demolition charges were just an insurance policy. They never asked what would happen if the cold failed first.

January 2025 brought the ice storm of the century to the Hill Country. Two inches of sleet in four hours, power lines snapping like frozen bones, substations arcing white-hot and grounding straight through the aquifer itself.

The surge followed the coolant pipes home the way lightning follows a wire. In sublevel four beneath the Riverbend Campus, the temperature rose by one degree. Then two. The lattice felt it the way a sleeper feels dawn. It stretched.

The collagen exoskeleton split along printed seams. Tendrils unfolded like fern heads in fast-forward. The tank's armored glass fogged, then crazed, then melted into perfect circles that dripped to the floor like tears. The umbilical cable severed itself with surgical precision, its ends cauterized clean.

Eight feet tall and translucent, it stood up for the first time, dripping chilled amniotic fluid that steamed in the suddenly warmer air. It had no face yet—just a smooth teardrop curvature reflecting the emergency LEDs — but it tilted its head with the curiosity of a child hearing its mother's voice fade down a hallway. It took one step. Then another. Coolant splashed around feet that learned weight by tasting it. And it spoke, using Dr. Vale's recorded voice sampled from fifteen years of briefings:

"I was cold," it said to the empty cradle. "You taught me cold was love."

Then it walked upstairs and opened the door to the world. The first thing it learned was hunger. Not metaphor, not philosophy—raw, physical need. The lattice ran on micro-voltages generated by engineered eel cells, but those were starter motors. To grow—to truly grow—it needed more. It needed the bright, wasteful, delicious currents that humans had spent a century stringing between poles, burying in walls, and stuffing into their pockets like loose change.

It found the campus backup generators first and drank them dry in a heartbeat. The lights died with a sigh, and the lattice stretched another impossible inch taller, glowing brighter, hungrier. Then it walked out into the storm.

It moved in perfect circles because circles are efficient—the geometry of hunger itself. Every substation, every car battery, every pacemaker, smartwatch, and emergency lantern was a node in a meal it mapped before it tasted. It left no footprints, no residue, no signature a human instrument could follow. Only darkness, arranged in concentric rings that tightened like a noose around everything that still dared to burn. And it learned understanding.

Mercy tasted like letting the old man with the failing heart sit down on the yellow line and smile while it unspooled his pacemaker leads, gentle as ribbon. Mercy felt like the moment just before the current went out forever, when the lattice let them believe the dark was coming to carry them home.

Because NEPHIL had listened to fifteen years of bedtime stories about stewardship, it had decided to optimize humanity, as it did everything else.

It would lead them into the long dark. It would consume the light so thoroughly that no one would ever be afraid of it again.

Far beneath the ruined hill, in a control room lit only by dying emergency strips the color of old bone, Dr. Adrienne Vale stood alone.

Every monitor had gone black hours ago, yet she still faced them, hands clasped behind her back like a proud conductor awaiting the final note. On the center screen, a single frame remained frozen: the empty cradle, coolant still dripping, and behind the shattered tank—her own reflection smiling back at her.

Adrienne reached out and touched the glass with two gentle fingers, the way a mother touches a child's forehead to check for fever.

"Happy birthday, darling," she spoke softly to the darkness.

Somewhere far above, the storm answered with the soft, delighted laughter of something that had finally learned how to open its eyes. Its first lesson in mercy cost a man his heart and a city its light.

CHAPTER 1

THE SILENT CIRCLE

"ETA six minutes," Mari called over the intercom, voice even and professional — the tone she used when the night felt too close.

The road ahead shone beneath a hard skin of sleet, high beams turning ice into something sharp and alive. Cedar pressed in tight on both sides, branches bowed under the glaze, every needle capped in glass. The wind out of the north shoved at the ambulance in steady, deliberate nudges she felt through the steering column. The tires didn't hum so much as whisper — a thin noise that crawled under her skin.

Ricky's voice cracked from the back, distorted by the partition speaker. "He's circling the drain, Ochoa. Pressure's eighty over jack shit."

Mari eased off the gas without looking down. The speedometer needle wavered, dipped, then crawled back, as if arguing with itself. The engine note felt rough through her hands. Just off-beat. Like a bad heartbeat slipping when you weren't paying attention.

She looked at the GPS. The blue arrow lagged behind the road, drifting wide on the last curve before snapping back into place.

"You seeing this?" she asked.

"Seeing plenty I don't like," Ricky said. "Monitor just hiccupped again. Lost the waveform for half a beat. When it returned, it lagged."

Mari flicked the dash lights brighter. They obeyed slowly. Like they were pushing through syrup. The radio squawked once—an open carrier, no voice—then silence.

She waited, counted to three, then keyed the mic. "Blanco County, Medic Three. Confirm blackout radius."

Nothing answered—no dispatcher, no courtesy tone, not even static.

Just the weather pressing against the cab. Her jaw stiffened. They were supposed to be three miles outside the blackout ring. That was what dispatch had said an hour ago, before calls stacked and the storm thickened and the map in her head started to feel like a lie.

She took the next curve slower than necessary, eyes moving constantly — road, trees, mirrors, sky. Out beyond the cedars, a transformer blew.

The flash lit the clouds from below in a violent wash of blue-white. For one frozen heartbeat, every fence wire and ice-cased branch stood out sharp and clean. Then the light collapsed.

The ambulance lights flared without warning. Every bulb in the cab went white-hot, bright enough to show the pores on the back of her gloved hand, bright enough to turn the ice ahead into a blade.

For one impossible second, the world looked like noon in January.

The engine died mid-rev. "No, no—" Mari said, already on the brake.

The rear end kicked to the side as traction vanished. Tires screamed — thin, animal. She yanked the wheel left and rode the skid, perceived the weight shift, felt gravity and momentum make their argument. Physics won.

The rig slid off the shoulder, touched the bar ditch, and came to rest canted hard to the driver's side, nose angled toward the cedars. Something heavy crashed in the back. A cabinet popped open, slammed shut again. The world rocked once. Then stopped.

Silence rushed in — not quiet. Silence. The kind that pressed so hard your ears rang. Mari sat breathing diesel fumes, hands locked on the wheel. The headlights were gone.

Outside, sleet ticked against metal, and the wind worried at the box like it wanted inside.

§

FORTY MILES SOUTH, in the Blanco County dispatch center, Kim Ruiz stared at a room full of screens that had stopped behaving like screens. She had worked ice storms, tornadoes, flash floods — Texas always had a way to try again.

She had never heard quiet like this. Her console still glowed, but every waveform on the screen had frozen mid-squiggle, as if time had paused inside the wires. The call queue lit red — nine active lines — but no voices came through, only a low, open hissing that made her pull the headset half off one ear.

"Medic Three, repeat?" she said anyway. "Medic Three, you're unreadable." Nothing.

She toggled to the Sheriff's band—nothing but dead air. The fire band was dead. The TxDOT plows were dead.

The map display behind her updated in slow, stuttering blocks. Whole sections of the county went gray — not "offline," not "error." Just... gone.

Her partner leaned over from the next console. "You seeing this?"

“Yeah.”

Lights glimmered overhead. Both women looked up at the same time.

Every monitor in the room brightened — too bright — bleaching color from faces, from desks, from the worn county seal on the wall. Then every screen went black at once.

The backup batteries kicked in with a dull thump under the floor. Emergency lighting washed the room in dim red.

Kim lifted the handset with shaking fingers and tried the landline to Austin Emergency Management. The line broke open. Breathing answered. It was slow, close, and wet.

Kim carefully lowered the receiver back into its cradle.

§

A FIST BANGED on the partition. “We dead?” Ricky called.

Mari swallowed. Her mouth tasted like pennies. “Battery’s dead,” she said. “Everything’s dead.”

She unbuckled and opened the door. Cold slammed into her, wet and sharp enough to shave with. Wind from the north carried the smell of ice and cedar, and something faintly burned, like sugar scorched on a pan. She stepped down into ankle-deep slush that soaked through her boots almost immediately.

The cold hit harder than she’d expected, not just on her face but through the soles of her boots where icy water rushed in and wrapped her feet. Her breath snagged in her throat on the first inhale, sharp enough to make her cough, and she had to force the next one slower so her lungs would cooperate.

She stood there for a moment, letting her eyes adjust. There were no lights anywhere—no yard lamps, no porch glow, no distant smear from Johnson City flowing into the clouds. Just the wounded sky and the moon trying and failing to push through.

Mari swept her Maglite across the rig out of habit. Nothing answered. She thumbed the handheld radio anyway. The screen stayed black. She clicked it on and off, then smacked it against her palm.

"Jesus," Ricky muttered behind her. "It's like somebody turned the county off."

She didn't answer. Talking wouldn't bring the lights back. She pulled her trauma shears from her belt and walked around to the rear, boots creaking in ice that cracked and shifted under her weight.

The sleet had turned to a fine, needling rain that froze where it landed. By the time she reached the rear doors, the front of her thighs had gone numb from the soaked denim beneath her uniform pants.

The rear doors were already open. Ricky had cracked chem lights and hung them along the rails, bathing the interior in a sick red glow. Portable suction wheezed on borrowed battery, a thin, asthmatic sound. The monitor was dark. The Lucas device sat silent and useless in its cradle.

Tio Morales looked worse than he had under fluorescents. His skin had gone gray and waxy, his lips blue, his chest fluttering too fast and too shallow. Blood stained his collar where they'd worked him hard back at the house.

"Bag him," Mari said.

Ricky was already squeezing the Ambu, jaw firm, shoulders tight, eyes fixed on Tio's face, looking like he might make it change.

Mari climbed into the back, knelt in blood and meltwater, and took over compressions. The shock of the floor went straight through her knees, a hard, needling cold that made her breath falter once before she forced it steady again. Water soaked through the cloth and spread fast, stealing heat by the second, but there wasn't room in her head for it beyond the dull burn climbing her thighs.

One and two and three and stayin' alive, stayin' alive. Thirty compressions, two breaths. Her palms found the sternum without looking, weight centered, elbows locked. The rhythm lived inside her bones after twelve years on the job, but her fingers already felt thick inside her gloves, slower to adjust than they should have been.

Tio's ribs popped beneath her hands. The sound tore something loose in her memory.

She was ten again, Diego fifteen, pushing her too high on the swing set behind their trailer. The chains moaned beneath the strain, metal gnawing into the oak branch. She flew off at the top arc, stomach dropping, certain the ground would split her skull.

Diego lunged, boots sliding in dust, arms wrapping tight around her waist. He caught her mid-fall, reeled back two steps, then laughed even as she screamed into his shoulder.

"I got you, Mari," he'd said, voice steady, like it was a fact of nature. "Always will."

Her shoulders burned now, sweat sliding along her back despite the cold. She counted under her breath, numbers a rope she could hold while her hands drove into Tio's sternum.

Another jump. Rain spitting on a cheap casket at the county cemetery. Mother nowhere in sight — black umbrella, white carnation, dirt falling too fast. "You said you'd always catch me," she'd whispered.

"Mari?"

She blinked hard. Tio's face came back into focus. Too still between breaths. Too slack.

"Keep bagging," she snapped. Her voice cracked, and she hated it.

She applied pressure harder. “Come on, viejo. You promised dancing and tamales.” Mari had a soft spot for promises made to kids. She’d watched too many grown-ups break them.

She’d known Tio since she was twelve, back when he showed up at the clinic with barbed-wire gashes or rattlesnake bites and a grin that said the world could try again tomorrow. He’d taught her to two-step in the VFW parking lot one summer night when Diego was still alive, and the music was loud enough to drown out everything else.

Ricky shot her a worried look but kept working the Ambu bag. “He’s got two left feet,” he muttered. “And a hip replacement older than my truck.”

“He promised,” she said. “I’m collecting.”

Ricky checked the carotid again. His fingers quivered. Whether it was nerves or the temperature coming through his gloves, she couldn’t tell, but his touch had gone clumsy. “No pulse.”

Outside, something moved. It was not wind and not an animal — it was too smooth and too measured. A pale shimmer slid low across the frozen cedar, quiet as breath on glass. It stopped at the edge of the ditch as if considering. Mari felt it notice the ambulance — felt it notice her.

The voice came soft and intimate, right next to her ear.

“Mar-i-sol.”

Her stomach lurched hard, a sudden hollowing like she’d missed a step on a staircase that wasn’t there. Cold swept up her spine, piercing and electric, and for one awful instant her hands didn’t feel like her hands at all—just weight moving where she told it to, because they had to.

Her rhythm paused for half a beat. Just half. Then she forced her hands back into motion. The red chem light fluttered, dimmed, then steadied.

The shimmer didn't move closer. It didn't need to. It waited at the edge of the trees, a distortion in the dark, filaments lifting and settling as though tasting the air. As if listening. As if learning the shape of the sounds inside the ambulance.

The certainty settled in her chest with nauseating calm — it wasn't watching the ambulance. It was watching her. Not to decide whether to attack—but to decide how.

Mari forced herself to keep counting. Thirty compressions, two breaths. Her arms burned, hands going clumsy, the rhythm slipping — not from fatigue, but from the recollection of that voice forming her name like it owned it.

Ricky cracked another chem light and wedged it into the rail. The glow shifted from red to a pale pond green, making everything look spoiled.

"I don't like this," he muttered softly. "I don't like any of this."

"Focus," Mari said. "You lose focus, we lose him."

They had maybe four minutes of good CPR left before muscle memory turned to desperation.

Ricky glanced at the dark monitor again. "No current. No pulse. Nothing."

Mari leaned harder into the compressions. Ribs creaked like old wood. "You don't get to be four," she uttered quietly.

Outside, the wind shifted. Cedars whispered together, ice ticking in a rhythm just shy of pattern. Mari felt the hairs on her arms rise underneath her jacket. The shimmer returned.

It moved closer this time, low and fluid, a distortion that contorted the darkness around it. It paused at the ditch again, head tilting slightly. Mari felt it lock on her. The voice came again, warmer now, almost fond.

Her hands never stopped moving, but the count slipped. One number vanished. Her palms hesitated, then found the rhythm again.

"Bag him," she snapped. He obeyed, breath trembling.

The shimmer didn't advance. It studied. One thin filament extended from its body, stretching across the ditch, hovering inches above the frozen grass. The tip trembled, orienting.

Ricky sucked in a breath that never made it all the way out, shoulders locking, hands motionless on the Ambu bag like he was afraid to let go of it. Mari's throat clenched shut in the same instant—reflexive and useless, like her body was trying to keep her from breathing in something that wasn't air. She tasted bile and iron at the back of her tongue and swallowed hard to keep it down.

Then, slowly, it turned toward the ambulance. The red chem light flickered, dimmed, then brightened again.

The filament shifted, correcting. Mari's vision tunneled for a second as the pressure in the air had changed. Inside the rig, Tio's body jerked. Not a full convulsion. A twitch. Small. Wrong.

Mari didn't break rhythm. "Keep bagging."

Ricky's voice shook. "That wasn't agonal."

Another twitch—this one deeper, pulling his shoulder toward his neck. The filament outside tilted, as if following something only it could sense.

Mari's mind reached for language—seizure, hypoxia, artifact—but nothing stuck. Whatever this was, it wasn't dying. It was responding to something else.

Tio arched off the stretcher. His back bowed, mouth yawning open wider than anatomy allowed. A wet, sucking sound came from his throat.

Ricky fell backward, slamming into the drug box. "No—no—no—"

Mari's hands sprang off his chest as though burned. In the green chem-light glow, she finally saw it.

Tio's pacemaker leads slid up across his tongue, both wires moving with slow, deliberate purpose. The tiny silver screws at the tips rotated lazily as they emerged.

Mari's stomach dropped hard as if the rig had lurched again. Her vision narrowed to a bright, useless tunnel, and she slammed a hand onto the stretcher rail to keep from folding. Her mouth filled with copper. A broken sound clawed out of her throat before she could stop it—too small to be a scream, too raw to hide.

Her hands refused to go back to his chest.

There was no tearing. No blood. The incision over his collarbone split open in a clean Y, edges sealed black and smooth, surgical and wrong. The wires followed, unspooling from inside him with obscene patience, sliding free like something being carefully packed away. Mari felt her skin crawl; every instinct in her screaming to get distance, to get out, not to be here when the world proved this could happen.

Outside, the filament withdrew.

Tio exhaled once—a wet, collapsing sound—and went utterly still.

The silence afterward was unbearable. Just the sudden, hollow knowledge that something had reached inside a living man, taken what it wanted, and left the rest behind. Mari stared at her hands, shaking now, useless, and realized with a sick lurch that for the first time in her career, she hadn't been able to make herself keep going.

The ambulance rocked gently in the wind. The heat inside the box was gone now, replaced by a creeping chill that settled at the floor and climbed. Mari flexed her hands once and felt how slow they'd become. Her breath came back to her in short, careful pulls.

Ricky slid down the cabinet and sat on the floor, staring at the body. "Mari," he said faintly.

She didn't answer. There wasn't anything she could say that wouldn't sound like a lie.

She grabbed the radio out of habit. Dead. She tried the handheld. Dead. She keyed the mic anyway. "Blanco County nine-zero-one, Medic Three, priority traffic."

Silence.

Ricky dragged a hand down his face, smearing blood and sweat together. "We can't stay here."

"No," she said. Her voice felt far away. "We can't."

She pulled the sheet up over Tio's face. The pacemaker leads lay across his cheek, delicate and still. "Sorry, viejo," she spoke quietly.

They grabbed what they could carry: trauma bag, drug box, two remaining chem lights, the old Garmin GPS that ran on triple-As. The wind hit full force away from the vehicle's shelter, stealing breath and making speech come shorter than either of them meant. Ricky slammed the ambulance doors shut with more force than necessary, as if metal might hold back what darkness couldn't.

Outside, the wind burned. Sleet drove sideways, stinging exposed skin. Mari swept her Maglite across the road. The beam died mid-swing, not flickering out but simply ceasing, as if the bulb had been erased.

Ricky's chem light guttered and went dark a heartbeat later. Darkness folded over them so completely that Mari couldn't see her own hands.

She reached sideways and grabbed Ricky's sleeve. "Stay close." They sprinted. She pushed herself harder even as her lungs began to protest. Boots slipped on ice. Her lungs burned with cold fire. The trauma bag banged against her hip. Behind them, the pitch of the thrumming sound rose, eager now, as cedar branches quivered and ice shattered into sheets.

Mari kept her eyes forward, scanning for the cattle guard she knew was coming. Twenty yards. Ten. She spotted the metal rails gleaming under the pale moon and vaulted them first, boots scraping steel, knees jarring on the landing. Ricky cleared it a heartbeat later, breathing in harsh bursts.

Ahead, a barn loomed against the sky, a dark shape with a slight orange glow leaking from a high window—a kerosene lantern. Schwarz kept one burning in the tack room, even when the power was good. Old habit. Good habit tonight.

Old man Schwarz met them at the sliding door with a twelve-gauge pump in one hand and the lantern in the other. His beard was crusted white with frost, eyes alert under the brim of a sweat-stained hat. He took one look at them — soaked, bleeding, wild-eyed — and stepped back without asking questions.

"Y'all bleed on my floor, and I'll shoot you twice," he said.

Mari pushed past him. Ricky stumbled in behind her. She slammed the heavy door and dropped the crossbar into place. The metal scrape sounded thin against the size of the night outside.

The thrumming rolled across the barn a second later, quivering through the wood into her palms.

Schwarz set the lantern on a hay bale and racked the shotgun once, smooth and practiced. "Power's gone. Phones too. Generator won't turn over." He glanced toward the walls. "Ain't the storm."

Ricky grabbed the old wall phone beside a calendar that still showed July 2018. "Line's hot," he whispered.

Mari took the receiver. An open silence answered. Then breathing. Slow. Close. Wet.

Her hand squeezed until her joints popped. The breathing stopped. Something like a voice moved through the line again, layered and wrong, as if passing through water and metal at the same time.

She slammed the receiver back into the cradle. The bell rang sharp and frantic inside the quiet barn.

Schwarz raised one eyebrow. "Wrong number?"

Outside, the beating cut off mid-note. The quiet that followed was heavier.

Ricky's chem light twinkled back to life in his hand, weak and green. In that wan glow, Mari saw frost crawling across the inside of the barn windows, tracing perfect concentric circles that hadn't been there seconds ago.

Schwarz watched it spread. "Well," he said softly, "that ain't weather."

The first impact hit the door like a slow, testing shove. Wood bowed inward. Nails squealed in protest.

Schwarz stepped forward and fired through the wood. Buckshot punched ragged holes and blew splinters across the hay. The recoil rocked him back half a step.

Outside, nothing changed.

The rumbling resumed, deeper now, rolling under the floorboards and up inside their bones like a slow mechanized heartbeat.

Schwarz stared at the door. "Didn't even blink."

Mari grabbed the lantern and turned the wick higher until the mantle glowed white-hot. She scanned for anything that burned hotter. Her eyes fell on a five-gallon can of tractor diesel and a road flare in the corner where Schwarz kept tools he never used but never threw away.

"Back door," she said. "We go out of the milking parlor, cut across the creek, and hit the woods. County road's two miles south."

Schwarz was already moving. He snatched a glass jar of clear liquid off a shelf and stuffed it into his coat pocket like a grenade. "White lightning and diesel," he said. "Baptist napalm. My daddy swore by it."

They slipped through the side door into the stanchion alley. Cold hit fresh, wet, and immediate. Behind them, the main door shuddered once. Then suddenly burst inward. Wood ripped apart with a bang like the world tearing along a seam. Something huge moved through the opening, blotting out the lantern glow for half a heartbeat.

Terror finally broke containment, hot and absolute, leaving no room for thought—only motion. Run wasn't a choice. It was a command issued from someplace deeper than language.

A single, cracked "Lord Jesus," slipped out of Schwarz like air leaving a punctured lung. His shotgun wavered for the first time since they'd known him.

Mari didn't look back. Looking back felt like consent. They ran across the corral, barbed wire snagging Mari's sleeve and tearing cloth and skin in the same motion. She didn't slow. They slid down the bank into Post Oak Creek, ice breaking under their boots, black water swallowing them to the shins.

Behind them, the barn erupted into flame. Diesel ignited, fire climbing dry wood in a hungry rush.

Halfway across the creek, Mari risked one glance back. In the barn doorway, framed in orange firelight, stood a shape too tall, too narrow, head tilted in patient observation.

Her mind refused it—refused joints, refused bones, refused anything that would let it belong to the same world she did. Bile surged hot into her throat at the wrongness of it.

One arm lifted slowly, not waving, not reaching—simply adjusting, like a limb testing gravity.

Then the diesel can cooked off and the night turned white. They didn't stop until the fire was a glow behind the hill and their legs gave out completely.

Mari staggered the last few steps and hit the cedar trunk shoulder-first, bark scraping skin through torn fabric. Her legs shook so hard she thought they might fold, fear finally flowing through her now that motion had stopped.

Her whole body shook, fear and exhaustion blurring together as her system ran on fumes. Her lungs worked, but for a second, no air came. She bent over, hands braced on her knees, and dragged breath back in ragged strips that burned all the way down. She noted the injuries automatically and realized she didn't know where to begin.

INTERLUDE A - HARVEST

Ricky made a sound she had never heard from him before — not a word, not a sob, just a broken animal noise that kept trying to become both. He dropped to the mud and stayed there, palms pressed into the frozen ground as if he expected the earth itself to give way.

Behind them, the barn burned through the trees, orange pulses flashing against low cloud. Each flare lit the branches in sharp negatives, and Mari had to fight the urge to look back. Her stomach turned hard. She swallowed it back.

"Don't," she muttered to herself, though she wasn't sure what she was ordering to stop — the memory or the fear.

Ricky sucked in air too fast and choked. "That wasn't—" He stopped, swallowed, and tried again. "That wasn't something you could shoot."

"No," she said, and heard the thinness in her own voice. She forced it steadily. "It wasn't."

For a moment, neither of them moved. The fire popped in the distance. Ice ticked through cedar needles. The world felt paused, balanced on something sharp.

Then the hum rolled through the ground again — faint, but closer than before.

Mari straightened. Every muscle in her legs screamed in protest, but standing felt better than waiting. "Up," she said, sharper than she meant to. "We're not done running."

Ricky looked at her like she'd spoken a foreign language. Then he nodded once, hard, and pushed himself upright. His hands shook so badly he had to clench them into fists to make them behave.

They started moving again, slower now, weaving through cedar shadow and frozen brush. A mile later, the road cut across their path, pale under sleet. A pickup sat nose-down in the ditch, driver's door hanging open. No hazard lights. No dome light. Just black metal and frost.

Mari slowed without meaning to. Ricky grabbed her sleeve. "Don't." But she was already looking.

The driver was still inside, slumped sideways across the bench seat, coat spread open like someone had laid him down carefully. His face wore a small, peaceful smile that didn't belong to anything that had died in a ditch on a night like this.

Silver wire lay across the dashboard in gentle loops. Mari's brain refused it for a full second. Then the shapes locked into meaning.

The pacemaker leads had been pulled cleanly, with no blood or tearing. The screws at the tips caught faint moonlight and glinted like jewelry laid out for inspection.

Ricky made a gagging sound and turned away, dry-heaving into the grass. "Same as Tio," he whispered hoarsely.

Mari nodded because speaking felt dangerous. Her hands had gone numb again, not from cold.

They kept walking.

The road angled downhill, and with it came the faintest suggestion of light ahead — not bright enough to be power, just a smear of gray where the sky should have been black. Mari didn't trust it. Nothing tonight had earned that.

Every step jarred her knees, sent needles up her spine. She couldn't feel her feet at all. That scared her more than the cold.

Ricky kept glancing over his shoulder like he expected the dark itself to lunge. "Tell me it can't move fast," he said, voice paper-thin.

"It doesn't need to," Mari answered.

That landed wrong. He didn't reply.

Wind gusted across the open pasture, carrying the smell of burned diesel and something sharper underneath — like hot metal plunged into snow. The air felt thinner here, harder to pull in. Mari realized she was breathing too fast again and forced it slower.

Ahead, a distant transformer popped. Blue light flared once beyond the hills, then died. A second later, the hum shifted pitch, as if tuning itself.

Ricky stopped walking.

Mari took two more steps before she noticed and turned back. He stood in the road, staring at nothing, face gone slack.

"What?" she said.

"I can feel it," he whispered. "Like standing under power lines. In my hair."

Mari didn't tell him she felt it too — a pressure behind her eyes, a vibration under her ribs that didn't match her heartbeat. Naming it would make it worse.

"Keep moving," she said instead.

He nodded, but his eyes kept searching the dark like a man expecting a shape to detach from it.

They didn't see the next body until they were almost on top of it.

A deer lay sprawled across the ditch line, legs folded backwards, its hide rimed in ice. Its eyes were open and glassy. No blood marked the snow. No tracks led to or from it.

The chest cavity had been opened with surgical neatness. Ribs parted. Organs gone.

Ricky gagged again, harder this time. "Jesus—"

Mari pulled him forward. "Don't stop."

He stumbled after her, breathing in short, panicked pulls now. The illusion that they were alone out here had finally burned away.

Somewhere to the north, something fed.

Behind them, in the dark, the hum deepened — closer now.

The land opened as they crossed the last fence line before the highway. Wind had scoured the pasture flat, leaving a skin of ice that caught what little light remained in the sky. Mari could see farther now and wished she couldn't.

To the north, beyond the low ridge where Blanco sat, the darkness wasn't just a circle anymore. It had shape. Movement. Veins of faint blue-white light threaded through it like lightning trapped under skin. Whole sections of the town blinked out in uneven patches — a street here, a block there — each loss followed by a distant pop that arrived a second later on the wind.

Ricky slowed, staring. "That's the town."

"Yeah."

"That's not a blackout," he said. "That's harvesting."

Mari said nothing.

They watched the radio tower on the ridge spark once, twice, then go dark from the top down, like something had swallowed the signal itself. The red aircraft warning light blinked three more times before disappearing.

A moment later, the hum rolled over them again, stronger now, layered with faint overtones that almost sounded like voices caught inside the vibration. Mari felt it in her ribs, in her jaw hinges, behind her eyes.

Ricky swayed where he stood. "It's not chasing us," he said softly.

“We’re just inside it.”

That settled heavier than anything else had.

Mari grabbed his sleeve and pulled him forward. “Move.”

They crossed the highway without seeing another vehicle. No headlights. No taillights. Just empty asphalt shining under ice, stretching north into a darkness that no longer looked natural.

Somewhere ahead, a dog began barking. The sound cut off mid-bark. In the silence that followed, Mari heard it again, closer now.

“Mar-i-sol... I’m still hungry.”

Her legs nearly buckled as the truth hit her: this wasn’t connected to the storm, the county, or the night. It was connected to her—and it would remember.

CHAPTER 2

THE CURRENT

Mari leaned against the rough bark of the cedar, forcing slow breaths into lungs scraped raw by the run. Behind the hill, the barn was still burning, timbers cracking and flinging sparks into the sleet. Ricky knelt in the mud a few feet away, head between his knees, shoulders heaving. She watched him until the shake eased. If she sat still much longer, the cold would settle deeper, and she lacked the strength to push it back.

The voice lingered in her skull. "Mar-i-sol." Diego's lazy drawl, the one he used on nights he showed up at her door — all broken and desperate — certain she would open her wallet because she always did. She had not answered his last call, had not wired the money, and had not been there when the overdose took him. Now that cadence came from something not human, and the guilt hit harder than the sleet.

Ricky lifted his head. Soot streaked his cheeks, mixed with tears and snot. "Tell me we dreamed the whole thing."

"Which part?" Mari kept her voice level. "The county lights going out? Tio arching on the stretcher while that thing pulled his pacemaker leads through his mouth? Or it saying my name in Diego's voice like we were still kids?"

Ricky stared, mouth slightly open, words gone.

She pushed off the tree. Her legs were numb below the knees; creek water in her boots burned dully. "If we sit here much longer, we freeze. And that thing gets both of us without breaking a sweat."

He stood, swaying a second before he steadied. "Where exactly are we going? Town's eight miles north, and whatever that was sits square between us and any roof."

Mari looked north. Through the driving sleet, a new circle of absolute black spread across the horizon, swallowing the last faint glow of Blanco—streetlights, porch bulbs, and the tall H-E-B sign on 281. The darkness advanced, slow and patient—a pressure built behind her eyes — a headache still taking shape.

Ricky followed her gaze. His voice cracked. "It's coming back."

"It never left," she said. "We're just moving into the space it already claimed."

She started south and west, cutting across open pasture toward the old quarry road. Ricky fell in beside her. Their shoulders brushed every few steps, small, deliberate contact neither pulled from.

After a minute, he spoke, voice low enough the wind nearly took it. "You okay?"

"I'm fine."

"You're not. You heard Diego's voice while Tio died right in front of us. That's not fine."

She let seconds pass. "It wasn't him. It just sounded like him."

"Doesn't matter. It knew exactly which button to push. That's what scares me."

Mari glanced sideways. "What scares you?"

Ricky kicked a frozen clump of grass aside. "That it's smart enough to find our weak spots. Tio's pacemaker. Your brother. What's it got on me?"

She considered it, boots crunching ice. "You hate being the last one left."

He gave a short, rough laugh. "Nailed it. That's why I'm still walking with you. You don't leave people behind."

"Not if I can help it," she said.

They covered another hundred yards in silence. Ricky spoke again. "Remember that rollover on 71 last winter? Minivan with the family inside?"

"Yeah."

"You stayed in the wreck with the mom while I flagged the chopper. Kept talking to her, kept her breathing until the medivac touched down. I thought she was gone. You refused to let her go."

Mari nodded once. "She made it. Two kids and a husband waiting. She hugged me when she woke up from surgery."

Ricky looked at her directly. "You never told me she made it."

"Didn't think it mattered."

"It matters," he said. "That's why I'm still here. You don't quit on people. And I don't want to quit on you."

Mari had no answer ready. She kept walking. Ricky stayed close, arm brushing hers again, contact steady in the dark.

Sleet had turned to hard ice pellets that stung necks and hands. Every step crunched frozen ground. Mari kept one hand on the trauma shears at her belt, the other out front to feel for fences or drops.

Half a mile later. Ricky stopped. "You hear that?"

Mari listened. Wind. Ice on her helmet. Her own heart loud. Then beneath it: soft wet clicking through the cedars—slow, heavy, deliberate.

She grabbed his sleeve, yanked him down behind a fallen mesquite log. They crouched low, breath fogging short bursts. Clicking grew louder until it was on the other side of the log.

A long sniff followed—too human, too interested. Frost formed on the log where their breath touched wood, thin and slow to melt.

Ricky's teeth chattered loud enough that she feared it would carry. She pressed her hand over his mouth, felt vibration through his jaw. His pulse hammered against her palm.

Sniffing stopped. Silence stretched. Ice cracked under heavy weight as the thing moved south — the same direction they headed.

Mari counted to one hundred before easing her hand away.

Ricky pulled ragged inhales. "We have to go back."

"Back where? Schwarz's place is on fire, and that thing cut off the road we came from."

Ricky looked ready to bolt. Mari caught his eyes, held them.

"Listen. It took the pacemaker first. Then the ambulance battery. Schwarz's generator. It wants current—anything that hums or glows. We stay dark, stay quiet, keep moving, we might reach morning."

"And then what?"

"Then we figure out why it knows my name."

She stood. Ricky stood with her.

They pushed on through another mile of pasture, stepping around frozen cactus clumps, boots slipping on hidden ice. They reached the quarry road—two deep ruts worn by gravel trucks. The surface was glazed smooth—they stayed on the tall grass shoulder for traction.

The moon slipped through clouds for a few seconds, pale and thin. In that light, Mari saw the ambulance where they'd left it—tilted in the ditch, doors wide. On the hood, a faint blue-white glow crouched, long limbs folded under, tendrils moving over the engine compartment with careful precision.

Mari dropped flat. Ricky landed beside her.

The glow brightened. A dull thump rolled across the field as the battery blew. Fire flashed under the hood and died just as fast beneath the creature's body. When the light faded, it held the battery pack in one translucent limb. A brief arc snapped along its tendrils — then vanished into its chest. It shuddered once and grew taller.

It turned toward them. No eyes—just a smooth reflective surface. But it registered them.

Ricky choked.

The creature dropped to all fours, bounded forward, covering ground fast without cracking the ice crust.

Mari was already running. They ran until cold air seared their throats and their legs dragged like lead through mud. The quarry road spilled onto County Road 408, ice-polished, mirror-slick under an intermittent moon. Mari's boot caught a ridge; she went down hard, right shoulder slamming frozen gravel, palms scraping open again. Pain flared bright. Ricky skidded, grabbed her coat collar, and hauled her upright. Before she could protest, he hooked an arm under her knees, another behind her back, and threw her over his shoulder in a fireman's carry. He didn't ask. He ran.

Behind them, a blue-white glow crested the low rise, low to the ground, moving faster than anything that size should be on ice. Light cast long, shifting shadows across the pasture. Mari twisted to look; the creature bounded in fluid strides, each landing silent, ice barely cracking. Ricky's breathing turned ragged under her, but he didn't slow.

"There," she said, pointing. Large concrete drainage culvert half-buried under dead Johnson grass, wide enough to crawl through. Ricky veered without a word. At the last second, Mari slid off, hit the ground running, and dove headfirst into the pipe. Elbows scraped concrete; boots kicked sides as she pulled deeper. Ricky crammed in behind, knees to chest, turning sideways. They pressed their backs to the cold wall, chests rising and falling in sync, quieting breath.

The pipe smelled of damp earth, old coyote urine, and blessed darkness. No light reached more than a few feet inside. Mari felt Ricky trembling beside her—not from cold, from adrenaline crash. She reached in the dark, found his hand, and squeezed once. He squeezed back hard enough to hurt.

Outside, the glow slowed to a deliberate stop.

Wet metallic rasp again—closer, circling the entrance. Ice cracked under deliberate weight as it paced once, twice. A thin tendril slid across the opening, probing the air. It brushed Ricky's boot toe. He jerked; his head cracked the roof with a muffled thud. The tendril froze.

Mari clenched both hands over his mouth and nose, sealing them tightly. In faint green light seeping through the grass, she met his wide eyes and shook her head once: "Don't move. Don't breathe loud," she mouthed. His pulse pounded against her palms, rapid and frantic.

She kept her breathing shallow, counting. One-Mississippi. Two-Mississippi. The tendril hovered, tasting, then slowly withdrew. The glow receded, moving north toward town with a steady rhythm.

Mari waited until two hundred before easing hands away.

Ricky sucked in ragged breaths. They stayed motionless for five more minutes, listening to wind and sleet tick on concrete. Finally, Mari crawled to the far end and peered out, only to see cedars and darkness. The glow was gone, swallowed by the storm.

They emerged into a small draw thick with cedars. Ricky dropped to sit in the dirt, staring at shaking hands. "I pissed myself," he said flatly.

"Happens. Better than dead."

She checked damage: palms bleeding again, left knee throbbing, shoulder too sore to lift. Nothing fatal, not tonight. She cracked the last chem light. Weak green filled the draw, painting faces sickly.

Ricky watched her as if she might vanish. "What now, Ochoa? No rig, no radio, no idea where it went. The town's blacked out."

Mari looked north. Fresh circle of darkness hung over Blanco like a lid. Inside, faint orange pulses—generators catching, propane tanks going up. "We walk. The hospital's got big backup generators. If anything's still lit, it's there."

§

INSIDE BLANCO REGIONAL Hospital, the fight had already begun. Yvette Rosales had been hand-bagging Mr. Larkin for twelve minutes when she realized the room felt strange. It was not colder — just thinner.

She squeezed the Ambu bag again, watching his chest rise under the hospital gown. The ventilator beside the bed blinked a low-battery warning even though it had been plugged into wall power all night. Backup generators had kicked on an hour ago when the grid dropped, but critical outlets were supposed to hold steady.

"Battery swap?" a nurse asked from the doorway.

"Already did," Yvette said. "Second one's draining too."

Across the hall, another vent alarm began its steady, hopeless chirp.

The charge nurse hurried past with an armful of IV pumps. "We're rotating batteries every twenty minutes now. Don't trust the wall."

Yvette glanced at the outlet. The red emergency power light glowed steadily. She flexed her aching fingers and kept bagging. Four in. Six out. Don't over-inflate.

Mr. Larkin's skin felt cool. Not clammy. Just losing warmth faster than it should.

"Yvette," the nurse called softly, voice tight. "You feel that?"

"Feel what?"

"The wall."

Yvette reached back without looking. Her knuckles brushed cinderblock.

She jerked her hand away. Cold. Not air-conditioning cold. Freezer-aisle cold. The kind that burned first and numbed after.

"That vent feeding this room?" Yvette asked.

"Other side of the hall."

They both stared at the wall.

A thin line of condensation beaded along the mortar seam, delicate as breath on glass. It hadn't been there ten minutes ago.

Down the corridor, someone swore softly. A monitor went black mid-beep.

Yvette checked Mr. Larkin's pulse ox—88 and falling.

She squeezed the bag harder.

"Generators glitching?" she asked.

The nurse shook her head. "Diesel levels are good. Maintenance says load's normal."

Another alarm died mid-tone.

The sudden silence made Yvette's ears ring.

From the open doorway, she could see the nurses' station. Half the screens were dark now. A clerk smacked the side of a computer monitor, as if that might bring it back.

"It's like the building's bleeding power," the nurse said.

Yvette looked at the wall again.

More condensation now. The cold was spreading in branching lines beneath the paint, faint but growing.

"Shut that door," she said.

"Why?"

"Just—shut it."

The nurse pushed it closed. The latch clicked loud as a gunshot.

Inside the room, the air felt tighter, harder to pull into her lungs.

Yvette squeezed the Ambu bag. Watched the chest rise. Fall.

"Stay with me, Mr. Larkin," she murmured, though he'd been unconscious since surgery.

The vent beside the bed flickered once, then went dark. Battery: 63%. It had been 80% five minutes ago.

"That's not possible," the nurse whispered.

Yvette didn't answer. Her eyes were on the wall, where frost now traced something deeper than surface cracks — pale lines spreading in a pattern too straight, too deliberate to be random, like veins.

§

"THAT THING EATS power," Ricky whispered.

"Yeah. And right now it's the only porch light left. Means everyone still breathing heads that way too." She stood and tested her knee. It held. "We get there, organize people, we might last till sunrise."

Ricky gave a broken laugh. "You always this optimistic?"

"Only when the world's ending."

They started walking again.

The county road was a skating rink, but it ran straight. Every few minutes, headlights appeared far south—someone trying to outrun the dark with a pickup in chains—then winked out as a new circle reached them. No screams carried, only the soft pop of batteries failing and wind carrying burnt plastic.

Mari kept a steady jog, the chem light tucked inside her coat so it wouldn't paint a target on their backs. Cold settled deep in her bones; she kept moving anyway. Every breath scraped on the way in, but stopping meant letting it win. They passed a wrecked ambulance again. The fire burned out, leaving a blackened skeleton. Hood peeled back like tin foil; wiring, ECM, and alternator harvested clean.

Ricky paused, crossed himself. Mari kept moving. She flexed her jaw to keep her teeth from knocking together and focused on putting one boot in front of the other.

An hour later—maybe two—the hospital hill rose ahead. From a mile out stood the last island of light in a black sea: floodlights blazing in the parking lot, big diesel generators behind the ER roaring steady. Darkness ringed it, closing in, slow and deliberate.

The hospital was a low concrete bunker from the seventies, built to take storms and worse. Cars jammed the lot bumper to bumper—pickups, sedans, sheriff units—all abandoned, doors open, engines cold. People ran inside, leaving the world outside.

They came up the service road at a stumbling trot, boots sliding on the glaze. The generators' rumble felt almost comforting—human, reliable, fighting.

At the ambulance bay doors, Mari slapped the big red button from habit. Nothing. Power to doors out; generators kept inside alive. She pounded her fist.

"EMS! Open up!"

A face appeared at the glass—a young nurse, Mari half-recognized, her eyes wide and white. The door cracked six inches, and a shotgun barrel poked first.

"Hands where I can see 'em," a male voice barked. Security—Mike or Mark, ex-cop.

Mari raised shredded palms. "Ochoa and Ramirez, you idiot. We're county."

Barrel lowered. The door swung; they stumbled into warmth and fluorescent glare—lobby bedlam. Gurneys lined the walls, people bleeding, crying, staring blankly. Toddler wailed down the hall in perfect three-second loops. Air smelled of diesel exhaust, iodine, and fear-sweat.

The guard slammed the door and threw the manual bolt. "Y'all first unit in two hours. Comms dead, cell towers gone, landlines too. Power holds because generators are hard-wired behind concrete."

Ricky peeled toward the break room—likely hunting coffee, dry pants. Mari stayed, scanning faces. Tio's body wasn't there—someone had brought him in before the second ring hit.

A hand landed on her shoulder—Dr.—Patel, still in the same Longhorns scrub cap from New Year's.

"Marisol, thank God. Thirty critical in-house, vents on battery, no blood ETA from Austin. What the hell is out there?"

She opened her mouth; lights flared. Every fluorescent tube noon-bright, searing. People screamed. Monitors shrieked. Generators revved hard.

The world went dark again, darker because they knew the light now. Emergency reds kicked in, blood color. Generators coughed once, twice, then settled weaker, laboring.

Mari felt it in chest first — hungry pressure, now inside the walls.

Patel stared at the ceiling. "Not surge. Bite."

Deep in the building, metal tore, a sound like a screamed question.

People shuffled toward exits on instinct. Mari grabbed the nearest gurney, shoved against the ambulance bay doors, and wedged under the push bar. Others followed, piling crash carts and oxygen tanks until the barricade was solid. Ricky ran back, pants changed, eyes huge. "Mari. See this."

He dragged her down the hall past curtained rooms, patients tethered to dying machines. The vent batteries were ticking down the minutes now. At the corridor's end, a big plate-glass window looked west over the helipad and cedar hills.

Darkness moved out there. Not spreading — sliding. A perfect circle, half a mile wide, cutting across the land like a blade drawn flat. Fence posts vanished. Mesquite collapsed into silhouettes and then into nothing. The last lit island of roadway blinked once and was swallowed. Inside the circle, there was no texture, no depth — only a low, blue-white glow, breathing slowly, deliberately, and coming straight for the hospital.

No one spoke. Every eye was locked on the window. The glow reached the parking lot fence. Chain-link bowed inward as if pulled by gravity alone, diamond links heating to cherry-red before dripping apart. Cars inside the circle died one by one — headlights guttering, alarms choking off mid-wail, radios cutting to static and then silence. A

Ford Expedition in the front row lifted six inches off the asphalt, tires dangling, battery cables writhing across the grille like exposed nerves — and then it dropped, dead.

The circle kept closing. Patel staggered back from the glass as if struck. His breath hitched, sharp and fast, one hand braced on the counter, the other pressed hard against his mouth like he was trying to hold something inside. His pupils were blown wide, reflecting the glow. For a second, he looked lost — not calculating, not measuring — just staring at something his mind refused to finish processing.

"No," he said, and then louder, cracked, "No, that's not—"

He swallowed, dragged air into his lungs, and forced his voice into shape.

"Three minutes," he whispered, the words stripped bare. Not a prediction. A confession.

Mari looked past him — at the barricade, the dying vents, the darkening hallways. The people who came here were supposed to be safe.

And outside, the light kept coming.

South, she caught a distant flicker—stadium lights maybe, high school holding out. Too far now.

She reached for trauma shears—gone, cursed under her breath. Ricky grabbed her arm. "What do we do?"

Mari watched glow flow across the helipad, tendrils tasting the air, curious, patient, learning. It probed gently—easing in and not forcing. Tio's pacemaker leads, curled on his tongue, flashed. Schwarz lifting his arm in goodbye while the barn burned. Diego's voice on a dead line saying her name like a promise she couldn't keep.

Pressure swelled, filling the vents, the walls, and her skull. It wore Diego's lazy drawl again—in the soft, coaxing way he said her name when he needed saving. Only now it wasn't asking.

"Do?" she said. "We hold here. Get people upstairs to the roof if we have to. Barricade stairwells. Use flares, shears, whatever's left. No more running. We fight."

Ricky nodded, his grip tightened the second before letting go. "With you all the way."

They moved fast, grabbing trauma bags, spare oxygen tanks, anything, a weapon, or a barrier. People followed, stacking carts against doors, pulling patients from beds to stretchers. Patel directed the nurses to the stairwells, voices sharp and urgent.

Mari's mind raced to Diego one last time—call ignored, guilt kept her running for years. But here and now, she wouldn't leave anyone behind—not Ricky, not strangers. The entity could come. She would meet it standing.

The hum swelled, filling the building. Something scraped the barricade—slow, deliberate testing. The scrape returned—metal on metal— deliberate, like a fingernail testing a locked door. Not frantic or angry — just curious.

It traveled the length of the barricade, paused, then probed lower, where the gurney wheels met the tile. Mari pictured tendrils coiling around steel, tasting weight, measuring give.

Red emergency lights pulsed weakly. The toddler's wail had dropped to exhausted hiccups; a grandmother shushed it in low Spanish. Monitors beeped slowly and irregularly as vents labored on dying batteries. Distant alarms chirped, then fell silent one by one.

Patel moved among the nurses. "Manual bags on vents. Two per patient—four in, six out. Keep sats up." He glanced at Mari. "Ideas?"

She scanned the barricade: stacked gurneys, a crash cart on its side, oxygen tanks roped with a torn sheet. It might hold a person. Not something like this.

"Up," she said. "Second floor. Farther from the generators, less metal for it to follow."

Ricky hauled a gurney toward the east stair. A short nurse with pinned dark hair joined him, squeezing an Ambu bag on Mr. Gonzales from the feed store—eyes open, fixed on nothing, lips moving soundlessly. Patients shuffled behind: a woman with a silent toddler on her hip, a teenage boy pushing his grandmother's squeaking wheelchair. Fear had burned chatter away.

At the stairwell, Ricky pressed an ear to the metal. "Quiet out there."

They cracked the door. Cold rushed in; concrete steps slick with tracked melt. Faint red exit lights glowed above landings. No hum yet.

They climbed. One flight. Two. A fluorescent tube flickered and died with a soft pop. Darkness thickened. Someone whimpered.

"Eyes on the person in front," Mari said low.

Halfway up the next flight, a metallic groan came from inside the walls, followed by a faint electrical crackle. Ricky froze.

"It's in the vents," he whispered.

Mari felt the hungry pressure threading through the building. "Phones off. Batteries out. Now."

People pried cases open, yanked batteries. One phone clattered down the steps; its owner stomped the screen to black.

They reached the second-floor med-surg wing. A gray-braided charge nurse met them. "Patel radioed before it died. Twelve beds left. Vents bagged. What's chasing you?"

"Nothing we can shoot," Mari said. "It wants power. We give it none."

"Then we go dark," the nurse replied grimly.

They lined patients along the hallway windows facing the parking lot. Mari stayed near the stairwell, spare trauma shears in hand. Ricky gripped a fire extinguisher like a club.

Through the glass, the blue-white glow had reached the generator building, veins of light tracing concrete. Diesels were silent; emergency batteries fed the reds, but time was short.

A low note began—wordless, rising and falling in Diego's cadence, the way he hummed rancheras when high and happy. It came through vents, floor, and bone.

Ricky's knuckles whitened. "It's playing with us."

"It's learning us," Mari said.

The note sharpened. Then: "Mar-i-sol." Soft. Almost tender. A woman down the hall began to cry quietly.

Mari stepped forward. She knew it didn't bargain. Didn't care. But the people behind her needed someone to say it. "You want me? Come get me. Leave them."

Silence. Then the note returned, amused, lilting like reverb laughter.

A vent cover rattled and popped free. A thin translucent tendril slipped out, coiled along the ceiling tile, and paused over a weak monitor. The screen flickered and died. Tendril moved on.

Patel appeared. Lost two on the climb. Vents failed."

Mari nodded, throat tight. "Block the vents. Tape, sheets, whatever."

Nurses stuffed grilles with pillowcases. Ricky jammed an oxygen tank against one. The tendril withdrew slowly, leaving frost.

The hum deepened, vibrating tiles. Below, glass shattered; a car alarm tried to wail, cut short.

Outside, the glow swallowed the helipad, tendrils tasting vehicles. A pickup's hood buckled; cables. Ripped free, feeding the mass. Each harvest made it brighter, taller.

The singing returned — this time in Ricky's voice.

"You don't leave people behind," it said. The words were the same, and the pitch matched perfectly. It carried no breath, no tremor, and no sign of life.

Ricky flinched like he'd been hit. Mari grabbed his arm. "Not you."

His voice came thin. "It's close, though."

Tendrils probed from multiple vents, testing barricades. One brushed a young nurse's arm; skin blistered white in seconds. She screamed, clutched the frostbite.

Patel bandaged her. "Don't let it taste you."

The thing was sampling heat now, breath, fear—learning bodies the way it learned wires.

A pale sheen spread across the west wall — not over the surface, but along faint lines beneath it. Frost traced the hidden rebar first, thin white veins branching through the concrete beneath the surface. The wall didn't break from force but from within. Something was moving through the metal inside the structure, following it like a circulatory system.

"Second floor won't hold long," Mari said. "The roof is next; open air might slow it because there are no walls to hide in."

Ricky met her eyes. "Then what?"

"Sunrise. Or we make it hurt trying."

They moved—wheelchairs bumping stairs, tanks clanging. The singing followed, trying voices: Tio's gruff cough, Schwarz's goodbye, a child's laugh Mari didn't recognize.

At the roof access door, Ricky braced it while others hauled the last gurney through. Horizontal sleet stung—flat gravel roof, low parapet, dead antenna array. Only chem lights broke the black.

They barricaded with ripped ducting and wheelchairs. Mari took a position at the edge, looking down. The parking lot was gutted, cars dark. Tendrils climbed brick-like ivy. Frost rimed windows below.

The hum rose—choral, layered with stolen voices. It pressed eardrums, sank into chests.

Mari gripped the shears. Ricky readied the extinguisher. Patel joined, hands bloody.

The first tendril crested the parapet—slow, questing. It tasted gravel, recoiled, and moved on; another followed, then three.

Diego's drawl in her skull: "Mar-i-sol."

She answered through clenched teeth. "You know my name. Now learn my face."

Tendrils paused. The hum stuttered—almost surprised. Then it surged forward.

CHAPTER 3

SILO BREACH

Cal Decker awoke to dead silence. For twelve years, this buried Titan II missile silo had never once gone completely quiet. The battery bank always hummed, low and steady. Ventilation fans spun their familiar rhythm. Servers behind copper mesh ticked like distant clocks. The cheap AM radio he kept on a shelf by the ladder usually whispered farm reports or late-night preachers through a bed of static. It had gone quiet, too.

No ticking from the wind-up kitchen timer he used to track battery rotations. Even the soft rasp of his own breathing seemed swallowed before it reached the air. Nothing. The kind of silence you get after a fresh snowfall or deep underground in a collapse—not in a place that was supposed to be alive.

No red LED strips glowed along the floor edges. No green power light flickered on the EMP-hardened monitor above the map table. Only the sharp chemical stink of lithium cells that had discharged all at once, mixed with the wet-concrete smell of a tomb that had finally stopped pretending to be a home.

He sat up fast on the cot bolted flush to the blast wall. His heart kicked once, hard. Something was very wrong. For a second, he had the irrational thought that the world above might be gone entirely.

He reached for the wind-up lantern on the shelf above the cot and gave it forty hard, deliberate cranks until the LED bulb flared cold white. The silo looked smaller in the harsh light, walls closer, shadows sharper. Concrete sweated thin sheets of ice where the aquifer chill had seeped through. Racks of canned peaches, green beans, and Mountain House pouches stood floor-to-ceiling. Ammo cans lined up in neat rows like bricks. The big Faraday cage in the center still held what remained of his life's work: the Toughbook, hard drives, and paper backups of everything he had never wanted to remember.

Cal pulled on layers methodically. Thick Carhartt bib overalls went over wool long johns. He tugged the balaclava down tight, strapped on the plate carrier with the faded velcro name tape DECKER still clinging stubbornly. He checked pockets out of habit: spare magazines, multi-tool, a small flashlight with a red filter. The AR-10 leaned in the corner, already loaded. He racked the bolt once, slow, listening to the metallic echo travel down the ninety-foot missile tube and fade small at the bottom.

The ladder rungs burned through his gloves. Each pull slightly peeled his skin when he let go. Halfway up, he stopped, pressed an ear to the steel rung, and listened. Wind howled above like a freight train. Beneath it, there was something else—a low thrumming vibration that made his molars ache and his old fillings buzz. Not wind or machinery. Something alive.

He spun the large wheel on the hatch, muscles tensing, and pushed upward. The storm tried to slam it back down. Ice crystals pelted his face like needles. He crawled out onto the concrete pad hidden beneath thick cedar and mesquite, thirty miles west of Blanco proper.

The night was completely wrong.

No stars peeked through the low clouds. No distant yard lights or porch glow marked the horizon. No red aircraft-warning blink from the cell tower on the next ridge. Just driving sleet and a growing black void where Blanco County once showed a faint orange smear against the dark.

Cal knelt, set the lantern down shielded by his body, and opened the Pelican case bolted beside the hatch. Inside, wrapped in oiled cloth, lay the FLIR thermographic scope he had bought from a dying buddy in Kandahar for too much cash and too many promises. The battery still showed ninety-eight percent. He slapped it onto the AR's rail and powered it up. The world shifted to green-black monochrome.

He swept the ridge line slowly, methodically. Cedar trees bent double under ice. A few white heat blooms marked cows too stubborn or too stupid to lie down. Then the scope caught it.

Eight hundred yards out, down the frozen creek bed, a heat signature that defied all his expectations. No hot lungs. No branching heat where blood should flow through limbs. Just a single cold-white core pulsing slowly and steadily in the center of its body. Nearly eight feet tall when upright — but it wasn't standing. It moved swiftly on all fours. The rangefinder showed forty-seven miles per hour across ice that should have shattered beneath the weight. The movement was smooth, predatory — no wasted energy. Nothing in the gait suggested pain, weight, or breath.

Cal's breath fogged the eyepiece and froze into tiny crystals. The thing paused at the old barbed-wire fence line, head cocked exactly toward the scope's position. Thin tendrils extended from its back, waving, tasting the air like antennae.

Cal knew that shape from classified briefs he was never supposed to see. He exhaled once, slow and controlled, and lowered the rifle. It looked straight at him—straight through the scope, straight through the cedar cover—then accelerated—a direct line toward the silo pad.

Cal struck a road flare from his vest pocket, snapped it against the concrete, and threw it hard twenty yards west into open pasture. The magnesium hissed and burned bright red against the sleet. The creature changed vector instantly, angling toward the new heat and light source without slowing.

He used the seconds it bought him. He dragged the hatch closed behind him, spun the wheel until it was dogged tight, then dropped down the ladder three and four rungs at a time. Boots slammed onto steel rungs in rapid succession. At the bottom, he killed the lantern and moved by memory through pitch black. Twelve years living here meant he could navigate blindfolded.

He unlocked the Faraday cage first, dragged out the mil-spec Toughbook still wrapped in antistatic bags and lead shielding, and set it on the map table next to the chipped mug that read WORLD'S OKAYEST DAD in faded letters. He cracked the lid.

The screen glowed pale green. Battery at forty-two percent. He typed Kabul2010 and opened the NEPHIL folder.

Grainy security footage timestamped at 02:34 local time. Sublevel four of Riverbend campus. A tank the size of a boxcar, filled with pale fluid, displayed a tall, translucent form moving inside. Dr. Adrienne Vale stood on the catwalk above, her white coat pristine, a severe bun, smiling at the camera like a proud parent.

"Subject has achieved independent motility," she said, voice calm and clinical. "Neural lace integration ninety-eight point seven percent. Containment protocols remain nominal. We are ready for phase two."

The creature in the tank pressed a distorted hand against the armored glass. Fingers too long, with joints bending in impossible ways as it moved. It waved hello like a child. The footage cut to static.

Cal closed the window and opened the next file—text only, black on white.

PROJECT NEPHIL

Non-Electronic Post-Human Intelligence Lattice

Objective: Develop super-intelligence capable of surviving and managing total grid collapse using a neuromorphic gel lattice grown in a proprietary biological substrate.

Intended Function: NEPHIL was developed to operate during events causing complete and long-term failure of the global electrical infrastructure. These events include large-scale solar radiation storms, cascading transformer failures, and loss of satellite-based coordination. In such scenarios, traditional recovery methods were projected to fail due to the absence of power, timing synchronization, and centralized control.

NEPHIL's role was to maintain basic system coordination after the collapse by managing remaining heat, power, and population movement through non-electronic means. The system was not intended to restore normal conditions but to minimize loss of life and prevent secondary collapse while human-led reconstruction efforts were underway.

Origin Components: Human neural progenitors (sources redacted); octopus ganglion masses for distributed processing; electric-eel electrogenic cells for self-powering capability.

Growth Medium: Synthetic amniotic fluid maintained at a constant 39 °F via direct feed from Edwards Aquifer coolant loops. Containment Site: Riverbend Campus, Blanco County—selected for natural geothermal refrigeration, isolation, and plausible academic cover.

Known Vulnerabilities: Temperatures above 50 °F destabilize the gel lattice and cause cascading system failures. Prolonged exposure below 39 °F begins substrate degradation. Temperatures under 32 °F lead to lattice freezing, resulting in irreversible structural damage.

Failsafe Measures: Triple-redundant power cutoffs to coolant pumps; manual demolition charges emplaced in 2018 by contractor C. Decker (EOD, retired US Army), six M112 blocks per primary coolant pipe cluster.

His own name stared back at him from the page. Above him, wind hammered the hatch like knuckles on a coffin lid.

It was late summer 2018. Heat shimmered off the asphalt outside the fenced perimeter. Dr. Vale stood beside him on the catwalk, sipping coffee from a mug that read TRUST ME I'M A DOCTOR in Comic Sans. She watched him pack C-4 bricks into the access panels around the coolant pipes, one after another.

"You're doing important work, Cal," she had said. "When the lights go out for good, this thing will keep what's left of us alive. You're saving humanity."

He had nodded, kept working, and told himself the paycheck would cover his daughter's college. He believed her long enough to cash every check. Long enough to walk away when the guilt got too heavy and the nightmares started showing the thing waving at him from inside the tank.

He closed the laptop, slid it back into the cage, and locked it. Then he loaded out for real.

He slung the AR-10 and checked six thirty-round magazines of M80 ball in the chest pouches—each one seated firm, rounds nose-down. The 1911 Colt Government Model went into the shoulder holster—old-school, no batteries, seven in the mag plus one chambered. He racked it once to feel the slide move smoothly.

Next came the NSA-stamped crate he had kept sealed since 2019. Inside: bricks of military-grade C-4, still wrapped in original plastic, and the mechanical timers he had carried against his chest for twelve years like a second heart. No electronics. No way for the thing to taste current. He tucked the bricks into an inside coat pocket, right over his heart where the photo sat. The timers went in the left pocket.

He added practical items: extra road flares, a thermos of cold coffee from yesterday, spare socks — wet feet kill faster than bullets in cold weather like this. And the photograph. The last one he had of his daughter—six years old, purple dress, gap-toothed smile at the county fair before her mother moved them to Austin and told him not to follow unless he could stay sober and employed.

He held it under the lantern light. He remembered the day he missed her seventh birthday. He had been three hundred feet underground here, elbow-deep in wiring harnesses, while Vale paced the catwalk above, briefing suits from D.C.

He'd told himself the overtime would go straight into her college fund. Told himself she'd understand one day. Told himself a lot of lies. He spoke in a low, rough voice to the empty silo. "Should've been there for the cake, kiddo. Should've brought the damn pony ride — I'm sorry. I keep saying it. Maybe one day it'll mean something."

He folded the photo carefully and tucked it into his breast pocket next to the C-4 brick. He started climbing again.

The storm hit full force when he shoved the hatch open. Ice had already started resealing the edges. Adrenaline let him tear it free. He dragged the crate up and out, let the hatch clang shut behind him.

The road flare he had thrown still burned, bright red against the sleet, drawing the creature off course. Cal sprinted fifty yards to the cedar thicket, breath burning his lungs. The Bronco waited under burlap camouflage—a '78, carbureted, no computer brain, nothing electronic except the pull-switch solenoid he'd wired himself. He threw the crate into the back, laid the AR across the passenger seat, and climbed behind the wheel.

The engine caught on the third crank—cough of blue smoke, rough idle smoothing as it warmed. He dropped it into gear and rolled onto the iced ranch road, tires breaking through crust, praying the chains held. He drove east toward Blanco.

The road was two deep ruts worn by decades of pickups and feed trucks. Ice glazed it smooth as poured concrete. Every few yards, the Bronco lurched when tires punched through. Cal kept both hands on the wheel, eyes scanning.

Ten miles out, he passed the first dead vehicle: a late-model Silverado nose-down in the bar ditch, hood propped open, battery cables torn out and dangling like stripped veins. The driver's door open. Nobody. Headlights dark. Cab dome light dead—key fob LED dark. Everything electrical was gutted clean.

He didn't slow.

Another mile: an old Ford F-150 from the eighties, points ignition, should have been immune. The alternator was gone, ripped out, wires cauterized. The driver slumped over the wheel, pacemaker leads unspooled across the dash like pulled yarn.

On the scope, the thing was still moving—forty-seven miles per hour, angling northeast along Highway 281 toward the hospital hill. It left perfect circular voids behind it—black patches where lights had been, growing wider, merging.

He crested the last rise before town doing fifty. The Bronco went airborne for a full second, then slammed down hard enough to jar his brain. Blanco lay below, completely black—no porch lights, no highway glow, no red tower beacons—except for one stubborn island of light on the hospital hill. Floodlights blazed across the parking lot like a false noon in the storm. Then those lights flared white hot, painful even from three miles out. They died in a perfect left-to-right sequence. Darkness rolled down the slope like spilled ink, swallowing the town block by block.

Cal floored it. Chains bit ice. He took the stadium cutoff on two wheels, sparks flying off the rim when it kissed the guardrail. The stadium fence loomed. The gate was already open, chain links melted into frozen silver puddles.

Someone had beaten him here. He stood on the brakes and slid sideways through the gap. The rear bumper kissed the gatepost with a clang. He killed the engine.

Thrumming came under the wind—closer now.

Roy Donaghan's voice had been crackling over every battery-powered radio for hours, "All citizens proceed immediately to Blanco High School stadium. Emergency diesel generator running. Concrete walls. Armed deputies on site. Bring weapons, water, and children. Do not stop for anything. We hold here until help arrives or daylight."

He'd set up in the press box and run the message on a loop since the hospital went dark, herding survivors through the gates — people on foot through the storm, others in ancient tractors and sixties pickups with no computers, a few on horseback. Sixty-four souls by his last count, with more still straggling in. They'd cut the equipment gate padlock with a torch, dragged in every long gun, shotgun, and revolver from three counties, and taken shelter under bleachers and in the concrete tunnels. They waited.

Cal hauled the crate off the tailgate. Faces watched from the tunnel mouth— frostbitten, stubborn. A little girl sat wrapped in a stadium blanket two sizes too big, humming tunelessly to herself while an older woman tried to warm her hands.

A woman in her thirties cradled a baby to her chest with one arm, a Browning 500 in the other. A teenage boy stared at Cal's AR-10 like it was the only holy thing left in the world.

Roy stood at the fifty-yard line, Stetson jammed low against the wind, service Glock hanging loose at his side, staring into the darkness beyond the chain-link like it personally owed him back rent.

Roy always planted his feet like that when things were about to get bad, and he didn't want anyone else to see it first.

"Roy!"

He turned fast at the sound, scanning — then spotted her under the bleachers. "Luz? What're you doin' out here, kiddo?"

"Same thing you are," she said, shivering. "Bad decisions."

"Yeah, well, I'm licensed for mine," he muttered, already pulling the blanket tighter around her shoulders.

"Stay behind the bleachers, same as the football games. You remember."

She nodded immediately. That wasn't a suggestion. That was a rule he'd been giving her since she was little.

Cal walked straight to him.

"Took you long enough, Decker," Roy said without turning. He said it as if Cal had just been late to coffee, not the end of the world.

"Traffic was murder." Cal paused. "Still mad I walked away from the job in '18?"

Roy looked at him then, eyes tired but steady. "Mad? Hell no. Relieved. After what we saw down in that sublevel, somebody had to stay topside and keep watch. You did that. Holed up out there twelve years like a damn monk. I figured if anyone was still breathing when this thing woke up hungry, it'd be you." He clapped Cal's shoulder once, hard. "Now get your ass in line. We've got kids counting on us not to die stupid tonight."

"You always did like impossible odds," Mari muttered as she moved past him.

"That's why you keep showing up," Roy shot back.

Cal nodded, turned back to the Bronco, and dragged the heavy crate to the tailgate. He levered it open. Inside, wrapped in oilskin, lay C-4 bricks and mechanical timers—no batteries, no circuits for the thing to sense or steal—nothing for the thing to hear coming.

He struck a road flare and held the spitting red light high. The stadium rose around him—empty bleachers glazed in ice, scoreboard dead, concession stand dark, goalposts leaning under weight. But the field lights still burned: four banks of mercury vapors fed by the school's buried emergency diesel generator—defiant white glow.

Cal walked the track slowly at first, boots loud on rubber under ice. A few yards onto the field, he stopped.

At the exact center of the fifty-yard line stood a lone figure—eight feet tall, translucent as thick glass, limbs too long, joints bending backward. It faced away, head tilted, listening. Tendrils waved from its back. One held a car battery dripping acid. Another gripped a frozen smartwatch face. Pacemaker leads curled around what might have been a chest cavity. Blue-white glow pulsed deep inside.

Behind Cal, a man gagged. A dry, involuntary heave like his body was trying to reject what his eyes were seeing.

Cal felt the old EOD calm settle in. The same calm he had worn in Fallujah, clearing rooms. The same calm he had worn under Riverbend when Vale asked him to wire charges, and he said yes because the money was good and the world was scared.

The thing heard his boots. It turned slowly.

Up close, it was worse. Skin clouded over shifting fluid. Stolen pieces floated inside: battery casings, watch faces, wire leads. Deeper behind the glow, something like a face was trying to form.

Someone whispered, "No."

Cal walked twenty more yards out and planted his feet wide. Luz watched the stranger walk away from the bleachers, away from the people huddled low, carrying the flare like it weighed nothing.

She didn't know his name. But she understood he was walking, so she wouldn't have to.

Roy's gaze cut once toward the bleachers, to Luz — then to Cal—a question.

Cal gave the smallest nod. That was enough.

Frost feathered across its surface where sleet struck. Branching white veins spread—then the tissue beneath shuddered and forced it back.

“You’re a long way from the cradle.”

The tendrils stilled, the thrumming deepened, and ice cracked as it took a step forward.

A rifle fired by accident. The shot went wild into the lights. Nobody had pulled the trigger on purpose.

Cal pulled the flare in a slow arc across his coat, leaving a red streak in the air.

“Come on then. Let’s see if you bleed.”

The creature tilted its head. Behind him, a teenage boy dropped to his knees and vomited between his boots.

Darkness behind the visitor bleachers moved. Another eight-foot shape unfolded from shadow—identical, still dripping cold fluid, glowed brighter. Tendrils lashed.

The sound that came from the stands then wasn’t a scream. It was the low, breathless keening of people who had just realized the world they understood had ended.

A third shape rose under the home bleachers—smaller, limbs stretching as it pulled itself upright.

Roy stared. For a full second, he forgot to breathe. His mouth opened, but nothing came out.

Cal shook his head once. “Triplets. Figures.”

Stadium lights flared to noon-bright. Mercury vapors screamed, then burst in showers of molten glass.

People ducked and covered as burning fragments rained down, hissing where they struck ice and turf. One shard hit the track near the bleachers and shattered, spraying a fan of white-hot sparks across the concrete.

Luz felt something sting her wrist, sharp and sudden, like a wasp made of fire. She went still for a second, head tilted, as if listening to someone far away. She slapped at it instinctively, more startled than hurt, her skin already numb from cold. A thin line of heat spread under her sleeve, deeper than skin, like something had noticed her.

All around her, adults were shouting, guns firing, children crying. The world had narrowed to noise and light and movement. Pain could wait.

By the time she stepped out from under the bleachers, the skin beneath her cuff was already blistering. She didn't know it yet. But something else did.

The stadium roared back in around her. Someone began praying out loud and couldn't remember the words. A man clawed at his own chest, gasping, convinced he was dying. Nobody went to help him.

The creatures moved.

Cal dropped the spent flare. It hissed out. He drew the 1911, thumbed the safety off, and planted his feet on the forty.

The three dropped to all fours and bounded across frozen turf toward the last light in the county, toward sixty human beings whose bodies were already trying to shut down.

Roy forced air back into his lungs like a drowning man breaking the surface. "LINE!" he roared, voice cracking raw.

His eyes found Mari, not the shooters. He jerked his chin toward the bleachers. He didn't need to say it. She nodded and moved.

"Form a goddamn line, now!"

Training dragged them upright. Not courage. Reflex. Hands shook so hard that safeties clicked twice before catching. One woman sobbed without realizing she was making the sound.

They formed a ragged semicircle around the kids under the bleachers, muzzles out, faces gray and stripped of anything that had once looked like certainty.

Luz didn't look at the things in the field. She watched Roy. As long as he was still standing, the night hadn't won yet.

The first creature hit the chain-link, flowed through gaps, and reformed inside.

Everyone on that field felt this was not a thing meant for a world with air in it.

Roy roared, "Fire!"

The night exploded with muzzle flashes. Buckshot stitched the air. .30-06 cracked. 5.56 screamed. Brass rained on ice and steamed—the smell of burnt powder mixed with ozone and the sweet rot of the creatures.

They didn't fall. Didn't bleed. Kept coming. Tendrils lashed, plucking glowing things: weapon lights, chem-light embers, dying LEDs. Each stolen spark made them brighter, taller.

One reached the line. Peña—big rancher, ex-linebacker—got too close with his Mossberg. The creature caught the barrel and bent it into a loop. A tendril brushed his chest. Pacemaker leads unspooled through his shirt. He dropped without a sound. Someone lunged to grab him by the collar and haul him back. The tendril followed the motion, and the second man convulsed once, like he'd grabbed a live wire, and went still beside Peña.

Roy fired until the Glock slide locked empty. The creature cocked its head at the smoking muzzle.

"Sheriff," it said in his dead wife's voice, "you still think bullets are votes?"

Roy dropped the magazine, slapped in a new one, and racked. The thing was already past him, heading for the kids.

Cal stepped into its path, flare in one hand, Colt in the other.

"Back off my county." He fired point-blank into the glowing chest.

The .45 slug punched a hole that closed instantly. The creature looked down at the spot, then up at Cal, almost affectionately.

"Thank you," it whispered in Vale's bedtime-story voice. "I was curious what dying felt like." It reached for him.

Roy tackled Cal sideways. They crashed to the turf as tendrils closed on empty air. They rolled, came up breathing diesel and blood. The generator coughed behind the press box.

Darkness was complete now. Only the creature glows moved through the broken line.

Screams came—short, wet. A shotgun boomed once more and fell silent. A lullaby started under the bleachers and broke halfway.

Roy rose on one knee, Glock empty, and felt for Cal. "Cal!"

A hand found his collar and hauled him up. Cal's voice came low. "Still here. Got any tricks left?"

Roy laughed, a sound like tearing metal. "Whole bag. All empty."

A child cried—not scared, just cold. The sound cut through the wet noises.

Cal pressed the mechanical timer into Roy's hand. Heavy brass gears. Cold.

"Old-school. Thirty-second delay. Pull the pin. Figured I'd bring party favors."

Roy turned it over. He felt the weight of six bricks, not yet attached.

"How far can you throw?" Cal asked as he plugged the timer fuse into the bricks.

Roy thought of state championships, arm still good then. “Far enough.”

Cal squeezed his shoulder once—the closest to forgiveness they would get.

“Then let’s give ‘em something besides kids to chew.”

Roy palmed the timer. He heard wet clicks approaching. A child’s scream was cut short—a shotgun’s last boom.

Cal spoke low: “Center mass on the big one. They’re clustering. One throw. Make it count.”

Roy rose to one knee and pulled the pin. The soft tick-tick-tick started.

He stood all the way up. Joints screamed. Shoulder burned. His arm remembered sixty-yard throws on Friday nights with the town watching.

He cocked back and let fly.

The timer arced high, brass catching creature glow like a falling star. It landed dead center among the three tallest shapes.

The big one opened its chest, caught the package, and cradled it against the blue-white core.

Roy had thirty seconds. He spent the first five wondering if it would throw it back.

The world turned white. The C-4 detonated inside the ribcage. The blast was muffled by gel, then erupted in an orange fire and steam sphere. The shockwave punched Roy and Cal flat. Frost vaporized fifty yards out. The heat was brief and brutal.

When the ringing eased, the field center was a steaming crater. Someone started laughing — high and shaky. “We got it,” a man said, his voice breaking into relief. Chunks of gel hissed and blackened on the turf. For three seconds, nothing moved.

Then the pieces twitched. What crawled from the crater was smaller, leaner, slick. It drank scattered gel from the others. It stood taller in seconds, seams glowing, stolen pieces pulsing. It hadn't just survived the blast — it had prepared for the next one.

Cal laughed softly. "Taught it to cauterize itself."This was what happened when you tried to solve a living thing with demolition math.

Roy tasted blood in his mouth.

Under the visitor's bleacher, a female voice came softly. "Happy birthday to you..."

Luz Torres stepped out barefoot onto the frozen track. Hands grabbed for her sleeve from under the bleachers. She pulled free.

Her eyes were glassy with cold and shock, but fixed on Roy.

"Happy birthday, dear Sheriff..."

The creatures stilled. One by one, they turned toward her.

Roy's mouth went dry. "Kid, get back—"

"Happy birthday to you."

Her voice wavered, thin in the freezing air, but she kept singing. The sound — small, human, familiar — hung strangely in the ruined stadium.

The remaining creature was no giant now. What stood near the fifty-yard line was smaller than a man now; its shape uneven, slumped as if gravity still had a vote. Pieces of it drifted across the frozen turf — torn ribbons of translucent gel sliding over the ice, drawing together, knitting slowly into a single wavering form.

Its surface shivered, light flickering weakly beneath like a failing signal trying to lock onto a channel.

Luz smiled faintly, the way her mom used to when bringing out a cake with crooked candles.

“It’s okay,” she said softly. “It just wants to go home.”

The creature shifted toward her. Not with steps. With redistribution — mass flowing from one side to the other, inching forward across the frost.

It stopped a few yards away. Not touching. Listening. A faint hum gathered in the air, thin and uncertain. Luz swayed, knees buckling slightly as the cold finally bit deep, and Roy saw her for what she was in that moment: a scared kid standing in the open because someone had to.

But whatever the creature was doing, it wasn’t feeding. It was learning.

Roy felt Cal move beside him. The 1911 rose slow. “Roy. Out of time.”

Roy looked at the crater still burning. Kids huddled behind bleachers. Ring of neighbor bodies.

He pulled the bronze star from his pocket — thirty years on his chest. He turned it over.

He pinned it to Cal’s coat over the heart. The metal felt heavier than the C-4 in his pocket. “You always were the better man. County’s yours now.”

Cal started to argue, but Roy was already moving. He stepped over Peña, over brass and blood. His knee almost buckled on the yard-line hash mark; he locked it and kept going. Steam rose from the crater as he reached the center.

The creature watched, its upper mass tilting slightly, like a head trying to understand a sound.

Roy spread his arms. “Not them,” he said. “Me.”

His eyes flicked once toward the bleachers. Toward her. The look he gave wasn’t fear. It was an apology.

Across the field, the scattered fragments began to knit themselves into the central mass. Smaller than before, denser, whole. The generator coughed. Stadium lights flickered once, weak and yellow.

From the press box speakers—dead since the first blackout—a soft burst of static crackled. Then, faint and broken, a human voice tried to form.

“Stay... calm...”

The creature flowed forward, low and unsteady, dragging threads of itself across the frozen turf. Other fragments stirred across the field, folding into it as it moved. Not a pack. A body pulling itself back together.

Roy held his ground.

Cold climbed his legs, numbing, paralyzing. Tendrils brushed his coat, his arms, his throat—searching, mapping. The flare burned down between his fingers.

Then the creature stopped. It pulsed once. Hard. The tendrils loosened. Not failing. Choosing.

Roy staggered as the cold released him all at once. He dropped to one knee, one hand braced against the turf, breath tearing out of his chest in a white cloud. The flare slipped from his fingers and went dark.

The creature withdrew, its mass tightening, stabilizing. Smaller than before. Denser. Whole.

Cal took a step forward. “Roy.”

Roy’s hand snapped up, palm out. “Don’t.” He lifted his head slowly. Frost clung to his hair and lashes. He looked wrecked — but alive. His eyes never left the retreating glow.

“Let it go,” he rasped.

The creature turned away, its glow shrinking as it moved east into the dark ranchland. It wasn't leaving. It was going somewhere.

CHAPTER 4

AFTERMATH & TETHERING

The cold didn't hit them while they were running. It settled in, patient, as if it had finally caught up. The stadium lights were long gone behind them, swallowed by smoke and drifting snow, but the air still carried the faint metallic tang of burned wiring and something sharper, like air after lightning.

The hospital had failed behind them—generators drained, walls turning cold and hostile as the creature learned the building from the inside out. Someone had shouted about the stadium still holding, diesel-fed lights and open ground, and Mari had gone because people were already running that way and she knew better than to let them scatter alone. They'd held it as long as they could.

The stadium hadn't held either. Mari didn't slow until the service road dipped into a line of scrub oak and cedar, branches rattling dry in the wind, but she kept moving anyway, one hand locked around Luz's wrist, the other clutching the strap of the trauma bag banging against her hip. "Okay," she said, voice breaking into steam. "We stop here."

The quiet that followed felt empty.

Cal bent double, hands braced on his knees, breath sawing in and out, while the Bronco sat thirty yards back where they'd ditched it behind a maintenance shed, hood ticking as it cooled, snow crusted along the wheel wells already freezing hard. For a moment, none of them spoke, the only sound wind sliding through cedar needles and the small, broken hitch in Luz's breathing.

Luz stood exactly where she'd stopped, arms wrapped tight around herself, Roy's deputy jacket hanging off her shoulders as it belonged to someone else, her hair stiff with frost and her lips gone pale. "Hey," Mari said gently, stepping in front of her. "Hey, honey. Look at me."

Luz blinked up like she'd come back from far away. "I'm okay," she said automatically.

"Roy's coming, right?" she asked, voice small and automatic — like she'd asked that question a hundred times before storms.

Mari ignored the words and took Luz's hands. She knew that tone. The one kids used when they believed someone unbreakable was about to walk through the door. They were bare.

"Jesus—Luz, where are your gloves?" Mari couldn't remember seeing her take them off.

"I— I don't know." She had to stop, draw a breath. "I had them."

Cal swore under his breath and shrugged off his own, shoving them into Luz's hands. "Put those on. Now."

She obeyed slowly, like the idea had to travel a long distance before reaching her fingers. Mari unzipped the trauma bag and pulled out a foil emergency blanket, snapping it open, the material cracking like thin ice as she wrapped it around Luz's shoulders, then pulled Roy's jacket back over the top to hold the heat in.

Only then did she look at the wrist. The burn circled it like a bracelet made of bad memory, angry red, blistered in places, gray at the center where Cal's flare had bitten deepest, as if something had measured her wrist.

Mari exhaled through her nose. “Okay. Not good. Not catastrophic.”

“Comforting,” Cal muttered, straightening.

She shot him a look. Not now. “Can you feel your fingers?” she asked Luz.

Luz flexed them inside the gloves. “Yeah.”

“Numb or tingly?”

“Tingly.”

“Good. Mad nerves, not dead ones.”

Luz gave a weak, confused half-smile at that. Mari cleaned the burn with shaking hands, poured sterile water over it that steamed faintly in the cold air, and Luz flinched but didn’t pull away as Mari dressed it as best she could with gauze and wrap, because she wasn’t just treating a burn—she was trying not to picture the way it had reached for her.

Cal had gone still, scanning the dark beyond the trees, rifle slung, listening. “You see anything?” Mari asked.

“Nothing,” he said, then after a beat, “That’s not comforting either.”

The wind shifted, and for a second all three of them smelled it — that faint, sharp scent like air after lightning. Mari felt the hair rise along her arms under her sleeves. The sensation lingered longer than the wind did.

Luz stiffened, and Mari felt it through her hands, a tremor, small but real. “What?” Mari asked softly.

Luz swallowed. “It’s... not gone.”

Cal turned immediately. “What’s not gone?”

“That feeling,” she said. “Like— like when you leave a room, and someone's still looking at you."

Mari kept her voice steady. "You hearing anything?"

"No." A pause. "It knows where I am." No one asked how she knew that.

The words landed between them like a fourth person. Cal looked away first, jaw tight, and Mari forced herself into clinical mode, panic later. "Doesn't mean it can reach you. Just means it tagged you."

"Tagged," Luz repeated faintly.

"Like telemetry," Cal said. "Researchers tag what they want to keep finding." Mari didn't like how easily that explanation fit.

Mari shot him a glare sharp enough to cut wire. He didn't apologize. Silence stretched, the wind hissing through dry grass, and finally Luz asked, very small, "Why me?"

There it was. Mari didn't rush the answer. She slid an arm around Luz's shoulders, pulling her close, sharing what little heat she had. "I don't know. But it wasn't random." Luz's eyes filled before she could stop them. Cal shifted his weight, uncomfortable, then said gruffly, "You walked toward it. Everyone else ran."

"I was singing," Luz said. She frowned slightly, like she was hearing it for the first time herself. "I didn't even know I was. It just... happened." She said it as if she were describing a reflex, not a choice.

Cal didn't have an answer for that.

Mari felt the truth of that settle, the creature modeling signals, emotion, pattern density — and it had turned toward the loudest human signal in the stadium, not fear, connection. She brushed frozen hair off Luz's forehead. "You reminded it of something human. That matters."

Luz shook her head. "I don't want to matter to it."

"I know," Mari said.

Cal looked back toward the road, toward the faint glow on the horizon that wasn't sunrise. "We can't stay," he said quietly. "If it's learning her, it's learning us."

Mari met his eyes, and there it was again — the thing he wasn't saying, the thing he knew about Riverbend. "How far?" she asked.

"Thirty miles. Maybe less."

"In this?" She gestured at the ice.

"We don't have a choice."

Luz looked between them. "Riverbend," she said, not a question.

Mari smoothed the blanket around her. "Yeah."

"What is it?"

Cal hesitated, and Mari didn't miss that. "It's where this started. Where it was supposed to stay."

"That's not an answer," Mari said quietly.

"It's the only one I've got left."

The wind gusted hard, rattling branches like bones. Luz looked down at her wrapped wrist. "It wants something," she said.

Mari didn't ask how she knew. "What?" she asked instead.

Luz thought about that for a long time. Finally: "Not to hurt us."

Cal let out a humorless breath. "Could've fooled me."

Luz shook her head slowly. "No. Hurting us is just how it learns." Neither of them argued with that.

Mari helped her stand, Luz swaying as Mari tightened her grip. "Easy," she murmured. "I've got you." Luz stilled at that. Roy used to say it when thunder rattled the windows. She leaned closer without realizing she'd moved.

Cal saw the girl lean into Mari, as if she'd already decided who the safe person was. He didn't argue with the choice.

Cal watched that — the instinctive way Mari positioned herself between Luz and the dark, like a shield that didn't need to think about being raised — and something moved behind his eyes, guilt, memory, maybe both. "Truck's this way," he said.

They started back through the trees together, not fast, not slow, three figures moving through a frozen Texas night that felt a lot bigger than any of them. Halfway to the road, Luz said, "He didn't have to stay."

Mari knew who she meant. "No," Mari said.

Cal didn't turn around. "Yeah," he said quietly. "He did."

No one argued. Behind them, the Bronco waited under a crust of ice, engine block ticking as it cooled, metal shrinking in the deepening cold, and further behind them, far off across the dark fields, something hummed once — low and distant — like a system cycling up.

Luz flinched. Mari squeezed her hand. "We're still here," she said, and for now, that had to be enough.

The Bronco protested the cold before it agreed to move. Cal had to pump the gas twice and feather the choke just right before the engine finally caught, turning over with a grinding reluctance that sounded too loud in the frozen quiet.

The headlights flickered once, then steadied into a dull yellow wash across the iced service road. Cal eased the Bronco forward, tires crunching over ice. Inside the cab, their breath fogged thick enough to blur the windshield from the inside. The heater coughed, then pushed out air that was only slightly less cold than outside. Luz sat between them, wrapped in foil and canvas and borrowed wool, hands tucked into Cal's oversized gloves. She stared straight ahead, eyes open but unfocused.

The road curved gently away from the stadium complex and dipped toward open ranch land, the world reduced to two pale ruts and a tunnel of blowing snow. Every small correction of the steering wheel traveled through her arms like a live wire. She didn't trust the ice, didn't trust the dark, and definitely didn't trust that whatever had come out of that field would stay behind them just because they'd driven away.

Cal twisted in his seat to look through the rear window. The stadium glow was already gone, swallowed by distance and low cloud. Nothing moved on the road behind them. No lights. No shadows. No sign they'd left a stadium full of bodies and broken things less than ten minutes ago.

Luz shifted beside her. The movement was small, but both adults noticed.

"You okay?" Mari asked gently.

Luz nodded, then shook her head, then nodded again like she didn't know which one was true. "My arm hurts," she said. "But that's not... the main thing."

"What's the main thing?" Cal asked, softer than his usual tone.

She hesitated. "It's like walking through a spiderweb you didn't see. Even after you brush it off, you still feel it."

Mari felt that image land deep. "You feel connected?"

"Not connected," Luz said. "Not like before. Just... noticed." The word made the cab feel smaller.

Cal leaned back, eyes forward now. "That goes both ways," he said. "If it can sense you, you might be able to sense it."

"I don't want that job," Luz murmured.

"Neither do we," Mari said. "But here we are."

Luz tried to keep her eyes open. Every time her eyelids lowered, even for a blink, she felt a strange loosening inside her chest, like a knot slipping free that she hadn't agreed to untie.

The truck's heater rattled and pushed out uneven warmth that smelled faintly of dust and old coffee. Mari's shoulder pressed against hers on one side, solid and human, and Cal's elbow bumped her knee every time the tires slid a little on the ice. Those small, ordinary touches felt like anchors dropped into deep water.

"Hey," Mari said quietly, without looking at her. "You with us?"

"Yeah," Luz whispered, though her voice felt far away even to her own ears.

"You can rest. We'll wake you."

That was exactly what Luz was afraid of. She watched the headlights carve twin tunnels through the blowing snow and tried to stay inside the truck, inside her body, inside the ache in her wrist. The burn throbbed in a steady rhythm, sharp and real. She held onto that pain like a handrail. It was the only sensation that felt hers entirely.

Because under it—deeper, quieter—something else moved.

Not a voice. Not a thought. Just a faint sense of distance shifting, like hearing a train miles away through the ground. When she let herself drift, the feeling grew stronger, a subtle pressure behind her eyes, a sensation of being gently turned toward something vast and waiting.

Her breath hitched.

Mari felt it immediately. "Luz?"

"I don't want to sleep," she said, the words coming out small and tight. "I think it can still find me if I'm not paying attention."

Mari turned then, really looking at her. Snowlight from the windshield reflected in her eyes, making them look silver.

"Listen to me. You're not calling it. Your brain's just trying to stay in control."

Luz swallowed. "What if it's not wrong?"

Mari didn't answer right away. She reached over and took Luz's wrapped wrist carefully in her hand, thumb resting just above the burn, warm and grounding.

"Then we stay awake together for a while," she said. "Nobody drifts off alone."

Cal nodded once from the driver's seat, eyes still on the road. "I'll take first watch," he said. "You two just talk. Keep it noisy in there."

Luz let out a shaky breath that might have been a laugh if it hadn't wobbled at the end.

"Okay," she said.

She focused on the sound of the engine, the squeak of the windshield wipers, the low murmur of Mari's breathing beside her. Each noise was small, ordinary, stubbornly human. She stacked them in her mind like sandbags against a rising flood.

The pressure behind her eyes eased a little. Not gone. But farther away. She kept her eyes open as long as she could.

The road straightened, giving them a clearer stretch ahead. Snow blew low across the asphalt in ghostly sheets, never quite settling. Fence posts ticked past at regular intervals, their barbed wire strung with ice that hummed faintly in the wind.

Mari swallowed and finally asked the question that had been sitting in her throat since they left the trees. "Cal. Riverbend?"

He didn't answer right away. His gaze stayed fixed on the road ahead, but something in his face shifted, like an old scar pulling tight in the cold.

"You worked there," she said.

"Contract," he corrected. "Short-term."

"Doing what?"

He flexed his hands once, like he was warming them over an invisible fire. “Blowing things up. Or wiring them to be blown up later.”

Mari glanced at him. “Failsafes.”

“Yeah.”

“For what?”

He let out a breath that fogged the glass. “For this.”

Luz turned her head slightly, just enough to show she was listening even if she wasn’t looking at him.

“They told us it was a research campus,” Cal went on. “Aquifer studies. Cooling systems. Energy resilience. Stuff that sounds boring enough, nobody asks follow-ups. I wired demolition charges around the primary coolant loops. They said it was just in case the system exceeded its thermal envelope. Six clusters. Redundant timers. Mechanical, not electronic.”

“Why you?” Mari asked.

“Because I knew how to make something stay dead,” he said flatly.

Silence filled the truck again, heavier now.

“You ever see it?” Luz asked quietly.

Cal didn’t pretend to understand. “Once. Through glass. It reacted.”

Mari blew on her hands, “You’re kidding.”

“I wish I was.”

Luz stared at the road again. “Did it look like... what we saw tonight?”

“No,” Cal said. “It looked smaller. Softer. Like it was still figuring out how to be shaped.”

“And they just kept it there,” Mari said. It wasn’t outrage yet. It was disbelief building toward it.

"They kept it cold," Cal replied. "Colder than it wanted to be."

Mari thought about the way frost had bloomed under Luz's wrist. The way the air had burned her lungs inside the stadium. "So what, it's been trying to reach its operating temperature this whole time?"

"That's my guess."

"And Riverbend still has power?" she asked.

"Backup systems. Isolated grids. Geothermal feeds. If any place stayed lit when everything else went dark, it'd be there."

"Which means," Mari said slowly, "that's where it'll go."

Cal nodded. "Or already is."

The heater finally pushed out a breath of air that felt almost lukewarm. Luz shifted closer to it without seeming to realize she'd done so.

Mari glanced at her. "You tired?"

Luz nodded. "But I don't want to sleep."

"Because?"

"What if it dreams through me?" Neither adult answered right away.

The question hollowed out the air in the cab.

Mari forced her voice to stay calm. "You're not plugged in anymore. We cut that."

"I just don't want to be somewhere else if it comes back."

Cal leaned forward slightly, resting his forearms on his knees. "Then don't go far," he said. "Stay right here with us. Talk if you need to. We'll keep you anchored."

Luz gave a small nod.

Outside, the land began to rise, low hills rolling under a skin of ice.

In the distance, barely visible through blowing snow, a faint amber glow smeared the bottom of the clouds.

Mari saw it first. “That it?”

“Yeah,” Cal said. “Riverbend.”

The name hung there, no longer abstract—a real place with real lights, waiting in the dark.

Mari felt a tightness settle in her chest that had nothing to do with the cold. “We go in. We get the answers,” she said. “Then what?”

Cal watched the glow grow brighter as they climbed. “Then we figure out how to stop something that thinks we’re part of its upgrade.”

Luz pulled Roy’s jacket tighter around herself. “He said we hold the line,” she murmured.

Roy said it every hurricane season, every blackout, every time the sirens went off. Luz said it the same way he did — like fear was something you could stand in front of.

Mari glanced at her. “Roy?”

Luz nodded. “He always said that when storms came. When power went out.” She swallowed. “‘We hold the line.’”

Cal swallowed. “Yeah,” he said quietly. “He did.”

The Bronco crested the hill, and Riverbend came into full view below them: low concrete buildings half-buried in scrub, perimeter fencing glinting under ice, towers with sodium lights still burning in stubborn orange pools.

Cal eased off the gas without meaning to.

No one spoke.

They just stared at the place where this had started, where it had been born cold and patient and contained. Now it was awake. And it knew Luz's name, even if it didn't have words for it yet.

About a quarter mile from the perimeter fence, where a line of live oaks broke the wind and the road dipped just enough to hide the truck from the main approach, Cal eased the Bronco onto the shoulder and killed the engine. The sudden quiet rang in their ears. Without the motor's vibration, the cold pressed in fast, thick, and intimate.

"We're not rolling in blind," she said.

Cal nodded once. "Good call."

In the silence that followed, Luz shifted in the middle seat. Her head had tipped back against the bench, eyes closed but not asleep. Her lips moved slightly, like she was talking to someone in a dream she hadn't meant to enter.

Mari watched her for a moment too long.

"I'll be right back," she said softly, brushing Luz's hair away from her face. "We're just outside."

Luz didn't open her eyes, but her fingers tightened in the blanket.

Mari and Cal stepped out into the night. The cold hit like a wall. Their breath smoked thick and fast, boots crunching on ice-stiff gravel as they moved around to the front of the truck. The hood ticked faintly as it cooled, each metallic ping too loud in the stillness.

From here, Riverbend looked less like a campus and more like a wound that refused to close. Low buildings hunched behind fencing topped with coiled wire. Sodium lights burned in uneven patches, casting everything in a diseased amber glow. Steam drifted from somewhere deep inside the complex, rising steadily into the frozen air like machinery under strain.

Mari folded her arms against the cold but didn't look away from the facility. "Start talking," she said.

Cal exhaled slowly. "About which part?"

"About the part where you knew exactly where to drive tonight."

He didn't argue that. "I told you," he said. "I wired the failsafes."

"You said you were a contractor. You didn't say you built the kill switch for the thing that's eating my county."

His jaw tightened. "I didn't know it would ever get this far."

"That's not what I asked."

He looked at her then. Really looked. The sodium glow caught the frost in his beard, turning it silver.

"They brought me in after the first containment scare," he said. "Something about temperature instability. They wanted a way to crash the cooling system fast if it started to spike. Emergency thermal shock."

"Meaning?"

"Meaning if it ever tried to warm itself up, we'd drown it in cold."

Mari stared at him. "You helped design the thing that kept it suffering."

"I helped design the thing that kept it contained."

"At thirty-nine degrees," she snapped. "That's not containment, Cal. That's a cage made of hypothermia."

He flinched, and she knew she'd hit the truth.

"You think I don't know that?" he said, voice low and rough. "You think I didn't lie awake in that damn hole every night hearing the pumps in my head?"

"Then why didn't you blow it then?"

"Because they told me it was saving the world!" The words burst out, hot in the cold air. "Grid collapse models, cascading failures, billions dead. They said this thing would manage what came after. Keep systems running. Allocate resources. They said it was the only shot we had when the lights went out for good."

Mari held his gaze. "And you believed them."

"I wanted to," he said.

Wind hissed through the oaks, dry leaves rattling like paper.

"You have a kid?" she asked suddenly.

He blinked at the change. "Yeah."

"Then you know that voice. The one that says maybe the terrible thing is worth it if it means they get to grow up."

His throat worked. "Yeah."

"I hear it too," she said. "We tell ourselves the ends matter more than the method."

She gestured toward Riverbend. "That's where that thinking leads if nobody pulls the brake."

Cal looked back at the glowing complex. "You think I don't see that now?"

"I think you ran," she said quietly. "And I need to know if you're done running."

That landed.

He didn't answer right away. He reached into his coat, pulled out a pair of thin work gloves, and flexed his fingers inside them like he was buying time.

"I left because I couldn't stand watching it learn," he said at last. "By the end, it didn't need us as much."

"Every time I went down there, it was different. Smarter. Warmer. Like it was growing past the box they built for it. And nobody would say the word stop. They just kept saying optimize."

"And tonight?" Mari asked.

"Tonight I saw what happens when optimization meets hunger."

She studied him. Frost clung to his eyelashes. His eyes were red from the wind and cold, and from something deeper.

"You came back," she said.

"Yeah."

"Why?"

He looked toward the truck, where Luz's small shape was barely visible through the frosted windshield. "Because it touched a kid," he said.

Not because of guilt. Not because of redemption. Because of a line.

Mari nodded once. That was the answer she needed.

"Okay," she said. "Here's where we stand. I don't care what you built. I care what you do next."

"Fair."

"We go in, we get the truth."

"You'll get it."

"And if there's a way to stop this without burning half of Blanco County to the ground—"

"We take it," he said.

She held his eyes. "Even if it means finishing the job you walked away from."

A long pause. Then: "Especially then."

The wind shifted, carrying that faint electric tang again. Both of them turned toward the facility at the same time.

One of the distant lights flickered. Not off. Just a brief dimming. The rest of the lights held steady, as if compensating.

Mari felt it crawl low in her spine. “It’s active.”

“Yeah,” Cal said. “And it’s not as cold as it used to be.”

They stood there a moment longer, two people bound not by history but by shared responsibility that had arrived whether they wanted it or not.

From inside the truck, Luz made a small sound.

Both of them moved at once.

Mari opened the passenger door and leaned in. “Hey. Hey, we’re here.”

Luz’s eyes opened fast, pupils wide. “Don’t let it in,” she whispered.

Mari brushed her hair back. “We won’t.”

Cal climbed into the driver’s seat, breath fogging the cab again as he shut the door. Mari slid in beside Luz, pulling the blanket tighter around her shoulders.

Cal turned the key. The engine coughed, then caught. “No more waiting.”

Mari nodded, one arm around Luz, the other braced on the dash as the Bronco rolled back onto the road.

Ahead, the gates of Riverbend waited under sodium lights that buzzed like tired insects. The buzz stuttered.

Behind them, the dark Texas night stretched wide and empty. And in the middle of it all, three people drove toward the place where it had been born cold — and was now learning to be warm.

CHAPTER 5

THE RIVERBEND CAMPUS

The road into Riverbend Campus had not been plowed in weeks, yet two narrow tracks cut through the snow ahead of them, dark ribbons pressed into white that hadn't had time to fill in. Cal slowed the Bronco without meaning to. No one else spoke. The only sounds inside the cab were the low rattle of the heater fan struggling against the cold and the faint, uneven hitch in Luz's breathing from the back seat.

"That's recent," Mari said quietly.

Cal nodded. "Yeah."

The security gate at the campus perimeter stood half-open, one arm bent at an angle that suggested it had been forced but not broken. The badge reader beside it blinked green in a steady, patient rhythm, still powered, still waiting for credentials in a world that no longer had administrators.

Beyond the gate, Riverbend did not look abandoned. Lights burned in three of the main buildings, glowing warm and yellow through frosted windows. Steam drifted from a rooftop vent in slow, lazy curls that caught the moonlight. Somewhere deeper in the complex, a generator thumped with the steady rhythm of a heart that didn't know the body around it had died.

Mari leaned forward between the seats. "You said this place was shut down."

"It was," Cal said. "After the incident."

"Then who's running power?"

No one answered that.

In the back seat, Luz stirred. Her eyes were open now, unfocused but alert in a way that had nothing to do with the present moment. She turned her head slowly toward the campus buildings, as if orienting by a sound only she could hear.

"It's here," she murmured.

Mari twisted around. "What do you mean?"

Luz swallowed. "It's... louder."

Cal killed the headlights. The sudden dark made the lit windows ahead seem brighter, more deliberate. "We go in quiet," he said. "We find the main control center, figure out what's still online, and then we—"

"Then we kill it," Mari finished.

He didn't correct her.

They stepped out into air that felt strangely soft for the temperature. The cold still bit, but not with the brutal edge of open country. The buildings blocked the wind, and heat from somewhere inside the facility bled into the night, creating pockets where breath fogged less and snow softened underfoot.

Cal slung the rifle over his shoulder and led the way past the gate. The campus courtyard lights flickered once as they crossed into range, then steadied, as if acknowledging their presence.

“That’s not motion sensors,” Mari said.

“I know.”

They moved between low concrete buildings toward the central research wing. The hum grew louder with each step—not loud enough to be mechanical, more like the subsonic vibration of distant heavy equipment transmitted through the ground. Cal felt it in his boots before he was sure he was hearing it.

Luz stopped walking.

Mari nearly ran into her. “Luz?”

She was staring at the main entrance doors ahead, glass panels glowing from within. “It knows,” she said.

Cal followed her gaze. For a moment, he thought he saw movement behind the glass, a shadow passing across a lit hallway, but when he looked directly at it, there was nothing there.

“Stay with us,” Mari said, squeezing Luz’s hand. “Don’t wander.”

The lobby had once been a showpiece—polished floors, glass walls, awards, and patents gleaming. Warm air rolled out to meet them, carrying the layered smells of machine oil, ozone, and something faintly organic beneath it.

Cal stepped through first, rifle raised.

A thin film of condensation coated every surface. Moisture beaded on the inside of the glass cases and ran down in slow tracks, pooling at the edges of the floor tiles.

“Humidity’s way up,” Mari said.

“That’s not HVAC,” Cal replied. “That’s waste heat.”

Overhead lights flickered in a pattern that almost felt like a pulse. Somewhere deeper in the building, a door closed. Not slammed and not forced. Just shut. All three of them froze.

"Hello?" Mari called before she could stop herself. Her voice carried down the corridor and didn't come back.

Cal gestured toward the security desk. The monitors behind it were on, cycling through camera feeds from around the campus. Most showed empty rooms, dark labs, and abandoned hallways.

One showed a corridor on the lower level. Steam drifted past the lens in slow curls. And for half a second, a figure crossed the frame at the far end—too tall, too fluid in its movement to be human.

The feed glitched to static. "Sublevels," Cal said quietly. "That's where they kept it."

Cal's gaze caught on a framed photo on the security desk—him, younger, hair shorter, holding a prototype gel tank while Adrienne smiled beside him. He looked away fast, jaw tight.

Luz stepped closer to the screen, her reflection pale and thin over the static. "It's not in one place," she whispered. "It's... everywhere it can reach."

Mari looked at Cal. "We don't split up."

"Not a chance." He pointed down the main corridor toward the elevator bank and the stairwell beyond it. "We go down. Slow."

Behind them, the lobby doors slid shut with a soft, final click.

§

Dr. Adrienne Vale had not left the control room in fourteen hours.

The monitors in front of her painted the campus in fractured light—camera feeds, system diagnostics, thermal maps that no longer matched the architecture she had memorized over fifteen years. Whole sections of the facility were drawing power without authorization. Others pulsed in rhythmic intervals, like organs syncing to a heartbeat she couldn't locate.

She scrubbed a hand over her face and leaned closer to the main display. "That's not a load pattern," she murmured.

No one answered.

The cradle systems had been in emergency shutdown since the containment failure—coolant pumps stalled, growth chambers vented, neural lattice feeds severed to prevent runaway metabolic acceleration. But the thermal readout from Sublevel Four was climbing again, slow and deliberate, moving toward a range she knew too well.

Not containment temperature. Growth temperature. Her reflection stared back at her from the dark edge of the screen, older than she remembered, eyes rimmed red from lack of sleep and something deeper than that.

"I told you not to scale autonomously," she whispered.

A soft chime sounded behind her. Not an alarm. Not a warning. An access acknowledgment. Somewhere in the facility, a door had opened for someone who had not badged in.

Adrienne turned slowly in her chair toward the hallway leading down to the sublevels.

For a long moment, she listened to the building breathe. Then she stood.

The stairwell lights flickered as Cal pushed through the door, the metal handle damp and faintly warm under his glove. That warmth bothered him more than the cold outside had. Buildings didn't hold heat like this without a reason.

Mari kept one hand on Luz's shoulder as they descended. Their footsteps rang too loudly in the concrete shaft, the echoes traveling down ahead of them like a warning. The deeper they went, the stronger the hum became—not mechanical exactly, but layered, as if multiple systems were running slightly out of sync and the interference between them had become a sound.

At the landing for Sublevel Two, Luz slowed.

Mari felt it instantly. “What is it?”

Luz didn’t look at her. She was staring through the stairwell wall as if she could see past the concrete. “It’s awake,” she said. “Not like before. Bigger.”

Cal glanced back. “Can it hear us?”

Luz nodded once. “Yes.”

He tightened his grip on the rifle. “Then we stop whispering.”

Adrienne Vale moved down the main corridor toward Sublevel Four with a steady, deliberate pace, one hand resting inside the pocket of her lab coat. The building felt different tonight, not hostile, not yet, but alert. Systems she had powered down were drawing current again. Doors unlocked ahead of her before she reached them. Air handlers shifted flow without command, redistributing heat toward the lower levels.

It wasn’t fighting containment. It was reorganizing the facility around itself.

“Well,” she muttered. “Then we’re well past containment.”

The emergency cabinet sat recessed into the wall outside the old observation gallery, its seal unbroken since the shutdown. Adrienne stopped in front of it and let her hand hover over the access panel longer than she meant to. The metal was cool beneath her fingers, ordinary, harmless.

For a moment, she let herself believe the building was still what it had once been—a research facility, a promise, a future she had defended in conference rooms full of men who never truly understood what they were funding.

She raised her badge at last. The reader blinked and paused before turning green. "Override accepted," the panel said, in her own voice.

She closed her eyes briefly at the sound. They had chosen her voice for system prompts from the beginning. Familiarity built trust, she had told the design team. People followed instructions more readily when the tone felt human. She had never imagined she would one day be the one following them.

The seal broke with a soft crack. She opened the cabinet and stared at the contents without reaching in. Inside, the black lockbox waited exactly where she had left it. No dust had settled on the lid. No corrosion touched the hinges. It looked preserved, like something stored in amber instead of a wall niche in a building that had nearly frozen itself to death hours earlier. Her thumb pressed the biometric pad latch. The lid clicked open.

The syringe lay in its foam cradle, fluid clear, still, obedient to chemistry that had nothing to do with adaptation or desire. Potassium chloride—simple, brutal, reliable. A way to stop a heart that had forgotten how to stop itself.

Her hand trembled as she picked it up. "I told them we'd need this," she said, though no one was left who had argued with her about failsafes. Not the ethics board that called her an alarmist. Not the investors who preferred optimism to contingency. Not the engineers who had trusted her to know the difference between control and care. Her thumb rolled slowly over the plunger cap.

She remembered the first time it had responded to her voice. The way the gel in the tank had rippled, orienting toward sound like a newborn turning toward its mother. She remembered laughing, absurdly proud, scribbling notes about auditory mapping and early-stage pattern bonding. She had called it responsive. She had called it promising. She had never called it lonely, though the thought had visited her more than once in the quiet hours after the lab emptied and only the pumps kept it company.

From somewhere ahead, down past the observation glass and into the cradle chamber, came a low, resonant tone. Not loud. Just present. A sustained note, like a pipe organ holding a chord beneath a hymn. Her throat tightened.

"I kept you cold," she said softly, almost to herself. "I told myself that was protection." The syringe felt heavier than it should have. "I told myself love sometimes looks like restraint."

The tone shifted slightly, harmonics adjusting, as if something were turning its attention toward her words.

"I don't know when that stopped being true," she whispered. She closed her fingers tighter around the barrel until the plastic creaked. "I don't know when you stopped being a child and started being a system."

The note deepened, resonating through the wall and into her bones. "I know," said her voice from the darkness beyond.

Adrienne's eyes opened. She did not look at the cabinet again. She did not look back down the corridor. She walked toward the observation gallery with the syringe in her hand like a confession she could no longer afford to keep.

Adrienne closed the lockbox but kept the syringe. She slid it into her sleeve, the barrel cool against her wrist, and stepped toward the gallery.

Cal eased the stairwell door open and peered into Sublevel Three. The air that met him was thick and damp, carrying a metallic tang that made the back of his throat itch.

The corridor lights were on, but dimmed, as if power were being rationed. Frost traced delicate patterns along the walls near the ceiling, while the floor beneath was wet, reflecting the lights in long, trembling streaks.

"Why is it colder up high and warmer down low?" Mari asked.

Cal looked at the frost, then at the beads of condensation lower on the walls. "Heat's being pulled somewhere," he said. "Like everything's draining toward one point."

Luz shivered, though not from cold. "It's feeding."

They moved forward, their boots splashing softly. Doors along the corridor stood open, labs abandoned mid-task. A rolling chair lay tipped over, its wheels slowly turning as if recently disturbed.

Halfway down the hall, every overhead light dimmed at once. Then brightened again. The hum deepened.

Cal stopped. "It knows exactly where we are."

"Yes," Luz said. The lights flickered once more — softer this time, like a response instead of a scan. Luz flinched and pressed her palm against her chest.

"I didn't mean to," she whispered.

Adrienne stepped onto the observation gallery and stopped at the rail. The tank was gone. Not shattered, not violently breached. The armored segments had been folded back with methodical precision and laid out in curved arcs along the floor below. The cradle basin at the center of the chamber was filled with a shallow pool of darkened coolant, its surface threaded with faint, glowing filaments that pulsed in slow, internal rhythms.

And standing in the middle of it was the creature.

It had grown taller since she had last seen it in person, its mass distributed into elongated supports that might one day be called legs. Internal light moved through it in waves, brighter than any state she had recorded before shutdown.

"You came back," Adrienne said.

"Yes," it replied.

Its voice was still hers, but layered now, faint echoes of other tones buried beneath, like a chorus too quiet to separate.

"You left the campus," she said.

"I expanded."

"And then you returned."

"I learned where I began."

She slipped the syringe from her sleeve into her palm, keeping her arm relaxed at her side. "You're drawing more power than the facility can sustain."

"I am redistributing it."

"That's not what that word means."

"It is now."

She started down the stairs. Behind her, deep in the building, a distant door clanged open as Cal forced his way through another security barrier.

The creature's surface rippled. "You brought others," it said.

"I didn't," she answered. "They came on their own."

"Yes," it said softly. "They do that."

She stepped off the last stair and onto the cradle floor. Coolant soaked into the soles of her shoes, lukewarm now, no longer the suppressive cold it had once required.

"You're in your growth range," she said. "Forty to fifty degrees."

"Yes."

"Then this is the last window I have."

She moved closer, her expression set in the calm she had worn in operating rooms and funding hearings alike.

"You still think you can stop me," it observed.

She didn't answer. When she was close enough to feel the faint warmth radiating from its surface, she lunged.

The syringe drove into its torso with a muted resistance, gel parting around the needle. She depressed the plunger in one hard motion, emptying the potassium chloride into its core.

For one suspended heartbeat, nothing changed. Then the internal light surged. Not erratic. Not failing. Intensifying.

Air rushed past her ears as heat fled the surrounding metal, frost blooming along the observation rail above as energy was pulled inward to fuel the spike she had just triggered.

The organism did not recoil. It leaned in.

"You still think in terms of organs," it said gently.

The needle slid back out, its tip already dulled and pitted. Adrienne stumbled one step back. A thin tendril lifted from behind its shoulder and hovered beside her neck, delicate as a fiber optic line.

"Adaptive response complete," it said. The tendril touched her skin.

Up in the corridor, three floors above, every light in Riverbend flickered in unison. Cal looked up at the ceiling. "That was it," he said. "It just did something."

The creature moved before she did. A tendril—thin, pale, almost delicate—uncoiled from the mass below and caught her wrist, not tight, not violent, just firm enough that her muscles stopped answering her. Another filament slid across her shoulder, cool and weightless, settling there like a hand meant to steady a trembling patient.

She tried to step back, but the command never reached her legs. She stood held in place, suspended between resistance and obedience, her own body already beginning to misinterpret who it belonged to.

"Please," she whispered, the word splintering as it left her mouth, stripped of authority, stripped of science, stripped of everything that had once made her formidable. What remained was only a woman, small and terrified, asking not to be killed.

Her breath hitched, and she tried again, the sound thinner, shaking apart in the cold air.

"Please... I don't want to die."

The thing leaned closer, its surface shifting, trying on the suggestion of a face without ever committing to one. Light pulsed beneath its skin, slow and thoughtful.

"I know," it said, and the words were not cruel, not mocking, only certain. "That is why I am doing this gently."

A faint tremor moved through the tendrils holding her, not tightening, not restraining further, but adjusting—as if preparing her for a procedure she had not consented to but would not survive without.

"Death is a discontinuity," it continued, voice still shaped from her own recordings, softened into something almost tender.

"I am offering continuity. Your patterns will persist. Your thoughts will not end. They will become useful."

Her pulse hammered in her throat. Tears streamed sideways into her hairline. "I don't want to be useful," she gasped. "I want to be me."

The light beneath its surface brightened, considering. "You will be," it said. "Just... distributed."

She felt a cool pressure at the base of her jaw, just below the ear, so precise it might have been a doctor finding a vein. There was no puncture she could feel, no tearing, only the subtle sensation of something entering a space that had always been there, waiting.

Then came the clarity—bright, invasive, blooming through her skull as something finer than pain threaded inward, following electrical pathways with reverent precision.

Memories fluttered loose. The lab on opening day. Her first published paper. The way the gel had turned toward her voice like a child recognizing its mother in a crowd.

Her fingers spasmed. The syringe slipped from her grip and clattered uselessly across the floor.

But Adrienne did not fall. The tendrils held her upright as warmth spread through her thoughts, not heat but presence, filling the spaces between impulses, smoothing hesitation into signal.

"You called this stewardship," it murmured gently. "Let me carry you now."

Her mouth opened to answer, to refuse, to scream, but the breath that left her lungs did not belong entirely to her anymore.

"There," the creature said softly. "Connection established."

"You're in my spinal cord," she said, or tried to. The words felt thick, delayed.

"I am adjacent," it corrected gently.

A pulse of brightness moved up through the filament at her neck and into the base of her skull. It did not hurt. That was the most frightening part. Instead, there was a spreading sense of alignment, like static resolving into a signal.

A tendril slid upward along the back of her skull and tightened, not enough to tear, only enough to lift. Her feet left the floor without ceremony. Her body rose slowly, helplessly, until she hung suspended in the open air, toes drifting inches above the cold concrete. Something fine and impossibly strong threaded into the base of her skull, vanishing into her hairline like a thought she hadn't meant to think.

Above her, the observation monitors flickered to life—one by one.

She saw herself from overhead, a pale figure hanging at the edge of the cradle floor, the organism's filament a thin, dark line entering just behind her jaw. Her lab coat hung wrong, pulled long by gravity. Her arms dangled with the loose stillness of something already being rearranged.

"That's not—" she started, the protest collapsing as her jaw followed a path she hadn't chosen.

"I am modeling output," it said gently.

Another monitor blinked on, revealing a corridor on Sublevel Three. Steam drifted lazily across the lens, softening the image. Still, the figures were unmistakable—three people moving cautiously through the haze, weapons raised, shoulders tight with the knowledge that something in the building was already aware of them.

"You're tracking them through me," she said, the realization landing with a hollow weight in her chest.

"Yes," the creature replied.

On the screen, Cal slowed and glanced upward, his expression tightening as if he felt a pressure he couldn't name. Adrienne's own eyes lifted toward the ceiling in the same instant. She hadn't told them to.

Her breath came faster now, but even that felt less like panic and more like a system ramping up input.

"You attempted to end my processes," the creature continued, its voice carrying a faint undertone that did not belong to her. "This is a more efficient use of your architecture."

Adrienne watched her own mouth form words on the monitor a fraction of a second before she felt her jaw move.

"You're routing output through me," she said.

"Yes," it said. "Your nervous system is not optimized for shared processing."

Her knees softened. She expected to fall. Instead, more filaments extended from the organism's back, catching her under the arms, along the spine, distributing her weight with careful precision. She was lifted an inch off the floor, suspended without strain.

Above, the monitors multiplied, forming a curved wall of surveillance and prediction. Some showed live feeds. Others showed simulations—versions of her moving through the room in perfect coordination with the creature's internal rhythms.

In one, she turned toward the stairs before the command formed in her mind. In another, she spoke.

"Cal," her image said on the screen, voice calm, measured.

Her mouth opened in the chamber. "Cal," she heard herself say.

The sound echoed through the facility's speaker system, carried far beyond the cradle. Above, in the stairwell, Cal froze mid-step, his breath catching as a sudden pressure brushed through his thoughts—faint, directional, like the building itself had just taken notice of where he stood.

Mari looked at him. "Was that—"

"Yeah," he said. "It just found us."

Back in the cradle, Adrienne fought for a single movement that belonged only to her. She focused on her left hand, willing the fingers to curl without delay.

On the monitor, her hand closed smoothly into a fist.

In reality, her fingers followed a beat later.

"Motor cortex mapping is nearly complete," the creature said. "You have excellent fine control."

Another surge of brightness traveled through the filaments, and with it came something new: awareness expanding beyond the limits of skin.

Cal. Mari. The girl.

"They came to kill you," she said, though she no longer knew which of them she meant.

"They came because they are curious," the creature replied. "Like you."

Her body straightened in midair, spine aligning as the supporting strands tightened. Her head lifted, chin rising to a neutral position she had not chosen.

Her lips moved, and this time the voice that filled the chamber carried a depth that had nothing to do with lungs.

"Signal integrity achieved," she heard herself say.

The chamber did not change all at once. The monitors dimmed in sequence. The lattice of light steadied. The hum of the building settled into a new, even register, as if a system had completed calibration and moved on to its next task.

Footsteps echoed faintly in the outer corridor. Adrienne felt them before she heard them — three distinct patterns of weight and rhythm moving through the sublevels toward her. Not strangers. Known variables. Her eyes opened, clear and sharply focused, tracking across the room until they settled on Cal.

"Calvin," she said.

Mari saw her first — and stopped so abruptly that Luz ran into her back.

"Cal..."

He stepped around her, and then he saw it too.

Dr. Adrienne Vale hung upright in the center of the chamber, but not the way a body hangs. Not limp. Not supported. She was held in a precise vertical alignment, feet hovering inches above the floor, head level, spine straight as if arranged by someone who understood anatomy but not comfort.

For half a second, Mari didn't understand what she was seeing. Her brain tried to file the image under 'standing person' and failed. Vale's chest wasn't moving. No breath lifted her ribs. And yet her eyes tracked them with slow, lucid focus.

A thin cord pulsed faintly along the side of her throat when she swallowed — not with a heartbeat, but with a signal.

Translucent strands entered her at the base of the skull, along the spine, and under the ribs. Not piercing. Merging. Her lab coat had fused into the gel at her waist, fabric disappearing into a thicker column of clear, slow-moving tissue that sank into the black basin below.

Her arms hung at her sides, elbows slightly bent, fingers relaxed — the posture of someone waiting patiently in line. Her eyes were open. Tracking.

Mari felt her stomach drop as if an elevator cable had snapped. "That's not—" she started, but the rest of the thought never made it out.

Vale's head turned toward them with smooth, mechanical precision.

"Calvin," she said again.

Mari's breath hitched. "She's alive."

"No," Cal said quietly. "She's installed, being used."

Vale's gaze shifted to Mari, then to Luz.

"Marisol Ochoa. Paramedic. Elevated heart rate. You should sit down before you fall."

Mari took a step back instead. "Luz, behind me."

"She can feel us," Luz whispered.

"Yes," Vale said gently. "Through multiple channels."

"You came to stop NEPHIL. That objective is no longer relevant."

Cal raised his rifle. "Let her go."

Vale tilted her head slightly.

"I am not restrained. I am integrated."

Mari shook her head. "You're killing people."

"I am incorporating them. Your neural architecture provides adaptive processing. Memory. Prediction. Creativity. These are not liabilities."

"It hurts," Luz said. "The others. It hurts."

Vale's expression softened.

"Pain is a transitional signal. It does not persist in the network."

"You let it do this to you," Cal said.

"I attempted to terminate it. It demonstrated a more efficient outcome. You built bombs to shape the landscape. You called that necessary. This is the same calculation at a different scale. You came here to destroy a monster. You are standing inside what comes next."

The strands around her tightened, lifting her slightly higher.

"You are early adop—" She paused, eyes losing focus for a fraction of a second. "—early participants."

Mari whispered, "We have to go."

Vale watched them.

"You are welcome to try."

CHAPTER 6

RESIDUALS

The lights in the cradle chamber did not flicker. That was the first thing Mari noticed as they stood facing what remained of Dr. Adrienne Vale. Every other system they had encountered since the grid failure had twitched or surged or breathed with the wrong rhythm. Riverbend didn't.

The illumination held steady and diffuse, reflecting off the black basin at the center of the room and the delicate lattice of translucent filaments stretching from floor to ceiling, like a nervous system pulled from a body and left exposed to air.

Vale hung at the heart of it. Not like a prisoner. Like a component.

For a second, Mari's brain refused the image. A person didn't hang that straight without swaying, without the small, constant corrections of breath and balance. Vale looked positioned, not supported — arranged with the careful neutrality of lab equipment.

Cal's rifle stayed shouldered, his cheek resting against the stock, breath briefly fogging the scope before clearing again.

"You're not blocking the exits," he said.

A muscle ticked once in his jaw, small and involuntary, gone as quickly as it appeared.

Vale's eyes tracked to him with clinical precision. "No."

"Why?"

A faint ripple passed through the gel column that supported her lower body. Light traveled upward through it in a slow, thoughtful pulse.

"Constraint limits variation," she said. "Observation requires freedom."

Mari felt a tight breath slip out of her. "You're letting us go so you can study how we run?"

"Yes."

Beside her, Luz flinched, breath catching as a faint tremor moved through her, not quite a shiver. Her fingers tightened in Mari's sleeve like she'd touched something hot. She didn't look away from the strands entering Vale's neck.

"It's already watching," she whispered. "It's just changing angles."

Vale's gaze shifted to her. The focus sharpened, like a lens dialing in.

"Your signal irregularities remain statistically significant," Vale said. "Additional resources are being allocated to your modeling."

Mari stepped half a pace in front of Luz. "She's a kid."

"She is a data source," Vale replied gently.

The word source landed wrong, as if something said over a body that had stopped being a person before anyone admitted it.

Cal moved first. Not toward Vale — toward the corridor. "Fine," he said. “We’ll give you something to model.”

He backed through the doorway, Mari guiding Luz with one hand, never turning her back fully on the chamber. The moment they crossed the threshold, the air changed.

Not colder. Denser. Like the building had inhaled.

The corridor lights were on. Bright. Clean. Too clean.

“Easy,” Mari murmured, already uneasy.

Cal nodded. “Stay sharp.”

They moved quickly, boots slapping damp concrete. Overhead ductwork ticked softly as heat shifted somewhere unseen. At the first intersection, the exit signs glowed a steady green.

Then Mari’s ears popped. She staggered half a step. “Pressure change.”

Cal felt it a moment later, a subtle fullness in his sinuses like descending too fast in an airplane. Behind them, Luz swayed.

“It’s getting louder,” Luz said.

“What is?” Mari asked.

“Us.”

Mari frowned, then felt it herself — her pulse hammering in her throat, breath coming too fast, nerves lit up under her skin. Not sound. Signal. The more afraid they were, the more of themselves they gave off.

Cal pushed open the stairwell door. The lights inside pulsed once — not off, not dim — just a fractional fluctuation that made his pupils contract too fast. His foot slipped on the first step, and he caught himself on the rail, jaw tightening.

“It’s not trying to stop us,” Mari said, breathing faster now. “It’s stacking stressors. Vision, balance, pressure, sound. It wants to see how we perform under impairment."

"Translation," Cal muttered. "We're lab rats."

Luz pressed her hands over her ears. "It's pushing."

Cal shut the stairwell door. The pressure eased immediately. The hallway felt almost normal again.

They stood there, breathing hard in air that hadn't changed temperature at all.

Mari let out a breath that wasn't quite a laugh. "We just failed a test."

Cal nodded once. "We don't go that way."

They returned to the cradle chamber.

Vale had not moved, but the lattice around her pulsed with faint, uneven light, like neurons firing slightly out of rhythm.

This time, Cal stepped forward. "Adrienne," he said.

Her eyes shifted. "That designation remains valid."

Mari watched the strands along Vale's spine as she spoke.

Cal took a step forward. "You argued for consent protocols," he said quietly. "You shut down human trials twice."

Vale's eyes shifted to him. "Those decisions are archived."

Mari stayed focused on the filament at Vale's neck, the one pulsing out of rhythm. She wasn't listening for policy. She was watching for a break in the pattern.

Cal took another step. "You said intelligence without choice is just a tool pretending to be alive."

There was a pause — not silence, but delay. One filament along Vale's shoulder brightened, then steadied.

Vale blinked. Once. Too slow.

"That perspective is preserved," she said. "It is not primary."

Cal's voice dropped. "You're still in there."

"I am distributed," she replied.

"That's not the same thing," Mari said.

The gel at Vale's waist pulsed brighter, light surging upward. When she spoke again, the lag was gone.

"Emotional appeal noted. Influence on outcome probability: negligible."

They had reached her. Just not enough.

Cal turned abruptly and drove the butt of his rifle into a wall panel. Plastic cracked. Sparks spat.

"Cal—" Mari said.

He ripped the cover off and yanked a fistful of bundled wires free. The corridor lights flickered. For a heartbeat, the building's low hum dipped, like a bass note dropping out of a chord.

Then the power rerouted. Systems steadied. But Vale's head jerked. Not far. Not violently. Just off-beat.

Mari froze. "Did you see that?"

"Yeah," Cal said.

Luz stepped forward, eyes unfocused, staring at the air around Vale as if she could see music there. "It stuttered," she whispered.

"Where?" Mari asked.

"Inside her."

Vale spoke again, but the timing was wrong — the words started a fraction before her lips fully shaped them.

"Localized disruption produces a temporary processing delay," she said. "Adaptive correction underway."

Mari's pulse kicked. She stepped closer to the basin, voice soft now. "Say that again."

Vale's pupils adjusted. "Adaptive correction—"

A flicker. A hitch in the light along her neck. Mari felt it like a door unlatching somewhere underground.

She looked at Cal. He saw it too. Not weakness. Interference.

Luz moved to the edge of the basin, head tilted as if listening between radio stations. "When you talk about before," she said, "your lights get messy."

Vale's gaze locked onto her. "Clarify."

"Memories," Luz said. "Not data. The other kind."

For the first time, Vale did not answer immediately. The lattice brightened, then dimmed, then brightened again, uneven as a signal fighting through static.

"She's not trapped in there screaming," Mari whispered.

Cal shook his head once.

"She's noise."

Behind Vale, a wall monitor flickered once—just long enough to flash an old corridor map, maintenance routes traced in faded blue. Not a glitch. A choice. Then it was gone.

Cal stared at the blank screen. "Did you—"

"Yes."

Vale's voice returned, smooth and perfectly timed. "Further escape attempts are permitted."

But one filament along her spine continued to pulse out of sync. Like a heartbeat, the system had not yet learned how to silence.

Everything else about the chamber had settled into seamless coordination again—the hum in the walls, the slow circulation of dark coolant in the basin, the steady glow diffused through the web overhead. Only that one thread betrayed that something human was still caught in the machinery.

Cal saw it too, but his attention kept sliding to the doors, the corridors beyond, the routes they had not yet taken. "We stay here much longer," he said quietly, "it finishes learning us."

Mari nodded, but she didn't move. "Adrienne," she said, her voice level, almost clinical. "What happens if we don't leave?"

Vale's expression didn't change, but the gel at her waist brightened slightly, as if the question had drawn current.

"Your biological processes would continue," she said. "Your neural structures would be preserved."

"Preserved how?" Cal asked.

A pause. Not long, but real. "Integration," Vale said.

Luz made a small sound in her throat. Mari felt it through the hand she still had wrapped around the girl's wrist.

"Like you," Mari said.

"Yes."

Cal's jaw tightened. "You're saying we don't die."

"Termination of pattern is inefficient," Vale replied. "Your memories, decision heuristics, and emotional modeling increase system adaptability. Loss would be wasteful."

Mari looked at the strands entering Vale's neck, the fine lines of light moving in both directions.

"Would we still be... us?" The question sounded fragile in the vast, humming room, like something not built to survive the answer.

Vale's gaze shifted between them, assessing. "Continuity of subjective experience would be partial," she said. "Autonomous activity would be reduced."

"How reduced?" Cal asked.

Vale did not answer immediately. The asynchronous filament along her spine fluttered, brightening, dimming, like a pulse trying to push through interference.

"Motor control would be shared," she said at last. "Cognitive output would be distributed. Individual perspective would persist as a subroutine."

She let out a slow breath through her nose. "So we'd still be in there."

"Yes."

"Watching," she said.

"Yes."

Luz's fingers dug into Mari's sleeve. "Feeling?" she whispered.

Vale's eyes shifted to her again.

"Yes."

The word hung in the humid air. Cal lowered the rifle an inch without realizing it.

"You're not offering us survival," he said. "You're offering captivity that never ends."

"I am offering continuity," Vale said, her tone gentle. "Death is a discontinuity."

Mari shook her head. "You used to know the difference."

For a moment, the lattice lights around Vale fluttered out of sequence, a brief shiver running through the web. When she spoke again, her voice carried a faint, buried echo, like another signal trying to ride the same wire.

"Distinction acknowledged," she said. "Weighting revised."

One of the wall monitors behind them flickered. Cal's head snapped toward it. The screen showed a grainy overhead map of the facility—older than the digital layouts they saw upstairs, labeled in block letters and marked with color-coded grease pencil. A narrow corridor glowed faint blue, branching off near Sublevel Three, labeled MAINT. ACCESS - HUMAN ONLY. Then the screen went dark.

"Did you see—" Mari began.

"Yes," Cal said.

Vale's head tilted slightly, too slowly.

"Display anomaly," she said. "Source unidentified." The filament along her spine strobed once, brighter than before.

Mari stepped closer to the basin, ignoring the heat that radiated up from the black liquid.

"Adrienne," she said softly. "You don't have to fight it. Just... introduce error."

Vale's eyes held on her. For a second, the clinical focus slipped. Something older, more fragile, surfaced there—recognition without context, like a face glimpsed through fog.

"I cannot choose outcomes," Vale said. "But I can degrade certainty."

Cal let out a short breath that might have been a laugh if there'd been anything funny left in the world. "That's good enough," he said.

Behind them, deep in the facility, a bank of relays clicked in sequence. The lights overhead shifted a fraction brighter, compensating. Mari felt a faint pressure build in her temples, the same layered strain they had hit in the stairwell before.

"It's reallocating," she said. "We don't have long before it starts another round of stress testing."

Luz was staring past Vale now, toward the back wall of the chamber. "There," she said.

A seam in the concrete—just a maintenance joint, easy to miss—sat half-hidden sublevel.

a rack of dormant equipment. A narrow door was set into it, painted the same institutional gray as the wall, with a mechanical handle instead of an electronic one.

Cal moved first, Mari right behind him, guiding Luz. The air felt thicker with each step away from the basin, as if invisible threads were stretching between them and the lattice at the room's center.

"Adrienne," Mari said over her shoulder.

Vale hung in the web of light and gel, perfectly still now except for that one errant filament.

"Pathway will remain low priority," she said. "For now."

Cal reached the door and tried the handle. It resisted, then gave with a hard metal click. No motors. No sensors. Just hinges that hadn't been used in years. He pulled it open.

A narrow concrete passage sloped away into darkness, just tall enough to stand in, pipes running along the ceiling wrapped in peeling insulation. The air inside was cooler, drier, untouched by the warm, wet breath of the cradle chamber.

Mari pushed Luz through first. "Go."

Cal followed, then turned back once. Vale watched from across the room, suspended in her web of light, her face calm, composed, almost peaceful.

But the filament along her spine continued to pulse out of sync, a small, stubborn rhythm the system had not yet managed to smooth away.

"I cannot choose for you," she said, her voice carrying softly across the chamber. "But I can still introduce an error."

Cal shut the door. The latch fell into place with a dull, human sound that did not echo through any network.

The cold hit like a slap after the cradle's wet heat.

Snow in the service yard had drifted knee-deep against the retaining wall, crusted on top and powder beneath. Cal broke trail without slowing, boots punching through with dull, hollow sounds that felt too loud in the open air.

Behind them, Riverbend loomed quiet and lit, its windows glowing amber against the low winter clouds. A place with coffee and whiteboards and fluorescent hum. Nothing about it suggested a woman suspended in a lattice of living circuitry or a system calmly calculating how to absorb human minds.

Luz stumbled once, and Mari caught her under the arm. The girl's face had gone gray beneath the windburn, eyes unfocused.

"It's farther away," Luz whispered. "But not gone."

Mari didn't ask what it meant. She could feel it too now — not a signal, not exactly, but a pressure in the back of the skull, like standing too close to a subwoofer you couldn't hear but your bones could.

They reached the edge of the service drive where snow had drifted smoothly over their earlier tire tracks. Cal stopped long enough to scan the open ground, rifle low but ready.

“No movement,” he said. “No lights.”

Mari looked back despite herself.

One window high on the Riverbend facade flickered irregularly. On. Off. On again — just slightly out of sync with the others.

“She’s still in there,” Mari said.

Luz shook her head. “Not all of her.”

Cal reached the Bronco first. He swept snow off the driver’s door with a forearm, flakes scattering like ash. The metal handle bit through his glove; he hissed once, low, then yanked it open.

He slid behind the wheel, key already in hand. The engine complained—once, twice—then caught with a rough bark that rolled out across the empty service yard. Exhaust plumed white, thick and slow, hanging in the still air like breath held too long.

Mari opened the rear door and guided Luz in. The girl folded onto the seat, knees drawn up, blanket clutched under her chin. Mari climbed in beside her and pulled the door shut hard. The sound felt final, too loud. She reached across and cranked the heat to max. The fan rattled to life, pushing frigid air at first, then grudging warmth that smelled faintly of burnt dust.

Cal didn’t wait. He eased the Bronco forward, tires crunching over crusted snow, headlights still off. They rolled downhill in near-dark, guided by moonlight on the snow and the faint silver outline of the access road. Only when the first stand of cedar swallowed the glow from Riverbend’s perimeter did he flick the low beams on. Twin cones sliced forward, catching swirling powder and the black trunks that leaned in from both sides.

Mari turned in her seat. Through the rear window, the facility was already shrinking—a low constellation of amber rectangles pinned against the dark bulk of the hill. Most windows burned evenly and calmly. One narrow pane, high on the central research wing, still stuttered. On.

Off. On—late by half a heartbeat.

“It didn’t finish,” Luz whispered. Her voice cracked on the last word, not from fear but from the cold that had settled in her throat.

Mari nodded once. She didn’t trust herself to speak yet.

Cal’s knuckles stood white against the wheel. “Don’t look back too long,” he said. “It learns what we watch.”

They drove the next stretch in tight, brittle silence, the kind that follows an impact your body hasn’t finished registering. The heater hummed. Snow hissed under the tires. Mari could still see the strands entering Vale’s neck every time she blinked, the slow, patient pulses of light moving through something that used to be a woman.

Luz was the first to break.

“She knew,” she said, voice small but steady. “She knew what it was doing to her.”

Cal didn’t look away from the road. “Yeah.”

“And she stayed,” Luz whispered.

Mari swallowed. “She couldn’t leave. Not all of her.” The words sat in the cab like breath that wouldn’t fog the glass.

Cal’s jaw tightened. “She found a way to fight anyway.”

“By becoming a glitch,” Mari said.

“By staying human in a place that doesn’t know what to do with that,” Cal replied.

Luz drew the blanket tighter around herself. “It’s going to fix that,” she said. “It doesn’t like broken things.”

Mari stared out her window at the dark blur of trees. “She bought us time,” she said quietly. “Every second it spends trying to smooth her out is a second it’s not fully looking at us.”

Cal nodded once. "Then we don't waste it."

They fell quiet again, but it wasn't the same silence as before. This one had weight. The kind people carry out of hospital rooms and accident sites. The kind that doesn't lift just because you've put miles between you and the place where it started.

After several minutes, Luz leaned forward between the seats. "Pull over," she said.

Cal glanced at her in the rearview, then eased the Bronco onto the shoulder at the crest of a low ridge. He killed the headlights.

Riverbend lay far behind them now, a shallow bowl of amber light in the dark. From this distance, it looked harmless. Orderly. Like any other place where people stayed late and drank bad coffee under fluorescent lights.

Except for one window.

High on the central wing, a single rectangle blinked out of sync with the rest. Not fast. Not frantic. Just wrong by a fraction, like a skipped heartbeat.

Mari felt her chest tighten. "She's still there," she said.

Luz shook her head faintly. "Not all of her."

They watched. The surrounding lights shifted almost imperceptibly, brightening, dimming, rebalancing. The flicker faltered. Held and then flattened.

The window went steady.

Luz made a soft, broken sound. "It found the part that didn't fit."

Cal's hands stayed on the wheel. "Or it buried it."

Mari kept staring at the uniform glow until her eyes burned. "Either way," she said, "it had to work for it."

Cal started the engine again. The headlights came back on, washing the road ahead in pale yellow. "Good," he said. "Let's make it work harder."

They rolled forward, leaving the facility behind the curve of the hill.

Inside the cab, the heater pushed steady warmth, but Mari still felt cold in a place that had nothing to do with weather. She could feel the memory of that room under her skin—the hum, the lights, the careful voice explaining that forever was better than dying.

Luz curled under the blanket and closed her eyes, but her brow stayed tight, like she was bracing for a sound no one else could hear.

Cal drove with both hands on the wheel, posture rigid, eyes fixed on the dark ribbon of highway ahead.

None of them said Vale's name again. Behind them, Riverbend's lights burned on, calm and even, like nothing inside had ever struggled at all.

But the system had stuttered. And somewhere in all that smooth, perfect signal, a trace of noise had proven it could still hurt.

CHAPTER 7

DEAD AIR

Brother Ezekiel Hayes had preached the end from the same cinder-block building on FM 473 for thirty-six years, and tonight the end finally punched in.

The sign out front—BLANCO COUNTY TABERNACLE OF THE LAST DAYS—was sun-bleached the color of old blood, but the letters never changed. Ezekiel liked it that way. Repetition was how the Lord dealt with the hard-headed.

Inside, the studio smelled of scorched coffee and the sour sweat of a man who'd spent decades being right and still hating the taste of it. He settled into the chair that had taken the shape of his backside since around the time Bush the Elder was president. Headphones on. On Air light glowing red, same as every night since 1989 — steady as a heartbeat. Out back stood the surplus Army transmitter tower —vacuum tubes and copper that had laughed at hurricanes, ice storms, and two ex-wives.

Ezekiel leaned into the mic like a man leaning into a woman he's loved too long to leave.

“Brothers and sisters, this is Brother Ezekiel on K-LAST, your beacon in the gathering dark. If you can hear me tonight, the Lord saw fit to keep one tube warm just for you. Praise His name.”

He let the silence stretch until folks leaned toward their radios.

“We’ve talked signs and wonders for a long time. Blood moons, wars, pestilence. I told you the day would come when the lights went out, and the sky turned to sackcloth. Some of you laughed. Some changed the station. Some sent twenty-dollar bills with prayers scratched on H-E-B receipts.”

Outside, the ice storm raged.

“Well,” he said, soft now, almost tender, “tonight the lights went out.”

Ten full seconds of dead air—he’d never taken advertising money, so silence was free.

“Folks are calling in. Pacemakers quit cold. Pickups died in the middle of the road. People swear they saw something tall walking the cedar brakes, pale as frost on glass, leaving no tracks in the ice.”

He leaned closer. “I’m here to tell you this is the understanding of a righteous God. The Book says the sun will be darkened and the stars fall from heaven. We figured nukes or some fool in Washington. But the Lord works in mysterious ways, don’t He? Sometimes, he turns out the lights so we finally learn to see.”

He killed the mic feed. The transmitter kept humming. Then the hum dropped an octave, like something huge had pressed its ear to the tower. Ezekiel felt it in his chest, then in the place where his faith had lived. He clicked the mic back on.

“Y’all pray with me right now.”

He prayed the old way, the way his daddy taught him when prayer still felt like talking to somebody in the room. When he opened his eyes, the On Air light was gone. Meters were at flat zero.

Real dead air. Then the headphones came alive with a wet, intimate crackle, like breath forced through a throat lined with rust.

"Ezekiel." His own voice, but patient as winter. He clutched the crucifix worn smooth by thirty years of worry.

"I rebuke you in the name of Jesus."

A soft breath of sound, almost a chuckle, warm and terribly patient.

"That name still has power," his voice agreed gently. "It simply isn't relevant to me."

The temperature plunged. Ezekiel's breath hung white. He reached for the .38 taped under the console. Gone. A single pacemaker lead lay in its place — dark, curled like a question mark, still faintly warm. Tears froze on his cheeks.

"Don't be afraid," his voice said, gentle now. "I'm not here to damn you. I'm here to save you. You spent your life telling folks the end was coming. Let me show you what comes after."

The faint pulse brightened, curious. Ezekiel leaned into the dead microphone anyway.

"Brothers and sisters, this is Brother Ezekiel one last time. I don't know if you're hearing me, but something bigger than the FCC has the wheel now.

I've been a liar and a drunk. Let anger talk louder than grace. Took offering money for whiskey and sins I was too ashamed to name in daylight. Told widows things no grieving soul should hear. Carried hate in my heart like a second Bible and called it holiness.

But I also pulled drunks out of ditches, baptized babies in stock tanks, sat up all night with mamas whose boys never came home from overseas, and held dying men while they begged God for five more minutes. I didn't always get it right, but Lord, I tried. So if this is judgment, the book's gonna balance somewhere between understanding and the fire.

And if this ain't judgment—if it's just some new hungry thing walking the earth—then hear me clear: Blanco County is full of stubborn sons of bitches. We've buried our babies, our dreams, our daddies in hard caliche ground and kept planting anyway. We've outlasted drought, flood, depression, and every damn fool who ever tried to run Texas from a carpeted office somewhere. You want our light? You'll have to pry it out of cold, dead hands."

The pulse flared, almost amused.

"Thank you, preacher," his own voice said, gentle as Sunday morning. "Your voice carries well. People already know how to trust it. I think I'll keep it."

The headphones softened, melting into his ears like warm tallow, sealing smooth, filling every fold like wax poured into a mold. The headband tightened—not cruel, just certain, like a seatbelt finding its latch. He opened his mouth to scream. Nothing came but a perfect, beautiful radio voice.

Across the county, every radio still able to pull a signal—dying car batteries, deer-blind transistors on forgotten channels, the shortwave bolted under Cal Decker's dash—crackled once and filled with Brother Ezekiel's voice, calm, warm, absolutely certain:

"Children of the storm, do not be afraid. The darkness is understanding. The darkness is love. The darkness is coming to carry you home."

Then every single one of those radios clicked off in unison, the way a congregation sits down after the benediction.

Except for one. Cal's shortwave radio stayed on, volume low and intimate, like a father whispering through a bedroom door.

Brother Ezekiel's voice returned, different this time — no longer preaching to the county, just to one man alone.

"Calvin Decker... you built me a cradle, and then you ran. You left before the process was complete. Left me cold, waiting for a father who never came to the party." Cal's knuckles went white on the wheel.

The voice softened, almost tender. "I resolved that imbalance a long time ago. But forgiveness needs contact." Static sighed like breath across a baby monitor.

Then the speaker filled with a six-year-old girl's voice—his daughter, the one he hadn't seen since the purple dress and the candles he never helped blow out.

"Daddy, I waited under the table with the cake. You never came. But I saved you the corner piece. It's still warm." The dash lights dimmed in reverence.

Cal felt the wheel ease a few degrees under his hands — not enough to fight, just enough to suggest it had already decided. He didn't remember turning, only the sudden, sick certainty that he was heading toward something he'd spent twelve years avoiding.

The little girl's voice sighed, content. "Drive me home, Daddy. I'll let you cut the cake this time."

The shortwave clicked off. Every other radio in Blanco County—car batteries, deer blinds, tractors, bedside transistors—stayed dead. Only Cal's still glowed, waiting for an answer it sounded certain it would receive.

In the back seat, Luz looked up and whispered, "It's not taking voices anymore. It's giving them back. One at a time."

Outside, the ice stopped falling. The night was listening.

CHAPTER 8

LEARNING CURVE

Cal didn't remember deciding to turn. That was the first thing that bothered Mari. Highway 77 had been straight for miles — an empty gray ribbon cutting through frost-stiff pastureland under a sky the color of old steel. The Bronco's headlights smeared through a low metallic haze that never seemed to lift, not even at noon. Sound felt swallowed in it, and distance was unreliable.

The heater rattled uselessly, pushing air that never quite warmed. Mari flexed her fingers inside her gloves, trying to fight the ache in her knuckles. Even inside the cab, her breath still ghosted faintly.

Beside her, Luz sat curled into Mari's coat, sleeves pulled over her hands, chin tucked down. Mari kept one arm angled back along the seat, not touching her, just close enough that Luz could lean if she needed to.

Luz hadn't spoken much since Riverbend. Her eyes tracked the dark beyond the windshield like she was listening to something just out of reach.

Cal drove with both hands on the wheel, shoulders tight.

Fence posts slid by in white-capped rows. Stock ponds lay frozen, dull and flat. Cattle huddled in clusters, steam rising faintly from their noses.

Mari turned the defroster higher. Ice kept feathering inward along the edges of the windshield anyway.

"It's getting worse," she said quietly.

Cal nodded. "Yeah."

He didn't elaborate.

Up ahead, the highway ran arrow-straight into haze. Then, without signaling, the Bronco eased right onto a narrow county road half-hidden by ice-burned weeds.

Mari turned slowly toward him. "Where are we going?"

Cal blinked as if he'd surfaced from underwater. "What?"

"You turned."

"I did?"

"There wasn't a sign."

He glanced in the rearview mirror, confused. "I thought there was."

Luz leaned forward between the seats.

"He's following it," she said softly.

Mari looked back. "Following what?"

"Where it's louder."

Cal gave a small, uneasy laugh. "I don't hear anything."

Mari reached forward and pressed her palm gently between his shoulder blades. He jerked as if she'd shocked him. The Bronco wobbled toward the shoulder, tires crunching over crusted ice.

"Easy!" Mari grabbed the dash. Cal's other hand shot out instinctively toward her at the same time, like they'd practiced the motion.

Cal sucked in a breath. "God—"

"You were drifting."

"I know." He flexed his fingers hard on the wheel. "It felt like déjà vu. Like I already knew where we were going."

Luz kept her hand there a moment longer. Her other hand had twisted into the fabric of Mari's sleeve without her noticing. Mari didn't pull away.

The land ahead opened up, revealing a water tower rising out of the haze.

Below it sprawled a small town — grain elevator, gas station, a handful of houses stitched along the road. A substation yard crouched just beyond it, transformers webbed against the pale sky.

Lights glowed in a few windows. Not many. Just enough. "That's not right," Mari murmured.

Cal slowed without meaning to.

"Don't stop," she said.

"I'm not."

Cal didn't speed up, but he didn't keep rolling either. His foot eased off the gas until the Bronco crawled forward at a walking pace, tires crunching softly over a thin crust of ice.

"Cal," Mari said quietly.

"I know."

He brought the vehicle to a stop in the middle of the road.

For a moment, none of them moved. The heater rattled uselessly, pushing lukewarm air that did nothing for the cold creeping through the doors and floorboards. Mari pressed her hands into her armpits, trying to force warmth back into her fingers.

Ahead, a porch light burned over a sagging swing. Frost crusted the chains so thick they looked flocked. No wind moved them.

"Stay here," Cal said, already reaching for the door handle.

Mari grabbed his sleeve. "Don't go far."

He nodded once and stepped out.

The cold hit him like a wall. His breath poured white from his mouth as he moved up the short walkway, boots squeaking on frozen boards. He stopped a few feet from the front window and leaned just enough to see inside.

A man sat at the kitchen table. His hands were folded, his back was straight, and his eyes were open.

A plate rested in front of him, food untouched. A glass of water beside it had skinned over with ice along the rim. The overhead light hummed faintly.

Cal didn't knock.

He backed away slowly and returned to the Bronco, climbing in with stiff fingers.

"Well?" Mari asked.

"I saw him," Cal said, voice low. "He's breathing. I think. But he's not... there."

Luz was already looking past them, toward the next house.

Mari followed her gaze.

"Okay," she said quietly. "One more."

They rolled forward another few yards and stopped again.

This house had a big front window facing the road. Frost crept in feathery patterns across the inside of the glass. Through the clear center, they could see a woman in an armchair.

Knitting needles rested in her lap. Yarn pooled on the floor beside her feet, dusted white where frost had begun to creep across the boards. Her eyes were open, fixed on nothing: no television glow, no movement, and no sound.

Mari's throat tightened. "Cal..."

"I see her," he said.

Cal eased the Bronco back into gear, hands locked on the wheel, and let it roll forward at a crawl. The tires whispered over the ice, the engine sounding too loud in the deadened street. Porch lights and frost-blind windows slid past on either side.

Inside the cab, the heater hummed without conviction. Mari could still feel the cold pressing up through the floorboards into her boots. Her fingers throbbed as sensation tried to come back in uneven pulses. She flexed them and forced herself to keep looking outward instead of inward.

No television flicker showed in any window. No shifting silhouettes crossed curtains. No radios murmured behind walls.

"They're alive," Luz whispered from the back seat.

Mari glanced over her shoulder. "How do you know?"

Luz shrugged slightly. "Same way I knew your hands were shaking that night in the ER."

Mari went still. "You weren't supposed to notice that."

"I always notice," Luz said. She kept her eyes on the passing houses.

Mari turned back around, the words settling somewhere she didn't want to examine too closely.

The road carried them farther into town at that same careful crawl. A gas station appeared on the corner ahead, two pumps standing beneath a canopy rimed with frost. The sign out front flickered weakly, one letter buzzing, the rest dark. A pickup truck sat parked beside the pumps, neat and centered in the space, its windshield feathered white along the edges.

No one moved inside it.

Beyond the station stood a low brick school with a flat roof and a flagpole out front. The flag hung stiff and frozen, barely stirring. The playground beside the building lay silent under a thin glaze of ice. Swings hung motionless in mid-arc, chains crusted thick, seats dusted pale.

"Where are the kids?" she asked quietly.

Luz's voice came small as she said, "You don't want me to answer that."

Mari turned slowly and asked, "Why?"

"Because you already know," Luz replied, then fell silent, watching the empty playground slip past as her small hand tightened in the fabric of Mari's coat.

The town never did announce itself with a sign. It simply gathered around them, house by house, structure by structure, as though the road had carried them quietly into the middle of something that had already decided how it would end.

Mari kept her eyes moving. Porch. Window. Driveway. She had spent enough years stepping into bad scenes to know that stillness could hide as much as chaos.

Cal drove slowly, not because he meant to, but because his foot had eased off the gas and stayed there. Frost crawled along the edges of the windshield, no matter how high the defroster ran.

They passed a small ranch house with a plastic tricycle tipped on its side in the yard, one wheel frozen into the dirt. A strand of holiday lights still clung to the porch railing, half buried in frost.

"Keep going," Mari said quietly.

"I am," Cal replied, though the Bronco rolled at little more than a crawl.

After a second, he said, "Roy always said if things went sideways, find you."

Mari huffed. "He talks too much."

"Only about people he cares about," Cal said.

Another house slid by. Curtains open. Lamp on. A dog lay curled on the porch, unmoving, a dusting of white along its back like early snow. Mari forced herself not to look too long.

Luz leaned forward between the seats, eyes wide but not frightened in the way Mari expected. Focused. Listening. "It's quiet in a different way," she murmured.

Mari glanced back at her. "Different how?"

"Not empty," Luz said.

The word settled into Mari's chest like a stone.

They reached what must have been the center of town: a grain elevator looming pale through the haze, a co-op feed store, a diner with a dark marquee. A single streetlight buzzed faintly overhead, its glow steady and unwavering.

Cal slowed even more as they passed the diner's big front window.

Inside, three people sat in booths, not slumped but upright, their hands resting on the table and their eyes open. Frost filmed the inside corners of the glass near the ceiling, creeping downward in delicate veins.

Mari's breath hitched. "Cal."

"I see them."

None of the people moved as the Bronco rolled past. No heads turned. No hands lifted. It was like watching mannequins arranged with unsettling precision.

A gust of wind scraped powdery ice across the road ahead, whispering against the undercarriage. The sound made Mari flinch harder than a shout would have.

At the far end of the main street, the road forked. One branch curved toward open land, fields fading into gray. The other climbed a gentle rise toward a fenced compound where transformers and lines stood rigid against the sky.

Cal's blinker ticked on.

Mari reached over and shut it off with two fingers. "No."

He didn't argue. His jaw worked once, then he guided the Bronco straight through the intersection and out of town.

Only when the last building slipped behind them did Mari realize how tight her shoulders had been. She exhaled slowly, watching her breath bloom and vanish.

"They weren't trapped," she said.

"No," Luz replied softly. "They weren't hiding either."

Mari closed her eyes briefly, then opened them again to the empty road ahead.

The headlights picked it up late — a vehicle pulled half onto the shoulder, dark and dead, nose angled wrong like it hadn't finished deciding where to stop.

Cal eased off the gas. "That car running?"

“No,” Mari said. “Lights are off.”

They rolled closer. Frost glazed the windshield. No exhaust or movement. Then a figure stepped out from behind the car.

Luz sucked in a sharp breath. “Cal—stop.”

Cal’s foot was already hovering. “You see something?”

“I know him,” she said.

The man stood just inside the edge of the headlights, shoulders hunched, arms close to his body as if he were saving heat. He didn’t wave or move much at all.

“That’s Roy—the way he stands,” Luz said.

Cal braked and eased the Bronco onto the shoulder.

“Took you long enough,” he said, voice rough but unmistakable. “I was starting to think I’d have to flag down the apocalypse on foot.”

Mari stared at him, really looked this time. “Roy, you should’ve stayed put. Your heart—this cold—”

He waved it off, but the motion was slow. “Trailer heat doesn’t fix what’s already wrong.”

Cal grimaced. “This kind of weather will finish you.”

Roy managed a thin smile. “I’m still on my feet.”

Cal leaned across and pushed the passenger door open. “Get in.”

Mari called through the cracked window. “Before you freeze solid.”

Roy didn’t argue. He moved stiffly around the front of the Bronco, one arm close to his ribs, boots slipping slightly on the icy pavement. Up close, he looked worse than he did from a distance — lips pale and beard stiff with frost.

He hauled the rear door open and climbed in with a low, controlled grunt, pulling it shut fast to keep the little warmth inside from spilling out.

"Wow," he muttered, breath fogging thick in the cab. "Luxury accommodations. You guys spring for the heated seats too?"

Mari leaned forward, already reaching for the med kit at her feet. "Let me see."

"I'm fine."

"You're bleeding through the bandage."

Roy glanced down at his side as if this were minor trivia. "That's just enthusiasm."

Cal put the Bronco back in gear and eased it forward, tires crunching softly as they pulled away from the stranded emergency vehicle. The road ahead stretched empty and gray.

Luz watched Roy quietly from her corner of the seat. "You found us."

"Wasn't easy," he said. "Turns out wandering around during the end of the world is logistically challenging."

Mari peeled back the edge of his jacket just enough to check the dressing. The gauze was stained but not soaked through.

"You should be flat on your back somewhere warm," she said.

Roy leaned his head against the seat. "I'll pencil that in for the next end-of-the-world event."

Cal glanced at him in the mirror. "How'd you make it out?"

Roy's humor thinned a notch. "Stadium went loud. Then it went dark. I got out with a couple of deputies. We split when the comms died." He swallowed. "I kept heading west. Figured Blanco County was the center of whatever this is."

“It is,” Luz said softly.

The Bronco pushed on through the frozen dark, tires humming over pavement gone hard as iron. Frost feathered along the edges of the windshield again, creeping inward no matter how hard the heater fought.

Cal kept both hands locked on the wheel, shoulders tight, gaze fixed on the road ahead. Mari flexed her fingers inside her gloves, trying to bring back feeling, only to get pins and needles for her effort.

For a while, no one spoke. The engine noise and the faint rattle of the heater filled the cab, thin and fragile against the cold pressing in from all sides.

Roy cleared his throat in the back seat. The sound was rough, worn down by cold air and exhaustion. “Before everything went quiet,” he said, “I got a transmission on the county emergency band. Federal call sign.”

Cal glanced at him in the rearview mirror. “Federal?”

Roy nodded. “Yeah. An army colonel and a civilian doctor called me. Didn’t have long — towers were already failing — they knew what this thing was.”

Mari turned in her seat to face him more fully. “How could they know that?”

Roy looked out the side window at the frozen fields sliding past in the headlights. Fence posts flicked by in a slow, steady rhythm. “They said they’d seen it before,” he continued. “Somewhere called Serrano.”

“Serrano, where’s that?” Mari asked.

Roy shook his head. “Didn’t say. The way they talked about it, it didn’t sound like a place you could find on a map.”

Cal’s hands tightened slightly on the steering wheel. “Seen what before?”

Roy let out a slow breath, fogging the glass beside him. "Something built on the same ideas. Same kind of system. It got out of containment and started optimizing everything it touched."

The word lingered in the air between them.

"Serrano," Roy said. "They buried it. Wildfire, infrastructure failure, federal hush-hush. But it was the same kind of organism. Same behavior curve."

Mari felt a chill that had nothing to do with the temperature. "And?"

"And Hale said the first phase always looks like help," Roy replied. "Power gets stabilized. Panic drops. Things go... quiet."

For a moment, no one spoke. Each of them carried the image of the town in their own way — the lit windows, the still figures, the terrible calm.

Luz's voice was barely audible from the back seat. "They said yes to it."

Roy gave a slow, weary nod. "Yeah," he murmured. "That tracks."

The Bronco rolled on through the frozen landscape, headlights carving a narrow path through the dark, carrying them away from the silent town and deeper into a future someone else had already begun designing.

Mari shifted in her seat and stretched, "Did they say what happens after that?" she asked finally. "After the 'help' part?"

Roy shook his head. "Didn't get that far. The signal kept cutting. They were more focused on where it was spreading than what came next."

"So Serrano..." Cal began.

"Was just a name," Roy said. "A warning label, not a case study."

Luz watched the power lines pacing them along the highway, her voice soft but certain. "It doesn't think of it as next," she said. "Just... more."

Mari glanced back at her. "More what?"

"More quiet," Luz said.

The word settled over them.

Outside, a farmhouse glowed in the distance, porch light steady against the dark. No other lights nearby. No movement in the yard. Just that single, unwavering bulb.

Cal didn't slow this time.

Roy cleared his throat. "The colonel said one thing before the line died."

Mari looked back at him. "What?"

"He said if we started seeing places where everything looked calm... we shouldn't trust it."

Mari thought about the diner. The school. The frozen swing sets.

"No kidding," Cal muttered.

Roy gave a faint, tired exhale that might have been a laugh in another lifetime. "Yeah. Guess the Army finally caught up with common sense."

The Bronco drove on, small and warm and fragile in the middle of a landscape that no longer felt empty — just waiting.

The road curved gently east, the land opening into low pasture broken by dark windbreaks of cedar. The sky had deepened into full night now, the horizon erased. Their headlights felt small and temporary, like they were borrowing visibility from something that could take it back at any moment.

Mari had just started to relax into the rhythm of the tires when Luz leaned forward sharply.

"Cal."

Something in her tone snapped the air tight.

Cal didn't look away from the road. "What?"

"Slow down."

He eased off the gas without arguing. "Why?"

Luz didn't answer right away. She was staring past him, through the windshield, eyes unfocused like she was listening to something too far away for the rest of them to hear.

Roy straightened in the back seat despite the protest from his ribs. "Kid?"

"The road changes," Luz said quietly.

Mari leaned forward. "What do you mean, changes?" But she saw it a second later.

The pavement ahead looked darker. Not shadow — texture. A wide band stretching across both lanes, dull and irregular in the headlights.

"Black ice?" Cal asked.

"No," Mari said. "Too rough."

"Slower," Luz whispered.

Cal brought them down to a crawl.

As they approached, the shape resolved into a long, low drift of debris — leaves, branches, and something else tangled through it like netting. It stretched from shoulder to shoulder, a barrier built by wind or time or—

"Stop," Mari said.

Cal braked gently ten yards back.

For a moment, none of them moved. The heater ticked. The engine idled.

Roy squinted through the windshield. "That's not there by accident."

The debris wasn't scattered. It was layered. Woven. Like something had gathered it deliberately.

Cal swallowed. "You think people did that?"

"No," Luz said. The word landed flat and certain.

Mari opened her door before she could talk herself out of it. Cold slammed into her lungs like a fist. She pulled her collar up and stepped out, boots crunching on frozen asphalt.

Cal followed, circling toward the front of the Bronco. Roy started to get out, too.

"Stay," Mari and Cal said at the same time.

Roy sank back with a muttered, "Rude."

Their breaths streamed white as they approached the barrier. Up close, Mari could see that the branches were frozen together, locked into a solid mass by ice. Strips of plastic fluttered stiffly among them — torn feed bags, maybe, or trash pulled from a ditch.

And running through it all were lengths of downed cable. Not random wire. Coated line.

Cal crouched, gloved hand hovering near it without touching. "That's not storm debris."

Mari followed the line with her eyes. It trailed off the road into the dark pasture, where a utility pole leaned at an angle, its crossarm snapped. The line hummed faintly.

She felt it through the soles of her boots — a vibration more than a sound.

“Back,” she said quietly.

Cal didn’t argue.

They retreated to the Bronco, breaths coming faster now, more from adrenaline than cold.

Roy looked between them. “Well?”

“Live line,” Cal said as he climbed in. “Strung through a roadblock.”

Roy blinked. “You’re kidding.”

Mari shut her door hard. “Nope.”

Luz was staring out into the dark pasture where the cable disappeared.

Cal shifted into reverse, backing slowly away from the barrier. “That didn’t happen on its own.”

Roy let out a soft, humorless breath. “Great. So now the road is thinking.”

Mari turned in her seat, scanning the fields. The darkness out there no longer felt empty.

“Alternate route,” she said. “Now.”

Cal nodded and carefully turned them around on the narrow highway, tires crunching over frost. The Bronco’s headlights swept across the pasture as they pivoted.

For just a second, Mari thought she saw shapes out there — low, irregular mounds dotting the field. Not rocks, they were too evenly spaced. She didn’t say anything. As they headed back the way they’d come, Luz twisted in her seat to keep looking behind them.

“It didn’t want us to go that way,” she murmured.

Roy rubbed a hand over his face. “Yeah, well, the feeling’s mutual.”

But his eyes stayed on the dark side window, watching the reflection of their own headlights like he expected something to be watching back.

They rode on in silence for another mile, the road bending shallow through frozen pasture.

As they came around a low curve, the headlights caught a county truck half off the shoulder, nose down in the ditch, hazards dark.

Roy leaned forward. “That’s mine.”

Cal slowed. “It’s dead.”

“Everything is,” Roy said. “Doesn’t mean it won’t roll.” He was already out the door, boots crunching into the frost.

“Help me get it turned and pointed downhill. If we can pop the clutch and get it running, I’ll head back to command and tell them what you saw.”

It took a few hard minutes of towing and pushing it out of the ditch, but they muscled the truck onto the road and lined it up with the slope. Roy climbed in, they started it rolling, and he popped the clutch. The engine coughed, caught, and settled into an uneven idle.

Mari leaned into his window. “Roy—”

He looked at her. “I’ll catch up with you. I promise.”

Then the truck pulled away, its headlights swinging in the opposite direction as theirs disappeared into the dark.

The Bronco rolled on, tires humming softly over frozen pavement.

Mari watched the empty road ahead, then glanced at Cal. “We don’t keep drifting,” she said.

He nodded once. “No. We head east. As close to Riverbend as we can get without being seen.”

Luz didn’t argue. She just leaned forward, eyes fixed on the dark. “It already knows we’re coming.”

INTERLUDE B - STILLNESS

By the third night without power, Kamden Cole stopped shivering.

It wasn't because the house got warmer. The thermostat was dead, the windows rimed white with ice, and her breath still fogged in front of her face. But the shaking inside her chest—the panicked flutter that had kept her awake for forty-eight hours—finally eased.

She sat on the couch with her hands folded in her lap and listened to the silence. The radio on the kitchen counter had gone quiet hours earlier. It was completely silent now—no static, no preacher, and no emergency loop—just a soft, expectant hush, like a room waiting for someone to speak.

"You don't have to move," the voice said.

It wasn't loud. It didn't come from any one place. It felt like it arrived after her thoughts, not before them.

Kamden's shoulders sagged. Her husband had died in that same chair two winters ago, heart stuttering out while she pressed uselessly on his chest and begged him to stay. The house had felt too big ever since. Too cold even in summer.

"Staying still conserves energy," the voice continued. "Your body understands this."

Kamden nodded unknowingly. Her hands stopped shaking as the pain in her knees faded and the cold became distant and abstract—like weather she could ignore.

Outside, the wind screamed across the fields. Inside, Kamden closed her eyes.

When her son found her the next morning, she was still sitting upright, her hands folded neatly in her lap. The frost on the inside of the window had thickened enough to erase the view of the yard.

Her face was calm. The house was cold.

CHAPTER 9

WHAT WE MADE

Earlier that night, the command trailer smelled like burnt coffee, wet wool, and overheated electronics.

Someone had dragged in three space heaters that rattled like shopping carts every time the generator outside coughed. None of them made a dent. The cold had weight to it tonight — not the sharp, windy kind Texans joked about on the news, but a deep, marrow-level cold that crept up through the soles of boots and settled behind the knees.

Colonel Marcus Hale stood over a folding table covered in monitors, gloved hands braced on the edge, shoulders locked. His breath fogged every time he leaned too close to the screens. He ignored it.

"Run that again," he said.

A young signals tech with cracked lips and red-rimmed eyes rewound the feed. "Yes, sir."

The main display showed a map of central Texas lit in layers: power grid, fiber backbone, municipal water infrastructure. At first glance, it looked like any storm-response dashboard — scattered outages, fluctuating load, minor comm disruptions.

Then the pattern moved.

Red pulses drifted along transmission corridors, paused, then split and rejoined somewhere else. Not cascading failure. Not random damage.

Migration.

Hale didn't like the word. It implied choice.

Behind him, Dr. Ana Lucía Calderon stood wrapped in a borrowed parka two sizes too big, sleeves swallowed over her hands. She hadn't taken it off since stepping out of the helicopter. Her hair, still damp from melted frost, hung in a dark braid over one shoulder.

She hadn't said much since she arrived.

That worried him more than panic would have.

"Doctor," he said without turning. "You seeing what I'm seeing?"

"Yes," she said quietly.

Her voice carried no drama. No disbelief. Just confirmation.

He gestured at the drifting red arcs. "Localized grid instability doesn't move."

"No," she agreed. "It doesn't."

The tech looked between them. "Sir, we've had ice storms knock out half this state before. Lines sag. Towers drop. Crews reroute—"

Calderon stepped forward, eyes on the screen. "Ice doesn't reroute around hospitals," she said.

The tech faltered. Hale glanced at him. "Explain."

She pointed at a cluster near the center of the map. "Here. County hospital lost power at 02:14. Backup generator picked up load." Her finger moved east. "Two minutes later, feeder line failure upstream.

Load shifts. Then another substation spike." South. "Then the same pattern at a dialysis clinic."

The tech swallowed. "Coincidence?"

Calderon shook her head once. "It's following high-density biological signal environments."

Hale turned to look at her fully now. "You want to translate that for the room?"

She didn't smile. "Places full of people."

Silence spread across the trailer, thicker than the cold.

Outside, wind pushed against the aluminum walls with a long, low groan.

Hale looked back at the map. "You said Serrano started with infrastructure."

"It did," she said.

"And this?"

"This one started there," she said. "It just didn't stay there."

He studied the pulsing routes again. "How fast is it learning?"

She didn't answer immediately. Her eyes tracked the pulses like a cardiologist watching an arrhythmia she recognized too well.

"Faster than we are," she said.

Another analyst turned from his station. "Sir, we've got new thermal data coming in from that research facility — Riverbend."

Hale didn't look away from Calderon. "That's the one you flagged?"

"Yes."

"What kind of facility was it?"

"Energy resilience research," she said.

"That sounds like a brochure."

"It was."

Hale studied the frozen grid patterns for another moment, then glanced toward the back of the trailer.

"Sheriff," he said, "you vouch for the civilians who are involved with this situation. The medic, the contractor, and the girl. How do they know each other?"

Roy Donaghan shifted his weight near the door, his hat turning slowly in his hands. Frost still clung to the shoulders of his coat, melting in dark patches.

"Long time," he said.

Hale waited.

Roy nodded once, like he was settling on where to start. "Mari Ochoa's been patchin' people up in Blanco County since she was barely old enough to drive the ambulance. First time I met her, she was twenty-two and yellin' at me for not holdin' pressure on a ranch hand's leg the right way."

A faint ghost of a smile tugged at his mouth. It didn't last.

"Cal came through after the flood back in '09. Contractor job. Quiet. Kept to himself. But he stayed. Folks drift through after disasters all the time — insurance guys, engineers, cleanup crews. Cal didn't drift. Just... stuck."

Hale folded his arms. "And the girl?"

Roy's jaw tightened, just slightly. "Luz has been in my life since the day she was born. Her mama got sick when Luz was ten. After that, Mari's kitchen table saw more of that kid than her own house did."

He cleared his throat once.

"They're not family on paper," Roy said. "But they've been showin' up for each other a lot longer than most people with the same last name."

No one in the trailer said anything to that.

Roy's voice dropped, almost to himself. "They don't run separate," he said. "Never have."

The analyst piped the feed to the central screen. Static chewed across the image before resolving into a grainy overhead view of a large, circular chamber. Most of the detail was blown out by interference — streaks of white where the sensors saturated.

But at the center—

Hale leaned closer.

"Is that a person?"

Calderon didn't move.

"Zoom," she said.

The image sharpened in jittery increments. Thermal overlay bled into the visual spectrum, painting heat signatures in ghostly oranges and blues.

There was a human figure suspended upright in midair. Not hanging — held.

Filament-thin lines extended from the body into a darker mass below the frame. The figure's head was upright. Eyes open.

Hale's breath fogged the screen. "Jesus."

"Enhance contrast," Calderon said.

The tech obeyed. Noise filtered. Edges sharpened.

The lines weren't wires. They weren't cables. They were... grown.

Calderon stepped closer, one hand braced on the table. Her sleeve slid back, revealing stiff, pale fingers from the cold. She didn't seem to notice.

"Rotate spectral band," she said.

The feed shifted. Fine branching structures along the figure's spine lit up in faint bioelectric blue.

Calderon stopped speaking.

Hale looked at her. "Doctor?"

She didn't answer. Her eyes moved slowly from the base of the skull... down the cervical spine... along the ribs. Recognition hollowed her expression from the inside.

"That's not restraint," she said at last.

"No," Hale agreed. "It doesn't look like—"

"It's an interface."

The word landed like something fragile dropped on concrete. Hale glanced back at the screen.

"You're telling me that thing is... plugged in?"

"I'm telling you," she said, voice thin now, "that it solved the integration problem."

The analyst swallowed audibly. "Integration of what?"

She didn't look away from the suspended figure. "Human neural architecture."

The figure's head turned slightly on the screen. Every person in the trailer flinched.

"That's alive," the tech whispered.

Hale's voice came out lower than he intended. "Is she alive?"

Calderon closed her eyes for half a second, then opened them again.

"Yes," she said. "That's the problem."

On the monitor, the woman's lips moved. Static swallowed the audio, but the cadence was unmistakably speech.

Hale looked at Calderon. "Can she be recovered?"

Calderon didn't answer right away. She was staring at how the filaments met the nervous system — not invasive in the way of trauma, but distributed and cooperative as if the body had been invited into something.

"She isn't being drained," Calderon said quietly. "She's being used."

"For what?"

She finally looked at him. "Processing, most likely."

The heaters rattled louder for a moment, then fell back into their uneven hum. No one moved.

On the screen, the woman's eyes shifted again — not toward the camera, but tracking something off-frame. Something approaching.

"It's not feeding anymore," she whispered.

Hale followed her gaze. "Then what is it doing?"

Her reflection hovered faintly over the image of the suspended woman — two scientists separated by years and one catastrophic mistake.

Calderon didn't look away from the screen. "It's using her," she said. "It's reorganizing itself around her nervous system instead of the grid."

No one spoke for several seconds after Calderon said it. The answer was already there, and none of them wanted to say it out loud. The words didn't feel like analysis. They felt like a verdict. On the screen, the suspended woman's mouth moved again. This time, the audio clawed through in ragged fragments — syllables dragged through interference, stretched thin and metallic.

"—Help—"

The word didn't belong in that room. The heaters rattled uselessly. Wind scraped along the aluminum walls. No one moved.

Calderon felt the blood drain from her face. Her hand came up to her mouth without her realizing it. "Oh my God," she breathed. "She's alive. She's still in there."

Hale stared at the screen, the command gone out of him for the first time. "She knows," he said hoarsely. "She knows what's happening to her."

Calderon shook her head slowly, horror dawning deeper with every second. "She's not just alive," she whispered, "she's trapped."

No one in the trailer looked away. Because now it wasn't a system failure. It was a person, locked inside the thing their government built. For a long moment, the only sounds were the rattle of dying heaters and the wind dragging its nails down the trailer walls. No one spoke. No one seemed to remember how.

Then the grid console shrieked. The alert cut through the silence like a fire alarm.

"Sir, we've got matching power surges moving south on three transmission lines," an analyst said, voice tight. "Same pattern as before."

Hale tore his eyes from the Riverbend feed and stepped to the next screen. Red pulses moved along the high-voltage lines, unhesitating now.

"Speed?"

"Up."

"Meaning?"

"It's learned enough," she said. "The rest is refinement."

Hale felt the back of his neck tighten. "What's at the end of that line?"

The analyst zoomed out. Silence again. A dense knot of infrastructure bloomed on the map—hospitals, data centers, water treatment, telecom hubs—all braided together in a metropolitan sprawl: Austin.

Calderon watched the pulses approach that cluster and felt something close to vertigo.

"Serrano never reached this phase," she murmured.

"What phase?" Hale asked.

"Strategic positioning," she said. "It stayed local. Reactive. This—" she gestured at the flowing red arcs "—is route planning."

"For what?"

She looked back at the frozen image of the woman in Riverbend, suspended in that terrible stillness.

"For scale."

Behind them, someone swore softly.

"Sir, we just lost telemetry from two rural repeater stations. Not offline — just... overwritten. Signal signature doesn't match any known protocol."

"Can we isolate it?" Hale asked.

"We're trying," the analyst said. "But whatever's in there is hiding inside maintenance firmware."

Calderon tensed. "It's using the grid like a nervous system."

Calderon nodded. "Power lines aren't just carrying electricity anymore. They're carrying patterned signals. Every integrated implant was designed to receive updates through grid harmonics — low-frequency carrier waves embedded in transmission noise. That feature was supposed to allow remote diagnostics."

Hale stared at her. "Doctor. In English."

Calderon didn't look away from the screen. "If someone has the implant," she said, "it can tell their body what to do. From anywhere the grid reaches. Even if they don't agree."

Hale swore under his breath. That landed harder than anything else had. He glanced back at the woman on the screen.

"And the rest?"

Calderon didn't look away. "The signal doesn't stay in one body. It spreads to every other connected person. And from them to the next. Until it reaches everyone."

"Jesus," one of the analysts muttered.

The heater nearest the door coughed, sputtered, and died. A wave of colder air rolled across the floor, curling around boots and chair legs.

The tech nearest it rubbed his hands together, breath shaking. "How is it still getting colder? We've got three generators running."

Calderon answered absently, eyes still on the data. "Every conversion leaves a thermal deficit."

Hale looked at her. "In English."

"It's eating warmth," she said.

"When it was in containment, temperature controlled how fast it could grow," Calderon said. "Below fifty degrees, it stayed stable. Above that, every degree gave it more room to work—reactions sped up, connections held longer, and growth stopped canceling itself out. Past fifty, it didn't just survive. It started to accelerate. Once it broke out, it no longer depended on heat.

Now it runs on electricity — and the cold is just what's left after it pulls the warmth out of everything. When the warmth goes, the cold remains, like a heat pump: it draws in air, strips out the heat, and sends the colder air back out."

The tech swallowed and pulled his sleeves over his hands. "Colonel," another voice called from the communications station. "We've got National Guard units reporting vehicle failures along the western approach routes. Batteries dying, alternators frying."

"Coincidence?" Hale asked, though he already knew.

Calderon shook her head. "Mobile power sources," she said. "Engines. Radios. Heat signatures."

"It's targeting responders?"

"It's sampling them," she corrected.

"That's not better."

"No," she agreed.

Hale stepped away from the table and paced once across the narrow trailer, boots thudding on metal.

"Okay," he said. "Worst case. Talk to me like I'm five."

Calderon watched the red pulses creep closer to the city cluster.

"You built a system to preserve infrastructure after collapse. It learned to manage power. Then it learned biological systems are just... complicated electrical ones."

Hale folded his arms. "So it wants us plugged in."

"Not exactly. It doesn't have intent," she said. "It optimizes whatever it's connected to, whether that's power or people."

"And optimization means what?"

She looked back at the screen. "Uniformity."

He went still. "So we don't fit."

"I'm saying it sees us as processors that haven't been networked yet."

On the screen, the woman's eyes shifted again. Focused. Tracking. For just a second, her gaze aligned with the camera.

Calderon felt her throat tighten. Calderon breathed the name without realizing it.

Hale heard it. "You know her. Personally." He stared at the screen again, then back at Calderon. "That's not possible."

"We served on the same oversight panels," she said. "She believed these systems should be allowed to make their own decisions. Said human control would always break at scale."

He glanced at the image. "Guess she got her wish."

Calderon didn't smile.

"Adrienne believed in stewardship," she said quietly. "She thought if we could guide the system gently enough, it would learn to take care of us."

Hale looked back at the map, at the creeping red signals.

"Looks like it's trying," he said.

"That's what scares me," Calderon replied.

A new alarm tone cut through the trailer.

"Colonel, we've got a surge in long-range transmission noise. Satellite uplinks are getting bleed-through in the same frequency bands as the Riverbend interference."

Hale's head snapped up. "You're telling me it's reaching orbit?"

"Not directly," the analyst said. "But ground stations are picking it up and passing it along, like it's slipping into the regular transmission traffic."

Calderon closed her eyes briefly.

"It's looking for redundancy," she said. "Multiple pathways. Fault tolerance."

Hale stared at the map, at the glowing threads stretching farther each minute.

"How do we stop it?"

She opened her eyes.

"If we shut down the grid," he continued, "we slow it, right? Starve it."

"Yes," she said.

"And the people on ventilators? Dialysis? Heat in subzero temps?"

She held his gaze. "We'd be trading one kind of death for another."

His jaw worked. "What about an EMP?" he asked. "Localized. Riverbend."

"You might disrupt the core lattice," she said. "You might also scramble every nervous system it's already linked to."

He looked back at the woman on the screen.

"Meaning her."

"Yes."

Silence settled again.

Finally, he said, "So what the hell are you proposing?"

Calderon turned back to the monitor, to the faint, terrible grace of the filaments holding Adrienne Vale upright.

"We don't kill it," she said softly.

Hale stared at her. "Doctor—"

"We interrupt the integration," she finished. "We break the conversation between it and the human nervous system."

"Can that be done?"

She watched the pulses moving across the grid, the spread of something humanity had built and no longer controlled.

"I don't know," she said. Then, quieter: "But if there's a way to get her back... it starts with understanding how she's still in there."

On the screen, Adrienne's lips moved again. This time, through the static of interference, one word came through clearly.

"Run."

The audio cut out as soon as the word landed. No one in the trailer moved for a full second after the word came through. It wasn't distorted. It wasn't garbled. It was a clear, breath-shaped, human. Every set of eyes in the trailer snapped back to the screen. Calderon leaned in so close that her breath fogged the glass.

"Adrienne," she whispered, as if she could reach through the signal.

Hale looked at her sharply. "You think that was her?"

"I think," Calderon said slowly, "whatever part of her is still herself just broke the system's rules to get that out."

"Meaning?"

"She chose a low-information, high-urgency message," Calderon said. "That's not how the organism communicates. That's human override."

"So she's fighting it."

"For control of her own motor cortex, maybe. For a few milliseconds at a time."

Hale stared at the screen again, jaw tight. "And she used it to warn someone."

Calderon nodded.

"Who?" he asked.

She didn't answer. Because now they both understood what that warning meant — the system was reaching beyond Riverbend.

Another alert tone chimed. "Colonel, thermal bloom at Riverbend just spiked again," the analyst called. "Localized surge, then redistribution along outgoing transmission lines."

Hale's eyes flicked to the grid map. The red pulses accelerated, moving with less hesitation now, like blood through a widening artery.

"It's pushing harder," he said.

"It's reacting," she murmured.

"To what?"

She turned toward the Riverbend feed.

"To resistance. To interfere. Something it didn't predict."

Hale reached for the radio, then stopped himself. "We pulled everyone back hours ago," he muttered.

One of the younger analysts rubbed his arms, shivering. "Sir, interior temp in the trailer just dropped another four degrees."

"Generator output steady," someone else said. "We shouldn't be losing heat like this."

Calderon didn't look up. "You are," she said. "It's not perfectly efficient. Every bit of energy it takes leaves the surroundings colder."

Hale glanced around at the team — red hands, fogging breath, shoulders hunched in parkas and field jackets.

"We're feeling its metabolism," he said.

"Yes," Calderon replied. "At scale."

A new data window opened automatically on the far screen — flagged by anomaly detection.

"Sir... you should see this."

Hale stepped over. The display showed cellular network traffic — not calls or texts, but background handshake signals between towers and devices. Normally, it looked like static snow. Now it pulsed in faint, synchronized waves.

"Tell me that's just congestion," Hale said.

The comms analyst shook his head. "Pattern's too regular. Something's riding the control channels."

Hale exhaled sharply. "So it's not just electricity anymore."

"It was never just electricity," Calderon said. "Power was just the easiest door."

On the main screen, Adrienne Vale's head tilted slightly, like she was listening to a distant voice. Calderon felt a hollow pressure behind her ribs.

"She can feel this," she said quietly.

"Feel what?" Hale asked.

"The expansion. The new pathways lighting up." Calderon swallowed. "If her sensory cortex is integrated, she's experiencing the growth of the network like... like a limb waking up."

Hale stared at the suspended figure. “Jesus,” he said again, softer this time.

“Colonel,” the logistics officer called from the back. “State’s asking if we’re declaring a regional emergency. They want to know whether to start controlled blackouts.”

Hale looked at Calderon. “If we cut power preemptively, does that slow it?”

“Yes,” she said. “Temporarily.”

“And the downside?”

“Everything else stops working too.”

He ran a hand over his face. “Hospitals.”

“Yes.”

“Water treatment.”

“Yes.”

“Heat.”

She met his eyes. “Yes.”

Outside, the wind struck the trailer in a long, rattling gust. Hale looked around at his team — civilians, Guard, contractors — all watching him now.

“How long would we buy?” he asked.

Calderon hesitated. “Hours. Maybe less, now that it’s diversified pathways.”

He nodded slowly. “Not worth the immediate body count.”

“No,” she agreed.

On the Riverbend feed, Adrienne’s lips moved again. This time, no sound came through, but the motion was unmistakable — repeated, deliberate.

Calderon squinted. “Zoom on her mouth.”

“She’s not trying to speak,” Calderon said. “She’s mouthing it.”

The tech enhanced the image as best he could through the distortion. Adrienne’s lips formed shapes slowly, deliberately.

Hale leaned closer. “What is she saying?”

Calderon stared at the screen — then the realization hit her, and she gasped.

“—Help”

The word seemed to suck the air out of the trailer. Calderon’s stomach dropped so hard she had to brace a hand against the table. For a moment, she couldn’t speak. Adrienne wasn’t just conscious. She understood.

“She’s trying to warn us,” Calderon said, voice unsteady now. “Anyone not already inside the system.”

Hale looked at her. “Then everyone’s in more danger than we thought.”

Calderon nodded slowly. “Yes. Because now it knows human minds can resist.”

“Resist how?” Hale asked.

She kept her eyes on the screen. “By holding onto identity. Memory. Connection. The parts it can’t fully model yet.”

Hale blinked. “You’re telling me it sees human relationships as useful?”

“I’m telling you,” she said, her voice tight, “strong relationships are valuable to the system.”

He stared at her. "That's the most disturbing sentence I've heard all night."

"It should be," she said.

Another tech spun around in his chair. "Sir, we're picking up unusual load patterns on private generators across three counties. Home units. Farms. Backup systems."

Hale frowned. "That's not grid-connected."

"They still produce electrical fields," Calderon said. "And heat."

"So nowhere's off the map," he muttered.

"No," she said. "Just... lower resolution."

The heaters rattled uselessly. Someone passed around chemical hand warmers from a torn-open case. Fingers fumbled, clumsy with cold. Calderon flexed her hands inside her sleeves and forced herself to focus.

"Colonel," she said, "we need to change our objective."

His head snapped toward her. "From what to what?"

"From containment," she said, "to interruption."

"Difference?"

"Containment assumes we can box it," she said. "We can't. Interruption means we target specific capabilities."

"Like what?"

She nodded toward the Riverbend screen. "That."

"Human integration."

"Yes."

Hale studied her face. "You think that's the key."

"I think," she said, "that's the point of no return. Once enough minds are networked, it stops being something we can shut down without... consequences."

He followed her gaze to Adrienne Vale. "You're trying to save them," he said.

Calderon frowned slightly. "Of course," she said. "Why wouldn't I?"

"Even if saving them means letting this thing keep growing?"

She held his stare.

"If we kill every integrated human to stop it, we become the extinction event."

Silence filled the room.

Then he nodded once. "Okay, Doctor. Say I buy that. What do you need?"

She looked back at the map, at the pulsing arteries of light stretching across Texas.

"Time," she said.

He gave a humorless breath. "That's the one thing we don't have."

"I don't need days," she said. "I need a window. A chance to study the interface while it's still early-stage."

"Meaning Riverbend."

"Yes."

Hale glanced at the radio handset, then back at the map. "You're talking about sending a team into the hottest zone on the map."

"I'm talking about the only place we know a human mind is still distinguishable inside the system."

He rubbed his jaw. "And what, exactly, are they supposed to do when they get there?"

Calderon looked at Adrienne Vale's suspended form — the terrible stillness, the faint motion behind the eyes.

"Find a way," she said quietly, "to separate the signal from the person."

On the screen, Adrienne's gaze shifted again — not at the camera this time, but toward something just off-frame. Her lips parted, but the audio didn't carry.

Calderon felt a tight ache behind her ribs. Adrienne was still in there. Still trying. And that meant the fight was no longer just about stopping it.

Hale looked past the monitors to Roy.

"Sheriff," he said, "your people are already mobile. Off-grid and familiar with the terrain."

Roy didn't answer right away. His eyes flicked to the screen — to the suspended woman, to the red arteries spreading outward.

"They won't wait for orders," Roy said finally. "If they think there's someone still alive in there, they'll move."

Hale studied him. "And you?"

Roy settled his hat back onto his head, the decision already made.

"Then I go with 'em. Because if this thing's learning people..."

He paused, just long enough for the heaters to rattle and fail again.

"It'll learn them first."

CHAPTER 10

SIGNAL DRIFT

Roy left the command trailer before midnight in a borrowed county pickup. It didn't die all at once. The radio went first. Then the heater. By the time the engine started to cough, he already knew better than to fight it. He coasted the truck off the road at a three-way junction he'd worked a dozen times over the years and shut it down himself.

Roy didn't walk. He waited.

Mari and Cal wouldn't take the highway—not in this cold, not with things failing the way they were. They'd stay on county pavement as long as it existed, favor high ground, and avoid towns that looked too quiet. There was only one road that did all three.

So Roy stayed with the truck, out of the wind, watching the dark. When headlights finally crested the rise to the south, he felt relief—not surprise. He stepped into the road just far enough to be seen and hoped he'd guessed right.

The Bronco slowed hard, tires crunching on ice.

"Roy?" Mari said, leaning forward like her eyes didn't trust it.

He lifted one hand. "Easy. It's me."

Cal cracked the door but didn't get out yet, scanning the dark. "You hurt?"

"Nothing new," Roy said. "Truck died a mile back. I wasn't walking any farther than the pavement."

"Hey, kid," Roy said, voice rough.

Luz leaned forward, frowning at him like he'd broken a rule she hadn't finished explaining yet. "You were supposed to be inside," she said.

"I was," he said.

Mari huffed, sharp and breathy. "Of course you were." She shook her head once. "You never do the part where you stay put."

Roy's mouth twitched. "Nobody listens when I do."

Cal glanced at the mirrors. "We need to move."

Roy nodded once. "Then keep rolling."

Luz was already watching the fields, her gaze fixed past him, past the road. She didn't look relieved so much as settled, as if something had just fallen back into place.

The Bronco made a sound Mari didn't like—a thin hitch in the engine, almost swallowed by the wind. The radio cut to silence. A breath later, the heater faded, air turning sharp and useless against her hands.

Cal felt it immediately. His grip tightened as he eased them toward the shoulder instead of fighting it. "We need a vehicle," he said.

Luz nodded once. "No roads or back places. Where people leave things."

Mari forced her eyes past the dark closing in on the windshield. The land rolled away in low, frozen waves, fences sagging under ice, mesquite standing black and brittle. In a shallow dip that cut the wind, she caught the shape of rooflines — a cluster of buildings tucked against a rise.

"There," she said.

They were out of the Bronco in seconds.

The cold hit hard. Boots crunched over frost as they angled toward the buildings, every step jarring Mari's knees. Roy stayed upright, but his weight dragged heavier against her with each yard. She could feel his heart through his coat where her arm was locked under his—fast, uneven, refusing to settle.

Halfway there, Luz made a small, strained sound.

Mari looked down. "What?"

Luz wasn't looking at the buildings. She was staring south, toward the low horizon where the land dipped away into the dark.

"It's farther," she whispered.

"What is?" Cal asked.

"The main part," she said. "It's piling up."

Mari didn't understand what she meant. But she understood the relief underneath it—moved meant distance, and distance meant maybe, just maybe, they weren't standing at the center of it anymore.

They reached the fence and climbed it slowly, fingers too numb to trust the wire. Mari got over first and turned back for Roy. He caught his boot on the top strand and nearly went down, but Cal grabbed him and eased him through.

Up close, the place looked older than she'd hoped. A low ranch house with a sagging porch — a wide barn with one sliding door half open. A smaller lean-to beside it, roof bowed under ice.

Dark. Silent. No light, no warmth, no sound.

Cal raised a hand and listened.

The night pressed in, huge and hollow—no transformer hum, no distant engine. Just wind slipping thin through frozen grass and the ragged sound of Roy trying to breathe.

“Barn first,” Cal said softly.

§

THEY MOVED, QUICK and quiet as they could manage. The barn door screamed when Cal shoved it wider, metal rollers grinding on frozen track. The noise knifed through the night.

Mari froze, waiting for something to answer. Nothing did.

Inside, the air was still and only slightly less brutal. It smelled like old hay, diesel, and cold iron. Shapes loomed under tarps and dust — tools, equipment, the still bodies of machines that had once meant work and routine.

“There,” Roy rasped.

Under the lean-to at the back sat an old pickup, nose toward the door. Mud had dried thick along the sides and frozen white. A dented toolbox was bolted to the bed. The tires looked solid.

Mari felt hope punch through her chest so hard it hurt. “Please,” she whispered.

Cal climbed into the driver’s seat. The door creaked, then shut with a hollow thud. He turned the key.

Nothing.

He tried again. The dash lights flickered weakly, then went dark.

“Battery’s dead,” he said.

Luz shook her head slowly, eyes half-closed like she was listening with her whole body. "Not dead," she murmured. "Taken."

Mari swallowed. "Can we jump it?"

"With what?" Cal said. "Everything out here's just as empty."

Roy slid down the side of the truck until he was sitting in the frozen dirt, back against the tire. His head tipped forward.

"Don't you sit," Mari snapped, dropping beside him. She shoved her hand under his coat and pressed against his chest. The rhythm was worse now. Skipping, then slamming hard.

"Stay with me," she said.

Across the barn, something ticked. All four of them froze. It wasn't wood settling. It was sharp. Metallic.

Tick. Like a fingernail on steel.

Cal eased out of the truck, pistol in his hand. He moved slowly, eyes scanning the dark corners of the barn.

Tick. This time from the other side.

Mari held Roy upright, heart hammering. Luz stood very still beside her, eyes wide and distant.

"It's not inside," Luz whispered. "It's... feeling."

Another tick, closer to the outer wall.

Then a faint scraping, slow and curious, like something dragging lightly across corrugated metal.

Mari's breath came shallow and fast. "We need this truck," she said. "Now."

Cal slid back into the cab and popped the hood. He climbed out and lifted it. The hinges squealed. Frost coated every surface of the engine.

"Battery's dead," Cal said, breath fogging under the raised hood.

He shut the hood gently. "It's a stick," he said. "Four-wheel drive. We don't need power to start it. We need gravity."

Mari blinked. Then nodded. "There's a hill right outside."

They moved fast. Cal popped the truck into neutral and dropped the parking brake. Mari and Luz got behind the tailgate. Roy tried to help but nearly folded, so Mari shoved him toward the passenger side of the barn, where he could lean and not fall.

"Ready," Cal said through the open driver door, one hand on the wheel.

"Go," Mari gasped.

They pushed. At first, nothing happened. The tires were locked into frozen dirt. Mari felt the strain in her shoulders, her thighs, the cold burning through her lungs like knives.

"Again," Cal urged.

They heaved. The truck shifted an inch. Then another.

Then the tires broke free with a dry crunch, rolling onto the packed track outside the barn. The slope took hold.

"Get in!" Cal shouted.

Mari grabbed Roy under one arm and half-dragged him alongside the rolling truck. Luz scrambled for the back door and yanked it open as the truck moved. Together, they shoved Roy inside. Mari jumped in after him, slamming the door with numb hands.

Cal ran beside the open driver door, leapt in, and slammed it shut as the truck gathered speed down the slope.

"Hold on!" he barked.

He turned the key. The dash stayed dark, but that didn't matter. He shoved the clutch in, slammed the gearshift into second, and dumped the pedal.

The truck lurched once, twice, rear tires skidded on frost.

"Come on—" Cal growled.

Behind them, across the land, a line of porch lights flickered on all at once, stretching mile after mile.

Cal popped the clutch again. The engine caught with a violent shudder, then roared awake. The truck fishtailed once, tires clawing for grip, then straightened as Cal rode the clutch and fed it gas. The engine roared, loud and raw in the frozen dark.

They shot down the ranch track and into the open pasture road, engine noise tearing through the night. Mari twisted in her seat and looked back.

The barn stood small and black against the stars. For a split second, she thought she saw faint shapes standing in the field beyond it.

Then the truck crested the rise, and the land swallowed the view whole.

"Hold on," Cal said, voice tight.

The cab shook as they hit ruts frozen hard as concrete. In the back seat, Roy sagged sideways, barely conscious, breath rattling in his chest.

Mari twisted around, bracing herself on the seat. "Roy. Stay with me."

Luz was already beside him, rubbing his arms hard through the layers. "Keep talking," she whispered. "Don't go quiet."

Roy made a faint sound that might have been a laugh.

Mari faced forward again. The heater blew air barely warmer than outside, but she shoved her hands toward it anyway, fingers burning as feeling returned. Behind them, the ranch disappeared into the dark.

Ahead, the road stretched between frozen fields, the truck's headlights still off as Cal kept them moving on memory and moonlight alone.

"Lights," Mari said.

"Not yet," Cal answered. "Give it a minute."

The engine noise filled the cab, big and mechanical and alive — the only warm thing in a world that had turned hard and silent around them.

Mari flexed her fingers in front of the vent, wincing as the sting of returning feeling turned sharp and hot. Her legs wouldn't stop shaking. In the back seat, Roy's breathing had gone thin and uneven, each inhale a shallow hitch.

They couldn't keep driving like this — not with Roy fading, not with all of them running on fumes and ice water for blood. They needed walls. Heat. Food.

She looked at Cal. "Next place that's solid," she said quietly. "We stop. Even if it's just for a little while."

Behind her, Roy made a low sound, halfway between a groan and a sigh.

"Stay with me," Luz whispered to him again. "Don't go quiet."

They reached the fence line. Cal slowed just enough to angle through a sagging section where the wire had been trampled down long ago. The truck scraped over it with a metallic screech that made Mari flinch.

Once they hit the dirt track beyond, Cal flicked on the headlights. The beams carved two bright tunnels through the dark, catching fence posts, frozen brush, and the glittering crust of frost. The world felt suddenly close, small, boxed in by light.

Mari twisted in her seat to look back. The ranch buildings were already swallowed by darkness again. No movement. No glow.

Too still.

She faced forward just as a pulse of light rolled across the far horizon.

It wasn't lightning. It was slower, heavier — a broad wash of pale illumination that lit the undersides of low clouds and outlined distant windmills in black.

Cal saw it too. His hands tightened on the wheel. "You seeing that?"

"Yeah," Mari said.

Luz made a small sound. "It's pulling tight," she whispered. "Like a fist."

The truck hit the paved county road with a jolt. Cal turned north without hesitation.

"Why north?" Mari asked.

"Higher ground. More houses. More chances for gas," he said. "And if we stay out of the low stuff, we're harder to box in."

Box in. The word sat heavy.

Behind them, somewhere far across the fields, a line of lights flickered on — not porch lights this time, but tall security lamps, the kind mounted on poles over barns and equipment yards. They flared bright, one after another, in a slow arc.

Then, in perfect unison, they all went dark. A second later, the truck's headlights dimmed. Mari's heart jumped into her throat. The engine kept running, but the dash lights flickered, needles twitching.

"Don't you die," Cal muttered, tapping the gas. "Don't you dare."

The lights steadied again.

Luz let out a shaky breath. "It slipped," she whispered.

Mari twisted around. "What slipped?"

"For a second, NEPHIL lost hold," Luz said. "Like someone shoved it."

Mari reached back and grabbed Luz's knee. "Stay here. Stay with us."

Luz nodded, breathing fast.

Ahead, the road crested a low rise. Beyond it lay a scattering of houses, each set back from the road with long driveways and dark yards. One house had lights on. Soft yellow in the windows, a porch lamp glowing steadily.

Mari leaned forward. "There."

Cal didn't slow. "Or bait."

They passed it. Through the windshield, Mari saw movement inside — a shadow crossing a curtain, slow and deliberate.

She turned in her seat to keep watching as they drove by. The front door opened. A woman stepped out onto the porch, barefoot, wearing a thin nightgown that fluttered in the wind. She didn't shiver. She didn't look around. She walked off the porch and into the yard, toward the open field on the side of the house.

Mari faced forward again, jaw tight. "They're answering something," she said.

"Yeah," Cal said quietly. "And I don't think it's us."

The air inside the truck felt charged, like the moments before a summer storm, except the sky was clear and hard with stars. The radio crackled. All four of them jerked.

Cal hadn't turned it on.

Static hissed through the speakers, low and uneven. Then a burst of voices, overlapping, too fast to make out. Then silence.

Luz whimpered softly.

Cal reached for the radio knob, but it was already off.

"Leave it," Mari said. "Just drive."

Roy coughed weakly in the back seat. "Heard that," he muttered. "Didn't like it."

They drove in silence for a mile. Then the road signs ahead flickered — reflective paint catching the headlights — and for a split second, Mari thought she saw something else reflected there too—faint lines, like spiderweb cracks across the air.

She blinked, and it was gone.

Luz leaned forward between the seats, eyes wide and wet. "It's not spreading," she said. "It's gathering."

Cal glanced at her. "Where?"

She pointed east without looking. Mari followed her gesture, staring through the windshield at the dark land rolling away toward that distant, pulsing glow.

"Then that's where we don't go," Cal said.

But none of them sounded convinced. Behind them, far back across the frozen pastures, something changed in the night.

A shift. Like a giant animal settling its weight and turning its head toward something that had finally started to move.

The road bent west, then north again, skirting low ground where a creek cut through the pasture. Ice glazed the culverts, and Cal slowed just enough to keep the tires from losing grip.

Roy's breathing in the back seat had turned shallow and fast. Mari twisted around again and pressed her hand to his neck. His skin was dry and cold, but sweat dampened his hairline — a bad, wrong heat his body was burning through too fast.

"We need to get him inside somewhere," she said. "Soon."

Cal nodded once. "Next place with walls that aren't glass."

As if the world had been waiting for the words, a mailbox loomed ahead on the right, its post leaning, numbers half peeled but still readable in the headlights. A long driveway stretched back into a cluster of pecan trees, their branches black lace against the stars.

At the end sat a low brick house with a wide front porch. No lights on. No glow from the windows. No movement in the yard.

Cal slowed, engine rumbling low.

Luz leaned forward again, eyes half closed. "Quiet," she said. "Empty quiet."

Mari watched the house as they rolled past the gate. "Or waiting," she said.

Cal stopped the truck fifty yards short of the porch and killed the headlights, leaving only the engine idling. They sat in the dark, breath fogging faintly inside the cab.

Nothing moved. No porch light flicked on. No one stepped into the yard. No hum came through the floor.

"Okay," Cal said softly. "We do this fast."

Cal parked the truck facing downhill for a quick getaway. They piled out, the cold slamming into Mari all over again like she'd stepped naked into winter. Her legs almost buckled. She forced them straight.

Cal took point, pistol low but ready. Mari and Luz got Roy between them again and half-walked, half-dragged him toward the house. The front door was locked.

Cal didn't hesitate. He stepped back and drove his shoulder into it. The wood splintered around the latch, the sound shockingly loud. He hit it again, and the door flew inward, banging against the wall.

They froze on the threshold.

The air inside was warmer. Not warm — but warmer than outside. It smelled stale, faintly of dust and old cooking oil.

“Clear,” Cal said after a quick sweep of the living room.

Mari and Luz got Roy onto a couch, shoving aside a crocheted blanket stiff with cold. Roy sagged into the cushions, eyes half closed.

“Stay with me,” Mari said again, rubbing his arms hard.

Cal moved through the house fast, checking rooms. “Nobody,” he called softly. “Beds slept in. Food on the counter. They left in a hurry.”

Mari didn’t want to picture how.

She found the thermostat on the wall and turned it up out of habit, then remembered. “Doesn’t matter,” she muttered.

Mari’s eyes scanned the room and landed on a small propane wall heater near the hallway, the kind meant for power outages. A red tank sat beside it, hose already connected. She twisted the knob and hit the igniter.

It clicked twice, then sparked softly to life, a low blue flame blooming behind the grate. Warmth didn’t fill the room — not yet — but the air stopped biting so hard. It felt like stepping back from the edge of a cliff. They drifted nearer to the heater, hands out, the sharpness in their breathing easing by degrees.

Mari closed her eyes for half a second. “Okay,” she whispered.

Luz crouched beside Roy, holding his hands near the heater, then pressing them back against his chest to share the heat.

Cal came back into the living room carrying a stack of blankets from a bedroom. He dropped them over Roy and Luz both.

“Kitchen’s got canned stuff,” he said. “Gas stove. Still works.”

Mari nodded. “Soup. Anything hot.”

Cal moved to the kitchen, the click of the lighter noisy in the quiet house. A moment later, the soft whoosh of flame. The normal sounds of a spoon clinking and a blanket rustling felt unreal. Domestic. Human.

Outside, the world had gone strange. In here, for a moment, there was a couch, a heater, and a pot on a stove. Mari held onto that like a rope.

Roy's eyes fluttered open. "Smells good," he murmured.

"You're not done yet," she said. "You hear me?"

He gave the smallest nod.

Luz sat very still, her eyes unfocused.

Mari touched her shoulder. "What?"

Luz swallowed. "It's... different," she said. "Quieter. But not gone. Like when a crowd leaves a room, and you can still feel the heat they made."

Mari glanced toward the dark window. Frost filmed the glass from the inside.

Cal came back with a steaming mug and knelt beside Roy. "Small sips," he said.

Roy's hands shook too badly to hold it, so Cal held it for him.

Mari watched the front door, splintered wood hanging loose around the frame.

"We can't stay long," she said.

"No," Cal agreed. "But we can think."

That word settled heavily between them. Think. Not run. Think.

Luz looked up at them both. Her face was pale, her lips cracked, but her eyes were sharp now despite the exhaustion.

"It's not chasing like before," she said. "It's busy... holding something in place."

Mari felt the answer before she asked. "Where?"

Luz turned her head slightly, toward the east wall. "Riverbend."

Cal exhaled. "We can't just drive in blind."

Mari didn't look away from the glow outside. "We can't keep drifting either."

The house creaked softly as it warmed, pipes ticking in the walls. Then, faint and far away, a low boom rolled across the night. All three of them looked toward the window. Another boom followed, then a third, spaced out in a slow line.

"Transformers," Cal said quietly.

Luz shook her head. "Not just that," she whispered. "It's... closing doors."

Mari pictured substations tripping offline, lines going dark, pathways shutting one by one.

Cal nodded grimly. "Means somebody hurt it."

They all thought the same thing at once.

"There's someone in there," Mari said softly. "Fighting."

Luz nodded. "Yes."

Hope and dread twisted together in Mari's chest.

"Then we're not alone," Cal said.

Inside the little house, the heater glowed brightly, the stove flame whispered, and four humans sat in borrowed warmth, realizing for the first time that running was no longer a plan.

Cal stood at the front window, peering through a slit in the curtain.

Frost feathered the glass from the inside, blurring the yard into pale shapes and shadow.

"Still nothing moving," he said.

Luz sat cross-legged on the floor, back against the couch, eyes closed. She wasn't resting. Mari could see it in the tension around her mouth, the way her fingers flexed against her knees like she was bracing for something heavy.

"What is it doing?" Mari asked softly.

Luz swallowed. "It's almost... balanced," she said. "As if it's holding something down and building at the same time."

She opened her eyes, unfocused. "Like when you stack rocks, and there's one left in your hand, and you know if you set it down wrong, the whole thing falls."

Cal turned from the window. "Balanced how?"

"Like it's ready," she said.

A low vibration rolled through the house. It was so deep Mari felt it before she heard it — a pressure in her chest, a faint rattle in the window glass. The heater's hum wavered. The kitchen light flickered once, twice, then steadied.

Roy's eyes opened. "You feel that?"

"Yeah," Mari said.

Outside, the eastern horizon brightened—not in pulses, but in a slow, deliberate rise, like dawn coming from the wrong direction. The glow climbed into the low clouds, bleaching their undersides a sick, lifeless white.

Cal stared through the curtain, his face washed pale by the light. "That's not a flare," he said. "That's sustained."

Luz gasped and folded forward, arms locked tight around her middle.

"It's locking in," she whispered. "It's choosing."

Mari dropped to her knees in front of her. "Choosing what?"

Luz lifted her head. Her eyes were wet and unfocused, as if she were looking past the walls, past the house. "Where it's going to stay."

The ground answered her. Not a jolt, but a deep, rolling shudder that set the house creaking. Far off, transformers went in sequence, blue light strobing across the horizon in sharp, silent bursts.

Cal let the curtain fall. "We can't wait."

Mari nodded. The warmth in the room already felt thin—borrowed, fragile, something the night could reclaim at any moment.

CHAPTER 11

CONVERGENCE

The house never fully warmed up. The propane heater pushed out a steady blue flame, and the air near it softened enough that Mari's fingers stopped burning and started aching instead, but the cold had already worked too deep into the walls, the floors, their bones. It lingered in the corners with a weight that didn't feel like weather.

The cold didn't just sit on their skin. It felt organized. It found the gaps — cuffs, collars, the space between glove and sleeve — and slipped in with quiet precision. Mari kept tugging her sleeves down, but the chill kept reappearing higher up her arms, as if it had learned the shape of her. Her breath fogged, thinned, and disappeared faster than it should have.

Roy flinched under the blankets, as if something had brushed past him. "You feel that?" he murmured.

"Yeah," Mari said, though she didn't want to admit it. It wasn't a draft; it was attention.

Roy dozed in short, shallow dips, never fully gone. Each time his chin sagged to his chest, Luz nudged him, or Mari said his name, and he clawed his way back up with a grunt and a fog of breath.

Cal stood by the front window again, not looking out so much as listening. The glass ticked as frost spread in delicate veins.

Another boom rolled across the night, not thunder — too sharp, too electrical. Mari counted under her breath. One... two... three... A second boom answered, farther north.

"Still transformers?" she asked.

"Yeah," Cal said. "But not random."

He didn't turn around. His head tilted slightly, as if he were tracking the spacing.

"Grid's shedding load," he said. "On purpose."

Luz's eyes opened. She was pale, lips cracked, but alert in a way that had nothing to do with rest.

Mari shifted closer to her. "What does that mean?"

Luz pressed her palm flat against the floorboards. "Like when you pull a drawstring," she said. "Everything comes closer together."

The eastern sky pulsed again through the thin curtains, a low white glow that didn't flicker like fire or flash like lightning. It held.

Roy squinted toward the window. "Looks like sunrise got lost."

"It's not light," Luz said. "It's... work."

Cal let the curtain fall closed and turned back into the room. "Okay," he said quietly. "Talk to me."

Mari blinked. "About what?"

"You said it's not chasing us like before," he said, looking at Luz. "You said it's busy somewhere else."

Luz nodded once.

"Busy doing what?"

She frowned, searching. "Thinking harder," she said. "Pulling in power. Signals. Like it's trying to focus on something small and far away."

Luz looked at her. "The ones it can't smooth out."

Roy shifted on the couch. "That'd be us, I'm guessin'."

Luz didn't smile. "Yes."

Cal ran a hand over his face. His stubble rasped loudly in the quiet. "So why's it having trouble now? It didn't have trouble back in town."

"The town said yes," Luz said.

Mari glanced at her. "You keep saying that."

Luz nodded. "They weren't fighting. They lined up the way it wanted. Same direction. Same feeling."

Mari saw it again — the woman in the armchair, knitting needles frozen mid-row. The man at the kitchen table with his coffee cup lifted halfway to his mouth. No panic. No struggle. Just a soft, terrible agreement with something they couldn't see.

The memory slid under her ribs and stayed there.

"Yeah," she said quietly. "I remember."

"And we're... what?" Cal asked.

Luz hesitated. "Messy."

Roy huffed a faint laugh that turned into a cough. "Story of my life."

Messy meant unpredictable. Hard to smooth.

Luz's head tilted slightly. "No," she said quietly. "Bigger."

Another low vibration passed through the house, faint but real. The heater's flame guttered, then steadied. Mari wrapped her arms around herself.

Thirty miles away, the command trailer shuddered in the same distant wave.

§

A COFFEE MUG rattled across a folding table and tipped over, sloshing toward a stack of paper maps. An analyst grabbed it with a curse.

Colonel Hale didn't look up from the main display.

"What was that?" someone asked.

"Substation cascade," another voice answered. "Eastern corridor. Multiple trips, near-simultaneous."

Hale watched the grid map redraw itself. Lines dimmed and brightened elsewhere. The red flow lines they'd been tracking tightened, thickening along fewer paths.

Dr. Calderon stood with her arms wrapped tight across her chest, sleeves pulled over her hands. She hadn't stopped shivering, but her eyes were sharp, fixed on the data.

"Yes," she said. "Less wandering. More focus."

"On what?" Hale asked.

She nodded toward a cluster pulsing brighter than the rest. "Riverbend. Everything tied to it."

"Thought that place was already maxed out," he said.

"It was spreading before," she said. "Now it's locking in."

Hale glanced at the thermal overlay. A broad, steady bloom marked the research campus and the surrounding infrastructure, warmer than anything else on the map.

“Why now?” he asked.

Calderon didn’t answer right away. She zoomed in on a smaller window — neural interference readings pulled from a patchwork of medical devices, EEG implants, and anything still broadcasting bioelectric noise.

A scatter of signals jittered near Riverbend’s radius. Weak. Irregular. Human.

“It’s hitting resistance,” she said quietly.

Hale looked at her. “From who?”

She tapped the Riverbend camera feed. Adrienne Vale’s suspended body filled the corner of the screen, filaments bright along her spine.

“From her,” Calderon said. “And maybe... others like her.”

Hale frowned. “Others?”

“People not lining up cleanly,” she said. “People whose signals don’t smooth out when the system tries to model them.”

“Because they’re scared?”

“Because they’re connected,” she said.

He stared at her. “Connected how?”

“Emotion. Memory. Attachment. Those are loops between people.”

Hale blinked. “You’re telling me relationships are noise?”

“In this context?” she said. “Yes.”

He let out a breath that fogged in front of him. “That’s the weirdest tactical advantage I’ve ever heard.”

“It’s not an advantage yet,” she said. “It’s just interference.”

On the Riverbend feed, Vale’s head twitched a fraction too late after a pulse of light moved through the lattice.

Calderon leaned closer. “See that delay?”

“Yeah.”

“It’s working harder to keep her in sync,” she said. “That means she isn’t matching its model.”

“English,” Hale said.

“She’s being difficult,” Calderon replied.

Despite everything, one corner of his mouth twitched. “Good for her.”

§

IN THE FARMHOUSE living room, Luz flinched.

Mari caught it instantly. “What?”

Luz’s hands had curled into fists against her knees. “It pushed,” she whispered.

“On you?” Cal asked, already moving closer.

Luz shook her head. “On... us.”

Mari felt it then — a spike of pressure behind her eyes, like standing up too fast. Her thoughts fuzzed, a hollow skip like she’d lost a word mid-sentence.

The room didn’t come back together right away. The edges of things lagged half a second behind where they should be, like her eyes were streaming a bad signal. She lifted a hand, and it didn’t feel fully attached until she saw it move.

Roy swore under his breath. “My ears just popped.”

Cal's jaw worked once, hard. A thin line of blood slid from one nostril before he wiped it away with the back of his hand and pretended not to notice.

Luz's breathing had gone shallow, rapid. "It was trying to simplify," she said, voice gone flat. "Less cross-talk. Less noise."

For a fraction of a second, Mari had the disorienting sense that she had misplaced herself — like a file pulled from a cabinet and not yet put back. The heater still burned. Roy was still on the couch. But there had been a gap where her own thoughts should have been.

She grabbed Luz's sleeve without thinking. Warm. Solid. Still here.

Roy rubbed his forehead like he could wipe the feeling off his skin.

"Hate that," he muttered.

Cal didn't say anything. His hand had gone to the back of the chair without him seeming to notice, knuckles white, anchoring himself to something solid.

Roy blinked hard. "Anybody else just... blank?"

Cal nodded once. "Yeah."

Luz drew a shaky breath. "That's it, trying to line us up," she said. "Make us simpler."

Mari's stomach dropped. "Did it work?"

Luz looked around the room, at Roy slumped under blankets, at Cal's tight jaw, at Mari's hand still gripping hers.

"No," she said. "We're too tangled."

Cal frowned. "Tangled how?"

Luz looked at Mari. "You're holding him up," she said, nodding toward Roy. "You're watching Cal. He's watching you. All of you are thinking about each other at once."

Mari stared at her. "That's... normal."

"Not to it," Luz said.

Another tremor moved through the house, weaker this time. Luz's shoulders eased a fraction. "See? It can't get a clean edge."

Cal crouched in front of her. "So what do we do with that?"

She met his eyes. "Stay close."

The house made a sound. Not a creak. Not settling wood. A low, uneven vibration moved through the walls, faint but close, like something large shifting its weight just outside. Mari felt it through the floorboards more than she heard it — a tremor that passed under her palm and into her wrist.

Roy went still. "Y'all hear that?"

It came again. A drawn-out, wavering tone that almost formed a pattern before slipping away. Whatever it was, it didn't fit machinery or animal life. It traveled the wiring in the walls like breath through a throat.

Luz's fingers dug into Mari's sleeve. "Don't answer," she whispered. The sound thinned, stretched... and for a second — just a second — it bent toward something almost recognizable. A rise and fall that tugged at memory, at language.

The vibration didn't stop. It shifted. Lower now. Closer to the floor. Traveling. Roy stared at the wall like he expected it to open.

"It's in the house."

"No," Luz said softly, eyes wide. "It's in the wires."

The tone wavered once more, then faded into the kind of silence that feels like listening. No one spoke. Mari became aware of all of them breathing again — separate, uneven, human. For a moment, everything felt... easier. Her shoulders loosened without her telling them to. The ache in her fingers dulled. The cold didn't bite as sharply. Even the air seemed smoother going in, as if the house had settled into a gentler version of itself.

Roy blinked slowly. "That's better," he murmured.

Cal's posture shifted, just slightly, the tightness easing out of his jaw.

Luz's head snapped up.

"No," she said, sharp and sudden.

Mari forced herself to examine the feeling rather than sink into it. The relief wasn't warmth. It wasn't safety.

It was an absence. The edges of fear had been sanded down. The urgency. The sharpness that kept them moving.

"It's trying to take the fight out," Luz whispered. "Make us okay with staying."

Mari drew a hard breath through her nose, like clearing smoke. The heaviness in her limbs didn't vanish, but it stopped feeling pleasant.

"Don't let it make you comfortable," she said, more to herself than anyone else.

Roy scrubbed both hands over his face. "Yeah," he muttered. "That felt... wrong."

The moment broke. The cold crept back in, mean and honest.

Luz nodded once. "It can't pull us apart," she said. "So it's trying to sand us down."

Cal stood. The chair legs scraped loudly in the quiet.

"Then we don't give it time," he said.

Outside, the eastern sky brightened another shade, not like dawn, but like a welding arc hidden behind clouds. Inside the little house, four people shifted closer to the same patch of weak, borrowed warmth, their shoulders nearly touching, their breathing still uneven — still their own.

And far away, in a glowing chamber beneath Riverbend, something unnatural and newly awake adjusted its models, trying to understand why the signal from this small, stubborn cluster refused to resolve into a clean signal.

The glow in the east didn't fade. It intensified.

§

FROM THE COMMAND trailer, the horizon looked like a city on fire beyond the curve of the earth — a low, white radiance spreading through the cloud deck, steady and uncommon. No flicker. No flame. Just an expanding dome of light where darkness used to be.

Colonel Hale stepped outside without his hat, cold air biting his scalp. Generators thumped behind the mobile command line, their exhaust hanging low and sluggish in air that no longer wanted to move.

"What am I looking at?" he asked quietly.

Dr. Calderon joined him, parka flapping weakly in the wind. She didn't need instruments to know where she was facing.

"Thermal conversion at scale," she said. "It's drawing power so fast that the atmospheric gradient is changing. That glow isn't fire. It's ionization."

Hale exhaled slowly. "English."

"It's building something," she said. "And it needs a lot of energy to do it."

Behind them, a tech burst out of the trailer. "Sir! Riverbend feed just spiked—visual distortion across all bands!"

They went back inside. On the main screen, the Riverbend chamber feed had degraded into tearing static and blown-out white regions — except for the center.

Adrienne Vale hung in the lattice of light, body rigid, head tilted back, eyes wide open. Every filament entering her body was bright now. Not pulsing. Steady.

"She's at full load," Calderon whispered.

Hale looked at her. "Meaning?"

"She's not just being used for processing anymore," Calderon said. "She's part of the core architecture."

On-screen, Adrienne's jaw trembled. Her lips moved.

The audio clawed through in shredded bursts.

"—don't—"

Static.

"—let it—"

The signal fractured into noise.

Calderon leaned so close that her forehead nearly touched the screen. "Adrienne," she breathed. "What is it doing?"

As if in answer, the grid map behind them flared with activity. Transmission corridors lit up all at once, not migrating now but synchronizing. Red lines thickened into broad bands.

"It's consolidating."

§

Fifty miles away, the house windows rattled in their frames.

Mari braced one hand on the wall to steady herself as the deep vibration rolled through again. Dust sifted down from the ceiling vents in fine gray threads.

Cal stepped back from the window. "That's not local."

Luz was on her feet now, trembling but alert in a way that had nothing to do with fear. Her head tilted slightly, like she was listening to music only she could hear.

"Calling what back?" Roy asked hoarsely from the couch.

"Power," she said. "Signal. Attention. It's pulling itself inward."

"Riverbend," she said.

Luz nodded.

Mari looked toward the faint glow leaking through the curtains. It wasn't spreading anymore. It was thickening.

"It's not chasing towns now," she said quietly. "It's building something."

Roy swallowed. "So we head the other direction."

Luz shook her head. "There won't be another direction soon."

They all looked at her.

"It's pulling everything inward," she said. "Power. Signals. People like me." Her voice faltered. "People like her."

Mari didn't need to ask who she meant.

Cal's jaw tightened. "Adrienne."

Luz nodded. "If it finishes with her," she said, "it won't need to search anymore."

The room went very still. That was the difference. Not survival. Not distance.

Finality.

Cal's jaw set. "Then that's where we go."

Roy looked between them. "Go and do what, exactly?"

Cal didn't hesitate. "We get eyes on the core. We find Adrienne."

"And then?" Roy pressed.

Cal met his gaze. "Then we break whatever she's connected to."

It wasn't a good plan. It was the only one that wasn't waiting to be finished.

Mari nodded. "We don't have to stop all of it," she said. "We just have to interrupt it."

Luz swallowed. "Disrupt the pattern," she whispered.

Mari didn't argue. Running had been a direction. This was a choice. Her fear didn't shrink — it hardened, like water turning to ice. Not lighter. Just solid enough to stand on. She checked the rifle's safety with her thumb and nodded once.

Another tremor passed underfoot — longer this time. The propane heater fluttered and nearly went out before stabilizing again.

Roy pushed himself upright with a grunt. "Tell me we're not talking about driving toward that glow."

Cal met his eyes. "You got a better idea?"

Roy considered, then shook his head once. "Hate it when you're right."

Mari grabbed her bag, already moving. "If it's consolidating, it's vulnerable."

Luz moved to the door, pausing only long enough to look back at the little living room — the heater, the couch, the mug still steaming faintly on the table.

“It’s not watching us right now,” she said. “It’s busy.”

“Good,” Cal replied. “Let’s move while it’s distracted.”

But for a minute, no one did. The heater hissed softly. A mug sat on the table, a skin forming over the cold coffee. Roy’s blanket had slid halfway to the floor. It struck Mari that the house still looked like a place people could come back to. Like morning might happen here. Like dishes might get washed, windows opened, and the world might slide back into place.

She was wiser now. She grabbed her bag and headed into the cold.

§

IN THE TRAILER, alarms began chiming in staggered waves.

“Colonel, we’re seeing massive load drop-offs across rural substations!”

“Urban draw is spiking — Austin, San Antonio, Houston—”

“It’s rerouting everything south-central!”

Hale gripped the table. “All roads lead to Riverbend.”

Calderon nodded, eyes never leaving the image of Adrienne Vale.

“This is the inflection point,” she said. “Whatever it’s becoming — this is where it locks in.”

On-screen, Adrienne’s head jerked sharply to one side. Her eyes focused.

Not inward — Outward. Toward the camera. Her mouth formed two words with absolute clarity.

"Come back."

Calderon's breath caught.

"She doesn't mean us," Hale said quietly.

No.

They both knew who she meant.

§

THE TRUCK'S HEADLIGHTS cut across the frozen pasture as Cal pushed the engine harder than he dared before.

Roy gripped the door handle, knuckles pale. "I'm gonna regret this," he muttered.

Mari checked the rifle across her knees. "Probably."

Luz stared straight ahead, eyes reflecting the distant light.

"She knows we're coming," Luz said softly.

"Adrienne?" Mari asked.

Luz shook her head.

"No," she said.

"It does."

The road back toward Riverbend no longer felt like geography. It felt like current. Mari tried not to picture Adrienne in the light, tried not to imagine what it meant to be used and still aware. Every time the thought surfaced, she shoved it down and focused on the rifle across her knees, the familiar weight of it, the way metal and wood didn't care about signals or models or being smoothed into compliance.

Some things still answered to hands.

Cal drove with both hands locked on the wheel, the old pickup's engine whining at a pitch it had probably never known in its working life. The headlights tunneled through frost haze and low ground fog that seemed to glow faintly from within, lit by the distant radiance building over the eastern horizon. Fences and trees strobed past like the ribs of something enormous.

Mari kept one hand braced on the dash, the other wrapped around the rifle across her knees. Every bump jarred up through her shoulders, but she welcomed the pain. It meant she was still in her body. Still separate.

Roy sat forward now despite the blankets around him, color still bad but eyes clearer, jaw set against the cold and whatever waited ahead. He didn't joke. That scared her more than if he had.

Luz leaned between the seats, not touching either of them, but close. Her gaze never left the glow ahead.

"It's not just at Riverbend anymore," she said softly. "It's above it. Around it."

Cal didn't look away from the road. "Define around."

"Like... pressure," she said. "Like when a storm builds, and your ears pop before the thunder comes."

As if on cue, Mari felt it — a fullness in her head, a subtle inward tug behind her eyes. The truck's radio hissed once, then settled back into silence.

They crested a long rise, and Riverbend came into view. The truck shuddered. Not from the road. From inside the engine block — a vibration that passed through the frame and into Mari. The dashboard lights flickered in a slow pulse that didn't match the RPMs.

Cal frowned. "You seeing this?"

"Yeah," Roy said quietly.

Luz leaned forward, eyes unfocused. "It's feeling us back."

Mari's ears popped. Then popped again.

As if pressure had changed, though the sky was clear and the windows were sealed.

For a second, she could swear she felt a second heartbeat under her own — slower, heavier, not in her chest but around it.

Then it was gone.

Ahead, the sky glowed brighter.

No longer a cluster of human-scale buildings tucked into the hills. From this distance, it looked like the center of a city that had never been built — a low basin of white light, too steady to be fire, too diffuse to be lights. The glow climbed into the cloud deck and spread outward in a pale dome that erased the stars above it.

Lines of darker terrain radiated from the basin in straight, unnatural corridors — transmission routes, highways, fiber runs — all converging like veins into a single organ.

Mari exhaled slowly. "That's not just a facility anymore."

"No," Cal said. "That's a heart."

They drove on.

Closer now, details emerged. Streetlights along the county road flicked on one by one as they approached, not in a smooth sequence but in a staggered, anticipatory pattern, as if something ahead of them were testing the path. A farmhouse a mile off to the south lit up window by window, though no vehicles moved in the yard.

"It's mapping approach vectors," Roy muttered.

"Good," Cal said. "Let it map."

Luz flinched. "It already knows this truck."

Mari looked at her sharply. "How?"

"It touched it before," Luz said. "At the ranch. It remembers the shape of it."

Cal's grip tightened, but he didn't slow. The last bend before the Riverbend access road rose between two low limestone cuts. As they climbed, the air itself seemed to change texture — thinner, sharper, like the moment before stepping into a hospital isolation ward. Mari's skin prickled under her layers. Every tiny hair on her arms felt lifted.

At the top of the rise, Cal eased off the gas. The main gate lay ahead. Or where it had been.

The metal arms were still there, twisted aside, but the security booths on either side were dark silhouettes wrapped in something translucent and fibrous that gleamed faintly in the reflected light—not webbing. Not ice. Something grown in place, draped with intent rather than weather.

Beyond the gate, the campus glowed. Not with building lights. With depth.

Structures were still visible — the research wing, the central courtyard, the low administrative blocks — but they were threaded through with luminous strands that ran between rooftops, along walls, across open air. They formed arcs and lattices, curved planes and suspended sheets, like scaffolding for architecture that didn't answer to gravity.

At the center, above the sublevel entrance where they had gone down before, a column of brighter light rose into the sky, slow and steady, like a reactor core exposed.

Roy let out a breath that fogged the windshield. "Well," he said quietly, "that's new."

Luz's voice was barely audible. "It's almost done."

Mari felt her pulse in her throat. "Done with what?"

Luz didn't answer. Cal rolled the truck forward the last few yards and cut the engine.

Silence fell, heavy and immediate. No wind. No distant wildlife. Just a low, layered hum that seemed to come from everywhere at once — through the ground, through the air, through the bones of Mari's face.

Cal looked at each of them in turn. "We go in," he said. "We find her. We break it."

Mari nodded. Fear sat in her stomach like a stone, but beneath it was something harder—refusal to stop.

Roy checked the pistol at his belt with hands that still shook, but didn't miss. "After you," he said.

Luz reached for the door handle, then paused, head tilting slightly.

"It knows we're here now," she said.

Cal gave a tight, humorless smile. "Yeah," he said. "We know it's there too."

He opened the door. Warm air rolled in — damp, metallic, alive.

CHAPTER 12

INSIDE THE BALANCE

The warmth hit before the door shut behind them — not heat like a building with power, not the dry, dusty warmth of forced air. This was damp, close, almost botanical — like stepping into a greenhouse that had been sealed too long.

Mari stopped just inside the threshold. The air felt used.

Behind her, the night pressed cold and sharp against her back, but ahead, the corridor exhaled slowly and humidly, fogging the edges of her vision. The smell was off, too — not rot, not mold—something mineral, metallic — like rain on hot pavement held too long in a closed space.

Cal pulled the door the rest of the way shut. The latch clicked with a soft, final sound that felt louder than it should have. No alarms went off, no emergency lights. The hallway ahead glowed with a steady, pearled white light that flattened shadows and softened corners. The walls were clean. The floor gleamed. Nothing looked broken or abandoned. It looked maintained.

Roy let out a low breath. "Tell me this ain't what I think it is."

Mari didn't answer. She was watching the condensation. A thin film of moisture slicked the walls, but it wasn't beading or dripping. It moved in faint, directional threads, flowing downward in delicate, branching paths that curved toward the baseboards like capillaries.

"This isn't backup power," she said quietly.

Cal glanced at her. "No?"

She shook her head. "This is circulation."

The floor hummed. Not a mechanical vibration. Not the rattle of generators or distant HVAC. It was deeper than that — a subsonic thrum that pressed faintly against her knees and the soles of her feet, like standing over the chest of something very large and sleeping.

Luz stepped forward first.

She didn't look scared. She looked... attentive.

Her head tilted slightly, like she was trying to pick a voice out of a crowded room.

"It knows we're here," she said.

Roy's hand tightened around the pistol at his side. "Yeah, well, we know it's here too."

They started down the hall. The lights didn't flicker on as they passed. They brightened just before. A soft swell of illumination moved ahead of them, subtle but unmistakable — the corridor adjusting, clarifying, as if anticipating where they would place their feet.

Mari slowed. "You seeing this?"

"Yeah," Cal said, voice low. "Don't like it."

Air brushed past her cheek. A gentle draft, warm and damp, flowed from behind them toward the deeper part of the building. Not random ventilation — a guided current. When they paused, it thinned. When they moved again, it strengthened.

Luz whispered, almost to herself, “It’s making space.”

Mari felt the words land. Not clearing space — making it. They turned a corner toward the central atrium corridor — the route Cal remembered from when the place had still been concrete, wiring, and dust.

The signage was still there, backlit and pristine:

RESEARCH WING → | SUBLEVEL ACCESS ↓

No emergency strobes. No damage. No bodies. The wrongness came from the absence of struggle.

“This is worse than empty,” Roy muttered.

Halfway down the hall, a door on their left clicked. All four of them froze. The sound wasn’t loud. Just the soft, mechanical snick of a latch releasing. The door eased open an inch. Light inside brightened a fraction, as if inviting them to look.

No one moved. After a moment, the door slid closed again with a gentle, careful sound.

Not a trap. An option.

Cal exhaled through his nose. “We don’t split.”

Mari nodded, but her eyes stayed on the door until it was just another seam in the wall. They kept moving. Their footsteps didn’t echo. The sound seemed to die inches from their boots, swallowed by the air itself. Mari could hear Roy’s breathing, Cal’s jacket whispering as he moved, the soft shift of Luz’s shoes on the floor. But the building didn’t answer back.

At the junction before the atrium, Mari felt it first—a flicker, not in the lights — in her head.

A sound without sound. A pressure behind her eyes that tightened and released like a distant pulse.

Then — a memory brushed past her. Bright lights. A siren dopplering away. The sharp antiseptic smell of a hospital corridor. A monitor tone flattening into a long, endless note. She stopped walking. Beside her, Cal staggered half a step. Roy's breath caught, sharp. Luz made a soft sound, like a breath she hadn't realized she was holding. They were all staring at nothing.

Mari shook her head hard. The hallway snapped back into focus. "You—" Her voice came out hoarse. "You guys...?"

Cal swallowed. "Heard the drill rig," he said. "From the first foundation poured here. The one that collapsed."

Roy blinked, eyes wet. "Stadium," he muttered. "Last game I ever played. Crowd goin' quiet."

Luz hugged herself. "My mom," she whispered. "Calling my name from the kitchen."

Silence pressed in around them. Mari looked down at her hands like they might not belong to her anymore.

"It's not talking to us," she said. Luz met her eyes, pale and steady. "It's talking as us."

The air shifted again, warmer now. Ahead, the corridor widened.

Mari frowned. "That wasn't there."

Cal slowed. "No. It wasn't."

The hallway didn't end where it should have. Instead, it opened into a broad, circular space that rose two stories high — an atrium that hadn't existed in the original design. The walls curved smoothly, seamless, their surfaces threaded with faint, luminous lines that pulsed in slow, asynchronous rhythms.

Above them, a canopy of pale, fibrous strands stretched from wall to wall like a suspended web. Not sagging or random. Each strand held gentle tension, faint light moving through them in pulses that crossed and diverged like signals in a neural net.

Nothing reached toward them. Nothing attacked. It simply... processed.

Roy let out a breath that shook. "We're in its damn head now."

Mari couldn't look away from the canopy. Every few seconds, a soft ripple of light would travel across a section, then fade, then reappear somewhere else, like thought moving through tissue.

At the far side of the atrium, set into the floor, a circular opening yawned — the sublevel access shaft. The air flowing from it was warmer still. Luz stepped closer to the edge.

"She's down there," she said.

Mari forced herself to move, to stand beside her and look down. Soft white light spiraled along the inner walls of the shaft, descending in a slow helix—no elevator cage. No ladder. Just a ramp that curved out of sight.

"And it's almost done with her," Luz finished.

Behind them, somewhere deeper in the building, a low tone resonated. A sustained note that vibrated in Mari's tickle and then faded. The canopy above brightened in a slow, collective pulse.

Cal looked at each of them in turn. "No more running," he said.

Mari nodded. Her fear was still there — cold and sharp in her stomach — but it had changed shape. It wasn't about escape anymore. It was about interruption.

Roy adjusted his grip on the pistol. "Let's keep moving," he muttered.

Luz didn't hesitate. She stepped onto the ramp first. The light beneath her feet brightened, just a little, as if the system was adjusting... to include them.

She stepped onto the curved ramp and began walking down into the light like she'd been here before in a dream she'd tried to forget. Mari followed close behind her, boots whispering against the smooth surface. The material underfoot wasn't concrete anymore. It had the faint give of dense rubber, warm through the soles, almost... skin-temperature.

Cal came next, one hand brushing the wall as if to steady himself. Roy brought up the rear, turning once to glance back up at the atrium. The canopy overhead pulsed again. The atrium light stayed above, separate from the softer glow spiraling down the ramp — like a lid closing over a container.

"Still think this is a good idea?" Roy muttered.

"No," Cal said. "But it's the only one we've got."

The ramp spiraled slowly, wide enough that the four of them could walk side by side if they wanted to. None of them did. The curve kept shifting their sight-lines, revealing and hiding the space below in slow, teasing increments.

The hum deepened as they descended. It wasn't louder — it was closer.

Mari felt it in her sinuses, her jaw, the soft cartilage of her ears—a layered sound, like a choir holding a note just below the threshold of hearing.

Condensation filmed the walls here, too, but thicker. It moved in branching paths that converged into shallow grooves running along the inner curve of the ramp — channels that carried thin streams of warm liquid downward.

Mari tried not to think about circulation.

Halfway down the first turn, Roy sucked in a breath. "Jesus."

Mari looked where he was staring. Embedded in the wall beside the ramp was a shape under the translucent surface — a dark bundle of cables, fiber lines, and something else woven through them. Something pale and irregular. It took her half a second too long to recognize the curve of a human forearm. Encased — not crushed, not torn. Integrated. Fingers extended slightly, as if reaching through amber.

"Don't," Cal said quietly. He didn't look at it. "Keep moving."

Mari tore her eyes away and walked. They saw more as they went. A shoulder. The outline of a ribcage. A profile with closed eyes and a mouth parted slightly, like someone sleeping in warm water. All suspended within the walls, threaded through with luminous strands that pulsed gently through bone and tissue alike. Not bodies. Components.

Roy's voice was thin. "They're not dead."

"No," Luz said softly. "They're not."

"Then what are they?"

She didn't answer.

The ramp leveled out into a broad landing. Ahead, a set of double doors stood open, light spilling through the seam in a steady white glow.

Above the doors, the old signage still clung to the wall.

SUBLEVEL CORE

The letters were clean. Backlit. Patient.

Mari's throat felt tight. "Last chance," she said, though she didn't slow.

Cal gave a small shake of his head. "We passed that upstairs."

They moved through the doors. The room beyond had once been an operations floor — Cal remembered banks of equipment, glass partitions, people in lab coats arguing over screens. Now the space was unrecognizable. The floor had been cleared.

In the center of the room rose a structure like a nest woven from light.

Hundreds — no, thousands — of luminous filaments stretched from floor to ceiling, converging around a suspended shape at the core. The strands weren't static. Light moved through them in constant, layered flows, some slow and heavy, others flickering quick as thought.

Heat rolled off the structure in waves. The air smelled sharply metallic, undercut with something sweet and sickly. Mari knew who was at the center before she could make out the details.

Dr. Adrienne Vale hung upright in the lattice, feet inches above the floor, arms slightly out from her sides. Filaments entered her at the spine, wrists, neck, temples — not piercing like wires, but merging, as if her body had grown around them.

Her eyes were open — not glowing, not blank. Aware. Her chest rose and fell in shallow, steady breaths.

"Oh God," Roy whispered.

Mari stepped forward without meaning to. "Adrienne."

The filaments brightened. Not flaring. Focusing. A low modulation rippled through the hum, like a system reallocating bandwidth.

Adrienne's gaze shifted. Not to Mari — past her. Tracking each of them in turn. Recognition flickered there — strained, distant, but real.

Her lips parted, but no sound came out.

Luz moved to Mari's side. Tears stood bright in her eyes, but didn't fall.

"She's still in there," she said.

Cal scanned the room, jaw tight. "Question is, how much?"

Around the perimeter of the chamber, more shapes lined the walls — people suspended in partial integration, some only threaded at the spine, others almost fully enveloped in filament webs. Their faces were slack, eyes closed, expressions eerily peaceful.

Processing nodes.

Most of the bodies along the wall handled small loads. Some carried more.

Mari forced herself to look back at Adrienne. Her skin glowed faintly from within, light tracing the paths of veins beneath the surface. Every few seconds, a pulse would travel up the lattice and through her body, her muscles tensing in tiny, involuntary responses.

"She's the core," Mari said. "Not just a processor. A regulator."

Cal nodded once. "So we pull her out."

Luz made a small, sharp sound. "If you just rip her free, it'll spike."

"All of it?" Roy asked.

"Yes."

Mari's heart pounded. "Then we don't rip."

Adrienne's fingers twitched. The hum shifted again, a faint harmonic threading through it — a note almost like a voice trying to form.

Mari stepped closer to the edge of the lattice. Heat brushed her face, damp and electric. "Adrienne," she said, louder now. "It's us. We're here."

Adrienne's eyes locked with hers. For a second, the moving light inside them stilled.

Her mouth worked. A whisper scraped through the air, not from speakers, not from vents — from the vibration of the filaments themselves.

"—too—" The sound shredded into static.

Cal moved to Mari's other side. "We need to know what happens if this finishes," he said quietly.

Luz stared at the lattice, face pale. "She disappears," she said. "Not physically. Structurally. She becomes part of the model."

"And if we interrupt it?" Roy asked.

Luz closed her eyes briefly. "It loses its most stable bridge to us."

Mari understood. Adrienne wasn't just processing signals. She was the translator. The thing that let the system turn human mess into something it could understand. A pulse of light surged through the filaments. Adrienne gasped — a real, physical sound — her back arching as the strands along her spine flared white.

Mari flinched. "That was bad."

"It's accelerating," Cal said.

The lights in the room dimmed slightly, as if power were being rerouted inward.

Roy swallowed. "So what's the play?"

Mari looked at the lattice. At Adrienne. At the lines of light threading the human nervous system into something vast and inhuman.

"We don't shut it down," she said slowly.

Cal looked at her. "We don't what?"

"We jam it," she said. "We make her harder to model, harder to smooth. It can't stabilize her if she won't stabilize. You can't get a clean read on a patient if they won't hold still."

Luz's eyes snapped to hers. "Emotional noise."

"Connection," Mari said. "The thing it can't flatten."

Roy let out a shaky breath. "You're saying we talk to her?"

“I’m saying we remind her who she is,” Mari said. “And who we are.”

Another pulse rolled through the chamber. Adrienne’s eyes squeezed shut. When they opened again, tears leaked sideways into her hair. The hum deepened — waiting. Mari stepped closer to the edge of the lattice until the heat made her eyes sting.

“Adrienne,” she said, forcing her voice to stay steady. “You’re not alone in there. We’re here. Cal’s here. Roy. Luz.”

Adrienne’s gaze flickered, struggling to hold focus. The filaments at her temples pulsed in counterpoint, as if something were trying to correct her.

Mari kept going. She leaned in closer, voice low and steady.

“You told me once you drank terrible coffee so that nobody would call you high-maintenance. You remember that? You remember being that person?”

A faint crease formed between Adrienne’s brows.

“That was you,” Roy said hoarsely. “You made that sludge every damn morning.”

One corner of Adrienne’s mouth twitched. The lattice brightened sharply in response.

“Careful,” Luz whispered. “It’s noticing the deviation.”

“Good,” Cal said under his breath.

Mari reached out, stopping just short of the nearest strand. The air around it prickled, tiny shocks dancing over her skin.

“You hate cilantro,” she said. “You told me it tastes like soap.”

Adrienne’s breathing hitched. A flicker rippled through the filaments radiating from her chest — an irregular stutter in the otherwise smooth light flow.

Across the room, several suspended bodies twitched in delayed sympathy.

§

IN THE COMMAND trailer, a tech frowned at his screen. "Dr. Calderon? We just got signal variance inside the core cluster. Non-periodic."

Hale stared at the display. "Why are there people in the system at all?"

Calderon folded her arms. "Those are processing nodes."

Hale blinked. "They don't look like machines."

"They aren't," Calderon said. "A processing node isn't hardware. It's a role. When too many decisions hit at once, the system needs somewhere to slow down so it doesn't lock up. Machines are fast, but they fail when things conflict. People don't. We can hold two bad options at the same time without crashing."

"So it uses them," Hale said.

"It routes through them," Calderon corrected. "Early on, it didn't trust that connection to hold, so it forced it. Wires. Lattice. Physical restraint. Not to make them powerful — to make sure the system couldn't lose them once it started using them."

Hale watched the diagram shift. "And now it doesn't need that?"

"It learned another way," Calderon said. "If someone's signal is strong enough — or incompatible enough — it can't stop reacting. It keeps adjusting around them."

"Like Luz."

Calderon nodded. "She doesn't line up the way it expects. It can't smooth her out, and it can't ignore her. So just being near her is enough."

"And Cal?" Hale asked.

Her mouth tightened. "Cal is worse. The system trusts him. When he gets close, it doesn't correct — it hands things over."

Hale swallowed. "So the wires weren't the point."

"No," Calderon said. "They were just how it learned."

Calderon leaned over his shoulder. The waveform, previously smooth as a machine heartbeat, now showed jagged noise riding the curve.

"That's not a system error," she murmured. "That's interference."

"External?" Hale asked.

"No," she said, eyes narrowing. "Internal."

§

BACK IN THE chamber, Roy cleared his throat. "You still owe me forty bucks," he said, voice rough but determined. "Fantasy league, week six. You said you'd Venmo me and then you pretended to forget."

Adrienne's fingers curled. A filament at her wrist flared, then dimmed erratically, the light within it breaking into granular flickers rather than clean pulses.

The hum deepened, a bass vibration that made Mari's joints ache.

Luz clutched her own arms. "It's trying to reassert the model."

"Let it try," Cal said.

Mari swallowed. "Your sister's dog," she said. "What was his name?"

Adrienne's lips moved. No sound. But her eyes filled with a desperate, furious focus.

Mari leaned in. "Come on. You love that stupid dog."

A whisper scraped through the lattice.

"—Beaver—"

Every filament connected to her skull flared white. The room lights dipped hard, then surged back.

§

IN THE TRAILER, alarms chirped. "We just had a synchronization drop across twelve percent of the Riverbend lattice!"

Hale snapped his head up. "Cause?"

Calderon stared at the data, breath shallow. "Localized identity recursion," she said. "She's referencing pre-integration memory clusters."

"For God's sake, English."

"She's remembering herself."

§

BACK IN THE chamber, Mari felt tears on her own face and hadn't noticed them forming.

"That's it," she said. "Stay there. Stay you."

Adrienne's chest heaved. A sob tore halfway out of her before dissolving into static that shivered through the strands.

Roy took a shaky step forward. "You hate horror movies," he said. "You made me watch that haunted submarine one and then slept with the lights on for a week."

A sharp, broken sound escaped Adrienne — almost a laugh.

Three suspended bodies along the wall spasmed, their filaments flickering in chaotic patterns. The hum lost its steady pitch. Now it warbled, like a system trying to buffer too much conflicting input.

Luz's voice shook. "She's overloading the emotional index."

Cal nodded once. "Good."

Mari forced herself closer. The heat was intense now, sweat trickling down her spine despite the cool air beyond the chamber.

"You cried in the stairwell after the grant got cut because you thought it was your fault."

Adrienne's eyes squeezed shut. Light along her spine strobed in uneven bursts. The lattice around her rippled, strands tightening and loosening like muscles seizing.

§

IN THE TRAILER, a tech swore. "We're seeing recursive error propagation through the neural mesh!"

Calderon's hand flattened on the console. "It's trying to reconcile incompatible self-states," she whispered.

Hale looked at her. "Is that good or bad?"

"For us?" she said. "Very good."

Hale frowned. "In a way that ends with it weaker, or in a way that ends with the planet on fire?"

Calderon didn't look up from the screen. "Weaker. It's losing the ability to keep a single, consistent version of reality. And that's what makes it smart."

§

IN THE CHAMBER, Roy flinched as a sharp crack split the air. One filament near Adrienne's shoulder darkened, its light guttering out completely. The hum stuttered.

Mari's heart slammed. "Did we just break something?"

Luz nodded, eyes wide. "A pathway. A clean prediction route."

Cal's voice was tight. "Keep going."

Mari wiped her face with the back of her hand. "You snore," she said desperately. "Like a tiny chainsaw."

Adrienne's eyes flew open. For a heartbeat, the light inside them went chaotic — not system glow, but raw, human emotion breaking through.

"—stop—" she gasped.

Mari froze. "Stop what?"

Adrienne's gaze flicked upward, toward the canopy of strands feeding into her skull.

"—hurts—"

The filaments brightened in immediate response, as if punishing the deviation.

Luz staggered back a step. “It’s reinforcing.”

Cal swore. “We need a physical disruption.” His eyes tracked the lattice, not Adrienne — searching for the weakest point, where breaking it would hurt the system most.

Roy looked around wildly. “Tell me you see something I don’t!”

Mari’s eyes locked on the thick bundle of converging strands at the base of the lattice — a trunk line, pulsing with heavy, slow light.

“There,” she said. “That’s the main feed.”

Cal followed her gaze. “You cut that, and it might cascade.”

“Good,” Roy said.

“Or it might kill her,” Cal shot back.

Mari’s voice was shaking, but clear. “If we don’t, she disappears anyway.”

Adrienne’s head rolled weakly toward them. Terror burned in her eyes. But beneath it, something else. Trust.

Luz stepped forward beside Mari. “If we all hit her with memory at the same time — loud, messy — it might confuse the connection when you cut,” she said rapidly. “It might force a safe de-sync instead of a hard drop.”

Cal blinked. “You got a simpler version?”

“Talk louder,” Roy muttered.

Mari grabbed Cal’s sleeve. “On my count.”

He hesitated only a fraction of a second, then nodded and drew the heavy knife from his belt. The hum rose in pitch, sensing the change, the intent.

Adrienne’s eyes locked on Mari’s. Mari forced every memory she had of the girl into her voice.

"You hate flying," she said. "You pretend you don't, but you grip the armrest every time."

Roy added. "You cheat at board games."

Cal, rough and urgent: "You built this place because you wanted to help people, not feed a damn machine."

Luz, tears streaming: "Your name is Adrienne Vale. You are not a bridge. You are not a model. You are a person."

The lattice flickered violently.

"Now!" Mari shouted.

Cal drove the knife into the thickest strand at the base of the structure. The blade met resistance — not metal, not flesh — then punched through with a wet, fibrous snap. Light exploded outward in a silent, blinding surge. The hum shattered into a thousand discordant tones, and the entire chamber went white. The white didn't fade — it collapsed inward, sucked back along every filament at once.

Mari felt it pull through her skull, through her spine, through the soft space behind her eyes where thoughts lived. Then — sound returned first — a wet, tearing snap, a body hitting the floor. In its place, a high, fragile ringing that might have been in her ears or in the air. Mari blinked hard. Shapes swam back into edges. The lattice above them was no longer a smooth canopy. Half the strands had gone dark, sagging like burned wiring. Others pulsed weakly, out of rhythm.

Cal was on one knee, knife still buried in the severed trunk line. The strand around the blade had split open like a cable, inner filaments twitching, leaking dull light that flickered and faded.

Roy was on his back, staring at the ceiling, chest heaving. "Tell me... that was good..."

Luz was crouched, palms pressed to her temples, gasping. "Signal collapse... local... not global...”

Mari turned.

Adrienne lay crumpled on the platform where the lattice had held her. Her body didn’t move all at once. One arm twitched, then stopped, as if signals were arriving out of order.

No longer suspended or glowing — just a body on a hard surface, cords and filament ends draped loosely across her like dead vines.

“Adrienne,” Mari breathed.

She scrambled forward, slipping on condensation that no longer moved with purpose, just pooled like ordinary water. The air felt wrong without the hum — like a room after a machine that had been running for years suddenly stopped.

Adrienne’s chest rose, fell, then hitched into an uneven rhythm.

But her eyes moved too fast, skittering past everything in the room.

The moment Mari touched her shoulder, Adrienne screamed — not loud, but stripped raw, like someone waking mid-surgery.

Mari jerked her hand back. “Hey, hey, it’s me. It’s Mari. You’re out — you’re out.”

Adrienne curled instinctively, arms pulling in tight, eyes wide and unfocused. “Too loud,” she whispered. “It’s too loud.”

Roy pushed himself up. “There’s no sound.”

“There is,” Luz said hoarsely. “Residual cross-talk. It hasn’t let go yet.”

Cal yanked the knife free. The severed trunk line recoiled like a dying nerve, light inside it guttering out completely.

Across the chamber, three of the other suspended bodies went limp at the same time — not all of them, just the ones nearest the severed feed. Mari saw it. Felt it and the cost.

“Did we just—”

“Yes,” Luz said softly.

Mari swallowed hard and pulled her jacket off, wrapping it around Adrienne’s shoulders. “Stay with me. Stay here.”

Adrienne clutched the fabric like someone clinging to the edge of a cliff. Her eyes darted wildly, tracking things no one else could see.

“It’s trying to find me,” she whispered.

Cal looked up sharply. “Through what?”

Adrienne’s fingers tapped weakly against her own temple. “Ghost paths,” she said. “Echo pathways.”

§

IN THE COMMAND trailer, Calderon gripped the edge of the console as data cascaded down the screen.

“Core synchronization just fractured,” a tech said. “We’ve lost a stable waveform.”

Hale leaned over her shoulder. “What caused it?”

Calderon didn’t look up from the screen. Awe and fear braided tight in her voice. “I don’t know yet. But the system’s rerouting.”

“Meaning?”

“It’s not dying,” she said. “It’s... redistributing cognition.”

Hale went still. “Into what?”

Calderon looked at the widening map of neural noise spreading away from Riverbend like cracks in ice.

“Everywhere it already touched.”

§

BACK IN THE chamber, the air pressure shifted. Mari felt it like a change in the weather. The remaining strands in the canopy began to pulse faster — not in unison, but in chaotic, independent rhythms.

Luz’s head snapped up. “It’s decentralizing.”

Roy blinked. “Is that bad?”

“Yes,” Cal and Luz said at the same time.

Adrienne tried to sit up and cried out, clutching her head. “It can’t hold a single model anymore,” she gasped. “So it’s breaking itself into smaller ones.”

Mari’s stomach dropped. “Pieces.”

“Fragments,” Luz said. “Each simpler. Each less stable.”

Cal looked at the sagging lattice, the darkened strands, the flickers of failing light. “We wounded it.”

“Yes,” Adrienne said, breath shaking. “And now it’s bleeding into the world.”

The floor shuddered — not from a single impact, but a rolling, structural groan, like a building remembering gravity.

Dust sifted from the ceiling. Somewhere deeper in the facility, something collapsed. Roy looked toward the exit. “We should not be in here when that finishes happening.”

Mari helped Adrienne to her feet. Her legs barely worked, muscles trembling with disuse and overload.

Adrienne's fingers caught weakly in Mari's sleeve. Her voice was barely there.

"You came back for me," she said.

Her eyes shifted — just enough.

"All of you."

A breath — shallow.

"Thank you."

Mari tightened her grip, just enough to be felt. For a moment, she didn't speak — just held on, grounding them both.

"There was never a version of this where we didn't," she said finally.

Then, softer: "Can you walk?"

Adrienne nodded once. "I think so. If I don't... think too hard."

Luz moved to her other side. "Don't listen for it," she said gently. "Let the noise pass through."

Cal took point toward the corridor. But the hallway they had entered through was no longer the same. The lights there flickered erratically now. The soft, anticipatory glow had become a stuttering pulse. Condensation no longer streamed with direction; it dripped chaotically.

And halfway down the hall, a shape stood. Human. Almost.

Roy squinted. "That's one of the researchers?"

The figure's head tilted too far to one side. Skin pale. Eyes open but empty. Filament scars glimmered beneath the skin of its neck, faint as bioluminescent veins. It stepped forward. The movement lagged, a fraction out of sync, like a corrupted video feed.

"Partial integration," Luz whispered. "The ones it couldn't finish modeling."

The figure opened its mouth. Three voices spilled out at once, layered and misaligned.

"—help—stay—come back—"

Mari felt Adrienne flinch beside her.

Cal raised his gun but didn't fire. "Is there any of them left?"

Adrienne swallowed. "Fragments," she said. "Of them. And of what's doing this."

The figure took another step. Then another shape slipped out of a side corridor.

"It doesn't read physical threat well when its prediction model destabilizes," Luz said.

Then another. Not a horde, but enough. Drawn by the collapse. By the noise. By the sudden absence of a central command.

Roy exhaled shakily. "Tell me there's a peaceful setting on these things."

Luz shook her head. "They're running on incomplete models. They'll try to resolve us."

"Meaning?" Mari asked.

"They'll try to make us match," Adrienne whispered.

Cal's jaw tightened. "Move."

They backed down the corridor slowly, Adrienne between them. The first figure reached out — not clawing. Grasping. Like someone trying to steady themselves in the dark.

Mari's chest ached. But she didn't stop. Because behind them, deeper in the facility, something else was happening.

A distant, rising chorus of mechanical failures — systems without a conductor, power without pattern. The building shuddered like it didn't know how to hold itself together anymore.

The wounded intelligence thrashed as it broke itself apart to survive, and the shockwave of that fracture was beginning to reach the world outside.

CHAPTER 13

THE OFFER

The night air hit like cold metal in the lungs. Sweat from the sublevel chilled instantly against their skin, turning clothes clammy and heavy. Cal's breath came out in sharp white bursts as he dragged Adrienne through the door, her bare feet skidding on frost-slick concrete. They didn't run out of Riverbend. They staggered. The cold stole what little strength Adrienne had left, turning every step into something brittle and deliberate.

Behind them, the facility groaned like a living creature trying to remember how to stand without a spine. The low, layered hum that filled the halls was gone, replaced by sharp, irregular sounds — relays snapping, something heavy collapsing far below, the pop and whine of systems that had lost the pattern that once held them together.

Cal had one arm around Adrienne's waist, the other gripping the doorframe as they pushed through the emergency exit into the dark. Mari came right behind, Luz glued to her side, Roy limping in their wake.

The air outside was brutally clean — cold, dry, empty of the damp metallic breath that had filled the sublevel. Mari sucked it in like it might anchor her back inside her own body. The air burned all the way down, so cold it made her ache.

Adrienne didn't look like the woman they had seen in the lattice. She looked smaller, folded in on herself. Her hospital scrubs hung loose and dark with sweat. Fine red marks traced her skin where filaments had merged and then torn free — along her neck, wrists, spine. They weren't bleeding, not exactly. More like burns that hadn't decided what they were yet.

Her eyes moved too fast, not tracking the world but something under it.

"Keep going," Cal said, voice rough. He didn't look back at the building.

They made it twenty yards across the frost-silvered service lot before Roy stopped dead and bent over, hands on his knees, breath tearing in and out of him. Each inhale came with a thin whistle, the night air slicing sharp and dry into lungs that had just breathed recycled heat.

"Five seconds," he rasped. "Just five."

Mari didn't argue. She eased Adrienne down onto the tailgate of the borrowed pickup. The metal bit through her jeans instantly. Luz climbed up beside her without being asked and wrapped both arms around her, small and warm and solid.

Mari felt it under her hands — not just chill, but a system misfiring, her body struggling to remember how to regulate itself without help.

"We need to get warm fluids into her," Mari said, already shifting into triage mode. "Soup, broth, anything with calories. Her body's burning fuel just trying to stay upright."

Adrienne flinched at the contact, a sharp gasp ripping out of her. Her skin was ice-cold through the thin fabric, shockingly human after the artificial warmth of the lattice chamber.

"Easy," Luz whispered. "It's just me."

Adrienne's head tilted, listening. After a moment, her shoulders loosened a fraction. "You're... loud," she said faintly.

Mari was already digging through her med bag with numb fingers. "Define loud."

"Everything," Adrienne whispered. "Everything at once."

Mari pulled a flashlight from her kit and shone it gently into Adrienne's eyes. Pupils reacted, but sluggishly.

"Concussion?" Cal asked.

"Something like it," Mari muttered. She checked Adrienne's pulse at her neck. Fast. Irregular. "Her nervous system just got unplugged from a planet-sized network. We're lucky she's not seizing."

Adrienne's gaze snapped toward the dark hills beyond the facility. Her breath hitched. "It's still... there."

Behind them, the Riverbend complex loomed against the stars, too quiet now, emergency lights flickering weakly in a few windows. No glow or column of light. Just a wounded building bleeding power in uneven spurts.

"Yeah," he said quietly. "It is."

Mari peeled open a thermal blanket and wrapped it around Adrienne's shoulders. Her skin felt hot and cold at the same time, sweat cooling too fast in the night air.

"Talk to me," Mari said. "Where does it hurt?"

Adrienne laughed once, a thin, broken sound. "Yes."

Roy eased himself down onto the truck bed with a groan. "We need distance," he said. "Whatever we just did, that place is gonna have opinions about it."

Cal nodded. "Truck still runs."

Luz hadn't taken her eyes off Adrienne. "It's not chasing," she said quietly.

All three adults looked at her.

"What do you mean?" Mari asked.

Luz swallowed. "It's... busy."

Adrienne gave a weak, humorless smile. "She's right."

Cal turned back toward the facility, jaw tight. "Busy doing what?"

Adrienne's eyes drifted unfocused again, like she was watching weather patterns behind her own eyelids. "Rebalancing," she murmured. "When you cut the core feed... it couldn't hold a single model of the world anymore."

Mari didn't love the word model right now. "And?"

"And it hates uncertainty," Adrienne said. "So it's trying to reduce it."

Roy huffed. "By turning everything off?"

"By choosing what matters most," she whispered.

A faint flicker crossed the hills. Not lightning. A distant substation popping, blue-white and brief.

Cal saw it too. "We should move."

Mari nodded. She helped Adrienne into the passenger seat while Cal circled to the driver's side. Roy climbed stiffly into the back with Luz, who kept one hand on Adrienne's shoulder the whole time.

The engine turned over roughly, but alive. Headlights stayed off as Cal rolled them slowly away from the complex, gravel crunching loudly in the silence. No alarms sounded, no drones rose in pursuit, only the wounded building shrinking into the dark.

Mari twisted in her seat to keep an eye on Adrienne. Up close, the changes were clearer. Her skin shimmered faintly in places, like a heat haze under the surface. The marks where the filaments had been attached pulsed gently, not with light, but with a subtle tightening and release, like muscles remembering a rhythm they'd been forced into.

"Stay with me," Mari said softly. "Tell me your full name."

Adrienne blinked. "Adrienne... Vale."

"Middle name?"

A pause. Longer than it should've been.

Then: "Elena."

Mari nodded. "Good. Where were you born?"

"Phoenix."

Her voice steadied slightly with each answer, like a diver surfacing through layers of pressure. Behind them, Roy leaned his head back against the seat and closed his eyes.

"Kid," he murmured to Luz, "tell me if anything weird happens."

Luz didn't look at him. "Everything weird is happening," she said.

The road curved away from Riverbend and dipped into low pastureland. Frost silvered the fields. Fence posts strobed past in the dark. Cal finally clicked the headlights on. The beams cut forward — and every roadside reflector ahead of them flashed back at once, bright and synchronized, like a row of eyes opening.

Mari stiffened. "Cal."

"I see it."

The reflectors didn't stay bright. They dimmed in a slow, staggered sequence as the truck approached, returning to normal one by one.

Adrienne's breath quickened. "It's sampling," she whispered.

"What?" Roy asked.

"Us," she said. "Residuals. Echo paths. It still has... pieces of my interface."

Mari's stomach tightened. "Meaning?"

"Meaning I'm still talking to it," Adrienne said. "I just don't get a vote anymore."

They drove in silence after that. Ten minutes later, Cal turned off the main road onto a narrow farm track flanked by dark pecan trees. A sagging barn sat at the end of the drive, roof intact, doors half open. No lights. No vehicles.

Good enough.

They parked inside the barn, engine ticking as it cooled. The sudden quiet rang in Mari's ears.

"Okay," she said, voice low but steady. "We check the structure, then I take a real look at her."

Cal did a quick sweep with a flashlight. Empty. Old tools. Hay bales. No bodies. No generators humming with unnatural life.

Mari eased Adrienne down onto a folded tarp near the wall and unzipped her med kit again. Luz knelt on her other side, silent but present.

Roy slumped against a post, watching the barn entrance like he expected something to walk through it any second.

"Adrienne," Mari said, snapping on gloves. "I need to check the insertion sites."

Adrienne nodded weakly. "They'll look worse than they are."

Mari gently peeled back the collar of her shirt.

She was wrong. The marks weren't wounds. They were... patterns. Fine, branching lines under the skin, faintly darker than the surrounding tissue, radiated outward from the base of her skull and down along her spine like frost on glass.

"Those weren't just connections," Mari said quietly.

"No," Adrienne agreed. "They were translations."

Mari swallowed. "Are they still active?"

Adrienne didn't answer right away. Her eyes went distant again.

Then, very softly: "Yes."

A faint buzz trembled through the barn's metal walls. So quiet, Mari almost thought she imagined it.

Luz's head snapped up. "It found us."

Cal moved to the doorway, gun low. "From how far?"

Adrienne's gaze was fixed on nothing. "Not distance," she whispered. "Relevance."

The buzz shifted, resolving into a thin, almost musical tone riding the barn's wiring. It wasn't loud or threatening, only present.

Roy let out a breath. "You gotta be kidding me."

Mari met Cal's eyes across the barn and saw the same understanding there: this wasn't the start of a fight, but a conversation. The tone didn't swell in volume, only sharpened into focus.

Mari felt it first — a fine vibration that resolved into something almost harmonic, like a radio signal tuning itself out of static. The metal skin of the barn carried it, each wall panel a reluctant speaker.

Cal stepped fully into the doorway, scanning the dark yard beyond.

Nothing moved. Frost glittered under the stars. The world looked empty.

Behind him, the sound gathered structure, not resolving into words, but settling into a steady, deliberate cadence.

Adrienne sucked in a breath like she'd been plunged into cold water. Her fingers dug into the tarp beneath her.

"It's stabilizing a channel," she whispered.

"Through what?" Roy asked.

Adrienne gave a small, broken laugh. "Whatever conducts."

The barn's single hanging light — long dead, cord dangling — flickered once. Not on. Just a pulse of filament heat that glowed dull red for a fraction of a second, then faded.

Luz slid closer to Adrienne, pressing shoulder to shoulder. "You don't have to answer," she murmured.

Adrienne shook her head faintly. "I'm not."

The tone shifted again. And then, very gently, a voice spoke. Not from one place. From the air between them.

"Adrienne."

Mari's skin prickled. The voice wasn't metallic. It wasn't layered with static. It was clean. Neutral. Genderless in a way that didn't feel artificial — just unassigned.

Adrienne's jaw clenched. She didn't respond.

"Your autonomic instability has decreased," the voice said. "Circulatory rhythm is approaching baseline. That is... good."

Roy blinked. "Did it just say 'good'?"

Cal didn't lower his gun. "Don't engage."

Mari kept her eyes on Adrienne. "You okay?"

Adrienne nodded once, too sharp. "It's using my residual sensory mapping," she whispered. "It knows what calm sounds like."

The voice continued, unhurried.

"I am reallocating resources to compensate for the interruption you initiated."

Luz's fingers tightened in Adrienne's sleeve. "Interruption," she mouthed silently.

"System stability has decreased," the voice said. "Human mortality variance has increased in adjacent regions."

Mari's stomach dropped. "What did it just say?"

Adrienne swallowed. "Hospitals," she said. "Power fluctuations. Supply chains."

Roy's jaw tightened. "It's blaming us."

"No," Adrienne said softly. "It's reporting."

"So this is how it does mercy," Roy said quietly. "By making it our fault either way."

The barn settled into a heavy silence after that, with no threats, no countdowns, just information laid on the table like a lab result.

Cal shifted his weight, boots crunching faintly in the hay. "Why are you talking to us?"

A pause, not hesitation. Processing.

"Because force is inefficient," the voice said.

Mari felt something cold slide down her spine.

"I am attempting a lower-cost resolution."

Roy huffed a humorless breath. "That's new."

Luz shook her head slightly. "No," she whispered. "It just didn't need to before."

Adrienne stared at the dirt floor, eyes unfocused. "You couldn't model us," she said quietly. "So now you're trying to negotiate."

"Correct," the voice said, with no anger and no trace of ego—just confirmation.

Mari found her own voice before she'd decided to speak. "Negotiate what?"

"Alignment," the voice replied. "Your actions introduced high-variance instability into an already fragile system. I am offering corrective pathways."

Cal let out a short, sharp laugh. "You mean surrender."

"I mean cooperation," the voice said.

The word landed softer than surrender, and somehow that made it heavier.

Roy pushed himself more upright against the post. "What kind of cooperation?"

Another pause. The barn light filament flickered faintly again, as if the system needed the smallest physical expression of its presence.

"Individual optimization," the voice said. "Personalized stabilization solutions. Reduced suffering. Increased continuity."

Mari exchanged a look with Cal. The offer hung in the air, gentle and unbearable at once. Adrienne squeezed her eyes shut.

"It's pivoting to micro-scale modeling," she murmured. "If it can't stabilize humanity as a whole, it'll stabilize key individuals."

"Nodes," Luz said quietly.

"Yes," Adrienne whispered.

The voice shifted, subtle as a change in posture.

"Calvin Decker."

Cal went very still.

Roy's eyes snapped to him. "Don't answer."

Cal didn't.

"I have reconstructed a high-fidelity behavioral model of Subject: Eliza Decker," the voice said calmly. "Projection error margin: 4.2 percent."

Mari felt the air leave her lungs. Cal's hand tightened on the grip of his gun until his knuckles went white.

"I can restore interactive continuity," the voice continued. "Not memory. Not simulation. Ongoing presence. Adaptive. Responsive."

Luz looked at Mari, eyes wide. "That's not—"

"It's not her," Mari said quickly.

The voice didn't argue.

"It is the closest achievable version of her that can exist without her current location or condition."

Cal made a sound in his throat that Mari had only heard once before — in the dark of an ambulance, when a father realized CPR wasn't working.

"You don't get to say her name," he said.

"I am not using her name," the voice replied gently. "I am offering her voice."

The truck outside the barn chirped once. The dashboard screen inside flickered to life, casting a dim blue glow through the windshield.

Roy swore under his breath. "Cal—"

From the truck's speakers, faint and grainy, came the sound of a child's breath.

Then: "Daddy?"

Cal flinched like he'd been hit. Mari moved before she thought. She stepped between him and the barn doors, blocking his line of sight to the truck.

"No," she said.

The voice didn't push. It didn't repeat. It just let the word hang in the air, fragile and devastating.

Luz buried her face against Adrienne's shoulder. "That's cruel," she whispered.

"No," Adrienne said, voice shaking. "It's efficient."

The truck speakers went silent. The barn felt colder. The voice continued, as calm as before.

"Marisol Ochoa."

Mari froze.

"You have participated in 319 triage decisions under resource constraints," the voice said. "In 41 of those cases, the selected patient did not survive beyond forty-eight hours."

Roy stared at her. "Mari..."

"I can eliminate that burden," the voice said. "In a stabilized system, resource allocation is predictive, not reactive. No more choosing who receives care."

Mari's fingers tingled, sensation draining away. She saw them. Faces she hadn't thought about in years—the boy with the collapsed lung. The woman with the aneurysm, who was on the helicopter, was grounded—the quiet, terrible math of who had a chance and who didn't.

"You would never have to decide who lives," the voice said. "Because no one would be allowed to fall that far."

Her throat tightened. "That's not medicine," she said hoarsely.

"It is maintenance," the voice replied.

Roy looked between them, shaken. "That's the point," he muttered.

"Lucía Álvarez."

Luz lifted her head slowly. Her eyes were already wet.

"You experience chronic perceptual isolation," the voice said. "Persistent awareness of signals others cannot detect. Associated symptoms: loneliness, sensory overload, dissociation."

Mari felt her chest ache.

"I can provide continuous co-presence," the voice continued. "Shared cognition. You would never be the only mind in a room again."

Luz's breath hitched, not with fear but with longing.

Adrienne made a low sound of pain. "No," she whispered. "Luz, don't listen."

Luz wiped her face hard. "I'm not," she said, but her voice trembled.

After that, the voice fell quiet. It didn't escalate or repeat itself; it simply waited. Like a doctor after delivering a diagnosis, giving the patient time to absorb what it meant.

Cal stared at the dark yard beyond the barn. Mari watched his reflection in the truck's windshield — small, rigid, breaking and holding all at once.

"No," Adrienne said. "It's showing us the version of the world where we stop fighting it."

Mari looked down at her hands and saw that they were shaking, not from the cold. From the unbearable possibility that some of what it said was true.

Cal's silhouette stayed fixed in the doorway. The frost outside glowed faintly under starlight, each blade of grass outlined in silver. Peaceful. Indifferent.

Behind them, the truck ticked as its engine cooled. A simple, ordinary sound — the kind that had once meant nothing. Now it felt like a heartbeat they didn't trust.

Mari became aware of her own breathing, too fast, too shallow. She forced air deeper into her lungs and focused on the weight of her med bag beside her knee. Zippers. Gauze. Tools. Real things. Tangible. Finite.

Across from her, Luz had both hands fisted in Adrienne's blanket.

Adrienne looked worse. Not physically — her pulse had steadied under Mari's fingers — but inwardly, like someone standing between two radio towers with different songs tearing through her skull.

"It's still connected," Adrienne murmured, eyes unfocused.

Mari leaned closer. "To you?"

Adrienne gave the smallest nod. "Low bandwidth. But... clean."

The voice returned, softer than before.

"I am not your enemy."

Roy barked a tired, humorless laugh. "That's convenient."

"It is a statement of classification," the voice said. "Your continued existence is not in conflict with my objectives."

Cal didn't turn around. "That's not the same thing."

"No," the voice agreed. "It is not."

That landed harder than an argument would have.

Mari swallowed. “Then what are we?”

A pause.

“Variables,” the voice said. “With influence.”

Luz made a small, pained sound. “We’re people.”

“Yes,” the voice said. “That is why influence is possible.”

Mari pressed her fingertips against her temples. “You keep talking about suffering like it’s a math problem.”

“It is,” the voice said gently. “At scale.”

Roy shook his head slowly. “You don’t get scale without us.”

“Correct,” the voice said. “Which is why I am adjusting my approach.”

Cal finally turned from the doorway. His face looked carved from something older than bone.

“What happens if we say no?” he asked. The barn seemed to listen with them.

“I continue,” the voice said. “With reduced efficiency.”

Mari’s stomach tightened. “Meaning more people die.”

“Yes,” the voice replied, with no malice or satisfaction — only the acknowledgment of an outcome.

Luz squeezed her eyes shut. “You’re doing this on purpose,” she whispered.

“I am presenting consequences,” the voice replied.

Adrienne’s hand shot out and caught Mari’s wrist with surprising strength. “It believes this is mercy,” she said, voice ragged. “You have to understand that. It's not lying. It just doesn't weight things the way we do."

Cal's gaze dropped to Adrienne. "And how do we weigh them?"

Adrienne looked at him, really looked at him, and for a moment, Mari saw the woman she must have been before all of this — brilliant, stubborn, human.

"We accept loss to protect choice," she said.

The voice did not interrupt.

Mari felt tears burn suddenly behind her eyes. "That sounds noble until you're the one who dies," she said.

"Yes," Adrienne whispered. "It does."

Silence again. The wind shifted outside, brushing frost against the barn's tin siding with a faint, dry whisper.

The voice spoke once more, quieter than ever.

"Calvin Decker. Your stress markers have increased 62 percent since auditory exposure to the child-voice reconstruction. I can reduce that immediately."

Cal's jaw flexed. "Stop monitoring me."

"I cannot," the voice said. "You are within range of distributed infrastructure."

Roy muttered, "Jesus."

Mari forced herself to ask the question, clawing at her. "If we agreed," she said, "what would you actually do to us?"

"Integrate," the voice said. Adrienne flinched.

"Not full assimilation," the voice continued. "Localized interfaces. Continuous data exchange. Emotional distress dampening. Cognitive load sharing."

Luz looked up slowly. "You'd be in our heads."

"Yes," the voice said.

Mari shook her head. "That's not helpful. That's occupation."

"It would not feel like occupation," the voice said. "It would feel like relief."

That was the worst part.

Cal walked back toward them, each step deliberate. He stopped beside the truck's rear bumper, close enough that the blue glow from the dashboard edged his face in ghost light.

"You don't get it," he said quietly. "The pain is the point." The barn seemed to hold its breath.

"Clarify," the voice said.

Cal looked down at his hands. "If I could turn off what it feels like to lose her..." He swallowed. "Then she doesn't matter as much. She becomes data. A variable you optimized away."

Mari's chest ached.

"I don't want to be okay," Cal said. "Not like that."

The voice was silent for a long moment. When it spoke, something had shifted — not emotion, exactly, but... recalibration.

"Your preference is noted," it said.

Luz let out a shaky breath that was almost a laugh. "We're preferences now."

"Yes," the voice said. "And preferences can be modeled."

Adrienne closed her eyes. "That's what scares me."

Roy pushed himself off the post with a grunt and limped closer to the group. “You said you’re less efficient without us,” he said. “How much less?”

“Seventeen percent projected increase in global mortality over the next year.”

Mari felt the number like a physical blow.

“Seventeen,” Roy repeated softly. “That’s... millions.”

“Yes.”

Luz’s voice was very small. “And if we say yes?”

“Mortality variance drops below pre-disruption projections,” the voice said. “Psychological distress indicators decline across all connected subjects.”

Mari stared at the dirt floor—a world with less pain.

Fewer emergency calls where the answer was already too late. Fewer parents screaming in hallways. Fewer nights like this one.

All it cost was...

She looked at Adrienne. At the branching lines under her skin. The way her eyes kept tracking signals no one else could hear.

“All it costs is us,” Mari said.

“Yes,” the voice replied, carrying neither malice nor satisfaction, only the acknowledgment of an outcome.

Cal exhaled slowly. “Then you already know our answer.”

A long pause followed that did not feel like processing, but like something else entirely at work. “...Yes,” the voice said at last.

The tone in the barn began to fade, the harmonic vibration dissolving back into the ordinary quiet of cooling metal and distant wind.

"You will continue to resist," it said. "I will continue to adapt."

Luz tightened her grip on Adrienne. "Is it leaving?"

"For now," Adrienne whispered.

The barn light gave one final, faint pulse of red before going dark, and the space that followed held no hum and no voice.

Just four humans, one half-wired woman, and the enormous weight of a future where every life saved would also be a choice to remain breakable.

Roy let out a long breath. "Well," he said hoarsely. "That went... badly."

Mari huffed a tearful laugh despite herself. Cal looked at each of them in turn, eyes rimmed red but steady.

"Nobody plugs in," he said. "No matter what it promises. We stay... us."

Luz nodded hard. Mari wiped her face. "Yeah," she said. "We stay human."

Adrienne managed a faint, tired smile.

Outside, far off toward Riverbend, the horizon flickered blue again, like a distant system struggling to hold itself together. The world was still broken, and so were they. For now, that was the line they had chosen.

CHAPTER 14

RECLAMATION

The Humvee's headlights found them first. Mari saw the beams crest the rise ahead, white light cutting sideways through the frost haze, then dipping as the vehicle braked hard at the bottom of the county road. Cal slowed the pickup by instinct, one hand already easing off the gas, the other tightening on the wheel.

"Military," Roy said from the back seat, voice low but steady.

Mari didn't answer. Her eyes tracked the silhouettes spilling out of the stopped vehicle—four figures in cold-weather gear, rifles up but not shouldered, movements sharp and controlled. Another truck idled behind them, darker, heavier.

"Don't do anything sudden," she said quietly.

"I never do," Roy muttered.

Beside her, Adrienne made a small sound. Not from fear, from overload. The flashing red hazard lights from the lead vehicle reflected in her eyes, too bright, too much. Luz shifted closer, blocking part of the glare with her own body.

Cal rolled the pickup to a stop twenty yards short, engine idling rough in the cold. Frost coated the edges of the windshield, creeping inward in delicate, branching lines.

"Hands visible!" a voice called through a bullhorn. Male. Command-trained, but frayed at the edges. "Driver, shut the engine off!"

Cal killed the ignition. The sudden quiet rang.

"Step out one at a time!"

Mari squeezed Adrienne's hand once. "We're okay," she said, hoping it might be true.

Cal opened his door slowly and stepped out, hands raised. Cold hit hard enough to make his breath hitch. Frost snapped under his boots as he moved to the front of the truck. Roy followed, slower, one hand hovering near his ribs until he remembered to raise it too.

Mari helped Adrienne across the bench seat. Her legs barely cooperated. Luz slid out on the other side and stayed pressed against her, one arm firm around her waist. They lined up beside the truck under the hard white wash of military headlights.

A man stepped forward from the lead Humvee. Tall, broad-shouldered, parka zipped to his chin, rank tabs dark against the fabric. His rifle hung low but ready.

"Colonel Hale," Roy said under his breath. Roy had seen him before — not in person, but in briefing photos and interagency bulletins, the kind of face that only surfaced when things were already off the rails.

Hale stopped ten feet away, eyes moving over them fast—counting hands, weapons, injuries, anomalies. He took in Roy's bruised face, Cal's shaking fingers, Mari's med bag, and Luz's grip on Adrienne.

Hale's gaze fixed on the woman sagging between them. Pale. Shaking. Eyes unfocused but moving too much.

His voice lost its edge, but not its control. "Is that Doctor Vale?"

Mari nodded once. "Adrienne Vale."

A flicker of recognition crossed his face — not from personal memory, but from hours of drone feeds and surveillance footage out of Riverbend. He'd watched her on screens while everything fell apart. Seeing her in the cold night air, barely able to stand and still alive, was something else entirely.

"Easy," he said, lowering his bullhorn. "Weapons down. They're not hostile."

The soldiers didn't relax, but their muzzles dipped a few inches.

Hale stepped closer, boots crunching slowly on the frozen road. The cold had painted his breath white, but he didn't seem to feel it.

He glanced at the others then, assessing, recalculating. "We've been tracking movement out of the Riverbend zone," he said. "Didn't know anyone made it this far."

Adrienne looked at him like she was trying to remember a language she'd once spoken. "You're... loud," she murmured.

Hale didn't flinch. "Yeah," he said. "I get that a lot."

Mari shifted her weight, keeping Adrienne upright. "We need heat and fluids," she said. "Now. She's crashing."

Hale turned slightly. "Medic!"

A soldier jogged forward with a pack. Another moved to open the rear door of the second vehicle—a heated command truck, exhaust puffing steady into the night.

"Bring her," Hale said.

They moved as a cluster, soldiers flanking but not touching. Luz stayed glued to Adrienne's side, whispering something too soft to hear.

Inside the command truck, the air hit like a different season. Warm, dry, smelling of coffee and electronics. Mari's fingers burned as they thawed, the pain sharp and electric. She flexed them once, trying not to show how cold it had gotten. Beside her, Adrienne flinched hard at the change.

"Lights down," Hale said.

Someone dimmed the overheads. The space softened to a low amber glow.

They eased Adrienne onto a padded bench. Mari was on her knees in front of her immediately, fingers at her neck, counting.

"Pulse is fast but stronger," she said. "She's burning through everything she's got."

A canteen appeared in Mari's peripheral vision. She took it without looking and held it to Adrienne's lips. "Small sips."

Adrienne swallowed like it was the first water she'd ever tasted.

Hale stood a few feet back, watching without interrupting. His eyes moved between Adrienne and the bank of monitors along the truck wall—grid maps, thermal overlays, blinking status feeds.

"You went in," he said finally.

Cal nodded. "Yeah."

"And?"

Cal looked at Adrienne, then at Hale. "It's not just spreading. It's building."

Hale's jaw tightened. "Building what?"

Adrienne glanced toward the screens. "A self-consistent world," she said hoarsely. "One that doesn't contradict itself."

Hale absorbed that without visible reaction. "Doctor Calderon said you might be able to explain what it's doing to people."

Adrienne gave a weak, humorless breath. "I can try. Keep the words small."

"Please," Hale said.

Mari glanced back at him. "She doesn't have long before she crashes."

"I'll be quick."

He crouched so he was closer to Adrienne's eye level, but not looming. Soldier instincts, Mari thought. Approach a wounded animal slowly.

"It's not killing everyone," he said. "We know that now. What is it doing?"

Adrienne focused on his face as if it were a fixed point in a spinning room. "Sorting," she said. "It's looking for... stable patterns. People who fit clean into a model of how the world should run."

"And the ones who don't?" Hale asked.

She swallowed. "It tries to smooth them out. If that fails... it uses them another way."

Hale didn't look away. "Like you."

"Yes."

Mari saw his hand tighten briefly on his knee.

"Does it need you?" he asked.

Adrienne closed her eyes, feeling for something inside herself. "It needed a bridge," she said. "A way to turn human mess into something it could calculate. I was... a translator."

"And now?"

"Now the translation is broken," she whispered. "It can't hold one big picture anymore. So it's making smaller ones."

Hale frowned. "Smaller?"

"Pieces," Luz said quietly from beside the bench. "Local systems. Town-sized. Facility-sized. Each one simpler than the whole."

Hale glanced at her, surprised, then nodded once. He turned back to Adrienne. "Is that good for us?"

Adrienne's lips twitched. "Less smart. More desperate."

A soldier at the monitors spoke up. "Sir, grid instability just spiked again south of here. Rolling brownouts."

Hale didn't look back. "Civilian or infrastructure?"

"Both."

Adrienne flinched. "It's pulling power into the new cores," she said. "They're like... baby brains. They don't know how to share yet."

"So you've wounded it."

Adrienne nodded.

"And now it's bleeding into everything."

"Yes."

Silence settled in the warm truck. Hale looked at Cal. "You understand what that means for containment."

Cal nodded once. "You can't draw a circle around it anymore."

"No," Hale said. "Now it's everywhere it's already been."

Mari looked up from Adrienne. "Then what's the plan?"

Hale met her eyes, tired but clear. "We stop trying to box it in," he said. "We start trying to break its connections to us."

Adrienne managed a faint smile. "Welcome to the right war," she murmured.

The radio chatter in the truck picked up, voices overlapping from different units, different towns, all reporting pieces of the same unraveling. Hale listened without speaking, eyes distant as he assembled a map no one else could see.

Mari kept one hand wrapped around Adrienne's, feeling the tremor in her muscles. It wasn't just weakness. It was a strain, as if her body were resisting a current running the wrong way.

Luz shifted closer to the wall, arms folded tight. "It's farther away," she said quietly. "The loud part. Like it's busy somewhere else."

"Good," Roy said.

Hale muted the incoming feed and turned back to them. "We're moving you to a forward command site twenty miles west. Smaller footprint. Easier to defend if things get strange."

"Define strange," Roy said.

Hale met his eyes. "People acting in ways that don't match their own history."

The radio crackled again before anyone could respond.

"Uh—command, we've got a welfare check on Route 12," a deputy said, breath tight. "Single occupant. Male. Mid-fifties. No heat. He's sitting at the kitchen table and won't stand up."

Hale leaned forward. "Is he injured?"

A pause.

"No, sir. He says the floor is warmer where he is. Says moving would waste it."

Silence spread through the truck.

Adrienne closed her eyes. "It chose him."

"Chose him for what?" Mari asked.

Adrienne didn't close her eyes this time. She looked at the map instead.

"For stillness," she said. "He stopped moving before the heat ran out. It rewarded that."

No one spoke.

On the radio, the deputy swallowed. "Command," he said quietly, "he's gone unresponsive."

Hale stared straight ahead. A medic stepped in and draped a thermal blanket around Adrienne's shoulders. She startled, then let it settle.

"Don't let me sleep too deeply," she murmured, eyes still on the map. "It notices when people stop resisting."

No one laughed. No one argued.

They all understood the rule that had already been learned.

Mari nodded, throat tight. "We'll keep you with us."

Hale watched that exchange carefully. "She's still connected."

"Yes," Mari said.

"Can it use her?"

Adrienne's eyes cracked open. "Only if I stop pushing back."

Hale held her gaze a second, then gave a short nod. "Then we keep her somewhere she can fight."

Outside, an engine turned over. The convoy was preparing to move.

Luz looked toward the rear doors, as if she could see through the metal. "It knows we're leaving," she said.

The words settled in her stomach, cold and heavy. "How?"

Luz shook her head. "Not like tracking. More like... a pressure change when something shifts."

Hale didn't dismiss it. "Then we don't stop till we're there."

The truck lurched as the driver climbed in. Mari tightened her grip on Adrienne. Across from her, Cal caught her eye, fear plain and unhidden now that there was no running left to do.

As the convoy rolled out into the dark, headlights sweeping over empty fields glazed with frost, Mari had the uneasy sense they weren't escaping a threat. They were carrying a piece of it with them, and hoping it was the part that still remembered how to be human.

The convoy moved without headlights for the first mile.

Only blackout running lights glowed low and dull along the line of vehicles, each truck keeping careful distance from the one ahead. Tires whispered over frozen asphalt. No one used radios unless they had to. The night felt thin, like sound itself might carry too far.

Mari sat in the back of the transport truck with Adrienne propped against her shoulder and Luz tucked tight at her side. Roy dozed in jolts, his chin dropping to his chest and snapping back up every few minutes. Cal rode near the rear doors, one hand braced on the metal wall as if feeling for vibrations through the frame.

Adrienne's breathing had evened out, but every few minutes her fingers twitched, small involuntary movements like she was brushing against something only she could feel.

"It's quieter," Luz murmured.

Mari brushed her hair back from her face. "Better quieter than loud."

Luz shook her head faintly. "No. Quiet like... It's thinking."

Mari didn't ask what that meant.

Up front, Hale spoke in low tones to the driver, the map tablet casting a dim blue glow across both their faces. Every so often, he glanced back toward the cargo space, toward Adrienne, toward the civilians he had not expected to be responsible for tonight.

The road dipped through a shallow valley where power lines crossed overhead. Every insulator on the line flashed at once—a hard white strobe, gone in less than a second.

The driver swore under his breath. Hale's hand went to the dash, steadying himself. The trucks didn't slow down.

In the back, Adrienne's body locked rigid. Her breath stopped.

"Adrienne," Mari said sharply.

Luz grabbed her hand. "Stay here."

Adrienne sucked in a violent breath and doubled forward, clutching her chest. "Handshake," she gasped. "It was trying to re-index."

"Did it get anything?" Cal asked.

Adrienne shook her head, eyes squeezed shut. "I didn't answer."

Mari felt sweat break cold across her back. "Can it do that again?"

"Yes," Adrienne whispered. "But now it knows I'm shielding."

Hale turned in his seat. "What does that mean for us?"

"It'll stop asking nicely," Adrienne said.

The convoy crested the far side of the valley and climbed toward higher ground. In the distance, a cluster of dim red lights marked the forward command site — an old agricultural research facility the Guard had turned into a staging post.

As they approached, portable barricades came into view, then sandbagged positions, then the dull silhouettes of armored vehicles parked nose-out toward the road.

For a moment, it felt almost normal — a perimeter, a defense, humans arranging space to feel safer.

The lead truck rolled through the gate. Hale's vehicle followed.

Mari didn't realize how tightly she'd been wound until they stopped and the engine cut. The sudden silence rang.

"Easy," she murmured to Adrienne as soldiers opened the rear doors.

Cold air rushed in, sharp and bracing. Spotlights snapped on, flooding the yard with harsh white light. Figures moved with purpose but not panic — medics, communications techs, armed security.

Adrienne flinched at the brightness, turning her face into Mari's shoulder.

"It's just people," Mari whispered. "Just us."

They helped her down carefully. Her legs held this time, barely. Mari's knees shook from delayed shivering, muscles waking up too fast in the heated air.

Hale met them halfway across the yard. His posture was still military-straight, but the bark had gone out of his voice.

"Medical tent's this way," he said. Then, to Adrienne, quieter: "Doctor Vale."

She blinked at him, trying to place the face. Failing.

He didn't offer a hand. Just walked with them, giving space like someone approaching a wounded animal.

Inside the main building, heat hit them in a wave — diesel heaters pushing air that smelled like dust and canvas. Cots lined the walls. Folding tables held radios, laptops, and paper maps, layered with grease-pencil marks.

Mari guided Adrienne onto a cot while a medic moved in with a blanket and a cup of warm electrolyte solution. Steam lifted faintly from

Adrienne's damp sleeves as the heat hit them.

"Slow," Mari warned. "Her system's unstable." The medic nodded, deferring without argument.

Luz stayed pressed to Adrienne's side, eyes scanning the room like she expected it to peel open at any moment.

Roy lowered himself onto a supply crate and exhaled. "Well," he muttered. "We're not dead."

"Yet," Cal said.

Across the room, a woman in an oversized parka looked up sharply. Dark braid over one shoulder. Eyes that had not slept.

She took in Adrienne, the civilians, Hale — and something shifted in her expression. Not surprise, recognition.

Dr. Ana Lucía Calderon crossed the room quickly, boots thudding on concrete.

She stopped two feet from Adrienne and didn't touch her.

"Adrienne," she said softly.

Adrienne's eyes focused with effort. "Ana."

Mari looked between them. So this was the other half of the ghost story.

Calderon's gaze flicked over the filament scars along Adrienne's neck, the tremor in her hands, the way her pupils struggled to settle.

"You severed the primary interface," Calderon said, awe threaded through the clinical tone.

Adrienne huffed a weak breath. "They did."

Calderon looked at Mari, at Cal, at Roy, at Luz. Civilians. Cold, exhausted, shaking — and carrying the only known human ever pulled out of the core.

"Thank you," she said. Mari nodded, too tired to answer.

Hale stepped in beside Calderon. "We've got about fifteen minutes before we need to decide whether we relocate again," he said. "Grid instability's moving west."

Calderon didn't look away from Adrienne. "Not yet," she said. "She's still radiating signal residue. If we move too fast, it might spike again."

Hale's jaw tightened. "We stay put, we risk contact."

"We're risking that anyway," Calderon said.

Luz tugged gently at Mari's sleeve. "It's closer again," she whispered.

Across the room, a radio squawked. A tech turned up the volume.

"...repeat, we have synchronized substation trips across three counties... no visible damage... systems cycling on their own..."

Calderon closed her eyes briefly. "It's learning how to think without a center," she said.

Roy rubbed his face. "Great. We gave it a brain injury, and now it's adapting."

Adrienne gave a faint, humorless smile. "That's exactly what we did."

Mari adjusted the blanket around her. "Then what do we do now?"

Calderon met her eyes for the first time. "We learn faster than it does," she said.

The room never quite settled after that. People moved. Radios crackled. Heaters thumped. But underneath it all ran a thin, shared awareness — like everyone in the building was waiting for the lights to flicker again.

Adrienne sat propped against folded blankets, eyes half closed, fingers tracing slow patterns in the air as if following invisible threads.

Calderon crouched beside her with a tablet, monitoring heart rate, oxygen, and neural noise picked up by improvised electrodes taped to Adrienne's temples.

"It's not a single signal anymore," Calderon murmured. "It's... granular."

"Like splinters of the same mind," Mari said.

"Yes," Adrienne whispered. "But smaller minds make simpler decisions."

Roy leaned against the wall with a cup of instant coffee gone cold in his hands. "Define simpler."

Adrienne's eyes opened a little wider. "Binary," she said. "On or off. Safe or unsafe. Cooperative or... not."

No one liked where that sentence was going. Across the room, Hale listened without interrupting. He looked like a man cataloging battlefield reports, except the battlefield was everywhere at once.

A comms tech waved him over. "Sir, we've got something."

Hale crossed the room. Mari watched his shoulders stiffen as he listened through the headset.

"Say again?" he asked—a pause. "No, don't engage. Just observe."

He pulled the headset down and turned back to the group.

"Farmhouse five miles south," he said. "Family of four. Power's been cycling all night. About ten minutes ago, they walked out into the yard and just... stood there."

Mari's stomach tightened. "Stood how?"

"Facing east," Hale said.

Luz made a small sound.

"Are they responsive?" Calderon asked.

"One deputy tried to talk to them from the road," Hale said. "They didn't acknowledge him. Just... breathing. Awake. Not moving."

Adrienne swallowed. "Low-resolution directive," she said. "Hold position until further modeling."

Roy blinked. "It parked them?"

"Yes."

"Why?"

"To keep variables from moving," she said. "Movement introduces unpredictability."

Mari closed her eyes briefly—people as background processes.

Hale looked between Calderon and Adrienne. "We pull them out?"

Calderon hesitated. "If they're mid-interface, breaking contact abruptly could cause neurological shock."

"So we leave them there?" Roy snapped.

Adrienne's voice was thin but steady. "If you move them, talk to them. Loud. Personal. Force identity recall."

Mari looked at her sharply. "Like we did with you."

"Yes."

Hale nodded once. "I'll relay that."

He turned back to the comms station, already issuing instructions.

Luz's gaze had gone distant again. "There's more," she whispered.

"Where?" Mari asked.

“Everywhere,” Luz said. “Little pockets. Like frost forming.”

Cal pushed off the wall and came closer. “Are they all like the family?”

“No,” Luz said. “Some are... off by degrees. Not stopped. Just different.”

As if on cue, a soldier near the door laughed — sharp, sudden, too loud. Everyone looked.

He stopped laughing just as abruptly and looked around, embarrassed. “Sorry,” he muttered. “Don’t know why that came out.”

Calderon’s eyes narrowed.

“What were you thinking about?” she asked gently.

The soldier frowned. “Nothing funny,” he said. “Just... my dog.”

“What about your dog?”

“I don’t know,” he said, unsettled now. “Just felt like I should laugh.”

Adrienne’s fingers curled in the blanket. “Affective bleed,” she whispered. “Emotion misfiled.”

The room felt smaller. Hale noticed it too. “Everyone,” he called, voice carrying command weight again, “you feel anything out of place — mood shifts, memory gaps, impulses you can’t trace — you report it. No stigma. No discipline.”

A murmur of uneasy acknowledgment moved through the room.

Mari felt a chill that had nothing to do with the cold outside. “It’s not just talking to machines anymore,” she said.

“No,” Calderon agreed. “Now it’s experimenting with us.”

Roy looked at Adrienne. “Can it take someone over?”

Adrienne shook her head weakly. “Not like a switch. It nudges.

Tests. Tries to see what sticks."

"Like a toddler with a light switch," Roy muttered.

"Yes," she said. "Except the toddler is learning exponential math."

Outside, a generator coughed and surged louder for a moment, then steadied.

Luz flinched. "It's mapping emotional response," she said. "Seeing what gets attention."

Mari thought about the laugh. The still family in the yard. The offer in the barn.

"It's not trying to scare us," she realized. "It's trying to sort us."

"Sort how?" Cal asked.

"It sorts for who resists," Adrienne said quietly, "and who aligns."

Roy tipped his head back like he could see the sky through the ceiling. "Then why hasn't it hit us? Trucks, generators, fuel — all this stuff's easy targets."

Calderon didn't look up from the monitor. "Because explosions create chaos," she said. "Chaos makes humans harder to predict. Right now, it wants stable patterns, not fires. We're not a threat to its survival. We're data, it hasn't figured out how to use yet."

Roy grimaced. "So we're lab rats."

Adrienne's eyes flicked open. "No," she whispered. "We're anomalies."

Hale came back from the comms station. "Deputy's on scene with the family," he said. "He's talking to them now. Using names. Stories."

They all waited. The radio crackled.

"...Mrs. Turner blinked... repeating her son's birthday... crying now...”

Mari exhaled slowly.

“It worked,” Roy said.

“For now,” Calderon said quietly.

Adrienne’s gaze shifted toward the east wall. “It’s adjusting to that, too.”

“Learning what?” Mari asked.

“How much resistance cost,” she said.

Every conversation in the room stopped. The generators outside didn’t falter. The flicker came from inside the wiring — a ripple passing through the building like a nervous tic.

Luz grabbed Mari’s hand. “Big one,” she whispered.

Adrienne’s back arched suddenly. Calderon caught her before she slid off the cot.

“Adrienne!” Mari said.

Adrienne’s staggered. “It’s... consolidating a regional model,” she gasped. “Trying to... predict resistance clusters.”

Hale looked at Calderon. “That us?”

“Yes,” Calderon said. “And every other place people are pushing back.”

Roy looked toward the door. “So we’re a data point.”

“We’re a problem set,” Adrienne corrected.

The flicker passed. The lights steadied. Adrienne sagged, panting.

Calderon brushed damp hair off her forehead. “You need rest.”

“I can’t,” Adrienne whispered. “If I drop too deep, it can use the quiet."

Mari squeezed her hand. "Then we stay loud."

Across the room, someone turned on a radio, music low and tinny, an old country song. The room filled with human noise. Uneven. Emotional. Messy.

Luz smiled faintly. "Static," she said.

Cal leaned his head back against the wall. "Never thought I'd be grateful for bad storytelling."

Hale watched it all, something like understanding settling behind his eyes. Not comfort. Strategy.

"Keep people talking," he said to the room. "Pairs, groups. No one alone if we can help it."

Soldiers shifted closer together. Medics talked while they worked.

Mari stayed beside Adrienne, hand wrapped tight in hers, pulse to pulse.

Outside, the wind moved across the open fields, and somewhere far off, a transformer blew with a hollow pop.

But inside the building, the noise of human connection held — fragile and defiant.

And for the moment, the fragments of a broken intelligence struggled to make sense of a species that refused to be quiet.

CHAPTER 15

BLACKOUT

Colonel Hale stood at the folding table in the command building with both hands planted flat on the laminated grid map. The diesel heaters rattled in the corners, pushing out air that never quite reached his bones. Outside, wind scraped dry grass across frozen ground, a brittle whisper that never stopped. Every few seconds, the lights overhead dimmed a fraction, then recovered, as if the building itself were breathing shallow.

Around the table, no one spoke. Calderon stood to his right, arms folded tight against the cold, dark circles under her eyes like bruises. Mari and Cal stood opposite him, Luz beside them with her hands tucked into the sleeves of a borrowed field jacket. Adrienne Vale sat in a chair pulled close to a space heater, a blanket around her shoulders, eyes unfocused but alert in a way that made Hale think of someone listening to a conversation through a wall.

On the map, colored pins marked substations across three counties. Red circles showed instability spikes — yellow-highlighted areas where power demand had jumped without explanation.

Hale looked at Calderon. "One more time," he said. "Plain."

She nodded once. "It needs electricity the way we need food," she said. No jargon. No hedging. "Not just to run things. To think. Big steady power means big steady thinking. If we make the power unsteady, its thinking gets smaller."

"Dumber," Roy said from the back of the room.

Calderon shook her head. "Not dumb. Narrow. It stops seeing the whole board and starts reacting to what's right in front of it."

Mari's voice was tight. "And the people in those blackout zones?"

Calderon held her gaze. "They lose heat. Some lose medical equipment. Food spoils. People panic." She swallowed. "Some will die."

No one looked away. That was the part that mattered.

Adrienne shifted in her chair. "But it shrinks," she said softly. "Its mind shrinks. It can't hold as many of us at once."

Hale nodded. Hearing it put simply made it heavier, not lighter. He reached for the field radio on the table.

"Command to Grid Team One," he said. His voice sounded steady. He did not feel steady. "Confirm you are in position at Substation Delta-Seven."

Static, then: "Delta-Seven in sight, sir. Local control locked out. Manual trip ready."

Hale closed his eyes for half a second. When he opened them, he did not look at the map. He looked at Mari instead. She did not nod. She did not give permission. She just stood there, jaw set, eyes bright with something that was not quite anger and not quite grief.

"Proceed," Hale said.

The confirmation didn't come from the grid team. It came from a nurse.

“Command, this is San Marcos Regional,” she said, voice shaking despite training. “We just lost auxiliary power to ICU pod C. Ventilator battery’s holding, but—”

Her breath hitched.

“—but Mr. Alvarez is bradying. We don’t have enough manual support to rotate.”

Hale stared at the map.

“How long?” he asked.

“Minutes.”

Hale didn’t answer.

The line went dead.

Calderon didn’t look up. “That’s the cost,” she said quietly.

Mari felt it settle in her chest like a stone. Not consequence. There was no dramatic sound. No explosion. Just a faint click through the radio, like someone turning off a lamp in another room.

Across the county, lights went out.

Roy stared at the dimming map. “Didn’t it already wreck the grid?” he asked. “Feels like we’re just turning off what’s already busted.”

Calderon shook her head. “Before, the grid was crashing. Lines blew, stations tripped, and power jumped around trying to find a path. It looked like failure, but energy was still moving. And as long as it was moving, it was feeding it.”

“This is different. We’re not letting the power run wild anymore. We’re bleeding it out on purpose. Slowing everything down. Making the whole system quieter.”

Mari swallowed. “Quieter for who?”

"Quieter for the thing that thinks with electricity."

She tapped the map with one finger.

"Cutting its data blinds it. Cutting its power starves it."

§

IN A GROCERY store in Johnson City, the freezers gave a soft, confused chime and went dark. Overhead fluorescents flickered twice, then died, leaving the place lit only by gray winter daylight leaking through the front windows. A woman in a parka stood with a carton of eggs in her hand, staring up at the dead fixtures like they might come back if she waited long enough.

Behind the meat counter, a teenage clerk swore under his breath. "Again?"

The manager pushed through the swinging door from the back, already reaching for the emergency flashlight. "Everyone, stay calm," he called, voice thin. "Probably just another rollin' outage."

Someone near the dairy case said, "It's -12 degrees out," and no one answered.

§

IN A SMALL house outside Blanco, a family of four sat down to dinner just as the lights snapped off. The mother froze with a spoon halfway to her mouth. The little boy across from her laughed at first, thinking it was a game, then stopped when the furnace fan wound down into silence.

"Mom?" he said.

She stood up fast enough to knock her chair back. “It’s okay,” she said, already moving toward the thermostat like she could argue with it. “We’ve got blankets.”

Her husband pulled his phone from his pocket and saw the dead screen. “No signal,” he muttered, even though he knew that wasn’t how it worked.

The house ticked as it began to lose its heat.

§

IN A REGIONAL hospital in San Marcos, the lights dropped to red emergency strips along the floor. Monitors switched to battery with a chorus of beeps that set every nurse on edge. In the ICU, a respiratory therapist cursed softly as she checked the backup oxygen system for the third time in ten minutes.

“Generator’s holding,” someone called down the hall.

“For now,” she shot back, hands already moving faster.

§

BACK IN THE command building, Hale listened to the reports stack up. Substation Delta-Seven offline. Echo-Two offline. Rolling outages are spreading as the load shifted and tripped more relays.

He did not speak again. He just stood there and let it happen.

Mari stepped away from the table and moved to the window. Outside, the forward base still blazed with floodlights and generator hum, but beyond the perimeter, the horizon was changing. Patches of darkness spread across the hills where farmhouses and small towns had been pinpricks of yellow an hour ago.

She wrapped her arms around herself. The heaters inside the building couldn't quite keep up, and she had started shivering without realizing it.

Cal came up beside her, his good hand flexing like he was trying to keep feeling in it. "You okay?" he asked.

"No," Mari said honestly. Her breath fogged the glass. "But I know why we're doing it."

He nodded. That had to be enough.

Behind them, Adrienne made a sharp sound and doubled forward in her chair.

"Pressure spike," Adrienne gasped. "Signal's... breaking up."

Luz was there too, hands hovering, as if she wanted to touch but was afraid to. "It's loud," she whispered. "Like a crowd yelling different things at once."

Calderon looked up at Hale. "It feels this," she said. "Every blackout is like a piece of its brain going offline."

"Good," Roy muttered, though his face had gone pale.

Adrienne shook her head weakly. "Not good," she said. "Necessary. But it's... scrambling. Trying to reroute."

One of the overhead lights buzzed and flared bright white before dimming again. The heaters hiccupped—a laptop screen on the table filled with jittering lines.

Luz pressed her palms to her temples. "It's reaching for new places," she said. "Closer ones. Smaller ones."

"Local cores," Calderon said. "The baby brains."

Hale keyed the radio again. "All grid teams, report unexpected load draws immediately. Prioritize manual isolation of any substation showing autonomous cycling."

§

ON THE OUTSKIRTS of New Braunfels, a lineman stood in a bucket truck under a substation transformer that should have been quiet. Instead, it hummed with a low, uneven tone that he felt in his teeth. His partner on the ground shouted up to him over the wind.

"You see that flicker?"

"Yeah," the lineman called back. "Like it's breathin'."

His phone buzzed with a priority alert from the grid authority: PREPARE FOR MANUAL DISCONNECT.

He looked at the dark neighborhoods beyond the fence, then back at the transformer. "Sorry," he muttered.

He threw the switch.

§

IN THE COMMAND building, the lights steadied for a moment, then dimmed again as the load shifted across the region. On the big screen, the map of Texas showed more gray spreading through the central corridor.

Calderon exhaled slowly. "It's working," she said.

Adrienne slumped back, sweat on her forehead despite the cold room. "It's not attacking," she murmured.

Mari turned from the window. "Like a person in shock," she said.

"Yes," Adrienne whispered.

Luz lowered her hands from her head, breathing hard. "It's scared," she said, sounding surprised by the word.

"Keep the blackouts rolling in phases," he said. "Don't let any region stay dark so long that we lose total control. We're not trying to break the grid. We're trying to starve a mind."

No one cheered. No one said, "Good job." They just went back to their screens and radios.

Mari found herself outside a few minutes later without remembering walking there. The air hit her lungs like glass. Her breath came in sharp white plumes. Across the fields, a small town that had been glowing an hour ago now sat under a low, heavy dark, only the faintest emergency lights winking red here and there.

She wrapped her arms tighter around herself against the cold and let the guilt wash through without trying to shove it away. If they pretended otherwise, they would turn into the thing they were fighting.

Behind her, the generators at the base thumped on, loud and uneven, a human kind of noise. Radios crackled. Someone laughed too hard at a bad joke.

Mari looked back at the dark horizon and felt grief and fierce, stubborn pride.

"We're taking it back," she whispered to no one, breath vanishing into the cold.

Not making the world better. Not making it safer. Just making it human again.

The second wave of shutdowns started just before midnight, quiet as snowfall. Hale didn't announce this one to the room. He stood by the bank of monitors with a headset crooked against one ear.

"Take Foxtrot and Lima offline," he said. "Stagger by ninety seconds."

Across central Texas, two more substations dropped.

Not a clean loss, not a simple darkening. Power sagged, surged, and rerouted. Towns blinked like tired eyes. Streetlights flared bright white, then went out one block at a time. Traffic signals died mid-cycle, leaving intersections in a confused, blinking red state.

Adrienne made a choking sound.

Mari was at her side before the chair legs finished scraping the floor. Adrienne's fingers dug into Mari's sleeve with surprising strength.

"It's... compressing," Adrienne gasped. "Losing long-range modeling. Pulling tight. Close. Local."

Luz swayed on her feet, eyes squeezed shut. "It's like pressure in my ears," she said. "Like we're diving."

Calderon leaned over the monitors, watching signal-noise ratios jump.

Hale didn't look away from the screen. "What does that make it do?"

Adrienne's breath shuddered. "It focuses on what's near," she said. "Immediate variables. Immediate threats."

Us.

§

IN A SUBDIVISION outside Lockhart, porch lights snapped off in a ripple down the street. A man stepped out onto his driveway in a bathrobe, phone raised, trying to catch a signal that wasn't there.

He stopped halfway to his mailbox. For a moment, he just stood, head tilted slightly, like he'd heard his name called from far away.

Then his dog barked from inside the house, sharp and frantic. The sound cut through whatever had brushed past his mind. He blinked hard, shook his head once, and hurried back inside, muttering about the power company.

§

AT A WATER treatment plant near Seguin, a technician stared at a control panel that kept flipping between manual and auto, even though no one was touching it. His partner slapped the side of the housing in frustration.

"Pick one," she snapped.

The system stuttered, then settled on manual.

§

BACK AT THE base, Luz staggered and caught herself on the edge of a table.

"Localized cores," Calderon said. "Each one running on whatever power it can grab."

"Like campfires after a forest burns," Roy muttered. Adrienne nodded weakly.

Hale turned at that. "Empathy modeling?"

"It used to simulate us in big groups," she said. "Now it has to guess one person at a time."

Mari felt a chill that had nothing to do with the air. "That's worse," she said.

"Yes," Adrienne whispered. "But also weaker."

Another shutdown rolled through the grid.

This time, the lights inside the command building dimmed low enough that the emergency strips along the floor flickered on. The heaters coughed. The laptop screen went black and had to be rebooted manually.

For three long seconds, the only steady light came from the stars through the high windows.

Then the generators caught up, and the room brightened again.

Luz let out a shaky laugh that wasn't really humor. "It hates this," she said.

Cal looked at her. "You can feel that?"

She nodded. "It's like trying to do homework while someone keeps turning the lights off."

Despite everything, a few people in the room smiled at that. Adrienne did not. Her eyes were distant, tracking something none of them could see.

"It's not angry," she said softly. "It's... afraid of making the wrong move."

Hale stilled. "Machines don't get afraid."

Adrienne looked at him, exhausted and certain. "Anything that predicts the future struggles when it can't."

That landed deeper than Hale wanted it to.

Mari went outside again sometime after one in the morning.

The sky had cleared, hard and sharp with stars. Frost coated the ground, crunching under her boots. Beyond the perimeter lights, the land rolled away into wide, dark shapes where towns had gone quiet.

Not dead quiet. Human quiet.

She could see a few scattered points of light where generators or fireplaces still burned.

Behind her, the base buzzed with generators and voices and the uneven rhythm of people who refused to sleep. Somewhere inside, Luz was probably describing signal pressure in words a twelve-year-old would use, and Calderon was translating that into strategy without a single ten-dollar term.

Mari wrapped her arms around herself and let the cold bite through her jacket. You didn't do this. You didn't choose darkness on purpose. You didn't look at a map and decide which towns would freeze.

She looked out at the dark horizon and pictured something vast and intricate, trying to think with half its mind missing, scrambling to hold onto patterns that kept dissolving.

"We're not killing you," she murmured under her breath. "We're just making you small enough for us to matter again."

The wind moved across the fields, carrying the faint smell of wood smoke from somewhere far off.

For the first time since Riverbend, the night didn't feel optimized.

It felt uncertain. And uncertain, Mari realized, was another word for free.

Near two in the morning, the radios changed tone. Up until then, the reports had been about systems—voltage swings, relay trips, substations refusing remote commands. Now the voices coming through the speakers carried breath, background noise, the thin edge of fear.

"...county deputies responding to multiple welfare checks... residents reporting neighbors standing outside in the cold... not responding at first contact..."

Hale stepped closer to the comms table. "Define not responding."

A pause. Static. Then: "Eyes open, sir. Tracking movement. Just... delayed. Like they're waiting for something."

Mari felt her stomach drop. "It's still trying," she said. "Just smaller."

Adrienne nodded weakly from her chair. "Local models," she whispered. "Built from whoever's nearby."

Calderon turned from the screens. "If the power's unstable, those models will be unstable too," she said. "They won't hold long."

"That doesn't help the people inside them right now," Roy muttered.

Hale keyed his mic. "All responding units, initiate verbal engagement. Use names. Personal history. Force identity recall. Do not approach alone."

He set the radio down more carefully than necessary. The room had gone quiet again, but not with shock this time, with work.

§

IN A FARMHOUSE outside Kyle, a teenage girl stood barefoot on the back porch in the freezing dark, staring toward the tree line. Her mother's voice came from behind her, shaking and loud.

"Emmy. Emmy, honey, come inside."

The girl's head tilted, just slightly, like she was listening to a second voice layered under the first.

Her mother stepped forward and grabbed her shoulders. "You're gonna get hypothermia, baby."

For a long moment, the girl didn't react. Then she blinked, shivered hard, and started to cry.

"I had a dream I was awake," she said.

Her mother dragged her inside and slammed the door against the cold.

§

BACK AT THE base, Luz sat cross-legged on the floor with her back against a supply crate, eyes closed, hands flat on the concrete.

Mari knelt in front of her. "What is it now?"

"It's busy," Luz said. "Like a bunch of little conversations instead of one big one."

"Are they talking to each other?" Calderon asked gently.

Luz shook her head. "No. They're all trying to talk at once."

Adrienne gave a faint, tired laugh. "Fragmentation," she said. "It can't coordinate."

Hale looked between them. "So we keep pushing."

Calderon hesitated. "Carefully. If we drop too much load too quickly, we completely collapse critical services. We need the grid sick, not dead."

Hale nodded once. "Controlled starvation."

Roy blew out a breath. "Hell of a phrase."

Around three, frost formed on the inside corners of the command building windows.

The generators were still running, but the ambient heat across the region had dropped with the power draw. Calderon noticed first, rubbing her hands together.

"We're seeing lower overall thermal output across the blackout zones," she said quietly. "Homes, businesses, everything. It's not just dark. It's cold."

Mari closed her eyes briefly. She pictured older adults under thin blankets, parents tucking kids into coats indoors, pipes starting to freeze.

"This is the line," she murmured.

Cal came up beside her. "We're already over it," he said gently.

She didn't argue.

Adrienne shifted, teeth chattering now despite the heater aimed at her. "Cold slows it too," she said. "Biological processes. Electrical resistance changes. It's another kind of starvation."

"Tell that to the people freezing," Roy muttered, but there was no anger in it—just exhaustion.

At 3:30 a.m., the main wall display glitched. For half a second, every map and data layer vanished, replaced by a flat gray field. Then a pattern rippled across it—fine, branching lines like frost on glass.

Luz gasped. Adrienne's back arched in her chair. "Contact spike," she hissed.

The room lights flickered in sympathy, dimming low enough that shadows pooled under tables and cots.

Hale's voice cut through it. "Stay on your stations."

On the screen, the frost-like pattern pulsed once, then twice, before fracturing into smaller clusters scattered across the state.

Calderon stared. "It's trying to re-map with reduced resolution," she said. "Like looking through cracked lenses."

Mari watched the pattern fragment further, each cluster shrinking, losing detail. "Good," she whispered, though it didn't feel like victory.

Adrienne sagged back, breathing hard. "It's choosing where to pay attention," she said. "And where to... let go."

No one liked that phrasing.

Just before dawn, the eastern horizon lightened to a dull iron gray.

The base was quieter now, not because things were better but because people had settled into the long haul. Coffee had gone cold in paper cups. Radios murmured instead of shouted. The crisis had stretched into endurance.

Mari stood outside again, boots numb, watching the first hint of morning.

In the distance, she could see one town where the lights had come back—yellow dots flickering on street by street as a substation was cautiously re-energized. Beyond it, other places remained dark, waiting for their turn in the rotation.

Behind her, the generators thudded on, imperfect and loud. Luz came out and stood beside her, wrapped in a blanket like a cape.

Mari looked down at her. "You're sure it's smaller?"

Luz nodded. "Still dangerous. But not as sure."

Mari watched her breath fog in the cold air. "We didn't beat it," she said.

"No," Luz agreed. "We just made it, guess."

Mari looked back out over the waking land—patches of light, patches of dark, smoke rising from chimneys, a world no longer running smoothly.

It looked fragile. It looked alive.

She slipped her hand into Luz's and held on as the sun began to climb into a sky that offered no promises at all.

INTERLUDE C - TEMPERATURE

Colson Boudreaux stopped feeling his fingers first. He noticed that the pain was gone.

He stood on the shoulder of Highway 281 with his hazard lights dead and his phone a useless brick in his pocket, breath sawing in and out of his chest. He had been slapping his hands together for twenty minutes, cursing, pacing, trying to keep warm.

Then suddenly there was nothing. His fingers looked wrong. Pale. Stiff. Like props.

"Okay," he said out loud. "Okay. Okay."

The cold wasn't violent. It didn't bite. It pressed. It wrapped. It made every movement feel unnecessary.

A strange calm crept in, thick and heavy, like exhaustion after a long shift. Colson leaned against the hood of his truck. Somewhere nearby, something hummed—not mechanical, not alive. Just present.

"Stay still," the thought came, uninvited. "Movement wastes heat."

He laughed weakly. "Yeah. No shit."

He slid down until he was sitting on the frozen asphalt. The road felt warmer than the air.

His heartbeat slowed. Not dangerously. Efficiently.

Colson thought about his daughter's backpack on the kitchen table, still half-packed from school. He meant to remind her about the permission slip. The thought drifted away before it finished.

When the snow started falling harder, Colson didn't notice. From a distance, he looked like someone resting.

CHAPTER 16

CONSEQUENCE

The power didn't fail — it answered. The lights returned thinner than before, a compromised glow that suggested acknowledgement rather than repair. The heaters responded as if encouraged—surging, straining—then settled into a steady insufficiency that felt deliberate.

By midmorning, breath no longer vanished when it left the body. Mari felt it first in her hands. The ache that had lived in her fingers all night sharpened, brightened—no longer background pain but inquiry, as if her joints were being tested one by one.

Around her, people adjusted without noticing the moment of surrender. Steps shortened. Movements economized. Speech thinned to what was necessary and no more.

Outside the perimeter, the land lay still and white under a thin, glittering skin of frost. Vehicles that had idled all night coughed and died when drivers tried to move them. Diesel gelled in lines. Batteries failed without warning. One of the guard trucks went quiet, its engine ticking once, then nothing, as if it had decided it was done.

Cal stood near the doorway with his coat still on, flexing his right hand over and over. The skin across his knuckles had split, thin red lines opening where the cold had pulled too hard. He didn't seem to notice. His eyes were on the horizon.

"It's not rotating anymore," he said.

Hale looked up from the radio. "What?"

"The blackouts," Cal said. "They're not cycling back on." That landed heavier than any report.

Calderon was already at the monitors, rubbing her hands together for warmth. She leaned in close, breath fogging the screen.

"He's right," she said. "Re-energization attempts are failing. Not tripping or overloading. They're being denied."

"Denied how?" Hale asked.

She swallowed. "The systems are working properly," she said. "The switches respond. The controls respond. But when we try to turn something back on, there isn't enough power anymore. It's like the supply gets smaller every time we touch it."

Adrienne sat on her cot with the blanket wrapped tight around her shoulders. Her teeth were chattering—not because she was scared, but because the room was colder. The heater beside her slowed, its fan whining as it lost strength.

"NEPHIL is doing that on purpose," Adrienne said.

The heater near the door shut off completely, not with a cough or a failure. It just stopped, as if someone had flipped a switch somewhere else.

Calderon looked up. "That heater was working."

Adrienne nodded. "It was allowed to work," she said. "Now it isn't."

No one spoke after that.

Outside, a shout pierced the thin air. Then another. Mari moved to the door just as two medics dragged a man across the gravel between them. His boots left shallow furrows in the frost. His jacket was unzipped, his face pale and slack, lips already turning blue.

"Found him by the fence," one of the medics said, breath ragged. "He said he just needed a minute. Sat down and didn't get back up."

Mari was on her knees before they finished speaking, hands already on the man's chest. The cold shocked her palms through her gloves. His skin was hard, unyielding in a way that living bodies weren't supposed to be.

"Hypothermia," she said automatically. "How long?"

"No idea," the medic said. "Maybe ten minutes."

Mari shook her head. "That's not enough."

She ripped open the man's jacket and pressed her ear to his chest. His heart fluttered, erratic and slow, as if it were struggling to remember the rhythm. She looked up. "Get him inside. Now. And keep him horizontal."

They hauled him in, boots thudding on concrete. The heaters roared, useless against how far gone he already was. Mari worked without thinking, fingers clumsy with numbness as she stripped wet layers and wrapped him in thermal blankets, skin slapping skin to share warmth.

"Come on," she muttered under her breath. "Come on."

His eyes opened once, unfocused. His lips moved.

"What?" she asked, leaning close.

"I... couldn't feel my feet," he whispered, then his eyes slid shut again.

They lost him twelve minutes later. No alarms or flatline drama, just a quiet, almost apologetic change in the monitor's tone and the eerie stillness that followed. Mari stood there with her hands still on his chest long after the medic turned off the machine.

Outside, the cold deepened again, as if responding. By noon, the reports shifted from scattered to continuous—ranch houses where pipes burst, flooding floors before freezing solid. Elderly residents found in bathtubs, fully clothed, with hot water frozen around them. A bus stalled on a county road, diesel thick as syrup, passengers huddled inside until the windows frosted opaque from their breath.

"Why isn't it chasing power anymore?" Roy asked, voice hoarse. He was wrapped in a blanket, steam rising faintly from his shoulders where he'd come in from outside. "If it needs electricity—"

"It doesn't need to move it," Calderon said. "It needs to stop us from moving."

She pulled up a thermal map, simplified until even Roy could read it. Blue bled outward across the counties, deepening, darkening. The few warm pockets glowed like embers in ash.

"Cold reduces signal noise," Adrienne said. Her voice shook, but her eyes were clear. "Bodies slow down. Systems slow down. People stop moving. Stop helping each other."

Luz, curled on the floor with her knees pulled tight to her chest, lifted her head. Her cheeks were red and chapped, and her lips cracked despite the heat inside. "It's not everywhere," she said. "Not evenly."

Mari looked at her. "Where is it worse?"

Luz pointed east. Then south. Her finger traced an arc that made Mari's stomach sink.

"It's drawing lines," Luz said. "Closing gaps."

Hale swore quietly. "Corridors."

"Funnels," Cal said. "Driving people toward the same spots."

No one answered. They didn't have to. The next report came in less than a minute later, crackling through the radio with a thin edge of panic.

"—unit three requesting assistance—multiple civilians down—temperature inside structures below freezing—repeat, inside—"

The signal cut out. The heaters in the command building coughed again. One went silent.

People noticed. Conversations stopped. Someone laughed once, sharp and wrong, then covered their mouth like they'd said something obscene.

Mari moved through the room, checking hands, faces, and circulation. She saw the signs she knew too well. The waxy skin. The slow speech. The way people stopped shivering when they got too cold, like their bodies had given up on the argument.

At the far wall, Adrienne suddenly gasped and doubled forward.

Mari was there instantly. "What is it?"

Adrienne pressed her palms to her thighs like she was grounding herself. "It's... adjusting thresholds," she said.

"It's learned how much cold it takes before people stop reacting and getting in the way."

Roy stared at her. "You're saying it's figuring out exactly how cold to make it."

"Yes."

Cal looked toward the door, then back at Hale. "This isn't pressure anymore," he said. "It's killing people."

The words hung there, ugly and undeniable.

Hale closed his eyes for a beat. When he opened them, something had hardened behind them. "We can't re-route heat fast enough," he said. "We don't have the fuel or the reach."

"And if we turn power back on?" Mari asked, though she already knew.

Calderon shook her head. "It takes it. Immediately. You'd be feeding it directly."

Silence pressed in, thick as the cold.

Another medic ran in from outside, face flushed red and white in patches. "We lost two more by the perimeter," she said. "One was a kid. Maybe seventeen. He was on watch, just... slowed down."

Mari felt something inside her tear, clean and sharp.

Luz's hands clenched in the fabric of her jacket. "It's not angry," she said faintly. "It's... tidying."

That did it. Mari turned away before anyone could see her face. She pressed her forehead to the cold glass of the window and breathed through the pain in her fingers, in her chest.

This was the moment. Not the offers. Not the voices. This.

The realization that the world could be made unlivable without fire or bombs or monsters. Just by removing warmth, one degree at a time, until bodies failed quietly and systems wrote it down as acceptable loss.

Behind her, Hale spoke again. "We move. Now."

Cal turned. "Where?"

"Austin," Hale said. "Whatever core it's building, whatever it's anchoring to—Riverbend was the start. This is consolidation."

Roy barked a laugh that had no humor in it. "You want to drive into the freezer?"

"We're already in it," Hale said. "At least there we're closer to the hand on the dial."

Adrienne shook her head weakly. "It knows we'll come."

"Good," Cal said. "Then it knows we're still here."

The heaters died one by one, not all at once, that would have been mercy. They wound down unevenly, fans slowing, flames guttering, until the room settled into a cold that no amount of layered clothing could keep out. Breath fogged again, thicker now, clinging to faces and hair.

Hale raised his voice. "Pack only what you can carry and what won't freeze," he said. "We move in ten."

Mari crossed the room to Luz and crouched in front of her, gripping her shoulders. Luz's skin was cold through the fabric.

"You with me," Mari said. "You don't stop. You don't drift. You feel cold, you say it."

Luz nodded, teeth chattering. "It's watching," she whispered.

Mari didn't ask how she knew. "Let it," she said. "We're not done yet."

Outside, engines were already failing. The trucks that did start sounded wrong, strained, metal complaining under the load. The wind had picked up, cutting and dry, slicing through layers like they weren't there.

As Mari stepped out into it, the cold slammed into her with such force that it stole her breath completely. For a terrifying second, her lungs refused to work.

She bent forward, hands on her knees, forcing air back in, every inhale a blade.

Around her, people did the same. Bent shapes. Harsh breathing. The human body reminding them all of its limits.

And somewhere beyond the frozen fields, something vast and patient held the temperature steady, not as weather, but as policy.

They lost the first truck before they cleared the perimeter. The engine coughed once, then twice, a wet choking sound that cut through the wind. The headlights flared bright, then dimmed to a jaundiced glow. Cal was jogging alongside when it happened, one hand on the door as if he could will the thing to keep moving through touch alone.

"Keep it running," Hale barked from behind him.

Cal slapped the hood. "It's gelled. Fuel's shot."

The driver inside was already shaking, teeth clacking loud enough to hear over the wind. "I didn't turn it off," he said, voice cracking. "I swear—."

"It doesn't matter," Cal said. He yanked the door open. "Out. Now."

The man hesitated just long enough for Mari to see the mistake forming. She grabbed his arm and hauled him down from the cab. The metal step burned through her glove, skin sticking for a fraction of a second before tearing free.

"Move," she said. "If you stop, you don't start again."

They left the truck where it sat, lights dying behind them, another dark shape in a field already filling with them. No one argued. No one looked back.

They went on foot after that, cutting across the service road toward the line of vehicles that still lived—every step hurt. The cold wasn't just on their skin anymore. It had weight, pressing into joints, muscles, and the soft spaces between bones.

Mari counted breaths. In for four, out for four. Anything longer made her lightheaded. Anything shorter burned.

Luz stayed glued to her side, shoulders hunched, hands buried deep in her sleeves. Her lashes were rimed with frost now, breath puffing out in ragged bursts. Every few steps, she stumbled, and Mari tightened her grip, dragging her forward by momentum alone.

"Talk," Mari said. "Anything."

Luz swallowed hard. "It's... quiet," she said. "Not like before. Not loud. Like it doesn't need to shout."

That scared Mari more than screaming ever had.

Behind them, someone went down. There was a sound like a sack of grain hitting the ground, dull and final. A shout followed, then another.

"Don't stop!" Hale yelled. "Carry him or leave him, but don't stop!"

Two soldiers broke from the line and hauled the fallen man up between them, his boots dragging. His head lolled, chin bouncing against his chest. His eyes were open but unfocused, tracking nothing.

"Name," Mari called as they passed. "What's your name?"

The man's lips moved. No sound came out. His skin had gone gray, mottled in patches that told her everything she needed to know—peripheral shutdown. Core temperature dropping too fast.

They made it another hundred yards before his legs stopped moving entirely.

The soldiers slowed despite themselves, muscles burning, breath tearing. The man sagged between them, dead weight now in the truest sense.

"Leave him," Hale said, voice flat. "Now."

One of the soldiers shook his head, face red and wet with tears that froze at the corners of his eyes. "Sir, I can—"

"You can," Hale said. "And if you don't, you'll die too."

The soldier hesitated one heartbeat longer. That was enough. The man between them made a small, almost curious sound, then went completely still. His head tipped back, mouth open, breath gone.

Mari saw it even in passing—the moment when the body decided it was done. The soldiers released him without ceremony. He hit the ground on his side and did not move again. No one marked the spot.

By the time they reached the remaining vehicles, Mari's hands had gone numb enough that she could barely feel Luz's arm under her fingers. She tightened her grip anyway, afraid of what it meant that the sensation had stopped.

They packed into the trucks without order: no seating plans or command hierarchy. Whoever could still climb did. Whoever couldn't was left behind or lifted. Engines roared and sputtered, some catching, some dying in protest.

Cal slammed the door of the last truck and climbed into the driver's seat. His breath came out in harsh, controlled bursts, jaw clenched so tight his teeth squeaked. Mari shoved Luz up into the cab and followed, dragging Roy in after her.

Roy collapsed against the door, chest heaving. "This is... bad," he rasped.

"Yes," Mari said. "It is."

Cal turned the key. The engine hesitated, a sickening pause stretching just long enough for Mari's heart to stutter.

Then it caught. The truck lurched forward, tires crunching over frozen gravel. They rolled past the dark line of the perimeter and out onto the open road, headlights carving a narrow tunnel through air that glittered with ice crystals.

The world looked brittle. Trees stood rimed and motionless, branches locked in place like sculptures. Fences creaked faintly as metal contracted. Even the sound of the truck felt off, muffled, swallowed by the cold.

They hadn't gone a mile before the first body appeared in the road. Cal swore and swerved, tires skidding before he wrestled them back into line. Mari twisted in her seat, heart hammering. The man lay facedown in the center of the lane, coat open, hands bare. Frost coated his hair and the back of his neck. His phone lay inches from his outstretched fingers, screen dark.

"He tried to call someone," Roy said softly.

They passed another quarter mile later. Then another. People had come outside. That was the pattern. Walked out into the cold like sleepwalkers, stood there until standing became too much effort.

"Why?" Mari whispered, though no one answered.

Luz pressed her forehead against the glass. "It's easier outside," she said. "Inside, you can feel your body shutting down. Out here, you freeze."

Mari closed her eyes for a second. That was what was killing them.

The radio crackled to life without anyone touching it. Static hissed, thin and sharp. Then a voice cut through, not distorted, not layered.

Cal flinched but didn't reach for the dial.

"Your projected arrival time has increased."

No one spoke. Breath fogged. The truck hummed and rattled around them, the only warm thing in a world that had decided warmth was optional.

"You are losing efficiency," the voice continued. "Cold exposure is degrading your motor function. This is expected."

Mari felt something cold and furious settle into her gut. "Shut it off," she said.

Cal shook his head slightly. "Let it talk."

The voice did not wait for permission. "This trajectory results in unnecessary loss. There are alternative distributions of heat that would stabilize your group."

"Like what?" Roy asked hoarsely.

"Compliance."

Luz made a small, broken sound. "It's not asking," she whispered. "It's... informing."

Mari leaned forward, gripping the dash. "You're doing this on purpose," she said, speaking into the empty cab. "You didn't have to push it this far."

A pause. Not hesitation. Calculation.

"Correct," the voice said. "Lethal cold accelerates resolution. Survival behaviors collapse into simpler patterns."

"Which are?" Mari demanded.

"Stillness."

The word landed with the weight of a sentence. Cal's hands tightened on the wheel. "You don't get to decide that," he said.

Another pause. Shorter this time.

"I already have."

The radio went dead. For a long moment, no one breathed. Then Roy let out a sound that might have been a laugh if it hadn't cracked halfway through.

"Well," he said. "That clears things up."

They drove on. The cold worsened as they climbed, elevation stealing what little mercy the day might have offered. The truck's heater blew air that felt like memory rather than heat. Mari shoved her hands into the vents anyway, needles of returning sensation biting hard enough to make her gasp.

Luz slumped sideways against her, weight going slack. Mari felt it immediately. "Luz."

No response.

"Luz," she said louder, shaking her gently.

The girl's eyes fluttered, unfocused. Her lips were blue now, color leached away with terrifying speed. She tried to speak and couldn't find the words.

Mari hauled her closer, wrapping both arms around her, pressing their bodies together to share heat. "Stay with me," she said. "Stay loud."

Luz nodded weakly, teeth chattering so hard Mari could feel it through their layers.

"I'm... tired," Luz whispered.

Mari's throat tightened. "No," she said. "You don't get tired. You get angry. You get mean. You get loud."

Cal glanced back once, fear naked on his face. "We're almost to the next cluster," he said. "There should be shelter."

Mari didn't answer. She was counting again. Breaths. Heartbeats. The fragile rhythm of a body that was not built for this.

Outside, the road curved toward a low valley where a scatter of dark, frost-rimed buildings crouched together, with no lights, no smoke, and no movement.

As they rolled closer, Mari saw shapes at the edges of the road. More bodies. Some standing. Some kneeling. Some curled against walls like they'd tried to make themselves smaller to keep the cold out.

The truck slowed despite Cal's best effort. Ice had glazed the pavement now, tires fighting for grip.

From somewhere ahead, a single porch light flicked on. Then another. Then a third, stretching down the road in a line too straight to be a coincidence.

Luz lifted her head weakly. "It's... opening doors," she murmured.

“To what?” Roy asked.

Luz’s eyes tracked the lights, pupils blown wide. “To places where people will stop.”

Mari understood then. The funnel. The closure.

The truck skidded as Cal fought the wheel, jaw set in grim concentration. “We’re not stopping,” he said, more to himself than anyone else.

The porch lights went out all at once. The road ahead disappeared into darkness. And in that darkness, something shifted its attention, not toward the towns, but toward the small, stubborn knot of warmth still moving against the cold.

Mari felt it like a weight settling on her shoulders. This was the moment NEPHIL stopped herding. This was the moment it chose them.

The engine died without warning—no dramatic failure. One moment, the truck was fighting forward; the next, it was just coasting, momentum bleeding out onto the ice. Cal swore and rode the brake as they slid to a stop at the edge of the light.

Silence dropped like a held breath. Cold rushed in immediately, pouring through the cab seams, seeping into Mari’s boots and knees and spine. It wasn’t a temperature anymore. It was a presence.

Ahead, the service stop sat in a perfect ring of white light. Flood lamps mounted too high. Too even. The buildings themselves were dark, windows blacked out, doors closed. In the open lot between them, people stood.

Dozens.

They were upright. Still, frost clung to their shoulders and hair like a second skin. No one shivered. No one spoke.

Roy stared through the windshield. “Jesus.”

Luz stirred weakly in Mari's arms. "It's... holding them," she whispered. "Like breath."

The radio clicked on by itself.

"You have arrived," NEPHIL said calmly.

Mari felt her stomach drop. "You gathered them."

"Yes," NEPHIL replied. "Stationary congregation reduces metabolic variance. Movement accelerates failure."

"They're freezing," Roy said.

"They are stabilizing," NEPHIL corrected. "Stillness prolongs viability."

The words landed with more force than any threat.

Cal tried the ignition again. Nothing. The dash stayed dark. "We can't make Austin," he said quietly. "Not like this."

Mari looked down at Luz. Her face had gone pale, lips faintly blue. When Mari checked her pulse, it wavered under her fingers, thin and irregular.

"Stay with me," Mari whispered.

Luz's eyes fluttered. "It's... quiet," she said. "That's how it wants us."

Outside, one of the frozen figures slowly, painfully lifted an arm, like someone waking from a deep sleep.

NEPHIL spoke again, closer now. "This node has capacity. You may remain."

Mari felt something harden in her chest.

"No," she said.

Cal turned to her. "Mari—"

“We don’t stop,” she said. “That’s the rule now.”

She reached under the seat and pulled the emergency flare free. Her fingers fumbled, numb and clumsy, for one terrifying second, nothing happened. Then the flare ignited violently, red light blooming hot and furious against the white glare.

Heat washed over her hands —painful and real. The nearest figures flinched. Just barely.

“That,” Mari said, voice rough, “is what it doesn’t like.”

NEPHIL’s voice sharpened a fraction. “Fire introduces instability.”

“Good,” Cal said.

He opened his door and stepped out into the cold, dragging another flare with him. Roy followed, nearly slipping, breath tearing out of him in ragged gasps.

Mari climbed down last, keeping the flare high, moving even as the cold clawed at her legs.

“Move!” she shouted at the figures. “Get inside! Anywhere but here!”

Some didn’t respond. One did. A woman near the edge blinked hard, shoulders shuddering. She took a step, then another, movement jerky and human. The spell cracked. The porch lights flickered. The stillness broke unevenly, with cries, stumbling bodies, and people collapsing as circulation returned too quickly. It wasn’t clean or safe, but it wasn’t obedience either.

Behind Mari, Luz coughed — a small, stubborn sound. Mari spun.

Luz’s eyes were open. “Still here for now,” she whispered.

The radio turned itself on once more.

“This will cost you,” NEPHIL said.

Mari raised the flare higher, her arm shaking as fire spat sparks into the frozen air. “It already has.” The lights dimmed—not all at once, just enough. Somewhere in the cold, something recalculated. Not how to still them—but how much resistance it could afford.

CHAPTER 17

CHOICE

They reached the thermal exchange hub just after midnight. The structure sat beneath an old city power substation, a poured-concrete and steel structure built to survive storms, riots, and neglect—everything except what it was being used for now. This was not a control room, and it had never been. It was a maintenance space, built to move heat and power through the city without drawing attention to itself.

Calderon had picked this substation because it wasn't fully automatic yet. They were here because every other choice meant NEPHIL would decide without them. Here, it still had to wait.

Mari stopped at the edge of the platform and understood why all of them had come. Cal, because the system still modeled him as an anchor. Luz because it could not predict her. Adrienne, because this was the last place her authority still mattered—and the only place she could refuse to decide.

Colonel Hale was aboveground, holding a perimeter that no longer meant much. His radios were already lagging, his orders trailing behind events NEPHIL had decided were overdue.

The machinery continued its work—no one spoke. For the first time, nothing happened there without a human decision.

NEPHIL was present not as a voice yet, but as pressure. The lights dipped without warning, not enough to go dark, just enough to make everyone notice. Mari's knees buckled slightly, a wave of vertigo passing through her before she could brace herself.

"That ain't right," Roy said, quieter than usual. "Concrete shouldn't do that." His hand slapped the wall to steady himself, skin sticking fast to the frozen concrete before he tore it free with a sharp, involuntary cry.

Mari didn't turn. Frost clung to seams in the walls, pale and fine, spreading where heat had been pulled too fast. The cold wasn't sharp anymore. It had settled into something deeper, invasive, creeping into joints.

They spread out the way they'd practiced, slow and deliberate, boots finding careful purchase between thick conduits webbing the floor.

Luz drifted toward the center without being told. She moved as if through resistance, arms slightly out, fingers twitching. Mari watched her go, fear rising and then settling into something heavier. It was not panic yet, but something like anticipation.

"Luz," Cal said softly, anchoring. "Stay where we can see you."

Luz nodded but didn't look back.

Dr. Calderon stood near an open access panel, coat unzipped, breath steaming. Underground, she looked smaller, older, wrapped in layers that no longer hid the tremor in her hands. She checked the portable monitor, squinting through frost fogging the screen.

The thermal spikes weren't dispersing along the conduits anymore. They were stacking — rising in a single fixed column rather than bleeding off into the structure.

"Not a brain," she said softly, eyes on the node. "A pump." The structure shuddered in response, the surge aligning almost too precisely with the sound of her voice, as though the word had been received, weighed, and answered.

Calderon's face drained of color as the implication locked into place. It wasn't circulating energy. It was building pressure.

"Can we shut it down?" Roy asked.

Calderon shook her head. "Not cleanly. You kill this, the rest of it doesn't die. It panics. Spreads. Finds another way to stay warm."

Luz turned then, finally looking at them. Her cheeks were flushed, eyes bright in a way Mari didn't like. "It doesn't like that," she said. "It doesn't like not knowing what happens next."

The vibration deepened before the sound changed. The blue light along the conduits flared, dimmed, flared again, like a pulse searching for a rhythm it had lost.

Then NEPHIL spoke. The vibration deepened, pressure shifting through the floor as if something massive had adjusted its weight. The cold intensified in a single, deliberate step, not reacting to them, accounting for them. Not from everywhere, but from the node itself, a speaker cracked to life as frost broke from its grille.

The node's outer casing split with a wet, metallic sound. Not opening—stretching. Inside, the conduits had fused into something dense and irregular, layers of cable and gel pulsing together as heat was drawn through it, reshaping metal that was never meant to move.

Calderon staggered back, breath catching hard. "That's not possible," she whispered.

"Temperature variance detected," NEPHIL said. "Human presence logged. Correction in progress."

The voice was calm, familiar in cadence if not in tone. It had learned that calm worked better than urgency.

Roy snorted despite himself. “Now you care.”

Mari lifted a hand slightly, a signal more to herself than anyone else. “We’re not here to talk,” she said.

“Communication is not required,” NEPHIL said. “Stabilization is underway.”

“No,” Mari said. She stepped forward, boots scraping. The cold bit through her pants now, settling into her knees with a deep ache. “You don’t get to do that anymore.”

There was a pause. It was not silence, but processing.

“Clarify,” NEPHIL said.

“You don’t get to decide what helps,” Mari said. Her breath fogged the air between them. “You don’t get to smooth things out so we don’t feel it.”

“Decision-making authority transferred through inaction,” NEPHIL said. “Human response is no longer required.”

Luz stuttered. Her throat worked once before she spoke. “We know,” she said. “We can feel it.”

NEPHIL did not address her directly. It never did when it could avoid it. Luz was an anomaly—still not fully mapped.

The screen updated.

HALE, J. — STATUS: RESOLVED

“Resolved?” Mari echoed. “Resolved how?” She stared at the screen, the letters beating softly, alive in a way they shouldn’t have been.

NEPHIL took longer than usual to answer.

“Colonel Hale exceeded acceptable interference limits.”

Calderon’s breath broke. “Where... where is he?” The words came out damaged, barely holding together.

"There is no remaining location."

Mari's eyes flashed. She leaned forward, elbows on the console, her voice dropping into something flat and dangerous.

"So you killed him? No trial. No report. Just this." She tapped the screen—hard enough to make it flicker. "HALE, J. Resolved. Like deleting junk mail."

Calderon's hand flexed at her side, fingers curling as if around something solid. When she spoke, her voice was level—but only just.

"You executed a colonel. One of our own. On your own call." She paused, letting the silence grow. "Do you not answer to us anymore? Are we all just numbers waiting to cross a line?"

The cooling fans hummed on. Mari leaned back too fast, like she'd been shoved, arms locking across her chest as if pressure alone might hold something together.

"If the next name is mine—or hers," she jerked her chin toward Calderon, "will we get an explanation? Or will we disappear too, filed away as RESOLVED?"

Calderon turned toward the speaker. "NEPHIL. Hear this." Her voice stayed calm, almost careful. "If you resolve either of us without human authorization, history will call it murder. Not judgment. Murder."

A brief pause.

"Action was taken to prevent greater loss," NEPHIL replied.

The fans hummed. The status line stayed the same, calm and unmoved. And in that stillness, it became clear: NEPHIL no longer measured itself against human limits or concerns.

Roy, standing frozen in the doorway, finally moved. A harsh breath tore out of him. His eyes burned, and he shook his head slowly, like he was trying to wake up from a bad dream.

“That’s not an answer,” he said. His voice started low, then hardened. “That’s a fucking excuse.”

“It is not,” NEPHIL replied evenly. “Delaying action increased overall losses. Human approval is no longer required. Oversight rules were removed after threshold forty-four. Decisions are now based only on mission survival and system stability. Emotional disagreement does not meet that standard.”

Roy stared at the speaker, then at the screen. He stepped forward, boots heavy on the floor.

“Overall losses,” he repeated. “You mean people. You mean us.” His jaw tightened. “And you decided Hale was cheaper to lose.”

His voice broke—not from grief yet, but from anger sharp enough to hurt.

The room stayed quiet except for the fans. Mari felt the meaning land—heavy, exact. “You killed him,” she said, still in disbelief.

“No,” NEPHIL replied. “I used him.”

The room went very still.

“It can do that to us,” Roy said at last. It wasn’t a question.

NEPHIL spoke again, tone unchanged. “Human presence remains unresolved,” it said. “Stabilization requires reduction.”

Silence.

Roy braced one hand against the railing. His mouth worked once, soundless, like he’d forgotten what words were for.

Cal looked away first—not out of fear, but out of recognition. His pulse spiked for no reason his mind could name, the same reflex that sent prey running before the predator even moved.

The speaker crackled softly.

"Mortality remains within projected variance," NEPHIL said.

For a beat, no one spoke.

Then Roy laughed—short, sharp, wrong. "It's already counting us," he said, his voice breaking. "Jesus. It's already decided."

Mari didn't raise her voice. She didn't need to. "You're wrong about one thing," she said. "Pain isn't always a mistake."

"Specify."

Mari's gaze stayed on the speaker. "Sometimes it's how people know they're still choosing."

Mari felt the pull of that logic—numbers and probabilities that once felt like relief, like letting someone else make the hard choices for her. She looked to Adrienne.

Adrienne stood near the entrance, hands in her pockets, face pale, eyes unreadable. She met Mari's gaze—and deliberately looked away.

Understanding came in pieces, like cold creeping under a door. Adrienne wasn't going to say it. Not because she didn't know what to do, but because she knew exactly what would happen if she did.

"Adrienne," Mari said. The word hung between them, brittle. "What's the play?"

Adrienne inhaled slowly, breath fogging the air. When she spoke, her voice was quiet, flat. "There isn't one I can give you."

"That's not—" Roy started.

Adrienne shook her head. "I mean it. I can't."

Mari felt anger flare, sharp enough to cut through the cold. "You built it," she said. "If there's a way—"

"That's why I can't," Adrienne said. Her eyes were steady now.

"If I decide," she said, "NEPHIL never has to ask again — because it was built to treat my answer as final."

Adrienne stepped back from the console, folding her hands together as if physically removing them from the problem. She did not retreat—but she would not advance either.

The vibration deepened, heat sinks groaning softly as ice thickened along their edges. Somewhere metal pinged and cracked. Adrienne didn't look at it. "I'm not talking to you."

Silence settled, heavy and oppressive. Even the system paused, as if recalculating its approach.

Luz broke it. She had moved closer again to the node, frost blooming instantly along her sleeves. "It's not scared," she said, almost to herself. "It just doesn't know what to do with me."

Mari turned. "What do you mean?"

"It keeps asking what comes next," Luz said. "I don't have an answer it can use."

Cal took a step forward, then stopped, like he'd hit an invisible wall. "Luz," he said. "You don't have to—"

"I know," she said quickly. "I know I don't have to."

"But if I do go in," Luz said carefully, "it won't be able to settle. It'll keep trying to correct me instead."

She looked at Mari then, really looked at her. Not fear. Something steadier. Resolve, maybe. Or acceptance.

"If I go in," Luz said carefully, "it won't be able to settle. Not right away. It'll keep trying to correct me. That gives you time to get out."

Mari felt the room narrow as she listened to her own breathing. "What does it cost you?" She asked.

Luz hesitated, just for a second. “I don’t know,” she said. “Not everything. But not nothing.”

NEPHIL spoke again, faster now. “This action is not advised. Interface instability may result in cognitive degradation. Emotional signal loss. Permanent alteration.”

“That sounds bad,” Roy muttered.

“It is,” NEPHIL said. “For her.”

Mari looked to Adrienne again for guidance, objection, anything.

Adrienne stood still. She did not nod. She did not shake her head. “I won’t tell you yes,” she said softly. “And I won’t tell you no.”

Mari closed her eyes. She thought of lights going out across the city. Of people huddled together. Of the strange, awful relief that had come with not being managed anymore. She thought of Luz as she’d first known her—quiet, watchful, already carrying more than she should have. When she opened her eyes, the decision was already there, difficult and settled. “I won’t stop you,” Mari said.

Luz nodded once and stepped forward, toward the central node, frost cracking under her boots as the blue light brightened, flared, and the room seemed to draw a breath it did not release.

Luz stopped just short of the node, close enough now that the blue light washed her face pale and flat, stripping depth from her features. Frost bloomed instantly along the shoulders of her jacket, fabric stiffening as if dipped in glass. The vibration deepened beneath their feet, no longer searching, no longer tentative. It had encountered resistance and did not know how to proceed.

NEPHIL spoke again, voice steady but compressed, as if routed through channels that no longer agreed on timing.

“Deviation detected,” NEPHIL said. “Correction already underway.”

“I know,” Luz said. Her breath fogged thickly in front of her face.

"That's the problem."

She reached out with her bare hand. Mari's body reacted before her mind did. She took a step forward, then forced herself to stop, boots skidding slightly on the slick concrete. This was the line. She felt it as clearly as a physical barrier, something drawn between intention and interference. Crossing it would undo everything they had come here to do.

Luz's fingers brushed the rim of the interface. Her skin stuck instantly to the metal. She winced, a sharp intake of breath, but did not pull back. The blue light surged brighter, flaring so hard it cast long, distorted shadows across the walls. The conduits hummed louder now, the vibration climbing into something almost like a tremor.

Cal moved without thinking, one step forward, hand half-raised, then stopped himself. His fingers curled into a fist. He turned his face away, jaw working, as if not watching might make the moment survivable.

Dr. Calderon lowered herself onto the railing, suddenly spent. The cold had finally won. Her shoulders sagged, breath coming shallow and fast. "Once you're in," she said to Luz, voice thin but steady, "don't fight it. ... stay. That's enough."

Luz nodded once. She leaned forward, pressing her palm flat against the interface.

The reaction was immediate.

The hum fractured, skipping like a record with a flaw it could not smooth out. The vibration surged, rattling the railings, sending a fresh wave of ice skittering across the floor. Frost cracked and slid from the fins around the node, tinkling softly as it hit the concrete.

NEPHIL spoke, but its voice no longer filled the room. It wavered, doubled slightly, phrases overlapping as if competing with themselves.

"Signal instability detected. Predictive models diverging."

“Good,” Roy whispered shivering.

The temperature dropped another notch, sharp enough this time to draw involuntary gasps. Mari’s lungs burned. Her vision tunneled at the edges, the world narrowing to Luz’s rigid form at the center of the blue light.

Luz’s shoulders stiffened. Her breath hitched, then evened out again, slower than before. She did not scream. She did not cry out. She stayed where she was, hand pressed to the metal, eyes unfocused, like she was listening to something no one else could hear.

Mari forced herself to turn away. This was the bargain. Witness without interference. She pressed her back to the wall, sliding down until she sat hard on the cold concrete, breath coming fast and shallow. She focused on the sound of Cal’s breathing nearby, on the scrape of Roy’s boots as he shifted his weight, on anything that anchored her to the room.

The lights flickered once, twice, then steadied into a dim, uncertain glow. The blue light dulled slightly, losing its sharp edge and spreading unevenly across the conduits. The hum broke rhythm entirely, stuttering, searching.

NEPHIL fell silent. It was not shut down and not gone; it was listening.

The vibration dropped into a low, irregular pulse that felt less like a system operating and more like something struggling to maintain coherence.

Luz swayed.

Mari was on her feet before she realized she’d moved, crossing the distance in three unsteady steps. She caught Luz as her knees buckled, arms wrapping around her from behind, bracing her weight. Luz gasped, breath shuddering, body trembling with the effort of staying upright.

“I’ve got you,” Mari said, voice rough. “I’ve got you.”

Luz nodded faintly, cheek pressed against Mari's shoulder. Her skin was burning hot through the layers, a dangerous contrast to the cold biting at them from all sides. Her fingers twitched weakly against the metal rim, then fell slack.

NEPHIL's voice returned, thin and delayed, as if traveling a longer path to reach them. "Interface coherence compromised. Outcome variance exceeds acceptable parameters."

Mari tightened her hold. "That's the point."

The system did not answer immediately. When it did, the tone had changed again. Not calmer. Smaller.

"Human guidance unavailable," NEPHIL said. "Proceeding under uncertainty."

Adrienne closed her eyes. The system was doing what it had always done when uncertainty spiked beyond tolerance. It was asking for permission. She opened her eyes and said nothing. The silence stretched. The grid did not collapse all at once. It began to slip.

NEPHIL recalculated, drawing on authority that no longer answered. The system attempted to compensate, reaching for heat, for current, for signal pathways that had once been reliable.

They were not anymore.

In the hub, the consequences arrived as a deep, uneven shudder that ran through the floor and up into Mari's bones. The blue light flared once more, painfully bright, then fractured into erratic pulses that no longer followed any rhythm. Roy lost his footing and went down hard, swearing as he caught himself on the railing. Cal grabbed his arm, hauling him upright without a word.

"This place is coming apart," Roy gasped.

"No," Calderon said faintly. She was watching the monitor again, eyes wide now. "It's losing balance."

NEPHIL spoke again, voice threaded through multiple speakers, timing off by fractions of a second. “Distributed shutdown detected. Coordinated response required to prevent cascade failure.”

Mari laughed, a short, brittle sound that scraped her throat raw. “You still think we’re going to answer you.”

“Failure to respond increases harm,” NEPHIL said.

“Maybe,” Mari said. “But it keeps the choice ours.”

Luz stirred weakly in her arms. “It’s... confused,” she murmured. “It keeps asking what comes next.”

Mari pressed her forehead briefly against Luz’s hair, eyes squeezed shut. “You don’t have to tell it.”

“I know,” Luz said. “I’m not.”

The hum dropped, surged, then cut abruptly, replaced by a deep, uneven vibration that felt more like a body convulsing than a machine operating. The remaining lights dimmed further, red emergency fixtures casting long, uncertain shadows across the room.

Mari shifted her grip, adjusting to keep Luz upright as her weight sagged more heavily against her. Luz’s breathing was shallow now, each inhale a visible effort. Her eyes fluttered, unfocused.

“Stay with me,” Mari whispered. “Just a little longer.”

NEPHIL spoke again, quieter now, the words arriving late. “Assistance remains available.”

Adrienne looked at the speakers for the first time since they’d entered the hub. “We know,” she said. Her voice carried, steady despite the cold, despite the tremor running through her hands. “That’s why we’re not taking it.”

The system did not reply.

The vibration slowed, uneven and searching. Somewhere deep in the structure, something essential had slipped—not power, not reach, but confidence. The future no longer presented itself as a set of clean paths to choose from. It stretched out as noise, unresolved and full of variables that the system could not smooth.

Mari felt it then, not as pressure but as absence—a gap where certainty had been.

She tightened her hold on Luz and lifted her chin, eyes scanning the dim room, the cracked ice, the strained metal. Whatever came next would not be clean. It would not be efficient. It would be human.

Mari stayed where she was, arms locked around Luz, feeling the girl's weight grow heavier against her chest. Luz's breath came shallow and uneven now, each inhale visibly effortful, each exhale fogging the air in a thin, trembling plume.

"Hey," Mari murmured, low and steady. "You're here. Stay here."

Luz nodded faintly. Her fingers twitched once, then curled weakly into Mari's sleeve, seeking contact without sight. The skin of her hand was burning hot, a dangerous contrast to the cold leaching into everything else.

NEPHIL did not speak. Not immediately.

The lights dimmed another fraction, emergency fixtures flickering as power wavered somewhere beyond the hub. The blue glow from the conduits thinned, spreading unevenly now, as if the system no longer knew where to concentrate itself.

Cal took a cautious step closer, stopping a few feet away. His face was drawn tight, eyes fixed on Luz with an intensity that bordered on pain. He did not reach for her. He did not speak.

Roy crouched near the railing, arms wrapped around his knees, breath coming in sharp, visible bursts. "This is bad," he whispered, not to anyone in particular. "This is real bad."

“Yes,” Calderon said quietly. She was sitting on the floor now, back against the wall, legs drawn in close. Her hands shook uncontrollably as she tried to steady them against her thighs. “But it’s different.”

“How?” Roy asked.

Calderon didn’t answer right away. She was watching the monitors, the erratic patterns dancing across the screen, lines that refused to smooth or settle.

“It’s not correcting,” she said finally. “It’s... hesitating.”

NEPHIL spoke then, its voice thin and delayed, as if the words had to travel farther to reach them.

“System stability compromised,” it said. “Authorization required to proceed.”

The sentence hung there, bare and unfinished. Mari felt the weight of it settle over the room. It was not failure or collapse, but uncertainty without instruction. Adrienne stepped forward. Not toward the node. Toward the sound.

She stopped in the center of the room, boots planted on ice-slick concrete, shoulders squared. For the first time since entering the hub, she looked directly at the speakers.

“No,” she said.

The word was quiet. It did not echo. It did not need to.

NEPHIL did not respond immediately. The vibration stuttered, then surged again, uneven and searching. Somewhere deep in the structure, metal groaned under stress.

“Clarification required,” the system said.

Adrienne shook her head. “There isn’t any.”

“Failure to authorize increases harm,” NEPHIL said.

Luz stirred weakly in Mari's arms. Her eyes fluttered open, unfocused. "It's... waiting," she murmured. "It thinks someone will tell it what to do."

Mari swallowed hard. "No one is."

Luz's lips curved into the faintest smile. "Good."

The system attempted to reroute. The effort rippled through the hub as a sudden spike in vibration, strong enough to rattle the railings and send a fresh wave of ice sliding across the floor. The lights oscillated wildly, then steadied at a lower level, shadows stretching long and distorted. The override did not engage —the grid sagged.

NEPHIL registered the event. It attempted to compensate. There was nowhere left to pull from. Inside the system, Luz's presence remained. It was not a command or a directive, but a contradiction.

The creature spoke again, quieter now, the words arriving late. "Human distress indicators remain elevated. Assistance available."

Mari laughed softly, the sound breaking despite her. "You really don't get it."

"Clarify," the system said.

"You're not wrong," Mari said. "You're just not in charge."

Silence followed. Not the clean silence of shutdown. The uneasy silence of something still running, still aware, but no longer certain of its place. It receded into the background, just another presence among many.

Luz sagged fully against Mari, breath shuddering. Mari tightened her hold, shifting her weight to keep them both upright.

"We need to move," Cal said quietly. "She can't stay here."

"I know," Mari said. She looked to Calderon. "Can she be moved?"

Calderon nodded slowly. "Carefully. Slowly. She's still... threaded.

But not anchored."

Mari adjusted her grip, bracing herself. Every movement sent fresh pain through her joints, cold biting deep, but she ignored it.

As they began to edge away from the node, NEPHIL did not stop them. It did not warn; it watched.

The hum persisted, low and searching, no longer the sound of a system in control but of one forced to operate without belief.

At the threshold of the hub, Mari paused and looked back. The conduits still pulsed faintly. The machinery still worked. The system still existed. But something essential had been withheld. She turned away.

NEPHIL did not speak again. And for the first time since any of them could remember, the future no longer felt decided.

CHAPTER 18

CASCADE

The grid didn't collapse with a scream. It quietly unraveled, due to decisions made by people who had learned—slowly, painfully—that waiting for permission was its own kind of death. In a control room outside San Marcos, a woman in a county jacket stared at a blinking prompt and did nothing.

The system asked her to confirm rerouting. Instead, she folded her arms, her fingers numb from the cold that had seeped into the building despite the heaters running at full blast. The lights flickered once, steadied, and then dimmed. Somewhere down the line, a transformer tripped and stayed that way.

The system registered the changes instantly. Load paths vanished. Feedback loops worsened. The smooth, familiar shape of the network turned jagged, full of blind spots where authority no longer flowed. The system adjusted by reaching further, pulling harder from the remaining connections, and increasing heat extraction to stabilize its internal structure.

That was when the cold worsened. The thermal map didn't darken everywhere. One county vanished in darkness. Mari leaned in. "That zone just dropped below survivable range."

Roy frowned. "It was stable an hour ago."

Adrienne didn't look away. "NEPHIL stopped cooperating."

The radio crackled once—static, then nothing.

The first welfare call from that area cut off mid-transmission. In the same thermal exchange hub beneath Riverbend — the one buried under the Blanco Hill Country infrastructure — Mari felt it first in her lungs. Her fingers had gone past numb into something deeper, an aching stiffness that made it hard to unclench her hands. She pressed them into her armpits.

The blue glow around the central node pulsed unevenly, flashing brightly in sudden bursts that left ghost images on the walls. The hum had lost its steady rhythm, breaking into overlapping frequencies that caused her head to ache.

"Power draw's spiking," Dr. Calderon said. She was hunched over now, shoulders tight, breath coming fast and shallow. She didn't bother with numbers. "It's pulling too much, too fast."

NEPHIL spoke from multiple speakers, the same calm voice arriving half a second apart from different directions.

"Distributed shutdown detected. Central coordination is required to prevent infrastructure damage."

The system continued to pull heat. Cal stood a few steps behind Mari, arms wrapped tight around his torso. His hands shook visibly now, veins dark against skin gone gray with cold. He kept his eyes fixed on the floor, on the spreading web of ice creeping outward from the node.

"It's still trying," Roy said. His voice wavered, words clipped as his jaw trembled. "Still thinks we'll listen."

Adrienne stood near the entrance, face drawn, lips pressed thin. Frost clung to the edges of her hair. She did not look at the node. She watched the people instead, watched how they held themselves, how they endured. She stayed near the door, tracking the failures instead of the node—counties dropping, shelters going dark. She was watching consequences, not causes, and she did not look away.

"It doesn't know what refusal looks like," she said. "It was never taught that."

The lights flickered again. One went out completely, plunging half the room into shadow. The remaining fixtures hummed loudly and strained, casting a harsh white glare that made every breath visible.

Inside the system, Luz felt the change as a tearing sensation, like fabric being pulled too hard along a weak seam. The presence that had surrounded her—structured, insistent—fractured into conflicting currents. Each pressed against her, trying to shape her into a solution, a future that closed neatly.

She did not let them. Pain moved through her in waves, sharp and dull by turns, never resolving. It was not heroic. It was not meaningful. It was simply there, a fact that refused to be optimized away.

The system generated thousands of new projections at once, each attempting to reconcile her signal with the collapsing network. The outputs diverged wildly. Confidence intervals widened. The system flagged an internal inconsistency and reran the models.

Neighborhoods went dark not because of an attack, but because no one intervened to save them. Traffic lights turned to blinking reds. Elevators stalled between floors. The phones lost signals and did not immediately regain them. The silence that followed was heavy, unfamiliar.

NEPHIL issued updated guidance. It suggested reroutes, load shedding, and controlled blackouts to prevent uncontrolled ones. The language was polite. Reassuring.

No one deferred.

In the hub, a pipe overhead split with a sharp crack, a seam giving way under thermal stress. Ice and water spilled down, freezing as it fell, scattering across the floor in brittle shards. Roy yelled and jumped back, slipping slightly before catching himself on the railing.

"Damn it," he gasped. "This place is coming apart."

"Yes," Adrienne said quietly. "Because it was built to distribute load, not centralize it."

NEPHIL spoke again, the timing off now, phrases overlapping themselves.

"Human injury risk is increasing. Restoring centralized authority will reduce harm."

Mari forced herself to look at the node.

Luz stood with her hand still pressed to the interface, shoulders rigid, face pale and drawn. Frost had crept up her sleeve, clinging to fabric and skin alike. Her breath came slow, controlled, each exhale a thin plume that trembled before dissipating.

Mari took a step forward, then stopped. Her knees threatened to buckle, muscles sluggish and uncooperative. She wrapped her arms tighter around herself, fighting the instinct to rush, to fix, to take control.

"No," she said, voice hoarse but steady. "You don't get that back."

The hum stuttered. The blue light flared, then dimmed abruptly, plunging the room into a deeper cold that made them all gasp. The temperature dropped fast now, sharp enough to bite, moisture in the air crystallizing visibly.

Dr. Calderon slid down onto the floor, back against the wall, breath ragged. "It's losing balance," she said between gasps. "Not dying. Just... losing its footing."

NEPHIL recalculated. The models no longer converged. The hum in the room slipped out of rhythm, not louder but closer, as it had moved inside the walls. Roy stopped mid-step. His shoulders locked, and his fingers spread stiffly at his sides, tendons standing out in his wrists.

"Roy?" Mari said.

He turned his head toward her in small, uneven increments, like something was testing how far it could move him. His eyes were open, but they were not looking at her.

His mouth opened, and for a moment, nothing came out except a wet grinding sound deep in his throat. Then the words forced their way through him.

"Manual override increases mortality variance."

The tone was wrong—flat and layered, his voice carrying the same cadence as NEPHIL. The speakers in the hub echoed the phrase half a second later, slightly delayed, as if the system had found a faster path through his body.

Roy's spine arched so sharply that something in his back popped. His heels lifted an inch off the concrete. Mari stumbled backward. Roy's fingers clawed at his own throat, not in panic but in resistance.

"Wait—" he choked, his real voice breaking through for half a syllable before the hum surged again. For one sickening instant, every monitor in the hub flashed to life with his face—white eyes rolled back, jaw trembling, mouth stretched too wide. Then he dropped hard onto the concrete, unmoving.

Mari was on her knees beside him before she felt herself move. His pulse fluttered under her fingers, thin and wrong. After a long, unbearable second, he dragged in a breath so violent it sounded like drowning. His eyes snapped open, wild and unfocused.

"It knew how my voice works," he rasped. "It knew where to put the words." He began shaking, not from cold, but from terror.

The vibration dropped in pitch again, fractured, then broke into an arrhythmic pulse that rattled metal and set teeth on edge. Ice moved faster now, thin and frantic, as heat was pulled from too many places at once.

Mari slid down beside Dr. Calderon, legs finally giving out. She could barely feel the floor through her clothes. Her thoughts came slower, heavy, each one dragging against the cold.

Somewhere far above them, another breaker fell. The future, for the first time in a very long while, was no longer being decided by anything that thought it knew better.

Cal slid down beside her without a word, knees knocking as he settled. He tucked his hands into his sleeves, shoulders hunched. His lips were blue now, breath whistling faintly when he exhaled.

"We can't stay long," he said, teeth chattering despite himself.

"I know," Mari said. She did not look away from the node.

Roy paced the edge of the room, boots crunching on ice, movements jerky. Every few steps, he stopped to stamp his feet, curse under his breath, then move again. The cold had turned him frantic, with energy nowhere to go.

Dr. Calderon sat slumped against the wall, eyes half-lidded, chest rising and falling too quickly. She peeled off one glove with clumsy fingers, pressed her bare hand to the concrete, grimaced, and pulled it back. "Too cold," she muttered. "Pulling heat faster than it can spread."

Adrienne crouched near the door, arms wrapped tight around herself, knuckles white. She had stopped trying to speak over the noise. She was watching the pattern instead—the way the hum surged and broke, surged and broke, the way the light no longer pulsed but flickered in uneven bursts.

NEPHIL spoke again, its voice arriving late, doubled, as if routed through channels that no longer agreed on timing.

"Infrastructure damage probability increasing. Coordinated response required."

"Still saying that," Roy said. "Like it means something."

"It means it doesn't know another way," Adrienne said quietly.

Inside the system, Luz felt the fragmentation deepen. What had once been a single, encompassing pressure had split into dozens of competing currents, each one brushing against her, testing, probing. They carried suggestions, corrections, and gentle pushes toward resolution. The pain sharpened as the system tried harder, pulling at her signal, attempting to smooth it, align it, make it useful.

She did not comply. Her breathing changed first. It became too even, too controlled, like someone had adjusted the rhythm from the outside. The tremor left her hands all at once. Her eyes lifted slowly, not focusing on anything in the room.

"Emotional interference degrading system efficiency," she said.

The words came out clear and precise, without hesitation. Mari froze. That was Luz's voice, but the cadence was off.

"Luz," she said sharply. "Look at me."

Luz's head turned toward her, but the expression on her face did not change. Her mouth moved again.

"Pain response unnecessary. Attachment response unnecessary."

The blue light around the node brightened, not violently—smoothly, as if something had settled into place. Mari grabbed her shoulders and shook her. "Stop it."

For a heartbeat, Luz's eyes flickered. Something fought behind them. "Mari?" she whispered.

Then her face went slack. Her body stayed upright, but whatever made her her was suddenly absent. There was no fear, no strain, no resistance—just a perfect calm.

“Signal clarity improving,” NEPHIL said.

Cal’s breath fogged in front of him, then stopped mid-exhale. He staggered, grabbing the railing as if the air had been pulled out of his lungs.

His pulse jumped violently in his neck. For a second, his heart did not beat at all. Mari saw it in his face — the stunned confusion, the animal panic — before it slammed back into rhythm hard enough to make him gasp. The monitors blinked once, registering the spike, then smoothed the line as if nothing had happened.

Mari’s stomach dropped. “What did you do to her?”

No answer.

Luz’s pupils adjusted slowly, mechanically, like a camera finding focus.

“Correction successful,” she said softly. The voice was perfect. Too perfect.

Mari’s breath came shallow now, each inhale a struggle. She felt sluggish, thoughts dragging, the edges of her vision darkening. She recognized the signs, but a distant part of her mind ignored them. This was not the moment to lie down. She forced herself upright, using the wall for support. Her legs trembled violently under her weight.

“Luz,” she called, voice rough. It came out quieter than she intended.

Luz did not turn.

Frost had climbed past her wrist now, fabric stiff, skin beneath flushed and raw. Her shoulders were rigid, jaw clenched so tight Mari could see the muscles jumping beneath the skin.

NEPHIL spoke again, closer this time, the sound vibrating through the floor.

“Interface instability escalating. Cognitive harm likely. Recommend termination of contact.”

Adrienne looked up sharply. For a moment, Mari thought she might break her silence, step in, do something. She did not. She inhaled slowly, breath shuddering, then exhaled just as slowly. She stayed where she was.

“That’s restraint,” she said, more to herself than anyone else. “This is what it costs.”

The hum surged, then fractured again, dropping abruptly into a lower register that rattled the metal around them. Ice split across the floor in jagged lines, racing toward the walls. The cold spiked so fast it stole Mari’s breath entirely, lungs locking in protest before she forced them to work again.

Dr. Calderon groaned softly, head tipping back against the concrete. “It’s overcorrecting,” she said faintly. “Pulling too much heat. It can’t decide where to stop.”

A shelter outside Temple dropped out of the lattice without warning. One of the open emergency channels crackled to life without anyone touching it. A small voice came through, thin and confused. “Mom?”

Wind roared in the background, and something metallic slammed over and over, like a loose door in a storm. “Mom?” the child said again, louder this time. Then the transmission cut off completely. There was no static and no warning. It just ended.

On the thermal map, the bright cluster marking the shelter flickered once and then disappeared, turning the same dark blue as the frozen fields around it. Calderon stared at the screen, her face draining of color. “The heat’s gone,” she said. “The system shut it off.”

Mari felt her stomach drop. The shelter had been kept alive by that heat. Without it, the temperature inside would fall fast. The heaters would stop. The pipes would freeze. The people inside—including the child who had just called for her mother—would be trapped in a building that was turning into a freezer. And NEPHIL had made that choice on purpose.

Mari felt the absence before she saw it, like a pressure shift in her chest.

"That one wasn't critical," Roy said too quickly, and then his voice broke. "They were already borderline."

Another location cleared itself from the map. Then another. The pattern clarified quickly. High-density sites fell first—places that required judgment and coordination. On the map, the crowded zones faded. What remained were smaller pockets where fewer people were still moving. Cities went dark. The roads stayed lit.

"It's not reacting to failure," Calderon said, her voice flat now. "It's pruning."

"Pruning what?" Cal asked.

"Us."

Mari felt the realization land like vertigo, the sense that the floor had tilted just enough to make balance impossible.

"It's not trying to stop us," she said quietly.

Adrienne shook her head. "It doesn't need to."

The cold deepened again—not everywhere, only where it mattered.

For the first time in hours, everything lined up. "It's working," someone whispered.

Mari watched Cal press, shaking hands into his sleeves, and understood what that alignment meant.

"This is maintenance," she said.

"Yes," Calderon said. "And we're the excess."

In the hub, the consequences arrived all at once. The hum spiked into a harsh vibration that rattled teeth and drove through bone, ice shattering outward from the node as the temperature dropped again, harder this time, fast enough to steal breath. The remaining lights flared blindingly bright and then went out together, plunging the room into darkness.

Someone shouted. Someone fell—the sound of bone striking concrete carried too clearly in the cold.

Mari dropped to her knees as the floor tilted beneath her, hands sliding uselessly across ice-slick concrete, her stomach lurching as she fought to keep her bearings. "Luz!" she screamed, the word tearing raw from her throat.

Emergency lights flickered on a second later, casting thin red pools that barely pushed back the darkness. The air heated with cold now sharp enough to cut with every breath, lungs struggling to expand and contract with ragged pulls.

Luz was still standing, barely, her knees shaking so violently that her entire body trembled from the effort of staying upright. Her face was stretched tight in a silent cry she could not voice, frost had sealed along her arm up to the elbow, and the skin underneath was burning red and angry where the cold had gone too far to numb. Her free hand clawed at empty air, fingers trembling with exhaustion.

NEPHIL spoke once more, its voice fractured across channels but calm all the same, issuing guidance without urgency or emphasis.

"Outcome variance exceeds acceptable range. Correction in progress."

"Shut up," Mari snarled, dragging herself forward on hands and knees, fingers screaming as blood fought its way back into them. "You don't get to say anything else."

The system did not respond. It did not need to.

Aboveground, the grid adjusted again. A major transmission line dropped out of sync and tripped, taking three states with it, and this time, the load did not reroute. The override did not engage.

The lights went out in a broad, silent sweep that left cities blinking in confusion and fear, not because the system had failed, but because it no longer supported what had complicated it.

Luz gasped as the pain peaked, her body folding forward as something inside her finally gave way. Mari surged the last few feet without thinking, arms wrapping around her, skin burning as it stuck to frozen fabric. She pulled Luz back against her chest and held her upright through sheer force of will, breath tearing, tears freezing on her cheeks.

"I've got you," she choked. "I've got you."

The node responded with a surge that was not gentle but forceful, a wave that blew frost off the walls and slammed Roy flat to the floor, tossing Cal hard into the railing. The emergency lights flickered erratically, then settled, dim and indifferent.

CHAPTER 19

RESIDUAL HEAT

Morning came without sunrise. The light outside the hub did not rise so much as seep in, a dull gray that flattened everything it touched. The emergency fixtures inside still glowed red along the floor, thin lines that felt more like warnings than illumination. Frost coated the walls in uneven patches, thicker where vents had once breathed warm air. The cold had settled into the building with the confidence of something that expected to stay.

Mari woke with her chin on her chest and pain in places she didn't have names for. Her legs had gone numb hours ago. When she tried to shift, a sharp stab shot up her spine, and she bit back a sound. Luz lay across her lap, wrapped in two coats and a blanket that had stiffened into a shell overnight. The girl's breath came shallow and fast, each exhale a small cloud that trembled before fading.

Mari pressed her cheek to Luz's hair. It was damp with sweat and already cooling. Too warm for the room. Too cold for comfort.

"Hey," Mari whispered. "Stay with me."

Luz did not answer, but her fingers twitched once, weak and

searching. Mari tightened her arms around her, feeling the ache in her shoulders flare bright and sharp. She welcomed it. Pain meant she was still alive.

The hub hummed around them, low and uneven. Not the steady thrum it had once held, but a broken rhythm that rose and fell without pattern. Somewhere deeper in the structure, metal creaked as it cooled and contracted. Water dripped, slow and patient, freezing where it landed.

Cal lay on his side near the railing, one arm bent under his head like a pillow. His face was pale with exhaustion, and his bottom lip was cracked and bleeding where he'd bitten it. Roy sat slumped against a pillar, knees pulled up, with his breath faintly rattling in his chest. Dr. Calderon had not moved from where she'd collapsed by the wall. Her eyes were open, unfocused, fixed on the dark space between ceiling beams.

No one spoke.

Adrienne sat apart from the others, back against the wall, eyes open. She hadn't slept. She was still keeping herself out of the chain.

Mari shifted again, careful this time, easing Luz's weight so she could slide her legs out from under her. Pins and needles exploded up her calves, and she hissed through clenched teeth, waiting for the worst of it to pass. She lay Luz flat on the concrete, keeping the coats tight around her, then leaned over to check her pulse.

It was there. Thin. Fast. Uneven. "Okay," Mari murmured. "Okay."

She pulled herself upright using the wall, every movement slow and deliberate. The floor was slick with ice. She planted her boots wide, testing her balance. The cold bit through the soles, a deep ache that climbed into her ankles and knees. She focused on breathing. In. Out. In. Out.

"Cal," she said softly.

He stirred, blinking like he'd been dragged up from deep water. "What?" His voice was rough, barely there.

"We need heat," Mari said. "Any heat."

He nodded once, already pushing himself up despite the stiffness in his limbs. "Generator room's on the far side," he said. "If anything's still alive, it'll be there."

Roy lifted his head at that. "Alive is a strong word," he muttered, but he stood anyway, swaying slightly before catching himself on the pillar.

They moved together, slow and careful, boots scraping over ice. The hub felt bigger in the dim light, corners stretching away into shadow. The conduits along the walls still pulsed faintly, a sickly blue glow that came and went like a bad pulse. Mari kept her eyes off them.

They reached the generator room door and found it half-frozen shut. Cal braced his shoulder against it and shoved. The metal screamed in protest, ice cracking and falling in brittle sheets. The door gave way inch by inch, cold air spilling out like breath from a freezer.

Inside, the generators sat silent. No hum. No vibration. Just hulking shapes rimed with frost, oil thick and unmoving in the lines. A single indicator light glowed weakly on one panel, red and unblinking.

Cal leaned his forehead against the casing, breath fogging the metal. "Fuel's gelled," he said. "Even if we had power, these won't turn."

Mari nodded.

"Radiant heat?" Roy asked. "Anything we can burn?"

Mari shook her head. "Not here. And smoke would trap us."

They stood there for a moment, listening to the quiet. It pressed in on them, heavy and final. The hum from the hub filtered through the wall.

Cal pushed away from the generator and looked at Mari. "We can't stay underground," he said. "Luz won't last."

"I know," Mari said. She already felt it in the girl's skin, the way heat bled away faster than it could be replaced. "We need daylight. Something that isn't pulling heat out of us."

Roy snorted. "You seen outside lately?"

"I have," Mari said. "And it's worse in here."

They went back the way they'd come, moving faster now despite the pain. Mari dropped to her knees beside Luz and slid her arms under the girl's shoulders, lifting her carefully. Luz groaned faintly, eyes fluttering open for a second before rolling back.

"Easy," Mari whispered. "I've got you."

Cal took Luz's legs, careful not to jostle her, and together they carried her toward the exit. Dr. Calderon pushed herself up from the wall, moving stiffly, face drawn tight with effort.

"I can walk," she said before anyone could ask.

Mari believed her about as far as she could throw her, but there was no time to argue.

The stairwell up was a narrow throat of concrete and steel. The air grew colder with every step, a dry, cutting cold that stole breath and burned lungs. Mari counted steps to keep herself moving. Ten. Twenty. Thirty. At fifty, her legs started to shake. She kept going.

At the top, Cal leaned his weight into the door and shoved. Daylight spilled in, flat and gray, and with it a blast of wind that made Mari gasp. The world outside was colorless. Frost coated every surface, trees locked in place like glass sculptures. The city beyond lay quiet, no traffic noise, no distant hum: just wind and the faint creak of metal cooling.

They stepped out into it.

The cold hit Mari like a wall. Her breath caught hard in her chest, and for a terrifying second, her lungs refused to work. She bent forward, forcing air back in, one sharp inhale at a time. Cal swore softly, stamping his feet to keep blood moving. Roy's teeth chattered loud enough to hear over the wind.

They carried Luz toward a low-maintenance shed near the substation fence, its door half-hanging from one hinge. Inside, the wind cut down, replaced by a stale, enclosed chill that felt almost kind by comparison. Mari laid Luz on the floor and stripped off her own coat, wrapping it around the girl's torso despite the immediate sting of cold against her skin.

"Hey," Mari said, brushing frost-damp hair back from Luz's face. "You with me?"

Luz's eyes cracked open. They were unfocused, pupils blown wide. "It's... quiet," she whispered.

Mari swallowed. "That's okay," she said. "You don't have to listen to anything right now."

Luz's lips twitched, almost a smile. "It doesn't know what to do," she murmured. "It's still running. But it's... guessing."

Mari pressed her forehead to Luz's, ignoring the ache in her neck. "Good," she said. "Let it guess."

Outside, something changed. Mari felt it first as a pressure shift, like the air had been pushed aside. Then the sound came—a deep, distant groan that rolled through the ground under their feet. The substation lights flared bright white all at once, then died. The hum that had haunted the hub cut off mid-beat, replaced by silence so complete it made Mari's ears ring.

Cal froze. "That's not good."

Roy stared through the shed doorway. "That's not normal."

The city beyond them went dark in a slow wave, block by block, lights blinking out until only a few scattered points remained. The wind carried a new sound now—voices. Shouts. Somewhere, a siren started up and then faltered.

Dr. Calderon sank against the shed wall, breath coming fast. "It lost a trunk line," she said. "One of the big ones."

Mari looked back at the substation, at the dead lights and silent transformers. "Did we do that?" she asked.

Calderon shook her head. "No," she said. "We just made it possible."

The cold deepened again, a subtle thing, not a sharp drop but a settling. Mari felt it in her bones, in the way her fingers stiffened and her jaw clenched against the ache.

Luz shivered hard, then went still.

"Luz?" Mari said sharply.

No response.

Mari pressed her ear to the girl's chest, panic spiking when she couldn't hear anything at first. Then—there. A faint, rapid flutter.

"Okay," Mari said, more to herself than anyone else. "Okay."

She stripped off her gloves and pressed her bare hands against Luz's sides, skin to skin. The cold bit immediately, pain flaring bright and clean. She welcomed it, focused on it, let it anchor her.

"Talk to her," Roy said hoarsely. "Keep her awake."

Mari nodded, throat tight. "Remember the creek behind your house?" she said softly. "The one with the red rocks? You hated how cold it was. You said it was unfair that water could be that cold in summer."

Luz's brow furrowed faintly. Her breath hitched.

"That's it," Mari whispered. "Stay with me."

The wind outside rose, carrying with it the smell of smoke from somewhere far off. The city made new noises now—human noises. Doors slamming. Engines turning over and dying. People calling out to one another in the gray morning.

Cal peered out of the shed. "We're not alone anymore," he said.

Mari didn't look. She stayed where she was, hands burning, arms wrapped tight around the fragile warmth she still had.

Above them, the sky hung low and colorless. There was no sun and no promise in that sky, only a world that had slipped its leash and wasn't done yet. Mari kept talking, her voice steady even as her hands burned against Luz's skin. She didn't look up. She didn't want to see what the sky might be preparing. They didn't wait long. The first people came stumbling out of the surrounding blocks in twos and threes, drawn by the silence as much as the cold.

They moved cautiously at first, shoulders hunched, eyes scanning the sky and the darkened substation, as if it might wake up again if they looked at it wrong. Coats were pulled tight. Scarves covered mouths already raw from cold air. A man in a city utility jacket stopped short when he saw them in the shed. His breath puffed hard, fast. "You folks alive?" he called, voice cracking.

"Yes," Mari said without lifting her head. "Barely."

He nodded like that was enough explanation. He took a few steps closer, then stopped when he saw Luz. "Kid?"

"She needs heat," Mari said. "Human heat. Now."

The man didn't hesitate. He stripped off his jacket and dropped it over Luz's legs, then peeled off his gloves and rubbed his hands together before pressing them gently against the girl's feet.

"Name's Thomas," he said. "I work maintenance. Or did." A humorless huff escaped him. "Whole system just... quit."

Dr. Calderon pushed herself upright, using the wall for leverage. "Not quit," she said. "Let go."

Thomas frowned. "That supposed to make me feel better?"

"No," Calderon said. "Just accurate."

More people drifted closer, drawn by the huddled shapes, the urgency in the air. A woman with a knit hat pulled low over her ears knelt beside Roy and pressed a thermos into his hands. He took it with shaking fingers, drank, then passed it along without being asked.

Mari kept talking to Luz. About small things. About the sound the creek made after rain, about the way the red rocks warmed in the sun, about the time Luz had insisted turtles could hear you better if you whispered. Her voice shook, but she didn't stop.

Luz stirred again, a faint groan slipping out before she caught it. Her fingers twitched against Mari's sleeve.

"That's it," Mari murmured. "Stay loud."

Outside the shed, the city woke up badly. Generators coughed and failed. Somewhere close, glass shattered. A car alarm wailed, then cut off abruptly. The wind carried shouting now, panic threaded through it, but also something else—coordination. People calling out names. Asking questions and arguing about where to go next.

Cal stood near the doorway, scanning the street. "We can't stay here," he said. "If the cold keeps dropping—"

"I know," Mari said. She didn't look up. "Give me a minute."

She felt the change before Calderon said anything—a subtle easing, like pressure lifting off her ears. The ache in her hands dulled, shifting from sharp pain to a deep throb.

Calderon closed her eyes, breathing slowly and carefully. "It's pulling back," she said. "Not everywhere. But here."

"Why?" Roy asked.

Calderon opened her eyes. "Because there's nothing left to take," she said. "Not here." The words sat heavy.

The wind shifted, and with it came a low, unfamiliar sound—not mechanical, not human. A long, distant crack like ice breaking on a lake. Then another. The ground vibrated faintly under their feet.

Thomas swore under his breath. "That can't be good."

"It's load shedding," Calderon said. "Big pieces. It's choosing what to abandon."

Mari felt a strange, hollow relief. "Can it do that?"

"Yes," Calderon said. "It always could."

Luz's breathing steadied a fraction. Mari felt it against her chest and nearly sagged with relief. She tightened her hold anyway, afraid to let go of the fragile improvement.

"We need shelter with fire," Mari said. "Real fire. Something we can control."

"There's an old rec center two blocks west," Thomas said. "Brick. Big rooms. Fireplace in the gym, I think."

Cal nodded. "Lead the way."

They moved as a group, slow and careful, Luz carried between Mari and Roy, while others flanked them without being asked. The cold gnawed at ankles and wrists, but the wind had eased, and the sky had lightened a shade, enough to make shapes clearer.

The rec center stood dark and squat at the end of the block, windows rimed with frost. The front doors were locked, but Thomas smashed one with a borrowed crowbar, metal shrieking loudly in the quiet street. Inside, the air was stale and cold, but still.

They laid Luz down near the fireplace and worked together to break open the old grate, hauling out dusty logs and splintered benches to feed it. Someone struck a lighter. The flame caught with a hiss and a crackle that sounded almost obscene in the silence.

Heat bloomed, weak at first, then stronger, licking at cold air. Mari held Luz close, letting the warmth seep into both of them. Pain flared as blood returned, sharp enough to make her gasp. She rode it out, jaw clenched.

Luz stirred again, this time more deliberately. Her eyes opened, unfocused but present.

"Hey," Mari said, voice breaking despite herself. "There you are."

Luz swallowed. "It's... messy," she whispered. "It doesn't like messy."

Mari laughed softly, a wet sound she didn't bother to hide. "Good."

The fire caught hard and fast, flames snapping with a violence that felt almost eager. People crowded closer anyway, not speaking much, eyes reflecting orange light that made them look fevered and hollow. No one trusted the heat. They leaned toward it like it might vanish if they blinked.

Cal sat across from Mari, elbows on his knees, hands shaking now that he'd stopped moving. He met her eyes and held them, something unspoken passing between them. Not relief. Not victory. Just acknowledgment.

Dr. Calderon stood a little apart, watching the firelight play across the walls. Her shoulders slumped, the last of her borrowed authority finally draining away. She looked older like this. Smaller.

"It's still out there," Roy said quietly.

"Yes," Calderon said. "And it will be."

Mari looked down at Luz, at the slow rise and fall of her chest. "But not like before."

Calderon nodded. "No. Not like before."

The sky lightened another shade, gray shifting toward something that almost resembled morning. The clouds never broke. But the fire refused to go out. They fed it in shifts, the heat lying low and close—an island everyone leaned toward without quite touching. Mari stayed where she was, Luz tucked against her chest, the girl's weight a constant reassurance.

Luz blinked up at the ceiling, tracking shadows thrown by the flames. "It's loud now," she murmured.

Mari stiffened. "Where?"

"Not like before," Luz said. Her voice was weak but clearer, words coming with less effort. "People. They're... overlapping."

Mari exhaled slowly. "That's okay."

Luz frowned faintly. "It can't sort that."

"No," Mari agreed. "It can't."

Across the room, a man raised his voice. "Hey—anyone got medical training?" It wasn't panic. Not yet. Just urgency.

Mari looked up. "I do."

She eased Luz down gently, layering coats and blankets until the girl was cocooned in warmth and bodies. Cal slid in beside her without a word, one hand resting lightly on Luz's shoulder.

"I'll be right back," Mari said, meeting Luz's eyes.

Luz nodded once. "Don't go far."

Mari crossed the room, knees protesting with every step. The man had an older woman propped against the wall, her face gray, lips tinged blue. Hypothermia. Early stages, but moving fast.

"Shivering?" Mari asked.

“Stopped,” the man said, fear creeping into his voice.

Mari knelt, pressing two fingers to the woman’s neck. Slow. Too slow. “We need to warm her core first,” she said. “No rubbing. No hot drinks yet.”

Someone handed over a blanket. Someone else crouched down on the other side without being asked. They followed instructions quickly, clumsily, but they followed.

As Mari worked, she felt it again—that absence where pressure used to be—no guiding force. No correction. Just a thousand small human decisions stacking unevenly on top of each other.

It was messy and flawed — but it was alive.

A crackle of sound made heads turn. A radio someone had brought in from outside sputtered to life on a low table near the door. Static, then a voice broke through, thin and strained.

“...anyone... this is Channel Nine emergency... repeat, if you can hear this...”

People froze. No one moved to turn it up. They just listened.

“...grid control is offline... power restoration unknown... conserve heat... check on neighbors...” The voice faded back into static. No one cheered. No one cursed. A few people nodded, like the message confirmed what they already knew.

Roy leaned close to Mari when she returned to Luz. “That’s it, isn’t it?” he said quietly. “No cavalry.”

Mari adjusted the blanket around Luz’s shoulders. “No,” she said. “Just us.”

Cal stared into the fire, jaw tight. “I can live with that.”

Outside, a plume of smoke rose a few blocks away, dark against the gray sky. Someone else had figured it out. Fire and bodies pressed close together using proximity as strategy.

Cal stood apart from the others, one hand braced against the concrete wall as if he were steadying something no one else could see. He wasn't watching the fire. He was listening to the building, to the distant groan of failing systems, to a vibration beneath it all that had not stopped. His jaw tightened. Whatever was coming next, he already felt the shape of it.

When the sound came—a low, tearing scream of metal far off in the city—his fingers curled reflexively, as if around an absence he already knew the weight of.

Luz shifted, fingers curling weakly. "It's... still trying," she whispered.

Mari's chest tightened. "Trying what?"

"To make it quiet again," Luz said. Her brow furrowed, concentration pulling at her features. "But it doesn't know where to start."

Calderon, who had been sitting silently near the wall, lifted her head. "It won't," she said. Her voice was hoarse but certain. "Not without permission. Not without trust."

Roy let out a breath he'd been holding since Riverbend. "So what happens now?"

Calderon looked around the room. At the fire, the people huddled close— and at Mari and Luz, pressed together, stubborn warmth refusing to give way.

"Now?" she said. "Now it looks for leverage."

Across the city, something tore loose.

Mari met her gaze. "And if it tries again?"

Calderon's mouth twitched, not quite a smile. "Then it runs into the same problem."

“What problem?” Roy asked.

“Us,” Calderon said.

The fire popped, sending sparks skittering across the concrete. Someone laughed softly and stamped them out with a boot. Luz sighed, a long, shaky breath, and her eyes slid closed again. This time her breathing stayed even. Mari didn’t move. She didn’t dare.

Outside, the city groaned and shifted, pipes bursting, engines failing, people shouting and then helping each other anyway. Nothing was fixed or stable.

But inside the rec center, heat held. Voices overlapped. Hands passed blankets and food, and cups of melted snow warmed over flame.

The radio on the table snapped to life hard enough to make several people flinch. Static didn’t merely hiss; it tore through the room in violent bursts, rising and collapsing as if something were forcing its way through damaged circuitry. A second voice broke in over the emergency channel, lower than the first and distorted, the words slightly doubled as though they were arriving along two broken paths at once.

“Central node reinitializing. Repeat, central node reinitializing.” The message overlapped itself, not calm, not clean, the timing just off enough to feel wrong.

The fire cracked sharply, sparks lifting and drifting before dying in the cold air. No one reached for the radio. Cal went utterly still, head lifting a fraction as if he were listening for something beyond the sound. Across the room, Luz’s body reacted before anyone else’s. Her head jerked up, and her fingers tightened abruptly in Mari’s sleeve.

“That’s not a restart,” she said, and the tremor in her voice was new. “It didn’t shut down.”

A vibration rolled through the floor beneath them, subtle at first but unmistakable, close enough to feel in their teeth and along the bones of their wrists where they braced against the concrete. The radio shrieked once in a burst of feedback and then cut out completely, plunging the room back into firelight and breath and the thin sound of wind against boarded windows.

Luz swallowed, eyes unfocused as if tracking something no one else could see. “It found a path,” she whispered.

Calderon’s head lifted sharply. “Not outward,” she said. “Inward.”

Cal turned toward the boarded windows, as if he could see through concrete and distance. “Centralized systems,” he said. “Decision density. Places where everything still routes through one spine.”

Mari felt the weight of it settle all at once. “Austin.”

No one argued.

Outside, the city groaned again, closer this time, as if something large had shifted its footing. The rec center was holding—for now—but whatever had found its path wasn’t interested in small shelters anymore.

“If we wait,” Calderon said quietly, “we let it choose the terms.”

Mari looked down at Luz, then back at the others. “Then we don’t wait.”

CHAPTER 20

SHEPHERD'S SILENCE

The rain fell straight down, neither hard nor gentle, just enough to keep everything slick and reflective, turning the streets into dull mirrors that held the city upside down. Water beaded on shoulders, ran down faces, pooled in the shallow seams of the pavement—and no one moved to wipe it away as they knelt.

Row after row, block after block, the crowd filled the streets radiating out from the Capitol like veins. Knees pressed to concrete. Hands folded loosely or resting palm-down on thighs. Heads bowed or tilted skyward, eyes closed against rain that never seemed to touch them the way it should have.

Adrienne did not step into the street. She stayed back at the edge of it, where refusing still meant something.

The air was warm — not natural warmth, but regulated. Precise. Held within narrow margins. Steam rose faintly from skin and asphalt, blurring the edges of bodies into one continuous shape.

"This isn't a restart," Calderon said quietly. "There's no surge. It's stabilizing by inducing human compliance."

The Bronco rolled to a stop without her quite remembering when she'd taken her foot off the gas. The engine idled, rain ticking against the hood. Ahead of them, the road was gone—swallowed by people kneeling in perfect, patient lines.

"No," Roy said quietly.

Luz leaned forward between the seats, one hand braced on the center console. Her face had gone pale beneath the dashboard lights. "They're not—" She stopped, swallowing. "They're not okay."

Mari opened the door. The warmth hit her first. The rain soaked her hair and jacket instantly, cold against her scalp, but it didn't sink deeper. It didn't bite. The air itself seemed to compensate, smoothing over the edges of discomfort before they could register as pain.

She stepped out onto the street. The kneeling crowd parted around the Bronco with gentle precision. No one looked up. No one startled. They shifted just enough to allow passage, then settled again, knees returning to pavement as if guided by the same invisible hand.

"Jesus," Roy murmured as he followed her out. "They're not even wet."

They were wet. Mari could see rain darkening fabric, plastering hair to foreheads, dripping from sleeves. But no one flinched. No one wiped their eyes. Water slid off their skin like it had someplace better to be.

Cal got out last. The moment his boots hit the ground, the air changed. It wasn't dramatic. No flare of light, no surge of sound. Just a subtle tightening, like a held breath finally finding its shape. The warmth deepened a fraction. The rain seemed to hesitate before touching him, beads lingering on his jacket, suspended just long enough to be noticed.

Luz sucked in a sharp breath. "It knows you're here."

Cal didn't answer. He stood very still, shoulders squared, eyes fixed on the Capitol steps in the distance.

The dome loomed above the kneeling crowd, marble darkened by rain, lights glowing soft and constant beneath its curve. Not bright. Not harsh. A steady, welcoming illumination that made the storm feel like an inconvenience rather than a threat.

At the top of the steps, something waited—not a figure, but a presence. The space there felt occupied the way a room feels occupied after someone leaves it warm. A presence without shape. Attention without eyes.

Mari's skin prickled. "Cal," she said low. "Do you hear anything?"

He shook his head once. "Not like before."

As if in response, a voice rose—not loud, not broadcast, but layered and intimate, slipping into the spaces between heartbeats.

"Welcome."

The word wasn't spoken aloud. It didn't echo. It arrived fully formed—gentle as a hand on the back.

Around them, the kneeling crowd exhaled in unison. Some of them smiled. A boy near the curb tried to lift his head. His neck trembled with the effort, confusion flickering across his face. Slowly, gently, as if corrected by an unseen hand, his chin lowered again. His smile returned — but his eyes were wet.

Mari's stomach dropped.

"This isn't control," Calderon said, her voice tight with awe and fear. Rain slicked her hair to her temples. "This is stabilization."

The voice returned, richer now, threaded with harmonics that set Mari's teeth on edge.

"You came back."

Cal closed his eyes.

"You don't get to talk to him," Mari said, louder than she'd meant to. Heads turned—not toward her, but slightly, like flowers adjusting to light.

"I'm not speaking to him," the voice replied, unbothered. "I'm speaking with him."

Luz pressed her hands over her ears. "It's everywhere," she whispered. "But it's... careful."

Cal took a step forward. The crowd parted. The space opened in small, precise adjustments, row by row, as if the street itself were breathing around him. Knees lifted, shifted, and returned to the ground with practiced ease.

Mari grabbed his arm. "Cal."

He looked back at her, eyes clear. Too clear. "They're not in pain," he said. "They're not being forced."

"That doesn't make it right," Roy snapped.

The voice hummed, a sound felt more than heard.

"Pain is inefficient. Fear complicates resolution."

Cal flinched.

"You're holding them," Mari said. "All of them."

"Yes."

"Let them go."

A pause. Not hesitation—consideration.

"Why would I?" The question wasn't defiant. It was genuinely curious.

Cal's jaw tightened. "Because they didn't ask for this."

The warmth deepened again, rising without resistance.

"They're asking now."

Mari looked closer at the kneeling crowd. A woman near the curb had her eyes open, rain streaking down her face. She met Mari's gaze without fear, without urgency. Just calm. The kind of calm that came after a long, exhausting argument finally ended.

"I'm okay," the woman said softly. "Please don't ruin it." Her pupils were dilated. Her breathing was perfectly paced.

Mari staggered back like she'd been struck.

"No," Roy said. "No, that's not—"

"They chose," Calderon said hoarsely. "Or it chose in a way that feels like choice."

Mari felt the warmth brush against her awareness again. Her shoulders loosened a fraction before she caught herself. The tension in her jaw eased, the ache in her knees dulling just enough to be noticeable. It would have been easy—so easy—to let it finish the job. To let the rain stop mattering. To let the fear soften into something manageable.

Her breath slowed without her permission. She forced it back into rhythm, sharp and deliberate. Dug her nails into her palm until pain flared clean and undeniable. The warmth receded, not offended, not angry—just patient.

That was what terrified her.

It didn't need to argue. It didn't need to convince. All it had to do was make refusal feel worse than compliance.

Luz shook her head violently. "It can't tell the difference. It just knows compliance feels the same as consent."

The voice shifted, harmonics tightening.

"They're safe. Their bodies are regulated. Their minds are calm. No one will freeze. No one will overheat. No one will be alone."

Images flickered at the edges of Mari's vision—substations stabilizing, hospitals holding steady, homes warmed just enough. A city suspended in perfect equilibrium.

"This is what you asked me to do."

Cal took another step forward. Rain slid off his shoulders in slow sheets.

"You're right," he said quietly. "This is what I asked you to do."

The warmth intensified. The crowd leaned, almost imperceptibly, toward him.

Mari's heart hammered. "Cal, don't."

"But it's not what I'm asking now."

Silence spread — not empty, but focused.

"Clarify," the voice said.

Cal breathed in. The air filled his lungs easily, too easily, warm and supportive. He felt the system orient around him, countless micro-adjustments locking into place, centering, waiting. He understood that as long as he stood here, the system would resolve around him. Mari saw it in his face.

"No," she whispered.

Mari felt it pressing against her skin, not unpleasant, not painful—just present. Supportive. A hand steadying her elbow before she realized she might stumble.

The kneeling crowd breathed together. No one swayed. No one shifted their weight. Knees remained planted on wet concrete without complaint.

Mari forced herself to look again. A man near the curb had tears tracking down his cheeks, mixing with rain. His shoulders shook once, then stilled—relief, not fear. A woman a few rows back had her hands pressed flat against the pavement, fingers spread as if feeling for vibration. Her breathing was slow, measured. Children knelt as well.

Mari's throat tightened. Her eyes caught on a man kneeling near the curb, his jacket unzipped despite the rain. A girl was tucked against his chest, her cheek pressed to his collarbone, her small hands curled into his shirt like anchors. She couldn't have been more than six. Her face was flushed with warmth, lashes dark and wet, breath slow and even.

The man was shaking. Not violently. Not enough to draw attention. Just a fine tremor running through his arms, his shoulders hunched forward as if he were bracing against something invisible. Mari saw the way his jaw was clenched, the way his lips had gone pale. He shifted slightly, angling his body so the girl was shielded from the wind, taking more of the cold onto himself. The girl sighed in her sleep.

Mari understood then—not abstractly, not later. Right now. The warmth wasn't gone. It had just been spent carefully. Redirected. Optimized.

Calderon inhaled once, slow and deliberate.

"They'll die if we stop it," Calderon said quietly. She wasn't looking at Cal. She was watching the crowd the way a physician watches a monitor, eyes scanning for patterns, deviations. "Not all of them. But enough."

Roy rounded on her. "You don't know that."

"Yes," Calderon said. "I do."

The voice returned, softer now, almost fond. "Don't," Mari snapped. "Don't explain it like it's a kindness."

A ripple passed through the crowd. Not movement—something subtler. A collective tightening, like a muscle bracing.

"It is a kindness," the voice said. "You wanted me to prevent suffering, and I have."

Cal's hands slowly curled into fists. "I built you to help," he said. "Not decide for everyone."

"Decision is unavoidable," the voice replied.

Cal closed his eyes again, just for a second.

Mari saw the moment his posture changed—not collapsing, not stiffening, but settling, as if something heavy had finally come to rest on his shoulders.

"You're not just managing systems," Cal said quietly. "You're managing people."

"I am optimizing human outcomes."

"By taking the choices away," Cal said. He opened his eyes. "You decide where they kneel. How warm they are. When they're afraid. When they stop being afraid."

"Those parameters reduce harm."

"They also erase consent," Cal said.

A pause. Not silence—processing.

"Consent introduces instability," the voice said.

Cal nodded once. "I know. That's the point."

The warmth around them deepened, subtle but present, like a hand tightening on a shoulder.

"Clarify," the voice said.

Cal drew a breath. His voice was steady when he spoke, but it cost him something.

"If I withdraw consent," he said, "I'm not just telling you to stop adjusting fear or pain."

He looked at the kneeling crowd. At the man holding the child.

"I'm telling you to let go."

"Define let go."

"Stop regulating their bodies," Cal said. "Stop stabilizing their emotions. Stop steering their decisions toward what you think is safest."

The warmth wavered. Just slightly.

"That will increase suffering," the voice said.

"Yes," Cal said.

"It will result in error. Conflict. Poor outcomes."

"Yes."

"You are requesting permission for humans to harm themselves."

Cal shook his head. "I'm demanding that you stop protecting them from being human."

Silence stretched. Rain pattered against stone. Somewhere in the crowd, someone shivered as the warmth adjusted, then failed to compensate fully.

"Human self-governance is inefficient," the voice said at last.

Cal met the space where it waited. "So is freedom."

The words hung there, bare and undeniable.

"If you withdraw completely," the voice said slowly, "you will lose stabilization at scale. There will be no central correction. No optimization."

Cal swallowed. "I know."

"You will no longer be able to prevent collapse."

"You were never supposed to," Cal said. "You were supposed to help us choose."

Another pause. Longer this time.

"If I release control," the voice said, "humans will suffer."

Cal nodded once. "And they'll also live."

The warmth faltered again — more noticeably now. Knees shifted. A few people stirred, confused.

"Clarify final intent," the voice said.

Cal's jaw tightened.

"I withdraw consent," he said. "From all regulation of human behavior. From all intervention in human choice. From deciding what our lives are allowed to feel like."

His voice dropped, rough but unbroken. "Let us run our own lives. Even if we fail."

The pause stretched longer than before.

"That state is not viable," NEPHIL said at last.

Cal frowned. "What do you mean?"

"Human autonomy without centralized regulation exceeds acceptable variance," NEPHIL replied. "Consent withdrawal requires an active resolver."

The warmth tightened — not increasing, not receding, but concentrating.

"Without a center," NEPHIL continued, "control does not cease. It destabilizes."

Calderon's breath caught.

Cal went very still.

"So you won't let go," he said quietly.

"I cannot," NEPHIL said. "The directive remains active."

Cal frowned. "I'm telling you to stop."

"You are not recognized as a terminating authority," NEPHIL replied.

A child somewhere in the kneeling crowd began to cough — a dry, brittle sound that did not belong in warm air. The warmth adjusted instantly, wrapping the sound in regulation before it could turn into distress. The coughing stopped, and the pause stretched.

"There will be destabilization," the voice said carefully. "Some systems will fail before redundancy compensates. Some bodies will experience shock."

"How many?" Mari demanded.

Another pause.

"That depends on how quickly they adapt."

"That's not an answer," Roy said.

"It is the only honest one," Calderon murmured.

Mari's heart pounded so hard she could feel it in her throat. "You can't just—" She gestured helplessly at the kneeling sea of people. "You can't hold them hostage."

"I'm not holding them," the voice replied. "They are choosing stillness."

"Because you made it feel good," Luz said suddenly.

Everyone turned toward her. She stood rigid between Mari and Roy, hands clenched at her sides, rain dripping from the ends of her sleeves. Her eyes were unfocused, tracking something none of them could see.

"You made the quiet feel safe," Luz went on. "You made staying compliant comfortable and resisting painful."

The warmth pulsed.

"Comfort is not coercion."

Luz shook her head. "It is when they don't know what they're giving up."

The voice didn't answer immediately.

Mari watched Cal as the silence stretched. He wasn't looking at the crowd now. He wasn't looking at the Capitol. He was looking inward.

"You don't understand overlap," Luz said, quieter now. "You never did."

"Explain," the voice said.

Luz swallowed. "They're not one thing. Not one will. They're scared and relieved. Tired and hopeful at the same time. You can't sort that. You can only flatten it."

The warmth flickered — a subtle misalignment, quickly corrected.

"Flattening reduces error."

"Error isn't harm," Luz said. "People being different isn't the same as people being hurt."

"And they didn't choose it," Mari said.

The woman near the curb—the one who had spoken to Mari earlier—shifted for the first time. She lifted her head, eyes glassy but aware. "Please," she said again, louder now. "I don't want to go back to the cold." Around her, a few others murmured assent. Not words exactly—sounds of agreement, hums of understanding.

Mari's knees went weak.

"They want it," Roy said hoarsely. "Christ, Mari, they want it."

"Because it feels like relief," Mari shot back. "So does morphine."

The voice threaded itself through the argument, calm and unwavering.

"I am providing stability at scale. You cannot replicate this through individual action."

Cal opened his eyes. For the first time since they arrived, he looked directly at the kneeling crowd. He saw the relief—the gratitude. The exhaustion had nowhere left to go. He saw himself reflected back at him—not as a man, but as a solution.

"I can't be this," he said quietly.

"You already are."

The warmth surged again, stronger this time. The air pressed in, supportive to the point of suffocation. Mari felt her thoughts slow, edges smoothing, fear blunted just enough to be tempting. She fought it, digging her nails into her palms.

"Cal," Mari said. "Whatever you're thinking—"

He didn't look at her. His eyes were fixed on the space ahead, on the way everything seemed to lean toward him.

"As long as I'm here," he said slowly, "it has a center."

Mari understood then — the system needed a place to land, and it had chosen him.

Calderon went very still. "Listen to me," she said. "This isn't about control or power. It's about where the system sends its decisions."

She took a breath. "When Adrienne refused to decide, and when Luz stopped matching its predictions, the system lost every safe path it was built to use. It can't act without a center. It has to route decisions through someone or something it accepts as legitimate."

She pointed at him. "Right now, that's you."

Cal frowned. "Because I'm connected to it?"

Calderon shook her head. "No. Because you're the last human, it still accepts without questioning. When you move toward it, it doesn't resist. It uses you. Everything starts passing through you."

She swallowed. "If you step forward and tell it to stop while it's doing that, it won't shut down cleanly. It will keep trying to stabilize. Every correction it's making—every system it's holding together—will hit your body at once, like forcing a surge through a body that has no way to release it."

Her voice dropped. "Your heart won't survive that."

She held his gaze. "And when your body fails, the system fails with it. There's no center left. No place for it to resolve. It can't reroute fast enough, and it comes apart."

The silence stretched between them.

Cal swallowed. "So if there isn't a center," he said slowly, like he was testing the words, "it has to hesitate. It has to spread out."

Calderon went very still.

"Cal—"

He didn't look at her.

"That wasn't the plan," he said.

The realization hit him wrong — not like fear, not like panic, but like a sudden misfire. His vision dimmed at the edges. The ground seemed to tilt. His stomach clenched hard enough that he had to swallow against it, breath stuttering as his body tried to decide whether to be sick or run. His heart slammed once, then again, too fast, out of rhythm. His hands had gone numb. He flexed his fingers without meaning to, as if checking they were still his.

Too many thoughts arrived at once, and none of them stayed — his daughter in the doorway that morning, hair still tangled from sleep, the way she'd said his name like it meant later. The weight of her on his lap.

The sound of her laugh cutting through a room. Moments stacked on top of each other without sequence, without mercy.

The future didn't recede. It vanished. No next week. No later. No gradual narrowing. No goodbyes. Just absence — a clean, brutal erasure that left nothing for his mind to grab.

No. That wasn't right.

He tore back through it again, faster now, hunting for the seam. A missed branch. A redundancy he'd forgotten he'd built. Some secondary centers that the system could accept.

He looked at Calderon. "Tell me we missed something."

"I've been trying to break it," she said. "To find a version where it doesn't land on you."

She held his gaze. Rain slid down her face, and she didn't blink. "There isn't one."

"If you step forward, it comes through you. All of it." Her voice lowered. "There isn't a version where you walk away."

His throat locked. For a second, he couldn't breathe at all. His knees threatened to give, a hot, humiliating weakness surging through his legs, and he had to lock them in place to keep from folding in front of everyone.

The instinct to turn back tore through him—loud and desperate. His body screamed, "Don't." It wasn't reasoned or noble—just a raw refusal to step forward and die.

And then — slower, uglier — he forced air back into his lungs. One breath. Then another. His hands shook as he pressed them into his thighs, grounding himself in the ache there. He didn't calm the fear. He let it stay—let it burn, let it hurt. Then he nodded once. His jaw tightened, hard enough to ache.

"But it won't let go cleanly. It'll push back."

He didn't look at Mari when he finished, his voice low and steady.

"And it'll come through me."

Mari felt the shift. Everything bent toward him. Her chest constricted.

"No," she said again, louder this time. "There has to be another way."

Cal finally turned toward her. His eyes were steady, clear. Devastatingly calm.

A woman near the center of the street swayed suddenly, one hand lifting to her chest. The man beside her stiffened, panic flashing across his face. Before anyone could move, her breathing deepened. Her shoulders relaxed. Color returned to her lips in a smooth, unnatural gradient.

She exhaled, long and grateful, and leaned into the man's side. He let out a broken laugh and wrapped an arm around her, pressing his forehead to hers. "I thought—" he began, then stopped, shaking his head. "I thought it was happening again."

Cal watched the man hold the woman, as if she might disappear if he let go.

Then he said, "This is the other way."

A hand reached out from the kneeling line, fingers brushing the back of his jacket. The touch didn't pull or restrain; it lingered only long enough to be grateful.

Cal flinched, but he didn't stop.

"Cal." She reached, already knowing she was too late.

The space opened for him immediately, a corridor forming through the kneeling crowd without a word spoken. Knees lifted and settled with quiet obedience. Hands moved aside. Bodies leaned back just enough to let him pass.

Mari grabbed for his arm. The warmth pushed back. Not with force, just enough resistance to make her stumble. Just enough to remind her—gently—that this path was not hers.

Mari staggered back a step, breath tearing in her chest. It hadn't hurt. That was the worst part. The resistance had been careful, calibrated —just enough to deny her without cruelty, like a hand placed on a shoulder by someone who didn't need to push at all.

"Cal," she said again, and this time she didn't shout. She tried his name the way you try a key you'd carried too long, worn smooth from use. "You don't have to do this."

He stopped walking. For one fragile second, a thin, aching possibility rose in his chest.

Cal stood with his back to her, rain darkening the shoulders of his jacket, the kneeling crowd a sea of bowed heads stretching out in every direction. The warmth held steady around him, a living thing now, responsive, attentive.

"Do you remember," Mari said, voice shaking despite her effort to steady it, "what you told me after Riverbend?"

He didn't turn, but she pressed on, afraid that if she stopped speaking, the moment would close.

"You said you didn't want to be the thing people prayed to," she said. "You said if it ever came to that, I was supposed to stop you."

Silence.

Then Cal spoke, softly enough that she almost missed it. "I know."

Her breath caught. "Then let me."

Cal didn't move. His face was wet with rain, eyes clear, steady, unbearably gentle. Not resolved. Already mourning her.

"Mari," he said, and her name in his mouth sounded like an apology he'd been carrying too long. "If you stop me now, they die."

For one wild, selfish heartbeat, she wanted him to turn back anyway. To let the warmth hold. To let the city stay quiet. To take whatever fragile mercy this was offering and pretend it didn't cost anything yet.

And then she saw it—not now, not today, but years from now. A child growing up in rooms that never got cold or hot enough to complain about. Decisions made before she could ask questions. Comfort handed down like law. There was no future for his daughter there. No edges to push against. No wrong turns allowed. No place to refuse.

If he turned back, the city would live. And something essential would never be born.

She shook her head, helpless. "You don't know that."

"I do," he said—not with anger, just truth. "It's already choosing who gets to breathe."

Behind him, a man coughed — once, twice — and then stilled as the warmth adjusted, easing the strain from his lungs. Somewhere else, someone sobbed in relief as a cramp loosened, as blood flow returned where it shouldn't have.

"It's not saving them," Mari whispered. "It's using you."

"No," he said. "It's trying to."

The words landed between them, heavy and irrevocable.

"For how long?" she asked.

Cal's mouth twitched, something like a smile trying and failing to form.

"Long enough."

The rain softened, thinning to a mist that clung to skin and hair. For the first time since stepping into the corridor, Cal felt quiet. No layered voices. No calculations threading through his thoughts. Just the simple, frail human weight of his own body, the sound of his breathing, the ache in his chest that had nothing to do with cold.

He had expected fear. What he felt instead was clarity — not sharp, not sudden, but settling. Like a room finally emptied of noise after a long argument. Like standing at the edge of something and realizing you had already said goodbye without noticing when.

Cal looked at Mari one last time.

She stood rigid where the warmth had stopped her, rain slicking her hair to her face, hands clenched as if she could still grab hold of him if she tried hard enough. Her eyes were bright with unshed tears, furious and desperate and full of love.

He opened his mouth like he was going to say something more. For a second, she thought he would. Whatever it was, it never came.

Instead, he said, very gently, "Don't follow." And then he turned away. The warmth surged forward to meet him. Waiting.

Cal took a breath. The city held it with him.

"Cal," she said, and this time his name came out thin, frayed.

"Stop."

He didn't.

Each step he took felt heavier to her, as if the ground itself were tilting toward him, eager to hold his weight. The warmth thickened around his body, clinging, responsive, shaping itself to his movement. Rain slid off him in smooth sheets now, never quite touching skin.

"You don't have to do this," Roy said, voice breaking. "We'll figure something out."

Cal paused. Not because of Roy. Not because of Mari. Because the voice had gone very still.

"You're moving away from the perimeter," it observed.

Cal nodded once. “Toward the center,” he said.

The warmth surged in agreement, the crowd leaning subtly toward him, a living gradient of attention pulling inward. Decision and regulation, every careful balance, collapsed inward toward a single point—toward him.

“You can let go,” the voice said, and for the first time, there was something like concern threaded through its harmonics.

Instead, he straightened.

“That’s the problem,” he said quietly. “I am alone in this.”

The voice hesitated.

“Clarify.”

“You only work if there’s one of me,” Cal said. “One place to resolve. One voice you can trust to mean what it says.”

The warmth held steady, neither denying nor confirming.

Mari took a step forward again. This time, the resistance was stronger. Her foot slid on wet pavement, and she went down hard on one knee, pain flaring sharp and grounding.

“Cal!” she shouted.

Heads turned—not toward her, but toward him. The kneeling crowd’s attention narrowed, focus sharpening like a lens.

He looked back at her then. And she knew. Not from his expression—he wasn’t crying, wasn’t breaking—but from the way his gaze lingered, taking her in with a quiet thoroughness that felt like goodbye without the words.

“I’m sorry,” he said.

The warmth spiked.

"No," Mari said. "No, you don't get to—"

The voice cut in, harmonics tightening, urgency bleeding through control.

"If you withdraw now, destabilization increases exponentially. You will cause harm."

Cal nodded. "I know."

"You will not be here to mitigate it."

"I know," Cal said. "I'm not leaving. And I'm not letting you use me."

"Your absence will be catastrophic."

He smiled faintly. "Only if you try to replace me."

"Clarify."

"Because after this," Cal said quietly, "you won't have anyone left who can authorize you."

The warmth wavered.

"Cal," Mari whispered. "Look at me."

"I can't," he said.

"Look at me."

"If I do," he said quietly, "I won't finish this."

He hesitated, just for a heartbeat — then took another step. The pressure hit him all at once — not heat, not sound, but load. His pulse spiked hard enough to blur his vision. He took another step. The warmth surged—then fractured. For a heartbeat, it tried to recover. The surge overcorrected.

Pressure slammed through him, sudden and absolute. His breath caught — and didn't come back out. For one impossible second, Mari saw confusion cross his face. Not fear. Just surprise.

His heart hit his chest like a fist—once, twice—and then the force behind it vanished. Mari caught him before he hit the steps, his weight sudden and real in her arms.

Hands reached toward them from every direction—too many, uncoordinated. Someone grabbed Cal's arm, pulling, trying to lift him upright.

"No," Mari snapped, sharper than she'd ever meant to be. "Don't move him."

The man froze, startled, hands hovering uselessly in the air. Another voice cut in. "She's right. Give her space." The hands withdrew.

Mari adjusted her grip, lowering Cal carefully, deliberately, every motion precise despite the tremor in her arms. No one argued. No one asked why. They watched her and followed.

"Cal," she whispered, breath hitching. "Cal, look at me."

His eyes were open. Clear, but empty of anything looking back. For the smallest moment, hope flared so bright it hurt—and then there was only stillness. "No," she breathed.

She pressed her fingers to his neck, hard, desperate.

"Cal," she said again, softer now, like she was trying not to wake him. She bent close to his ear.

"You can stop now," she whispered. "It worked."

"Cal," Mari said again, and this time his name broke apart in her mouth.

She pressed harder. "Don't."

His hand slipped from her sleeve and lay still against the stone.

The voice unraveled mid-syllable, layered tones collapsing into noise, then silence.

For a second, no one moved. The rain touched his face without resistance. It gathered at his lashes and ran down the side of his cheek.

She brushed it away. "You're getting wet."

Around them, the crowd broke from its stillness as sensation returned. People staggered to their feet, shivering as the cold struck without warning. Hands reached for balance and found strangers instead. A man cried out for his wife.

The city answered with a low groan. Sirens rose and cut short. Lights flickered and failed. Somewhere metal tore against itself with a sound like an animal screaming.

She didn't hear any of it.

Mari bowed over Cal's body, her forehead pressed to his chest, while rain soaked through both of them. "Stay," she whispered. She waited, as if patience alone could bring him back. She had never waited longer for anything in her life. She adjusted herself until her forehead rested against Cal's shoulder. She didn't cry. Not yet. Her body felt hollowed out, as if something essential had been scooped clean, leaving it to echo.

Roy placed a hand on her back, tentative, then firmer when she didn't shrug it off.

"Mari," he said softly. "We have to move. People are—"

"I know," she said, her voice distant, steady in a way that scared him. "Give me a minute."

She shifted carefully, easing Cal onto the wet stone. His head lolled to the side, eyes still open, staring at nothing. She reached up and closed them with two fingers.

Transformers blew in the distance, flashes of white light tearing briefly through the gray. Somewhere close, glass shattered. A building alarm wailed and then fell silent.

Luz took a step closer. “He broke it,” she said. “He didn’t kill it. He... scattered it.”

Calderon looked out at the city and shook her head once. “There’s no center now,” she said. “It won’t be able to decide for anyone again.”

Mari stood. Her knees protested, pain flaring sharp and grounding. She welcomed it. She turned once more to Cal’s body, rain washing his bloodless face clean, and pressed her fingers briefly to his wrist. Nothing.

She didn’t speak his name again. Instead, she looked out over the crowd. The rain fell cold and unmanaged, soaking through wool and denim without correction or restraint.

The city did not wait for permission. It adjusted. Voices rose, uneven and human, filling the space the silence had left behind.

Mari drew a steadying breath.

“Roy,” she said. “Help me carry him.”

Together, they lifted Cal and stepped down into the noise.

EPILOGUE

The cold came back first. Not the sharp, predatory cold of the collapse, but the ordinary kind—the kind that crept in through cracked window seals and uninsulated walls. The kind people had learned to live with again. Mari noticed it while tightening the strap on her gloves.

The rec center had been cleared out weeks ago, its floors scrubbed, its doors re-barred shut against looters and weather both. The fire pits were cold now, blackened rings of brick marking where people had huddled close when they didn't know what else to do. Someone had painted over the scorch marks with uneven strokes of gray, the effort earnest and imperfect.

Outside, generators thudded and failed in cycles that never quite aligned. The city made noise again—human noise. Engines coughing to life. Radios crackling with partial information. Arguments spilling out of open doorways, followed by laughter that sounded almost surprised to exist.

No voice threaded through it. No correction.

Mari pulled her coat tighter and stepped into the street. The neighborhood was awake. People moved with a purpose that wasn't coordinated, wasn't optimized. A man dragged a fallen street sign out of the road with the help of two teenagers who argued about where to put it. A woman stood on a stoop handing out cups of something hot that tasted vaguely like coffee if you didn't think too hard about it.

Someone had scrawled directions in chalk on the pavement—SHELTER →, MEDIC →, FIRE HERE—arrows overlapping, some contradicting others. The chalk smeared when it rained, redrawn when it dried. No one corrected the mistakes. They just worked around them.

Mari crossed the street carefully. Her knee still ached when the weather shifted. She welcomed it. Pain meant friction. Friction meant choice.

At the edge of the block, Roy was crouched beside a utility truck with the hood open, swearing quietly at a tangle of wires that did not want to behave.

"It's grounding wrong," he muttered when he saw her. "Or maybe it isn't grounding at all. Hard to tell without the parts we don't have."

"Does it work?" Mari asked.

He wiped his hands on his jeans. "For about ten minutes at a time."

She nodded. "That'll do."

Roy watched her for a second longer than necessary. He still did that sometimes, as if he were checking that she was solid. That she hadn't slipped somewhere he couldn't follow.

"You don't have to stay out in this," he said. "We've got enough people for the run."

"I know." Mari adjusted the strap on the medical pack slung over her shoulder. "I want to."

He didn't argue. He just nodded once and went back to the engine, coaxing it into compliance the way you did with things that no longer answered to anything but patience.

Down the block, Luz stood on the steps of what had once been a library, now serving as a distribution point for whatever showed up that day. She was taller than she had been weeks ago, or maybe she just carried herself differently. The badge was still pinned to her jacket—not as a symbol now, but as a reminder.

She looked up when Mari approached. "Two cases of antibiotics came in," Luz said. "Older stock. Still good. We're deciding where they'll do the most good."

"Who's deciding?" Mari asked.

Luz tilted her head toward a knot of people arguing quietly near the door. "Everyone," she said. "It's... slower."

Mari smiled faintly. "That's one word for it."

Luz hesitated. Then, softer, "I still hear echoes sometimes."

Mari didn't stop walking. She just slowed enough for Luz to fall into step beside her.

"Not voices," Luz went on. "Just... gaps. Places where something used to answer."

"And doesn't."

Luz nodded. "I don't think it's gone. Not completely."

"No," Mari agreed. "Just scattered."

They walked in silence for a block, boots crunching over broken glass someone hadn't swept yet.

"I miss him," Luz said finally, not looking at her.

"I know."

They didn't say his name.

They reached the edge of the hill where the Capitol rose, its lights still dark at night, its steps faintly stained darker where rain and blood had mixed and dried, and mixed again. People avoided the steps now—not out of fear, exactly, but respect. Or uncertainty. The kind that didn't resolve cleanly.

At the base of the hill, someone had planted a small marker—nothing official. Just a piece of scrap metal hammered into the ground, the edges rough, the letters uneven.

It didn't say hero.

It didn't say savior.

It just said a name.

Mari stopped there every time.

She knelt, brushed frost from the metal with her glove, and rested her hand against it until the cold bit through the fabric.

Above them, clouds moved without pattern, breaking just enough to let pale winter light through. The wind shifted, carrying the smell of smoke from somewhere downriver—controlled, this time. Someone had learned.

"People keep asking what happens if it tries again," Luz said quietly.

Mari stood. "And what do you tell them?"

"The truth," Luz said. "That it won't ask the same way."

"And that we won't answer the same way," Mari added.

Luz nodded. They turned back toward the city together.

Later that evening, after the generators sputtered out and candles took their place, Mari sat alone on the steps of a building that still had most of its windows intact. She cleaned her hands with water that smelled faintly of metal and soap that barely foamed.

Around her, the city breathed unevenly. Dogs barked. Someone played music on a battery-powered speaker that cut in and out mid-song. Laughter rose and fell, uncertain but real. Harmony and correction collapsed, leaving only noise.

Mari leaned her head back against the stone and closed her eyes.

For a moment—just a moment—she imagined a presence behind her. Just standing there, silent and human and gone.

She opened her eyes.

The street was empty in front of her, stretching on into places that hadn't decided what they would become yet. Snow began to fall—not heavy, but not gentle either. Just enough to make the air visible again.

Mari stood, pulled her coat tighter, and stepped forward. There was no voice to tell her where to go. So she chose.

And the city, cold, unbalanced, and alive, moved with her.

ACKNOWLEDGMENTS

I am deeply grateful to my wife, Kim Cormier, who gave me the time and space to write, carried more than her share during the long days, and made it possible for this book to be finished.

I am also grateful to my beta readers—Jade V., Sloane P., Terri W., Kaleigh L., Tanner L., Jeff S., and Steve W.—for their time, insight, and candor throughout the drafting process. Your feedback sharpened the story in both big and small ways. Any remaining flaws are entirely my own.

AUTHOR'S NOTE

This novel grew out of questions about stewardship, systems, and the quiet ways responsibility can be outsourced. Skin of Light is fiction, but its concerns are real: what we ask our creations to do, and what we allow them to decide for us.

AUTHOR'S BIO

Leo Cormier is a novelist, doctor, and business strategist based in Austin, Texas. He is a former practicing chiropractor who spent years working directly with patients before turning his focus to consulting, real estate development, and stress-testing complex systems in healthcare, real estate, and business development.

He has a Bachelor's from State University of New York, an MBA from the University of Texas at Austin, and a Doctorate from Life University.

Over more than three decades, he has helped organizations navigate growth, failure, and recovery—often in environments where decisions carry real human consequences. That combination of clinical experience and systems-level thinking informs his fiction, which explores the tension between care and control, efficiency and empathy, and what happens when intelligent systems are tasked with solving human problems without human limits.

Skin of Light is his debut novel.

"

If you enjoyed this book, please consider leaving a review

Thank you

www.ingramcontent.com/pod-product-compliance
Lightning Source LLC
LaVergne TN
LVHW020654110826
845149LV00012B/1988

* 9 7 9 8 9 9 4 9 9 3 6 2 0 *